For Gerry —
Hope you enjoy it.
It was fun to write.
Barry

A NEW WORLD WON

A NEW WORLD WON

Barrington King

Five Star
Unity, Maine

Copyright © 1999 by Barrington King

Barrington King also writes under the pseudonym
Barrie King.

All rights reserved.

This novel is a work of fiction. Names, characters, places, and incidents are either the product of the author's imagination, or, if real, used fictitiously.

Five Star First Edition Romance
Published in conjunction with
Kidde, Hoyt & Picard Literary Agency.

Cover photograph © Alan J. LaVallee

June 1999
Standard Print Hardcover Edition.

Five Star Standard Print First Edition Romance Series.

The text of this edition is unabridged.

Set in 11 pt. Plantin by Al Chase.

Printed in the United States on permanent paper.

Library of Congress Cataloging in Publication Data
King, Barrington.
   A new world won / by Barrington King. — 1st ed.
     p.   cm.
   ISBN 0-7862-1886-X (hc. : alk. paper)
   1. United States — History — Revolution, 1775–1783 — Participation, French — Fiction. I. Title.
PS3561.I4728N49 1999
   813'.54—dc21   99-17836

For Sarah

BOOK I
THE OLD WORLD
1776

CHAPTER ONE

*Bordeaux,
   September, 1776*

Sophie Armonville looked up from the big leather-bound ledger over which she had been bent for hours. Debits and credits, red ink and black, had been brought down to the lower right-hand corner of the page. She rubbed her stiff neck, her sore wrist, sighed. A sea breeze ruffled the surface of the river, and along the esplanade the lamps of Bordeaux harbor began to glow one after another in the wake of the lamplighter, as he dragged his ladder from one post to the next.

She scratched a sulfur match against its box, lit a candle, turned the ledger page. She was about to toss away a scrap of folded paper stuck between the blank pages, when her fingers felt some slight object within. She opened the paper and a dried wildflower fell out. She held it in her hand, trying to recall, and then the memories came flooding back. . . .

Someone was tapping on the window. She turned to look into the face of her cousin Hyacinthe pressed against the glass. What had brought him from Paris to Bordeaux? She arose to unlock the door, forgetting, in her pleasure at seeing Hyacinthe, the dried flower and scrap of paper held tightly in her hand.

"Evening, cousin," Hyacinthe said lightly, exploring her face with shrewd gray eyes. "You work late."

"If I did not I would soon be drowning in bills of lading and exchange."

He rolled his eyes at this, wandered about the room and then perched his slim, elegantly dressed form on a table: Hyacinthe, her island refuge of wit and charm in a sea of grim Huguenot merchants.

"A young widow," she added provocatively, knowing he would have some impertinent reply, "cannot afford to let business slip. The merchants of Bordeaux would show me no quarter."

"Indeed?" he said, raising a blond eyebrow, swinging a silk-stockinged leg. "This is France, my dear Sophie, and the year is 1776. I told you when we first met that no woman is freer in our society than a young widow, particularly if she has your . . . attributes."

"But as you pointed out to me then, this applies only in Paris, not in Bordeaux."

"Even that is changing. Why, I know any number of young provincial widows . . . You know, the problem is that you don't go out in society. I would wager it's straight from the counting house every night to supper and a cold bed."

She should have been offended. Instead she laughed, but she could think of no light and bantering reply.

"Sophie, what *are* you clutching in your hand? Your knuckles are quite white."

She held out her hand to him then and opened it. The dried wildflower had been reduced to powder. He took the crumpled scrap of paper from her outstretched hand and smoothed it out.

". . . a life of passion and adventure . . . ? *Cousine,* if you wished to mystify me, you have certainly succeeded."

"I wrote that," she managed to say with only a slight tremor to her voice, "ten years ago, when I was fifteen, in Martinique, in a letter to a girl friend, that I was too shy to send. I tore up the letter, but saved that scrap with those few words . . ."

"And?"

"And I wrapped a wildflower in it and placed it ten years ahead in this great family ledger of accounts that I brought with me to France, on that unhappy voyage."

"What does it mean, 'a life of passion and adventure . . .'?"

"That before ten years were up I would have just that. Now these words, that I came upon not two minutes ago, are but mockery. Oh, Hyacinthe, how I wish I could go back to my beloved Martinique, with its warm sun, the water deep blue and emerald green, the frangipani blossoms . . ."

"Ah, Sophie," and he took both her hands in his.

"Well, you warned me that first day what would happen if I turned my back on life . . ."

Hyacinthe lowered his eyes.

". . . and you have had the good grace never to mention it again."

He raised his eyes, and she wondered what he would say next.

"I suppose," he said, "that you know the harvest festival takes place tomorrow at Château Ivran. The governor will be there, all the local nobility, the leading wine merchants. You are, of course, invited."

"Of course." What had brought about this abrupt change of subject?

"And you will go?"

"As usual, I will send Etienne in my place. That is quite sufficient to show the firm's interest."

"You must go yourself this year."

"Why should I?"

"Because I have promised a friend of mine that you will be there."

"You have promised a friend?" She was astonished.

"An American. He has a serious business proposition for someone in the West Indian trade, and I didn't see why that someone shouldn't be you, dear cuz."

"An American?" She was even more astonished.

"They are not all wild savages, you know. He is quite presentable."

"I couldn't."

"Why not? Nothing to wear?"

"*Mon cher cousin,* I have suitable clothes."

"Well then?"

"You will be there, of course."

"Afraid not. On the king's business tomorrow."

"Always the king's business. And what might that be?" She grew bolder. "A naval officer who never goes to sea, who sleeps all day and spends his nights with beautiful women and powerful men of the upper nobility—or so I am told."

She was delighted to see that for once Hyacinthe was at a loss for words. She was even more delighted to discover that the sea breeze of this unusual evening had passed across what she had thought the dead ashes of her life and brought forth a glow.

It was a glorious September day, as warm as mid-summer, and she had had the roof of the carriage turned back, a thing she never did. It called attention to oneself, and a woman who competed in business with men kept out of the public eye. Then why had she done so today? And why had she taken such pains with her hair and with the choice of her dress? Had the emotions of the previous evening rekindled some small hope that she might yet enjoy, if not a life of passion and adventure, at least one in which there was some place for pleasure? She had even considered a brightly colored dress, but in the end she had chosen a brown taffeta. It was not seemly for a woman in her position, and a widow as well, to wear bright colors. Besides, she was going out on business, business that her irresponsible cousin Hyacinthe had made it almost impossible for her to avoid.

"There will be dancing," the boy seated opposite her in the carriage said. "Will you dance?"

"What? Of course not."

She said nothing more, for she had no desire to engage in banter with Paulot, the West Indian lad who served her as office boy, messenger and male escort when, as today, she was obliged to venture out. Her carriage had joined the stream of vehicles making its way down the long drive to the dark mass of Château Ivran. On either side the vines had been stripped of their grapes and the leaves were beginning to turn to the red and gold of autumn. From the distance came the sound of an orchestra.

"Madame Armonville!" boomed the voice of the majordomo, costumed in wine-colored velvet, as he struck the stone floor with his staff.

Sophie had not expected to be announced and was disconcerted to find all eyes up and down the long hall of the winery turned on her, nor did the eyes of many of the men turn immediately away. She felt blood rush to her face. To her relief, old Beaumont, the president of the wine merchants' guild, came forward to greet her.

"It has been too long, Madame Sophie, that our gatherings have lacked the grace of your presence." He bowed and kissed her hand. "Welcome, welcome. Now come, let me present you to the governor."

Friends and acquaintances, men and women, came up to her in the course of the hour, greeting her with affection, kisses by the men on her hand, by the women on her cheeks.

In her single-minded effort to revive the fortunes of Chardin and Co., had she become a narrow, suspicious person, seeing her fellow merchants and their wives as no more than competitors, and not fellow human beings with their own troubles and joys? She had always been cordial with them, but always with a purpose. Suddenly she could barely restrain tears.

Glasses of the best wines from Sauternes, Pauillac, Médoc, Pomerol were thrust into her hand to taste, to consider buying a few barrels of, until she became a little tipsy from only a sip of each; or perhaps it was the air itself, reeking with the fumes from the huge vats of fermenting grapes that half filled the long whitewashed hall, and that within a week would transform the grapes of Château Ivran's vineyards into wine.

"The one day of the year when the three social classes of Bordeaux come together as in no other part of France: the land-owning nobility, the bourgeois merchants, and the peasants who till the earth and harvest the crop. We are bound together like brothers by our devotion to the vine. Indeed, I believe the juice of the grape courses through our very veins."

She barely listened to Beaumont's discourse, which she had heard more than once. It was true that the local nobility and the merchant class rubbed elbows on this day, and the vineyard workers were at least close at hand outside, where an ox was being roasted for their benefit. Of brotherhood she reckoned there was very little. But her thoughts were elsewhere. Where was this American? How did one recognize an American?

There was some commotion at the door. The noisy, jovial crowd parted to let past a cavalry trooper, white with the dust of the road, who made his way straight for Governor de Saint-Foix's entourage. The governor studied the paper that was handed him, and then one of his aides broke away to

A New World Won

summon a stranger to his presence. She knew everyone of quality in Bordeaux by sight, and he was unknown to her: tall with bronzed skin, as if he had been on a military campaign, dark hair knotted into a pigtail, with no trace of powder, a narrow hawk-like nose, deeply-set dark eyes. Although he was dressed by a Parisian tailor, his movements lacked the studied grace of a Frenchman of the upper classes. Here then was her American.

The stranger conferred briefly with the governor and then withdrew. Within minutes word had spread through the hall: a ship had arrived off Bordeaux flying an unknown flag, claimed to be that of the new nation of America, and had asked permission to enter the harbor. The stranger who had conferred with the governor was the American agent in Paris. He had confirmed that word had just been received that Britain's American colonies had declared their independence; and he had vouched for the good behavior of captain and crew, with which the ship had been granted permission to enter the harbor.

Suddenly, to everyone's surprise, a young nobleman, the Comte de Saluzes, leaped onto a table.

"America has declared her independence from the British crown. Long live liberty! Long live France and King Louis!"

"And what does the comte suppose will happen to his class," said one of the merchants in Beaumont's circle, "when liberty pays a visit on our own King Louis?"

The American agent in Paris. Hyacinthe had done ill not to inform her. She had not worked into the night for five years restoring the fortunes of Chardin and Co. to have its good name tainted with revolutionary politics. She would out of politeness have listened to his business proposition, but there was now no question of their conversing with every eye in the hall on him. To her dismay, the American began moving in her direction; but then he paused, bowed ever so slightly in her direction and moved away. Sophie inclined her head as slightly in response. He too recognized that the situation was impossible for conversation and had extricated himself gracefully.

"Looks like he just stepped out of the forests," said one of the merchants with whom she stood.

"Yes," said Sophie absently. To her surprise what she felt was not relief at having avoided embarrassment, but disappointment at having even this innocent little adventure taken from her.

Despite the awkward situation, Sophie found herself enjoying the day more and more. Everyone seemed genuinely pleased at her unexpected entry into society, and she was obliged to receive many compliments, both professional, on how she had turned about the fortunes of Chardin and Co., and personal, on how striking was her appearance.

As the day cooled off, the festivities moved outside where long tables laden with the good food and wine of Bordeaux had been set up under big striped tents. She dared not participate in the dancing, but she longed to. How little pleasure she had known since that fateful day she had arrived from Martinique to be met at the Bordeaux dock by her uncle. Five of what should have been the best years of her life had vanished, never to be seen again. And what she had to show for those years seemed now not the fruits of industry but dust and ashes.

"May I ask you to dance, Madame?" It was the governor's aide, a quite charming young nobleman who had been helpful to her on several occasions when she had had business with the government.

"I would be delighted, Major Richard, but I fear that

bourgeois custom does not permit me the pleasure."

He laughed. "You put it well. May I sit with you then and chat of this and that until I am summoned back to duty?"

"If you promise not to speak of frivolous matters, only serious ones, then I suppose that might be permitted."

He laughed again and sank to a cushion next to her on the grass, resplendent in his uniform. He looked into her eyes, smiling.

Ma foi, she thought, he is testing to see if there might not be the possibility with me of an affair of the heart. Well, she had encouraged him with her bold words. What had come over her?

"Since we are to speak only of serious matters," the major said, "what is your view of the American declaration of independence?"

"If it also frees Canada from British rule, then I am for it."

"Canada?"

"Where I was born. My family had its offices in Quebec before France lost Canada to the British."

"Really? Doing what?"

"Trading in furs, timber, salt cod."

"I know little of trade."

"And I know little of court etiquette, Major. So, there you are. Our classes rarely come together."

"Not true. Marriages between the nobility and the bourgeoisie are ever more frequent."

"As the wealth of the nobility decreases and the dowries with which the merchant class sells its daughters for titles grow ever larger."

There. She had brought up the bitter bile that had been within her for five years, and as one relieved of seasickness, she felt well again. She was drunk, not on wine—though she had had more of that than was prudent—but on words. For years she had rationed her words like coins, never to be dispensed without a purpose; but this afternoon purposes and profits were forgotten.

The major was visibly uncomfortable, and so was she. She quickly changed the subject.

"Tell me something of this American," Sophie said.

"He is to be taken with some seriousness. Others that this Continental Congress has sent us have been crude, interested mainly in lining their own pockets . . ."

"A failing unknown among our own officials."

". . . and unable to speak our language. Morgan Carter's French is impeccable."

"How so?"

"There is a rather strange story about that. . . . But tell me, will you be returning to Bordeaux by barge?"

"By barge? *Je ne comprends pas.*"

"It has been arranged that the barges they use to carry the barrels of wine to the port will tonight take back those guests who wish to while away another hour or two in sailing up the Gironde. There will be a cold supper served, and no doubt there will be music. The moon will be full."

"I regret that I must decline. There are some business matters that I must attend to. . . . Ah, I see the carriages are already being brought up for the return."

The sun was setting now over the vineyards. Major Richard arose with a sigh and helped Sophie to her feet.

"May I hope to see you again in less formal circumstances?"

"No, Major Richard, that cannot be, but I hope that we may remain friends."

He bent over her hand and lowered his lips to it.

"I will always be at your service," and he offered his arm and led her back to her carriage. His advance had been softly turned aside, and as she would have expected of a French nobleman he had accepted her rebuke with grace.

There was a jam of carriages at the entrance to the château, and after half an hour it showed no signs of soon becoming unsnarled.

"There is a back road along the canal that I could take," said the driver, turning to Sophie, "if Madame wishes."

"Do so. Anything to get out of this crush."

They were soon through the vineyards and to the canal, where carriages were drawn up alongside a line of gaily decorated barges. Those guests who had chosen to return by water were clambering aboard them and, as they filled with passengers, one by one they raised their sails and cast off.

"Stop. I have decided to return by boat."

Paulot's face registered surprise. She was surprised herself.

"Well, don't just sit there. Help me down. Quick. The boats are leaving."

Paulot leaped aboard the last barge that remained and took Sophie's arm as she stepped over the gunwale.

"Now, you are to return to the carriage and meet me on the quay at Bordeaux."

Reluctantly Paulot climbed back onto the dock as the man at the tiller cried *"embarquez!"* No one else came aboard, and moments later they were moving away. She looked about her. She knew none of the passengers as more than a casual acquaintance. Then her eyes fell on the American, who immediately came across the deck toward where she stood with her back to the rail. She wished their eyes had not met, yet her gaze remained fixed on him.

"Excuse me for approaching you without permission, but you seem to be alone."

"Yes, I decided at the last moment, on impulse, to return by water."

"As you are without escort, may I join you?"

"That would be . . . welcome." What else could she say, yet she felt the need to justify herself. "I have no friends on board, and it would make my situation less awkward."

"There are seats in the stern, if you would like."

"Bien volontiers," and once again she accepted an offered arm. She had been told that Americans had no manners, but she would have to give at least this American good marks.

Seated on cushions in the stern of the barge, apart from the dancing, singing crowd, with glasses of cool white wine that he had brought, she waited for Morgan Carter to speak of business matters.

She watched as he lifted the delicate glass to his lips and slowly tasted. He turned his dark eyes on her as if about to make some serious overture.

"Yes?" She at last said nervously.

"Tell me what I should think of this wine."

Sophie laughed. She put her nose into her glass, lifted the glass to the twilight sky, took a sip of the wine, rolled it around in her mouth, ran her tongue over it, breathed in deeply through her nose, swallowed and exhaled.

"It is excellent. An especially fruity Graves. Château Carbonnieux."

"And the year?"

"The vintage is '73."

"Astonishing."

"Monsieur, if one trades in wine and cannot make such distinctions, then one is soon out of business."

"Nevertheless. I have tried to learn, but my progress is slow. At least I recognized it as a Graves."

"You are interested in wine?"

A New World Won

"I am interested in many things about your country. You ship wine to the West Indies, I believe."

"Yes."

"And receive in return?"

"Coffee and indigo."

She regretted that they must now turn to business. It was a pleasure to talk to someone who was not either in commerce, a tradesman or a government official, someone whose tanned skin and strong good looks were in such contrast to the pallid and sedentary merchants she saw every day. She had been starved for the simple pleasure of light conversation with a man. And now her little adventure, her day of freedom, was coming to an end.

"Madame . . ."

"Yes?"

"Might I fetch you a bit of supper?"

"Oh, yes. Though I shouldn't, after that feast that was put before us at the château."

She watched him move away, dark-haired, tall, his powerful form more easily imagined in buckskins than the breeches and silk stockings of fashionable Paris that he wore.

He returned, smiling on her, with plates of cold chicken, bread, cheese and pears.

"An excellent choice," she said. "Tell me, where did you learn to speak French so well?" She wanted not only to put off for a while longer any talk of business but to hear something of the strange story that Major Richard had referred to.

"Any skill that I may have in the language is due to Charles Dupont, the best friend that I ever had; but it pains me to speak of him."

Indeed, a look of pain came across his face, which she could see better now that the Japanese lanterns strung overhead had been lit.

"If you would rather not . . ."

He fell silent. The party in the bow had settled down to supper. A young man had begun playing a guitar, while looking earnestly into the eyes of his female companion. The canal had joined the wide expanse of the Gironde, and a rising full moon, red as a glowing coal, was reflected in its waters.

"I was a student of law, a subject for which I had little aptitude, at the College of William and Mary in Virginia. Charles Dupont arrived one day, sent by the King of France to collect American plants for the royal gardens at Versailles. While he waited for his expedition to the interior to be outfitted he gave some lectures on botany at the university, with the aid of an interpreter. He would, naturally, need a guide for his expedition; and I, quite sick of the law, volunteered to accompany him. My home was far up the James River, and I knew the forests well.

"For more than three years we wandered the face of the continent, collecting plants and sending them back to Williamsburg to become acclimatized and to await Dupont's return to France. As we journeyed day after day, there was little to do but talk; and as Charles would learn no English, this was perforce in French. And so I became quite fluent in the language.

"*Hélas,* as his mission was almost complete we were ambushed by a party of renegade Indians. Charles was killed, and I barely escaped with my life. So it was I, and not Charles Dupont, who accompanied our plant collection back to France. At the botanical gardens I was offered, if I would stay, a position as botanist to the king. The life of Versailles—and Paris, of course—pleased me well enough, and I accepted. So, here I am."

"*Ah, oui?* Then you are not the political agent of America in Paris?"

"That too. Since I was already there and spoke the language, unlike those who had preceded me, I was asked by the Continental Congress to assume that post, a request no patriot could refuse. I cannot say, however, that I have had great success in persuading your government to support our cause."

"I'm sorry . . . both about the loss of your friend and your lack of success in Paris." This was said with such obvious sincerity, and almost intimacy, that she grew embarrassed and felt her face redden. To cover her confusion Sophie arose, plucked a branch from the greenery with which the barge had been decorated and handed it to him.

"I will test whether your story is truthful. What plant is this?"

He held the branch up to the light. "Winter jasmine, *Jasminum nudiflorum*. Its leaves will fall in late autumn, but then, about New Year's, its bare branches will put forth yellow blossoms."

"Astonishing."

"Madame, if one is a botanist and cannot make such distinctions, then one is soon out of business."

They both burst into laughter. How long had it been since she had had just simple fun? They talked then of one thing and another until the lights of Bordeaux grew near.

"Monsieur, if you wish to speak of business matters, there is but little time left."

"I did not think it proper to put before you, as a stranger, the serious matter that I am charged with. I hope I am not now totally a stranger."

"I value your consideration."

"Then might we meet tomorrow or the day after?"

"At my office?" As soon as she said it, she knew that would not do.

"I feel sure the British have someone watching me. Is there not some private place where we might converse without fear of being seen?"

"There are no places, monsieur, where one is not observed by someone. And you doubtless understand that I could not be seen in unusual circumstances with a man who is neither husband nor close relation—and who has this afternoon drawn considerable attention to himself among all the merchants of Bordeaux."

"But are there not other circles where it would be natural for us to be seen together? Frankly, madame, I am nearly at the end of my rope. Will you not, somehow, give me a hearing?"

His face in the light of the Japanese lanterns seemed so honest and anxious, that she paused in her resolve to proceed no further. She thought about what he had said for several moments.

"There is, I suppose, one possibility. My aunt is married to the Comte de Marivaux. Their château is a few leagues from Bordeaux, rather remote from the highways. My visits there are quite commonplace; and since your face would not be known in that neighborhood, and your accent in French would be considered there nothing more than that of a Parisian . . ."

"Madame, I cannot thank you enough."

"Wait, I have not quite finished. My aunt would have to be fully informed, and in agreement. Tomorrow, then, would be quite out of the question. And should she agree that we pass an hour in conversation there, our arrivals and departures would have to be quite separate."

"Any conditions whatever that you apply. But will not your aunt's husband, the Comte de Marivaux, be hostile to the American cause?"

"Certainly, he is no republican." Sophie smiled at the

thought. "On the other hand, anything that discommodes the English, one of whose musket balls lodges in his side, meets with his approval. In any case, he is in Paris on some legal business."

"Then I will await your word, showing my face no more in Bordeaux. A message can reach me at my inn, The Golden Pheasant."

That night, as she lay sleepless in bed, Sophie could feel but astonishment at not only having agreed to meet a man she barely knew over a matter that might be fraught with dangers, but at having proposed to involve her aunt and uncle in it.

CHAPTER TWO

The next day was a Sunday, the day of the week that Sophie had for the last five years dreaded most. It was the day when she was alone with herself: the bustle of the quay stilled, the office empty, the ledgers closed, the shutters of Chardin and Co. drawn. She went to the window of her bedroom and threw open the shutters.

The quay below was piled high with lumber, bales of cotton, barrels of wine, but deserted of human activity. Then she noticed a slim figure leaning against a bollard made from a long-ago captured British cannon. The figure turned at the clatter of the shutters being thrown open and looked up at the open window. He bowed slightly to the female figure high above him in the window, and only then did she realize who it was. She withdrew into the darkness of her bedroom, slipped a silk dressing gown, a gift from someone in the China trade, over her night dress of fine-spun cotton, picked up the heavy ring of iron keys to every door and chest in the offices of Chardin and Co., and in bare feet ran down the three flights of stairs.

"*Chère cousine,*" Hyacinthe said softly, passing his lips over the back of her outheld hand, "you are looking most exotic this Sunday morning for a merchant of Bordeaux."

"I am?" Sophie glanced down at her half-exposed breasts, the flowing Chinese gown, her bare feet. But her mind was elsewhere. "When I first saw you, for a second I thought you were your father. He met me on that same quay when I arrived in France from Martinique."

"A day I remember well, Sophie."

There was a look in Hyacinthe's gray eyes that she found vaguely disturbing.

"Would you like some coffee?" she said tentatively, when those gray eyes did not leave hers. She could hear her own breathing in the stillness of the room.

"Instead, Sophie, why don't we get out of these dark chambers that smell of commerce? Why don't we go—I have a fiacre and a frisky little mare nearby—to a place I know along the river's edge, with a garden shaded by willows, where one can lunch admirably."

"Ah, Hyacinthe, you are most seductive. Were I not your cousin . . ." What was she saying? She felt herself blushing to the roots of her hair.

"Then I am to take it you will go?" The look that accompanied these slowly-spoken words was a mixture of, she thought, surprise at her daring, delight that she would go and, most of all, regret that they were, indeed, of a degree of consanguinity that made any thought of . . .

She turned away in waves of blushes. "I will go dress." As her bare feet pattered up the narrow dark stairs, it seemed to Sophie that her bold words to Hyacinthe had some other meaning than a woman's teasing—which in itself surprised her—were some kind of declaration that she no longer turned her back on life.

"*C'est charmant*", she said, "*tout à fait charmant*". And it was. The slow-moving Garonne flowed past almost at their feet, reeds along its edge, ducks floating placidly on its surface. The dappled shadow of willow leaves played across the tablecloth, a slight breeze from time to time lifted the napkins, blew strands of Sophie's dark hair into her eyes. She swept them back each time with her hand but made no effort to pin them into place.

They had ordered a *friture* of fish no bigger than one's little finger, fried and served on skewers, a green salad and a bottle of Graves brought up chilled from the inn's well, quite acceptable, but certainly nothing like the Château Carbonnieux of the night before. . . .

She knew quite well why Hyacinthe had been lounging on the quay below her window, why he had brought her to this charming little inn on the banks of the Garonne. Well let him remain in suspense a while longer.

"You say, Hyacinthe, that you remember well that day I arrived at the Château Marivaux for the first time, a girl-widow from Martinique betrothed to a great nobleman, bringing with her a dowry large enough to command such a marriage. And then . . . Tell me what you felt."

"I will never forget," he said, "the nobility of your bearing as you entered the drawing room, your head held high, though you had just been informed by father in the carriage that brought you from Bordeaux that your family's fortune, your dowry, and a great marriage with it, were all lost. And you, what did you feel?"

"Some disappointment that my grand marriage was not to be, some relief that I would not have to endure such a marriage."

"How so?"

"The Marquis de Chanteloup—whom I had met only once—clearly was marrying me for the dowry . . ."

"There were, if I may say so, other attractions than dowry."

". . . but my motives were perhaps no purer. It was the only chance I would ever have to enter the grand world of the nobility. I had married once for love, a young naval officer, hardly more than a boy; and I did not aspire to do so again.

The sensation that it would cause for a bourgeoise girl to marry the admiral of the fleet in which my late husband had served was not far from my mind, I must confess."

"And were you in love with your young André?"

"At seventeen and eighteen one is in love with the idea of love. Certainly, there was passion enough in the few scattered weeks we had together before he died of the fever in Guadeloupe . . ." She was astonished that she would say such a thing to Hyacinthe.

"And how did you find me that day of the family council, with my bourgeoise Chardin mother trying to get you to marry the son of a well-to-do Bordeaux merchant, my noble father, the Comte de Marivaux, having none of it, you saying you would marry no one but reopen the Bordeaux branch of the family business as your estranged brother Antoine had done in Quebec, and I trying to mediate and angering both my parents."

"You surprised a provincial girl with the boldness of your speech. From that moment I regarded you with greater interest."

"And?"

"I thought you very handsome, although perhaps too delicate of feature." Now, here under the willow tree by the river's edge, it was she who spoke boldly. What had been unloosed in her at the wine festival? "I thought your costume was of a nicely understated richness and noted that you wore no wig, but had had your own hair lightly powdered. It was the first time I had seen that new Paris fashion."

"I suppose what I really mean," Hycinthe said, examining the elaborate silver embroidery of his cuff, "is how you now view the advice I gave you that day."

"Ah, that." Sophie had known perfectly well what he had been driving at, and she was surprised at her coquettishness in pretending to believe he had referred only to his appearance.

"I believe you remember what I said that day?"

"Word for word. After your parents had left the room, you said that in Paris lack of dowry could be overriden, particularly if a woman had beauty, intelligence, wit . . . and independence of mind; that such a woman could do well for herself in Paris, where a young widow might enjoy great freedom and still be considered virtuous."

"And you gave me many good reasons why you would not go to Paris and throw yourself on the marriage market."

"And you said, Hyacinthe, that if you could not persuade me, I should at least not close the door entirely; that once I was immersed in business, the years would pass quickly, and that I might awake one morning and find that I no longer had any choices. . . ."

Hyacinthe looked at her longingly, and she knew that it was for all that might have been and never could be; and then he poured the last of the wine into their glasses, as though to close the subject.

Sophie finished the strong sweet coffee, put down the little flowered porcelain cup, leaned back in her chair and sighed.

"Your thoughts, cuz?" Hyacinthe had lit a clay pipe of aromatic tobacco.

"I have so much enjoyed this place and your company, Hyacinthe. I . . . I could cry for all my wasted Sundays." It was her answer to the question Hyacinthe had been too gallant to ask.

He reached across the table and put his hand on hers. "It is not too late, Sophie."

"Ah," she replied, and suddenly she no longer felt like crying.

"And now?"

"And now, I suppose we should be going."

"Haven't you neglected to tell me something?" Hyacinthe said with a slight frown, a touch of annoyance in his voice.

"And what might that be?" Sophie said with a mischievous smile.

"Did you or did you not meet my American?"

"Oh, yes. We met."

"*Mon Dieu,* Sophie! And?"

"We may meet again, possibly even tomorrow."

The carriage rumbled along the rough cobbles of the quay, passing the cathedral, the archbishop's palace, the church of St. Michel, the elegant façade of the new stock exchange, rising just beyond the docks. Ropes flung from a ship's deck coiled through the air to be caught by practiced hands that flicked them around bollards, and the ropes grew taut and groaned with the pull of the ship's weight.

And then the carriage entered the dark wine merchants' quarter of Bordeaux, the streets lined with the offices of the merchants, above warehouses piled high with barrels. The smell of wine was everywhere. They passed various churches, the carved stone façades of the houses of the richer merchants, squares containing the statues of eminent men, and on through poorer quarters, until they were through the city gate and out into the country.

The hooves of the horse beat a quick pleasant rhythm on the hard dry earth. Pine woods, a few villages in the distance marked by their church steeples, cattle in the fields, hay carts drawn by oxen, and the empty vineyards sped by, the harvest in these fields already over.

Sophie smiled. From this soil sprang the vines that produced the wine that had made her family's fortune and that had almost propelled her, the great-granddaughter of a Huguenot ship's carpenter into the upper reaches of royal and Catholic French society. And the land that had produced this wealth was not even pretty: bare, dusty, rocky, and altogether plain, but from here sprang the greatest wines that France—which meant the world—produced.

She seemed to herself to float on a rising swell of contentment, like the warm waters of Martinique she had known as a girl, and this against all reason and common sense. Not only had she agreed to meet clandestinely with the agent of a rebellious colony, at some risk to her business but—should her meeting this handsome, well-spoken American become known—at some risk to her personal reputation as well. Her feeling of contentment at having a little adventure gave way again to panic, and she came close to telling the driver to turn back. But then she thought, *Mon Dieu!* am I not due a little adventure after what fate has dealt me these last eight years?

Tame deer raised their heads to watch the carriage go by; a huntsman, a brace of pistols stuffed in his wide leather belt and surrounded by hounds, doffed his tricorne. The château itself, foursquare and dark, was no thing of beauty, built in the days when a nobleman's home had to serve as well as his fortress. Much of the Marivaux lands had long ago been sold, but the château had stubbornly been held onto generation after generation, the visible symbol of a title that went back to the time of the Crusades.

"Well, my dear," her Aunt Marthe said, looking up from the large piece of embroidery on which she was working, "I was beginning to think I shouldn't see you at all this day."

Sophie leaned over and kissed her aunt on both cheeks. "I'm late, I know. I even thought to send you a note that I would not come after all, but that would have been even more awkward for you, with the gentleman . . ." Her voice trailed off. Where, indeed, was he? "It was wrong of me to propose this meeting, and to impose the possible consequences of my own poor judgment on you."

"Sophie, do come sit down beside me. You are as nervous as a cat."

Sophie obeyed, folding her hands in her lap to conceal their shaking.

"Now you must compose yourself, you who are always so cool and careful and sure of yourself."

In her aunt's eyes and voice Sophie sensed criticism of her dry mode of life. Had she changed so much since she arrived that day from Martinique? Yes, she had become the widow Armonville—as she was known to the merchants of Bordeaux—the widow Armonville, whose family no longer bothered even to hint that it was still not too late to consider the advantages of marriage.

"There, that's better," her aunt said, not knowing that Sophie's turmoil inside was even greater than its outward signs. "Your American gentleman arrived about an hour ago, and I found him quite charming."

"What did he say to you?"

"That you had a question of trade with America to discuss, which it were better to discuss in private—much the same as you wrote me—and I find nothing irregular in that. A certain amount of confidentiality is quite natural in trade."

"What has most caused me two sleepless nights," Sophie blurted out, "is that by meeting here with the representative of a country in rebellion against its king I might do harm to the good name of Uncle Meurice. I was far too quick and careless in proposing such to Monsieur Carter, but afterwards I saw no way to withdraw my offer."

"Put your mind at rest, Sophie. This is a matter of trade; and has not the king sternly enjoined the nobility to avoid all contact with commerce, as though it were the plague? Therefore, I shall say nothing of this to Meurice, nor, you can be sure, will the servants—who answer to me."

"You have eased my fears somewhat, but," and she looked around the room as though he might be lurking somewhere, "where is Monsieur Carter?"

"I suggested that, while awaiting you, he might wish to take a stroll. I think you might find him in the summerhouse, where there should be privacy enough."

The summerhouse had been built by the Comte de Marivaux at the far end of the formal gardens he had had laid out. The gardens occupied space that had been a parade ground, and the round wooden gazebo atop the wall, resembling a Chinese pagoda, had taken the place of cannon that once commanded the road below. It had been more than a hundred years since the King of France had put down the last rebellion by the nobility and vowed they would never again take up arms against him nor make further war among themselves. Even Meurice, Comte de Marivaux, had finally had to admit that his fortifications were a threat to no one but, as his sensible wife Marthe insisted, merely an embarrassment to a gentleman who prided himself on his modern views.

Morgan Carter was seated on one of the cushioned banquettes that circled the inside of the summerhouse, looking out across the countryside. Sophie approached quietly, so that he did not turn until she was almost upon him.

As he rose to greet her, she weighed again her first impressions, which on the whole she found confirmed. His physique was that of someone used to action but his voice . . .

He bent to kiss her hand. "Madame Armonville."

. . . that of someone also used to quiet reflection. She pictured him moving astride a horse through the vast forests of America.

"Monsieur."

"I have been watching the road, and you were not followed."

"And who would follow me?" she said lightly.

"Perhaps someone who saw us together day before yesterday."

"A world of those."

"But one of whom might be in the employ of the British crown."

"Is not such a degree of secrecy a bit excessive?" She hoped he was not one of those romantically involved with intrigue for its own sake, as she supposed Hyacinthe to be.

"Madame, the enterprise with which I am entrusted by my country is of such importance that I dare not take the slightest risk that can be avoided."

She was somewhat chastened by his reply. She was unused to sincerity in those who dealt in political matters, and five years in foreign trade had not left her naive. But she could read in his clear brown eyes that his devotion to the cause for which he worked was complete. However, she must not let that influence her judgment.

"You must be the judge of how best to carry on your affairs," she said, "as I must be of how I carry on mine."

"Shall we sit? It is most pleasant here, and the gardens are beautiful, but . . ."

She laughed. ". . . but you were surprised to see them composed not of flowers but of vegetables, at this season those of the fall variety—cabbage, cauliflower, eggplant, carrots, broccoli, red and green peppers, et cetera. It was a fancy of my uncle's, who is of an original turn of mind."

"So it would appear," Morgan Carter said, seeming still

somewhat perplexed, and he looked out again across the formal garden patterned in colors as intricate as those of a Persian carpet.

They sat across from each other on the banquette, and neither spoke. He stared at her intently, and she lowered her eyes and studied his strong sunburnt hands lying quietly on his knees. They were used to physical labor, and there was a long scar across the back of one of them. A gentleman in France would not have such hands, yet he had the manners of a gentleman. He was still a puzzle to her. She wondered how she appeared to him but couldn't imagine.

Finally the silence had lasted so long that she grew amused, realizing that he was as nervous as she.

"Don't you want to tell me," she said quietly, "what you have come so far to say?"

Still he hesitated.

"Surely, one who speaks with the king's ministers cannot be intimidated by a mere woman."

"Would that being in the presence of a minister of the king were as pleasant as being in your presence. I do not grovel easily, which is what they expect of a foreigner and commoner."

She felt some pity for him. To convince the cold, conniving noblemen who were the king's ministers to support the infant American republic in its rebellion was indeed a difficult task.

"With me you have conducted yourself well," she said gently. "I cannot tell you what I will do until I know your proposal, but I can promise you an honest answer."

"Our rebellion against Great Britain must surely fail unless we soon begin to receive regular shipments of arms and ammunition."

She drew in her breath. She had walked right into the

lion's den. The shock she felt gradually subsided, and she wrestled with how best to frame her refusal to become involved. It saddened her to have to do so; and she was forced to admit how much this little adventure, now aborted, had meant to her. Here she was alone, and not unhappy to be so, with one of the most attractive men she had ever met; and he had begun by proposing that she should enter into a business arrangement that could not only lead to the ruin of both her company's fortune and reputation, but even to war between France and Great Britain. If anyone had told her that her cousin Hyacinthe tapping on the window of her office two nights before would lead to this . . .

"Have I said something that displeases you?"

"It is not that, but don't you see that what you propose to me is not possible?"

"You will not even hear me out?"

"It would not be mannerly of me to get up and leave, and if I stay I suppose I have no choice but to listen. However, I warn you that I can think of no argument that could change my mind."

"Not even if I told you that a powerful minister has secretly promised me that although the French government cannot provide transport directly, it would avert its eyes to the private shipment from France of arms and supplies for the American army?"

"I put little faith in such promises. One minister promises, another minister having more influence with the king overrules him."

"This is the most influential minister of all."

"Then you mean Foreign Minister Vergennes."

"Although I had sworn to reveal it to no one, it is he."

He had got up and now was pacing the summerhouse.

"Pray do sit down. I am nervous enough as it is." What

had made her reveal her emotional state, when her aim should be to bring the conversation to a rapid close?

"I beg your pardon," he said, sitting down. He looked at her as though there were something about her he had not noticed before.

"Do you always wear such somber colors?" he said to her surprise.

"I already encounter some disapproval for not wearing black for the rest of my life."

"The rest of your life? Surely you intend to . . ."

"Marry again? Were I to express the wish my family would be all too glad to select a suitable husband for me."

"But you have not done so?"

She should show her disapproval of such a personal question. Instead she said, "A suitable husband would be a well-to-do merchant of Bordeaux. I hear talk of commerce all day. I could not bear to hear it at night as well."

"Then you have not entirely excluded . . ."

Then she did raise an eyebrow. "Monsieur, that is an altogether intimate matter." But she knew that it was she who had overstepped the bounds.

"I must beg your pardon again."

"Shall we return to the subject? Since Vergennes has given his approval, there is nothing to keep you from hiring as many ships as you can find arms and supplies with which to fill them."

"The minister laid down two conditions: all shipments must be made by one firm, to reduce the risk that the British will find us out; and that firm must be already in the West Indian trade. No direct shipments to America will be allowed. The cargoes must be unloaded at Martinique or some other French West Indian territory and there transferred to vessels flying the American flag. These are vexingly difficult conditions."

He looked so terribly serious. She supposed he was under great strain, and with good reason. The survival of his country might depend on his success.

Now it was she who got up. Placing her hands on the summerhouse railing, she looked down, wanting to find words that would encourage him yet not commit herself to his venture. Below the high wall a stream wound its way to the Garonne, its banks thick with water plants, dragonflies flitting over the surface of the clear water in which fat trout moved lazily. She turned to him.

"You haven't had an easy time of it, have you?" The words were spoken in a low voice, with a warmth that made him raise his eyes to her and that made color come to her face.

"A botanist and woodsman is ill-equipped for the task that has been given me."

"I can give you the names of several merchants in the West Indian trade who have a taste for risk—provided the profits are large enough."

"I cannot guarantee profits, but I believe they are there to be made. But why not your firm? I would much prefer that. Its repute is high, and already I have come to trust you. I could never be sure with those who take risks only for large profits."

"I am flattered, Monsieur Carter, but even were there no risk involved I could not agree to your proposal. From the time of my great-grandfather, who founded the firm, there are two cargoes that Chardin and Co. will not accept: slaves and arms."

"As to the first, I could not agree more heartily. Of all trade that mankind has ever engaged in, that is surely the most wicked. Even as regards the second, my sympathies are with you. The weapons of war rarely are used to any purpose but promoting the ambitions of kings, paid for with the lives of the foot soldier, the common man."

Caught up in his emotion, he arose from the banquette and again began pacing the floor, the tails of his elegantly-cut Parisian coat swinging as he turned.

"Do you not see that there is for once in human history a justification for a resort to arms? Do you not see that were we to be subdued by the British crown the cause of freedom would be dead for centuries?"

"For a botanist and woodsman you speak most eloquently, but I cannot see how you expect me to take such risk."

"I would have thought one of Huguenot lineage, whose co-religionists long suffered persecution under the kings of France would . . ."

"Monsieur!"

She rose to her feet and faced him angrily. How dare he bring the martyrdom of her ancestors into his argument!

"And did not the British drive you and your family from Canada?"

"You do not play fair, Monsieur."

"I play any card that I can, Madame. The fate of my country is at stake."

"Yes, I do understand that. Let us sit down and calm ourselves. You must understand that I work not only for myself, but for aged relatives who have shares in the company and whose earnings are their sole support. I cannot afford to be frivolous. I must consider carefully each move I make."

"Then may I suppose that I have some small cause for hope?"

Indeed he did not play fair. She had not meant what he supposed . . . or had she? Tears sprang to her eyes.

"*Je suis désolé*. Please forgive me. I have made a total mess of things."

She had tried to blink away the tears, but he had seen them. The anguish etched on his face struck her to the heart with some strange mixture of pain and joy.

"No," Sophie said, "you haven't. You've only made me face matters honestly."

He looked up, uncomprehending.

How could he understand? She was wandering the beaches of Martinique again, at an age when she thought she was capable of daring anything.

"I cannot risk the good name of Chardin and Co. . . ."

"I must accept your decision," he said gravely.

". . . but it might be possible to form a separate company."

She would savor for a long time the look of astonishment that crossed his face.

"Am I to understand . . ."

"Even though the French government may turn a blind eye, the British will not," she said, returning to business quickly to hide the powerful emotions that had gripped her. "If ships are taken on the high seas?"

"I will insure against that eventuality." His anguished face had broken into a broad smile.

"The rates would be high."

"I have sufficient funds."

"The ships would be under lease, and again the rates would be high."

"Whatever is required."

"Yet another condition. Only if my senior captain—my oldest adviser—agrees, would I even consider proceeding."

"My fate is in your hands."

They sat looking at each other, silent now, and she supposed that he was as stunned as she by what had passed between them.

★ ★ ★ ★ ★

She lay back in the carriage, drained by emotion, trembling and damp with perspiration. What had she done? How would she explain to Etienne and, most of all, Archambault? He would laugh at her as a foolish woman who had been bewitched by a handsome foreigner. No, he would not do that. He would give her grave and good advice. Archambault in his younger days had been more than willing to take risks, perhaps still was. He might tell her there was a great fortune to be made . . . or lost.

Why had she done it? Had she been bewitched? Did she really trust Morgan Carter as he claimed to trust her? She knew these were questions for which she had no answers. What she did know was that she had just experienced a most passionate hour, not passion as she had understood it at age seventeen, when she had been in love with love itself, and with eighteen-year-old André Armonville as its object, but passion nonetheless. Could five years of denying herself everything possibly have made her a woman who was capable of knowing passion and adventure on some higher plane? What a tremendous, if most disturbing thought.

CHAPTER THREE

Sophie passed through the office with no more than a few words, pleading a severe headache. She could not bear to face the uncomprehending stares of Etienne and Paulot, could not even think of returning to work that afternoon. Tomorrow Archambault would arrive and would advise her what to do. She threw herself onto her bed without undressing and soon fell asleep.

When she awoke it was dark. She got up and lit a candle, changed to her nightgown and brushed out her hair. Then she went to the window to close the shutters, as she had every night for five years. Moonlight shimmered on the Garonne, stern lights flickered on ships at anchor in the river, and all up and down the quay shutters were closed. She decided not to close her shutters this beautiful moonlit night, and for a long time she lay in bed watching the moon make its path across the sky and letting her thoughts wander in unexpected ways.

The next morning, after a quick sponge bath, she dressed and took her grandfather's old brass telescope out of a dresser drawer. Then she pulled down the ladder that led to the roof, climbed up it, and pushed open the cobweb-covered door. How many years had it been since anyone had been out on the walkway from which her ancestors had watched anxiously? Times had changed. Now fortunes were not made on the arrival of a single ship from the New World, or lost on the disappearance of one. But for the moment she shared their anxiety. Before she could lift the glass to her eye she saw that the *Aphrodite* was already in port. Good old Archambault had brought his ship into harbor at first light.

"I have a treat for you, Madame Sophie," said Archambault, "a gift from our ship's agent in La Rochelle. Some little mince pies, just reheated in the cook's oven," and he whisked a napkin from a plate of pastries. "Also a bottle of cognac older than either of us."

"At eight o'clock in the morning?"

"And why not? Our ship's safely in port, and I've brought you a fine cargo from Martinique."

"You're right." She took a bite from a mince pie and raised her glass. "To your health."

"And to your prosperity," but he said it quietly and not in his usual booming voice. "You always were pretty, Sophie, but never so lovely as now. It's almost as if finally . . ."

"You're looking well yourself, Archambault," she interrupted. She buried her nose in the cognac glass, pretending to test the brandy's quality. He had aged. Transatlantic voyages were not child's play, and he had been at them since he began working for her family as a cabin boy forty years ago. He would not be able to go on much longer. Each year she had put aside a sum of money for his retirement, for he had always spent every sou he made.

"Archambault, I need your advice."

He swirled the cognac in his glass and pulled at his graying red beard. He seemed preoccupied.

"I've always come to you for help."

"That's true. Since your parents died you have."

"Even before that. They were not easy to approach."

"That's true too. What is it, Sophie?"

She drew in her breath. "I've been approached with an offer of the exclusive right to ship arms to the American rebels—with the concurrence of the government of France."

Archambault whistled softly to himself and rocked back and forth in his chair.

"As you may know, I did a certain amount of that kind of thing on my own account when I was young. Done on a large scale, well, it could be the making of a vast fortune. It all depends on the quality of the persons who have made you this offer."

"An American. The agent of their Continental Congress in Paris."

"You've met him?"

"We've had two conversations. I think he is an honest man."

"There are not many of those in the arms trade, let me tell you. How did you meet this American?"

"Through Hyacinthe."

"Not the best of recommendations, I must say." He could tell that he had upset her. "On the other hand, it can't be denied that Hyacinthe is well-connected in high places."

"Well, what do you think?"

"What do you think, Sophie?"

"I think it is the right thing to do."

"To transport arms?"

"To support the cause of freedom. We Huguenots, too, have known the tyranny of kings. Many of us sought refuge in America."

"Well, I can't say that I would mind sticking a finger in the eye of King George, but just be careful, Sophie, that you don't confuse matters of the head with those of the heart. Many of us also sought refuge in England, and this offer that has been made to you is smiled on, you say, by that government that was our persecutor."

"You don't need to give me lessons in logic, Archambault, just tell me what I should do." What exactly did he mean, matters of the heart? What else but that she should not let emotions sway her judgment. He certainly did not mean any feeling she might have for Morgan Carter. . . .

And it was exactly at this moment, she would remember afterward, that Sophie first admitted to herself that there might be such a feeling. Was that not why she had spoken sharply—and unfairly—to Archambault? He was looking at her in a curious way, and she wondered if he might not have been as fast as she to suspect what might be in her heart.

"*Je m'excuse,* Archambault. I did not mean to speak rudely to you. But do give me your advice, which you know I value above any other." She felt her face flush.

"There are other things to be considered first, Sophie."

He ignored her hand raised to prevent him refilling her glass. His face was unexpectedly grave. The cognac, his subdued air . . . He had been about to deliver some unpleasant news when her urgent plea for advice had intervened.

"What is it, Archambault?"

"You had better read this."

He handed her an envelope sealed with red wax.

"From the Governor of Martinique? Do you know its contents?"

"I have suspicions."

She tore open the envelope. Her eye flew across the page.

". . . illegal transactions . . . smuggling . . . suborning an officer of His Majesty's service . . . present yourselves before me within four months and show cause why Chardin and Co. should not be henceforth barred from the West Indian trade . . ."

It was like a bolt of lightening out of a clear sky. With a trembling hand she passed the single sheet of paper to Archambault.

"Who is responsible for these lies, and what motive lies behind them?"

"In Martinique they say the Comtesse de Brieux wishes to seize your firm as she has the lands of others."

"Is this the same woman whose husband was banished by the king to his estates in Martinique?"

"The same."

"But this is absurd. The nobility are not allowed to engage in trade."

"She would not be seen to. There would be a middleman, of course."

"What of our lawyer?"

"In her pay, it is said."

"And Jean?" She could not believe that her agent in Martinique, old Etienne's twin brother, would betray her.

"In prison on charges of smuggling and other illegal transactions."

"Outrageous! We must free him. We must prove our innocence. But if our lawyer is bought . . ."

"And any other, I fear, that you might hire. The families of both Brieux and his wife are rich, very rich. Your choices are few."

"Have I, indeed, any choices at all?"

"You could go there personally to defend yourself."

"How? Four months given to answer the charges and of that half is already gone. Were I to leave next week there would barely be time to reach Martinique before the time is up."

"And that with good winds."

"If we lose the West Indian trade the house of Chardin is ruined . . . after a hundred years . . ."

Archambault laid his large rough hand on hers. "All the way across the Atlantic I was dreading this moment. And I cannot pretend to you it is not a serious matter . . . one that could well be the ruin of Chardin and Co."

"And the end of your livelihood."

Archambault waved that thought aside. "It's you I'm worried about."

"And they will blame it all on a woman being in charge." There were no tears in her eyes now. "Somehow I will find a way . . ."

She stared out of the big stern window of the captain's cabin, open to another warm September day. The white flag scattered with the gold fleurs-de-lys of the kings of France rippled in the breeze. What justice could she expect under that flag?

There was a knock on the door.

"Entrez."

Her cousin Hyacinthe stepped over the sill followed by a taller man who had to bend over to enter the cabin: Morgan Carter. The two men stared at her in surprise.

Sophie rose to her feet. She felt outrage. This is what it meant to be a lone woman in a man's world. She faced powerful enemies with no help but that of an ill-tempered old man, a boy and . . . She looked suspiciously at Archambault, but he seemed as surprised to see their visitors as they were to see Sophie.

"You did not expect to find me here so early, did you?" she said, addressing Morgan Carter. "I told you that I must consult my senior captain before I gave you an answer. I take it ill that you have tried to precede me to parley directly with him."

"Hold, cousin," said Hyacinthe, throwing up a hand. "The fault is mine. It is I who persuaded Monsieur Carter, who only with reluctance agreed to accompany me. I thought I might do a service by giving Captain Archambault the opportunity to see for himself that the person putting forward this proposal is a gentleman of quality."

"The judgment of a woman on that matter being insufficient."

"I did not stop to think."

"Since when did a member of His Majesty's secret service—which you so manifestly are—not stop to think?"

The two men stood before her like contrite schoolboys. At least Morgan Carter had the grace not to try to excuse himself. He was as visibly shaken by what she had said as if her words had come from someone whose good opinion he put the highest value on . . . or was she reading too much into the look in his eyes?

"In any case, it no longer matters. I can be of no help to you." She tossed the governor of Martinique's letter on the table before them. "Archambault has already been hinting that my only solution now is marriage."

"I never. . . ." Yet it was Archambault who saved the day. "Now see here," he began again, his voice booming out as of old, "you are all guests under my roof, and I'm also captain of this ship. By God, I won't have this. What we ought to be doing is figuring out how—under Madame Sophie's direction—we snatch victory out of the jaws of defeat, for the benefit of us all. Now sit down."

They did as they were told. The quick glance that she and the American exchanged was charged with her still smoldering anger, his appeal for forgiveness and—it had to be admitted—some amusement on both their parts.

After Hyacinthe and Morgan Carter had read the Governor of Martinique's ultimatum, Hyacinthe spoke.

"May I, Madame President, have the floor?"

She nodded her head curtly. He would have to show her something more than cleverness.

"I think I see a solution. The Comtesse de Brieux has played a card, and we hold no higher card in that suit. We must, therefore, trump it."

"That is?"

"We must lay upon the governor's order an order of a higher sort, that makes the governor's impossible to execute. I can assure you that, although the government will never admit to it, the king himself has given his consent to the supply of arms to America. If the firm of Chardin, or another under its control, is the instrument of this policy, then the Comtesse de Brieux has been trumped."

It sounded too simple. She avoided Morgan Carter's eyes and sought those of Archambault, but he was gazing out the stern window. After her tirade he was keeping out of the line of fire.

"Sophie, if you were to agree to Monsieur Carter's proposal," Hyacinthe continued, "then I would be in a position to go straightway to Paris and plead that a special courier be sent to Martinique with instructions that the trade of Chardin and Co. not be interfered with."

Hyacinthe, she saw, was for once dead serious. His career was at stake. He had given promises on which he must make good. For Morgan Carter even more rested on her answer. For her the fate of the house of Chardin was on the table. Even Archambault had a stake in her reply. Outside the firm of Chardin and Co. a fifty-four year old ship's captain would not easily find employment.

"All well and good, Hyacinthe, but who will manage this business in Martinique? That is the tricky part. Certainly not old Jean, even supposing he were released from jail."

"You might."

"Me? Go to Martinique?" She had not expected this.

"You would, in any case, be in a better position there to

protect your interests. There is no guarantee that I will be able to obtain ministerial orders to the governor that will prevent the Comtesse de Brieux from despoiling you of your property."

"Still . . ." There was logic in what Hyacinthe said; and had not Archambault earlier, and quite independently, suggested the same course? And with yet another gray Bordeaux winter soon to come, would she, who had no close family ties, rather not be in her beloved, warm and sunny Martinique? Then why was she reluctant? She could but suspect that it had something to do with Morgan Carter. True, he would soon be returning to Paris; but the thought of putting an ocean between them . . . She put such speculation out of her mind.

"Should you decide for Martinique, you might by and by see me there," Morgan Carter said awkwardly, as if it were a matter of embarrassment to him, "for as soon as I am convinced the flow of arms will be a steady one, it is my intention to go to the French West Indies myself, to keep an eye on the transfer of these arms to American vessels."

The speed with which things were developing she found quite unnerving, and she was not at all sure that this thought of going to Martinique had not just occurred to him, or that he and Hyacinthe had not agreed upon some scheme to advance the interests of governments, in which she was merely a pawn. She cut short this ungenerous thought as well.

"Tell me, Hyacinthe, something of this Comte and Comtesse de Brieux. Surely, you know much about them."

"Much that is not fit for your ears, Sophie. Two of the great land-owning families of France are joined in those two creatures; and although the king has clipped their wings—I do not think they will be allowed to return to France as long as Louis XVI lives—they still wield influence behind the scenes."

"And the crime for which the count was banished?"

"I will spare you the details, but the comte was famous, or I should say notorious, for his entertainments. Of a summer evening, I am told, guests of both sexes might be seen swimming or chasing each other through the woods while quite naked. The king's own private life is above reproach, but he certainly recognizes the moral level of a certain segment of the upper nobility and turns a blind eye to much. In this case the king was outraged to hear not so much of what was going on, but to hear this scandalous behavior linked some of the grandest names in France with village girls. Beyond that, there were rumors of rough treatment of some of these young women, one of whom went to a magistrate with her story. The comte was arrested, but before the matter could be pursued, and further damage done the reputation of the noble class, already everywhere under attack, the king intervened. He issued a *lettre de cachet,* by which His Majesty may override the law, ordering the Comet de Brieux to his estates in Martinique along with his lady."

"What of the comtesse?"

"They say that the count's lust for unusual gratification is equaled only by her lust for property. Since her comet-like passage through the skies of Paris society was extinguished in mid-flight, she has vowed to rule in Martinique as Marie-Antoinette rules in France. She purchases or extorts vast properties, forms a circle of sycophants, presides over a dissolute court—and now, it would seem, aspires to take over the West Indian trade."

"I see." A shudder of loathing ran through Sophie's body. In the normal course of events a young woman of Bordeaux would not hear of the acts of such monsters, and here she was toying with the idea of confronting them on their own ground.

"Now, what of this trade that you would have me undertake? Where are these military supplies?"

"As you are aware," said Morgan Carter, "there exists a gloomy old fortress to the north, at the point where the Gironde flows into the Atlantic. It is used as a depot for army materiel, and I carry an order from the minister of war authorizing sales from this stock up to the amount of one million livres."

"One million livres! But that is a vast sum."

"Cannon and muskets do not come cheaply."

"And where does this money come from?"

Hyacinthe opened his wallet and dramatically threw a piece of paper on the table. "A draft for two million livres on the Bank of Paris, where that amount has been deposited by . . . shall we say persons friendly to the American cause."

Sophie picked up the paper, incredulous. "The name of the payee is blank."

"You may put there any name you please, Sophie. It is for you to choose."

The point of no return was upon her. Things had moved so quickly these last days that there had been no time for reflection. But she could still, even now, turn back from this mad venture, return to the safe and comfortable routine she had known for five years. But could she? There was still the Comtesse de Brieux.

She looked at their faces. Hyacinthe smiled, inscrutable, as became his profession. Archambault looked as if he had misgivings, perhaps regretting that he had, in the first place, proposed her going to Martinique. As for Morgan Carter, his eyes implored her—to do what? In the end her decision was made by a girl of fifteen, whose promise she must now either keep or forever abandon.

"Archambault, bring me pen and ink."

With a trembling hand she wrote across the bank draft at the point where the payee's name was to be inserted: "The New World Trading Co."

Hyacinthe got up from his chair and brought the bottle of old cognac and four glasses from the sideboard.

"May I propose a toast? To a new partnership that will astonish the world."

They clinked their glasses, and it was Archambault's turn.

"To the next hundred years of Chardin and Co."

"Très bien!"

Then Morgan Carter's. "To Madame Sophie Armonville, who has this day set us on a course that must lead to . . . a new world."

"Bravo!"

She was too overcome with emotion to look into his eyes. It was her turn, and she lifted her glass. There was so much that she wanted to say, conflicting things even, none of which could be said in the few words of a toast

"That Fortune may smile on us, for we will surely need her to."

They touched glasses again, and as they did she looked up. There were tears in Morgan Carter's eyes.

"Brave words all. Let us hope we can do honor to them," she said brusquely and sat down.

CHAPTER FOUR

Sophie Armonville awoke on the fifth day of this astonishing voyage on which she had embarked, the shutters once again open to the dawn, to find that she had been turned inside out. For five years she had been constant activity on the outside and dead within; now she was total calm on the outside and great excitement within.

Most of all, lying motionless in her bed, she felt her body: arms, legs, hands, feet, hips, breasts, neck, face, eyes, mouth, the mass of dark hair that wound around her neck and spread out over her shoulders. Before, she had gone to bed each night her mind filled with columns of figures, bills of exchange, barrels and crates and bundles to be loaded and unloaded; and now she had awakened to find in her bed the body of a woman, still young, who did not give a damn for profit and loss.

This calm did not leave her, as she feared it might, but stayed with her as she bathed and dressed and descended the stairs.

Paulot leaped up to bring Sophie her coffee. Etienne remained hunched over his ledger.

"What news?" She had no intention of explaining her absences.

"We have a cargo for the *Artemis*," Etienne mumbled into the ledger.

"Not possible. I've leased the *Artemis*, the *Ariadne* and the *Aphrodite* for a very handsome price."

"*Sacrebleu!* You've what?" Etienne threw down his pen. "To what firm?"

"The New World Trading Co."

"Totally unknown."

Etienne nodded his head solemnly, as if to say that the pressures on a woman of running a business had led to just what he had expected: she had taken total leave of her senses.

"And I am going to Martinique."

Paulot spilled her coffee on the rug.

The days that followed were among the most difficult of Sophie's life. Each day could be faced when she had known that all her days would be the same, succeeding one another endlessly, as her life slowly dwindled away. But now that hope was reborn that she might yet live with passion, she burned with impatience. She counted each day that passed with her still in her office as a day lost to life. She slept fitfully and often awakened from dreams made up of childhood images of Martinique: white sand beaches, palm trees, the cloud-capped volcano, paths like green tunnels through the banana leaves.

Even the weather conspired to darken her mood. While she dreamed of tropical beaches, dark clouds covered the formerly brilliant September skies of Bordeaux. A fine drizzle fell continuously, and the fog grew so heavy that the lights along the quay were left burning all day.

Hyacinthe had returned to Paris, taking with him the articles of incorporation for their new company, to try and persuade his minister to issue orders to the Governor of Martinique to allow free passage of its ships. It would be better that such an order precede her to Martinique, but whether such an order could be obtained at all was impossible to know. Archambault had sailed with the *Aphrodite*, supposedly for Spain; but once at sea he had turned back and headed for Fort Colbert. There Morgan, for so she now called him to herself, was selecting the arms and ammunition most needed by the American army to make up the first cargo.

She tried not to think too much of Morgan, for she was not entirely sure of her feelings toward him, and certainly she was not sure of his toward her. What she did know was that she was most reluctant to have an ocean put between them.

Once more Sophie was sitting late at her accounts, not so much because she needed to as to tire herself to the point that she could sleep, when a tapping came at the window. It was Major Richard, the governor's aide. She got up to unlock the door. What could he possibly want of her at this hour of the night?

He came through the door apologizing profusely for any inconvenience, his black cloak and black tricorne hat, pulled down to his nose, streaming with water. He was not in uniform, and Sophie had a premonition of disaster. Well, when she had filled in that blank on a note for two million livres, she had signed away, for vague hopes of happiness, her so carefully secured place in the merchant community. So be it.

"A touch of brandy, Major?"

She needed time to arrange her defenses.

"Nothing could be more welcome."

She took from a cupboard the remains of the bottle of old cognac that Archambault had insisted she take with her when she left the *Aphrodite*. She poured a bit of the amber liquid into a brandy glass and turned it slowly over a candle. When it was sufficiently warmed, she wiped the soot from the glass and handed it to Major Richard.

"I assume, Major, that this is not a social call of the usual kind."

"No, and it is one that I am making at some risk."

"Risk to whom?"

"There are things I would tell you that I should not."

She had understood him well enough. The risk was to his own career.

He put his nose into the glass she had handed him and inhaled.

"This is extraordinary," he said, even before tasting it.

"Older than our combined ages, Major. Now, what is it?"

"You will protect me?"

She did not think that Morgan Carter would have demanded such an assurance. She nodded her assent.

"The American. I do not know or care what your relationship is to him."

He paused, but she did not respond. She reckoned he cared. Despite five years of living alone and—as Hyacinthe had put it that first night—going every night up to a cold bed, she was a woman; and she had known from the first instant that afternoon at the Château Ivran that Major Richard had become infatuated with her. So much the better. She was surprised at her own coolness.

"We, naturally, have had him watched. He was seen going aboard one of your ships . . . while you were aboard. This was reported to Paris."

"I do not deny it."

"You must understand that dozens of reports of this kind are sent on to Paris each week. Hardly ever is there a response. But this time . . ."

"This time?"

"The governor has been ordered to put this American under arrest."

"And have you done so?"

"We cannot find him. I have been instructed to interrogate you tomorrow on his whereabouts—and what business you had with him aboard your ship. But first, I wanted to warn you, to hear from your own lips . . . Sophie. . . ."

"I can tell you this, Major Richard. I do not know his whereabouts; and as for the meeting aboard the *Aphrodite*, he had some preposterous proposal to make that no sane person in business would consider for an instant—and so I shall reply to you officially tomorrow."

"You delight me. I had hoped to hear this from you." Richard rose to his feet. "You have nothing to fear. Count on me for that. Now, it would be unwise for me to linger." He kissed her hand with fervor.

When Major Richard had gone Sophie could barely keep on her feet. To overcome her faintness she downed the remains of his brandy. Then she put on her cloak, went straight to the stables, up the ladder and awakened her driver Claude who, thank God, had not been in town carousing. They had a long night before them.

The road to Fort Colbert was little more than two ruts through the barren landscape, and these had now turned to mud. Every few hundred paces the driver was obliged to descend and, lantern in hand, lead the horses around deep pools of muddy water covering the track.

Hours passed as they inched their way toward the fort, while she endured the torture of imagining ever more terrible fates being prepared for this man she had known for only a matter of days. Had she ever, in fact, felt such concern for anyone? She had dared not ask Richard on what charges Morgan was to be arrested, for that would have been to show too much interest. Of one thing she was sure: he must flee.

Her brief dream of freedom, a passionate life, of returning to her childhood paradise, with Morgan one day near her—was it over? Was the flower that had blossomed so suddenly and unexpectedly in the barren confines of her office on the Bordeaux quay destined to wither away after only a few days?

At last the light at the gate of Fort Colbert came into view. The lantern hung from a guardhouse where a barrier bristling with sharp points of steel blocked the road. She descended from the carriage. The rain had ceased and the moon was emerging from the clouds. Turning, she scanned the desolate empty landscape and assured herself that she had not been followed. A sleepy sentry confronted her with fixed bayonet.

"What is this?" the sentry said roughly. "Have you lost your way?"

"No. I have urgent business."

"Give me the name of the officer with whom you have this urgent business."

Sophie was momentarily puzzled, but then realized that she had been taken for the mistress, or worse, of some officer in the fort. What could she say?

"I cannot."

"Then turn your carriage around and be gone."

"Allow me to speak to the officer of the guard."

"Ca, c'est impossible."

How was she to deal with this peasant lad, pale and undernourished, in an ill-fitting uniform. He clearly had orders not to disturb his sleeping officer. She had nothing to lose.

"If you do not let me speak to the officer of the guard I shall report you to Colonel Duffet."

She had happened to hear Hyacinthe mention the name of the commandant of the fort, and this had an immediate effect. The boy struggled with himself for several seconds. He was in trouble whatever he did, and he was trying to decide which form of trouble was likely to be the least painful. He turned on his heel and, affecting a military bearing as best he could, marched back to the guardhouse.

A few minutes later a dishevelled officer appeared at the barrier. Sophie had thrown off the hood that shadowed her face in hopes of winning favor with what she had of youth and beauty. But instead of some hardened veteran, a lieutenant not much older than the sentry stepped into the lantern light.

"What is your business, Madame?"

"There is an American inside with whom I have urgent need to speak."

"This is a French military fort. There are no Americans here."

How stupid of her. Of course they would not admit that an American was at the fort, and even should this young lieutenant be aware of Morgan's presence he would have been kept completely in the dark as to his mission.

"There is an American here. And do not bother to deny that there is also a ship loading at your dock, for I am its owner."

"You are the ship's owner?" said the young lieutenant incredulously. He had given away the show and quickly realized it.

She felt sorry for him, but her stakes were far larger than his.

"I assure you that I am. You must tell Colonel Duffet that Madame Sophie Armonville is here on a serious matter and desires admittance."

"At three o'clock in the morning? I dare not."

"It will not go well with you if you refuse me."

She held her breath. She had put the lieutenant in the same spot as the sentry. Would it work again?

Without another word the lieutenant turned and disappeared into the fort. Sophie climbed back into her carriage, for the night was cold and damp, and fell weakly onto the cushions. It was a full half hour before the lieutenant returned.

"You may follow me. Your carriage and driver must wait here."

"Very well, but at least get my driver some hot drink."

Bleary-eyed, Claude smiled at her in appreciation.

To say that Fort Colbert was gloomy, as Morgan had, was to understate the case. It was more like a dark and dismal medieval prison than one of the king's fortresses. In place of stairs there was an inclined plane designed to permit the movement of artillery pieces from one level to another; and at each turning a single lantern gave out just enough light to allow passage to the next level.

Their ascent ended on the cannon-lined ramparts, at a door in one of the fortress's towers. The lieutenant opened the door, and when she stepped inside closed it behind her. She was alone in what appeared to be a guardroom, bare but for a few chairs and a table on which a lighted lamp had been placed; but then she heard footsteps quickly approaching.

Would it be Colonel Duffet, half-asleep and angry? An aide? Morgan himself? Or perhaps Archambault, raised from his bunk on the *Aphrodite* to verify her identity?

The door flew open. It was Morgan, enveloped in a black cloak, his head bare. His presence seemed to fill the room. Throwing the door shut behind him he came straight to her and, to her utter surprise, gripped her by the shoulders with his large strong hands.

"Sophie . . . Madame . . . are you in danger, has some misfortune befallen you, has someone . . . ?"

"No, no. I am well, not in the least danger."

From the look in his eyes she would not have wanted to be the someone who threatened her. He released her shoulders from his grip.

"It is you who are in danger," she said in a low voice. "I came to warn you."

"You came over that hellish road all through the night just to warn me . . ."

"That the governor has received orders from Paris for your arrest."

"Ah. That, at least, I can deal with. But when they told me you were here, I truly feared . . . I should never have brought you into this dangerous business."

"You argued passionately enough that I do so."

"Then you were but a merchant of Bordeaux, who happened to be a woman, but now . . ."

"Can we leave this musty room? Its stale air makes me feel faint. Perhaps we could walk upon the ramparts."

She did feel faint, but she also needed to stop this flow of words. Ever since that night when Hyacinthe had tapped upon her window things had moved too fast for her. For now, she did not want him to say more.

They walked silently for a while along the ramparts. A huge lantern that hung from a tower, to mark the fort's location for ships at sea, swung in the breeze, and the shadows of their cloaked figures thrown on the interior walls of the fort were like giant birds of prey swooping down.

"You must not concern yourself with my safety," she said. "Any danger to me will be slight enough; and had I not longed for a little adventure, you would not have persuaded me to join your enterprise. You cannot imagine how dull my life has been."

She hoped that this little speech would distract him from any expression of his feelings toward her. She was not ready for that—if, indeed, he had any such intention.

"I would have thought that there was some excitement in international trade."

"For those who cross the seas, there are months of boredom and some moments of deadly peril. For those who remain behind figuring profit and loss and overseeing the loading and unloading of cargoes, there is only the former. But what of your cargo—our cargo?"

"The *Aphrodite* is fully loaded now and can sail when the captain gives the word."

"You could sail with her. You certainly cannot now remain here."

Why had it not occurred to her that his fleeing, as he must, need not part them, indeed might speed quite the opposite? Hope was reborn again.

"Now there is no question of my going to Martinique."

"What is this you say?"

"Don't you see that I must return to Paris? Someone has overturned my agreement with the foreign minister, or attempts to do so. I must return and set things right again. This order for my arrest, from wherever it comes, is meant to frighten me off. One shipload of arms is nothing. The ships must follow one after the other, as we agreed."

Sophie felt numb. Better not to know hope than have it constantly snatched from her. Out of anger and frustration she grew reckless.

"I understand full well what we agreed to, but are we not in this together? That was my understanding of your recent words to me. Otherwise do you think . . . Did you not understand that I too sail for Martinique?"

His eyes looked pleadingly into hers, pleading for understanding that duty . . . Yes, duty. Already she could see that this was to be her rival, and already she may have lost.

From the courtyard below came a commotion and then the improbable sound of someone riding a horse up the gun ramp. Level after level, the sound of iron on stone grew louder until into the light of the signal lantern rode a scarecrow of a figure, horse and rider covered in mud. Slowly Hyacinthe slid down from his mount and fell to the pavement. Sophie and Morgan caught him as he fell.

Back in the guardroom orderlies brought hot water, soap, towels, brandy and a cold chicken pie, and only after he had washed, drunk and eaten did Hyacinthe speak.

"I may have, *ma chère cousine,* and my distinguished colleague, set some sort of record. From Paris to Bordeaux in three days and most of three nights, with—if my addled brain has it right—eighteen changes of mount. The insides of my thighs and my posterior are not a sight to please any of the refined ladies of my acquaintance."

Sophie could but laugh at this totally unacceptable remark. But what impressed her was that within the slight frame of her foppish cousin there apparently dwelt a man of steel.

"One can suppose that you bring some news?" Morgan said, adopting Hyacinthe's light tone, but clearly as impressed as Sophie at this feat.

"I do. And I can only assume that your presence here, dear Sophie, is in connection with the order that has been issued for our friend Morgan's arrest."

"That is so."

"Wiser heads have prevailed. If you will fill my glass and attend on me, I will give you the story."

"At your disposal," said Morgan.

Once again she was pleased to see with what grace these two men dealt with the situation in which they found themselves.

"But first we should offer a toast to Madame Sophie Armonville, who made her way to this place over perhaps not so many leagues but against all tradition."

Sophie was touched by Morgan's acknowledgment that what a young widow of Bordeaux had done this night was, if not the equal of her cousin's feat, worthy of praise.

"Enough of compliments," she said, turning to Hyacinthe. "What is your story?"

"Soon told. Our plans have been discovered by the British secret service, and the British ambassador in Paris, Lord Stormont, has called on Foreign Minister Vergennes and told him in no uncertain terms that the supply of arms to the Americans—particularly the large-bore cannon not yet available to the rebels, which are loaded aboard the *Aphrodite*—could be a *casus belli*, provocation sufficient for Britain to declare war on France."

"*Mon Dieu!*" was all that Sophie could respond.

"The story is not yet finished, cuz. There was panic among that hutch of rabbits which passes for the government of France, and certain ill-advised orders were issued. Vergennes, however, confident of the king's favor, has sent me to tell you that the *Aphrodite* is to sail at once, that all that has been agreed to stands, and that Monsieur Carter is to return to Paris to consult with him. After that Morgan will probably have to absent himself from France for a while, so that the government may credibly say to the British that they were not, as they promised, able to effect his arrest."

"Hyacinthe," began Sophie, but her cousin's head had fallen on the mud-splattered jacket of his uniform. He was sound asleep.

Morgan spread his cloak on the floor, picked up the sleeping Hyacinthe, as though he were a child, laid him upon it and wrapped it around him.

"A few hours sleep will restore him."

"Shall we leave him, then?"

Morgan turned down the lamp until only the faintest glow pervaded the room.

Out on the ramparts the wind had died down, and the first

hint of pink marked the horizon.

"When will our ship sail?" she said at last.

"The *Aphrodite* is yours, and when it sails is for you to command."

She supposed he meant it straightforwardly, but Aphrodite was also the goddess of love. . . .

"I would propose that she sail this very morning, as soon as there is enough light. I believe the tide is right, and who knows what transpires in Paris? She may have to outrun the French fleet as well as the British. But if there is a man alive better able to do that than Archambault I do not know his name."

"I will send someone to warn him," Morgan said, turning; but she caught his hand.

"No, wait a moment." She had much to say, but there was no time to arrange her thoughts, her words. "You are cold. Come, share my cloak," and she threw it over both their shoulders.

"When will you sail for Martinique . . . Sophie?"

They leaned on the parapet together looking out to sea.

"As soon as it can be arranged . . . Morgan. And now I cannot object to your returning to Paris, since the minister has ordered it. And if you must absent yourself from France . . ."

"Where will I go? God willing, to Martinique."

"I believe you will find me there."

She had said, this time, exactly what she had meant to say. Whether even now there was to be anything between them she could not know. The obstacles were many: two strong wills, two different dreams, great distances soon to separate them, and perhaps great dangers. What she did know was that there would be between them either nothing or everything.

★ ★ ★ ★ ★

Sophie came down from her apartment, having bathed and changed from her muddy clothes and shoes, just as the sun was setting. The *Aphrodite* would be well out to sea now, with a cargo that could change history; that is, if they were not stopped by the French navy or, God forbid, intercepted by the British fleet.

By now the quiet office routine of years had been reduced to chaos. The boy Paulot stared at her as if she were a madwoman. Old Etienne had abandoned his ledger and stood staring out the window, his hands clasped behind him.

"Have you been able to book passage?" she said to Etienne's back.

"Oh, yes. But you'll have to go to La Rochelle. The royal packet sails from there in six days' time."

"Splendid."

"No, Sophie," said the old man, turning to face her, "it is not splendid. What you are doing is willful, unreasonable, perverse and," his voice shaking, "ruinous."

"And also my own affair."

"Not only yours. Aged relatives depend on the firm's prosperity."

"As I am so often reminded."

"Your father on his deathbed asked that I see you safely to harbor."

"Which you have done and done well." Sophie softened her voice. Despite his rough manner, she knew that Etienne had only her best interests at heart and could not understand what had come over her. "I am now twenty-five years old and must follow my own destiny, if I am to have one."

"Take me back to Martinique with you," the boy cried out.

"Martinique, indeed," snarled Etienne, turning on

Paulot. "If it were not for my brother Jean, and Archambault willing to take you aboard, it would have been the prison of Fort Royal for you."

"He is right, Paulot. You are going to have to put your homesickness aside. Your future, and you can have one, is here in France. But do not forget, Etienne, that it is your brother Jean who is now in that very prison—however false the accusations brought against him through the stratagems of the Comtesse de Brieux—and part of my purpose in journeying to Martinique is to secure his release."

"At his age he won't last long in such a prison."

"Then the sooner I arrive the better. How fast is this packet?"

"Fast enough. They're built for speed, not comfort. It will be rough sailing," and this seemed to give Etienne some satisfaction.

She looked around the room that had known her for five years, now stripped of all her personal belongings. Yet it seemed undiminished, filled with mahogany furniture from the West Indies, a sofa, chairs, a long oval table, matching mirrors, a pair of tall armoires, a writing desk, the wide four-poster bed. Several generations of Chardin women had known this room, that bed. Had they known passion, even some happiness here, or only the comfort of a well-ordered bourgeois life?

She looked around the room for the last time, then she closed and locked the two trunks that held all that was truly hers, mostly clothes and mementos from Martinique and Canada kept through the years. All the rest belonged to a stranger whose life she had lived.

She had already made her farewell to Etienne and thrust a pouch of coins into Paulot's hand. She went to the top of the servants' stair and called down to her driver, "Claude, I am ready."

Her carriage arrived at La Rochelle at dusk. She could easily pick out among the ships tied up along the quay the long dark shape of the frigate that would bear the king's correspondence to the West Indies. The inn on the quay where Etienne had arranged her lodging was, and it did not surprise her, opposite the stern of *La Bonne Nouvelle*. The inn itself was also just what she would have expected of Etienne: modest but comfortable, managed by a couple whose three sturdy sons would provide whatever protection a young woman traveling alone might need.

It came as a great surprise then, this night she had meant to pass alone before sailing with the morning tide, that the innkeeper came to her room to inquire whether she would receive a gentleman with a message which he would leave personally or not at all.

"Show him up."

The young man who entered her room, in the blue and white uniform of the French army, she immediately recognized by his bearing and speech as a member of the upper nobility. This was the sort of junior officer who would find himself a colonel before his twenty-fifth birthday.

"Madame, may I introduce myself. Captain d'Amboise. I am instructed to deliver to you personally this letter."

She took the envelope from him and knew at once from the faint scent of a certain cologne that it was from Hyacinthe. It was his custom to pass a cologne-scented handkerchief across his correspondence with members of the female sex.

"And how fares my cousin, Captain?"

"He is well, and he has charged me with also saying to you

that he is making every effort to have that other message of which you are aware dispatched; but the outcome is as yet uncertain."

That would be the hoped-for instructions to the governor of Martinique lifting the ban on the firm of Chardin and Co. "I am greatly obliged to you, Captain, for this service."

"It has been my pleasure. Now, Madame, if I may take my leave, I have other duties to perform, and none nearly so pleasant as this," and his lips lightly hovered for an instant over her extended hand.

As soon as Captain d'Amboise had gone she sat down and broke the seal on Hyacinthe's letter.

"Paris, 1st October, 1776

"My dearest cousin,

"I hasten to reply to your letter informing me that you are sailing from La Rochelle in three days' time. Only the departure of a royal courier within the hour gives me any hope that this will reach you before you sail.

"Sophie, it is not my place to speak to you as a sympathetic uncle might, but of those you have none. Neither have I by my conduct and way of life earned the right to offer advice of any sort to an honest young woman. Nevertheless, we have always held each other in affection, and I believe that you know that where you are concerned my counsel could never be anything but sincere.

"I have over the years watched you more than you know. I was there, by chance, that day you arrived from Martinique, still hardly more than a girl, but so full of life that I believed you would have the spirit to make a success of whatever your heart and mind directed you to. My disagreement with the course you chose has been no secret to you, though neither of us ever spoke of it.

"And then one night I did reenter your life and found that you were still that young woman of spirit I had known, and I have seen since your first steps toward reclaiming the life that was taken from you. Knowing that much, I am emboldened to say do not turn back, have courage, take the risks, live and be free. These are very general words of advice—and not ones that would be approved of from an uncle. I do not know all that is in your heart, so I will say no more, but I have had a feeling that some such words as these might be useful to you at this moment.

"Sophie, I wish you a calm voyage, a safe harbor and, at last, the happiness you deserve.

"With my love and affection,
"Hyacinthe."

Sophie put the letter on the table and went to the window, looked out on the lights of the ships in the harbor. Somehow Hyacinthe had sensed that she was standing at the entrance to the life that she had always desired, yet hesitating to enter. Why had she not spoken to Morgan? Why had he not spoken to her? For now she knew that their feelings for each other, if not yet fully formed, were mutual. She began to cry, and this time there was no stemming the tears, tears made up of regret, frustration, fear and happiness. She threw herself on the bed and let the tears flow. After tonight there would be no more tears. This was the only chance for happiness she would ever have, and she meant to fight for it with all her being.

CHAPTER FIVE

Sophie was up at dawn, anxious for the future to unfold itself as quickly as possible. The thought of six to eight weeks aboard the frigate *La Bonne Nouvelle*, the not knowing when—or even whether—she would see Morgan in Martinique, the uncertain fate of Chardin and Co., all weighed heavily upon her. At least, she told herself as she breakfasted on coffee and a brioche, the curtain had risen on the drama she had begun by accepting Morgan's proposition. In little more than an hour she would leave France for Martinique and a most uncertain future. Well, let the play begin.

"Welcome aboard, Madame Armonville," Captain Joubert said, and he bowed and kissed her hand. "I will try to make the voyage as comfortable for you as possible."

"I am a good sailor, captain, and not unused to the sea. My first voyage was all the way from Quebec to . . ."

Her voice trailed off. A carriage had pulled up on the dock, a door opened, and a pair of long legs emerged.

The captain's gaze followed hers. "From Quebec to?"

"Martinique. . . ."

Morgan Carter descended from the carriage. Before there was even time for Sophie to say what were the feelings that made her heart beat so violently, he was up the ladder and standing beside them.

"Excuse me, madame," he said, looking at Sophie as though he had never seen her until that moment. "I have a rather urgent message for Captain Joubert," and he handed the captain an envelope.

"From the Minister of the Navy." Captain Joubert broke the seal and opened the letter. While he read, Sophie stared wide-eyed at Morgan, still in the grip of strong and conflicting emotions.

"So, Monsieur Duplessis, you sail with us. Since my minister commands, without having to trouble himself with practicalities, I must comply. But it is only through the sudden illness of one of my prospective passengers that a spare cabin remains; and I must warn you it is but the size of an armoire. I suppose you have a trunk."

"Yes sir, strapped to the back of the carriage."

The captain turned to one of his officers and ordered it brought aboard. "Now, madame, monsieur, if you will excuse me, I must see us underway."

"What is the meaning of this? Monsieur Duplessis, indeed!" Sophie whispered as soon as the captain had left them. She now had her emotions more under control and understood them better. An hour before she had been longing for Morgan's presence, but having him at close quarters for six or eight weeks under false pretences was not what she would have desired at all.

"The letter from the minister so names me, though it hints that my real identity is otherwise."

"You knew I was aboard?"

"That is why I sped from Paris in hopes of beginning the exile that has been decreed for me aboard the same ship." Her stern look caused him to pause. "But perhaps I should have thought more of the circumstances this would create."

"It is awkward to have to treat you as a stranger in front of others." She could not say the truth: that a woman who is beginning to feel something akin to love needs the liberty to retreat from the object of this new feeling from time to time.

"Well," he said with a smile, "we could be strangers who

are seen to become friends with the passage of the days, as sometimes happens aboard ship."

She could but smile slightly but did not answer directly. "You, of course, learned from Hyacinthe that I sailed aboard *La Bonne Nouvelle*."

"He urged me on, it is true, but there was also the consideration that I would be well advised to travel aboard a French warship, to preclude the possibility of falling into British hands."

She now saw Hyacinthe's letter in a somewhat different light, not only as an exhortation to dare to live her desires but also as a bit of matchmaking. It was not the first time that she had felt an uneasiness that Morgan and Hyacinthe were attempting to direct her actions. To dare to live her desires might mean that she would come to love Morgan, but she must be free to make that choice.

"Have I displeased you?" He surely knew that he had.

"No, of course not. I made it quite clear that I hoped to see you in Martinique." True enough, but Sophie resolved to treat Morgan for the time being with some reserve.

As they spoke to each other in lowered voices, sails were unfurled and their ship began to move away from the dock, its bow turning toward the narrow entrance to the harbor.

"Those two towers that guard the harbor entrance, Monsieur Duplessis, are the Tower of the Chain and the Tower of St. Nicholas," Sophie said in a normal speaking voice. If they continued to converse it could not be in whispers. Whether she wanted it or not, the charade had begun. "Between them a great chain is drawn at night to close the harbor."

"La Rochelle seems a pleasant city," Morgan replied, assuming his role, "and I regret that my last-minute arrival made it impossible for me to visit its sights. I'm sure it has an interesting history."

"La Rochelle has a sad history, particularly if one is Huguenot. A hundred and fifty years ago it was a Protestant city that did not recognize the authority of the King of France. To end this independence Cardinal Richelieu had it besieged, but it only surrendered when the last survivors were too weak to fight on. Of the inhabitants five out of every six were dead of starvation, including many from my family—so that the flag of the King of France could fly from the Tower of St. Nicholas, as it does today."

"Such is the way of kings, as we in America know only too well," Morgan said, lowering his voice. "We too have pledged our lives for our beliefs, but there are few among us, I reckon, who would have the courage to endure what you describe."

"And it availed them nothing. Let us hope your country's struggle has a happier outcome."

"It must."

Hyacinthe's wish for a calm voyage could not have been better fulfilled. A day out from Bordeaux an autumn calm fell upon the Atlantic, with just enough breeze to move them steadily along. The ocean was a deep blue and, day after day, the sky cloudless. It seemed to Sophie that they were already sailing in tropical waters.

She was pleased with Morgan's discreet behavior toward her, both as regarded the fiction that they were strangers and—for they could have found occasions to whisper together—his leaving her at peace to make her own decisions on how and whether their relations would develop. What conversation she had with him was in his chosen role as a Creole merchant in the West Indian trade, a piece of ironic humor she quite appreciated. The suspicions that had caused her reserve toward him were melting away.

"Tell me," she said, as they strolled the deck one moonlit

evening, "what caused you to choose New Orleans as your place of origin, Monsieur Duplessis?"

"I determined the first day that none of the ship's officers or the other passengers were familiar with the place, and therefore whatever statements I might make about my native city were unlikely to be contradicted."

She laughed and wished it were possible for her to put her hand in his. "And through your conversations with me you have now learned enough about the West Indian trade that you are unlikely now to make any serious slips in that regard; and should you, I will come to your rescue."

"It has been rather good sport, and with my experience as American agent in Paris I flatter myself that I have developed some skill in deception. Nonetheless, I look forward to the day when we reach Martinique and I can call you Sophie again and we can resume genuine relations."

And then he did take her hand in his. She left it there for a few seconds for the sheer pleasure of the feel of his touch, but then withdrew it.

"We must remain careful, Morgan. You—and I—have much at stake."

"But surely, by now, no one would find it strange that the handsome young widow from Bordeaux and the gentleman from New Orleans might have developed a certain attraction for each other."

She laughed and then realized that he had taken her quite off guard. He had touched her in a way that could have but one meaning and then spoken to her in the same vein in his fictional guise. Thus it was several seconds before she became fully aware that he had made his first declaration to her. She was not yet ready to respond, half from fear of committing herself, half from wanting to enjoy slowly each stage of what was happening between them.

"There may be something in what you say, but I think I had best now withdraw. The evening is becoming chill."

Sophie fled to her cabin, threw herself upon her bunk and read Hyacinthe's letter over again. And then she began to laugh. Morgan had, until this evening, shown her every consideration, had left how their relations developed entirely in her hands. When she continued to hesitate, he had made a subtle declaration, and she had sidestepped. The matter, then, still rested in her hands. So be it!

The next day the captain announced that a feast was in order: not only was the last of the game to be consumed at the captain's table but the last fresh vegetables as well. After that they would perforce eat sailors' rations. Captain Joubert, who prided himself on his table, had selected two particularly fine wines for the occasion, and these flowed copiously.

There were seven of them at table: the captain, Sophie, the first officer, the ship's surgeon, an army colonel who was returning to his regiment in Martinique, the colonel's new wife and, at the end of the table, Morgan, who was unusually quiet. Had she discouraged and disappointed him? She would soon rectify that.

Captain Joubert, a wiry little man with a face reddened by twenty years at sea, raised his glass.

"To France, the only nation on earth where the arts of good food, good wine and good conversation are daily joined at table."

"Bravo! Bravo!"

Sophie clinked her glass with that of the colonel's wife opposite her. She was nineteen and living the first great adventure of her life, marriage followed in two days by a voyage to the New World. The first days at sea the new bride had emerged in the morning from her cabin all blushes and averted eyes. This was a refined torture for Sophie, who quite unexpectedly found herself thinking quite often of physical love, which for her was but a years-old memory of a few brief weeks.

The two women retired together to a corner, leaving the men at table with cheese and fruit and the last of the wine.

"Do you think I shall like Martinique? I believe you know it well."

"I thought it a paradise, but then I lived there as a child." Child? When she left Martinique she was about the same age as the colonel's bride.

"Is this your first visit since?"

"Yes," said Sophie cautiously. She would no doubt be seeing more of the colonel and his lady in Martinique. "And I would not be going now but for a vexing legal matter."

"I would not have the courage to travel alone."

"One does what one must. You are lucky to be just beginning a life of companionship."

"Oh, I must confess," the young woman said, lowering her voice and blushing, "I find marriage to be bliss."

Well and good, thought Sophie, but what of twenty years from now, when the colonel—who was fifty if a day—is a retired general of seventy and you are still young? This innocent would then, no doubt, be dallying with the likes of Hyacinthe. She disapproved of such marriages—of all arranged marriages.

"I wish you all happiness," but Sophie's mind was elsewhere.

She had inevitably thought of her aborted marriage to the Marquis de Chanteloup, to which her family had consigned her, as this girl had been consigned to the arms of a fifty-year-old colonel. Though certainly not eager, she had not been unwilling; but now she thanked her stars that fate had delivered her from that marriage. She looked in Morgan's direction but could not catch his eye. She wanted to reassure him with a warm look. Yes, what great good luck that the house of Chardin had gone bankrupt.

"I shall try to be a good wife."

"You will be an adornment to your husband's career," Sophie said with unintended sarcasm. Now she saw that Morgan was nodding, which was unlike him.

The men arose with a scraping of chairs, but Morgan got to his feet with difficulty.

"Is something wrong?" the captain asked.

"A little unsteady. Too much rich food and wine I think. I'll just lie down for a few minutes, and I'll be fine."

He looked across the cabin at Sophie, and she could at last give him the warm look that she so much owed him.

"Ladies and gentlemen," said the captain, "I think some fresh air will do us all good after that meal."

Following their daily stroll, the others retired to the only pastimes available on board ship, cards or reading. Sophie remained on deck with her thoughts, expecting Morgan. But he had still not appeared an hour later when the lookout called from high above that there was a ship to starboard on the horizon. The ship's officers were soon on deck, and the captain took out his telescope.

"French flag. She's disabled. Looks as if part of her rigging's been shot away. We'll have to go to her aid."

The ship's officers were quickly at their places, shouting orders to the men at the ropes. Sails were soon furled and unfurled and trimmed, and the *La Bonne Nouvelle* changed course for the vessel floating helplessly on the water.

Afterwards, Sophie was surprised at how long it had taken her to consider one possibility. She had only just begun to when the captain, peering through his glass announced, "*Aphrodite*'s her name."

As they drew closer Sophie sought out Morgan, who had emerged from his cabin still looking, she thought, a little feverish.

"What shall we do?" she whispered.

"Nothing. It would serve no purpose for Archambault to know we are aboard *La Bonne Nouvelle*. The important thing is to keep the nature of the *Aphrodite*'s cargo hidden—and that you are the owner."

"You are right. We must not place Captain Joubert in a compromising position. Go now."

The signalman had begun to read to the captain signals being received from the other ship, while Sophie listened as discreetly as she could.

"Repairs underway . . . do not need your help . . . under sail again within hours . . . attacked by British frigate . . . saved from capture by nightfall . . ." She expelled the breath she had been holding. Archambault was making sure that no one from the French warship came close to the *Aphrodite* and its clandestine cargo.

But then, ". . . two dead, one wounded . . . do you have a surgeon aboard?"

It seemed to take an interminable time for a ship's boat from the *Aphrodite* to cross the stretch of calm blue sea that separated it from *La Bonne Nouvelle* and for the crew to lift aboard the wounded man strapped to a stretcher. It was a sailor she knew by sight, his chest wrapped in a blood-soaked sheet. The surgeon moved with great speed and precision to take charge of the situation. But after an hour he emerged from below and went directly to the captain.

"I regret to say I was not able to save him. I did the best that I could, but he had lost too much blood."

When their party returned to the captain's table that evening for a light supper, everything had changed. It was, said the colonel, like the first day of Lent after Mardi Gras. They all understood that more was meant than soup and black bread after their noontime feast. The dark shadow of war and violence had fallen over their calm sunlit voyage.

Morgan did not appear at the table. She had left him on deck, brooding over the possible capture of the *Aphrodite*—probably more damaged than Archambault had been willing to admit—and the loss of the first precious cargo of arms for the American rebellion. Beside her, Colonel Girard's young wife was silent and had little appetite, no doubt comprehending for the first time that her husband's business was killing.

"Well, captain," the colonel said, trying to stir up some conversation, "what may we expect if we ourselves meet the British?"

"We will no doubt meet them, and given their barbarous behavior on this occasion, who can say that they will respect even the ensign of His Majesty's navy?"

He caught himself up short, realizing that such talk would only further frighten his guests, and changed subject to the weather. Here he fared not much better, opining that, from the feel of the sea and the look of the sky, confirmed by his barometer, there was a storm somewhere over the horizon.

The surgeon, on Sophie's other side, was lost in his own thoughts.

"I much admired your calm and skill today, Doctor Beauchamp," she said at last.

"Skill? There is no skill to match the destructive power of war. What I did amounted to little more than watching that sailor die. Only occasionally is one able to cheat death. . . ."

The surgeon's mate had entered the captain's cabin, and thrusting his head between Beauchamp and Sophie whispered, "Doctor, they have found Monsieur Duplessis lying on the deck half-conscious and running a very high fever."

Thus began hellish days for Sophie, as she awaited each morning the surgeon's emergence from the dispensary. There Morgan lay tossing in a bunk, ravaged by fever and delirium. The surgeon's comments were always guarded, but one morning it seemed to her that his countenance was especially grave. She threw discretion aside and pressed him with questions.

"Then you do not think he will live?" she finally said, twisting her silk scarf into a tight knot with her two hands.

"I did not say that. One can never be sure . . ."

"That is, unless there is a miracle . . ."

"Madame, your concern for a fellow passenger is admirable, but you must not make yourself distraught."

"Yes, you are right," Sophie said weakly, and turned away from the doctor before he could see her tears. She went to her cabin and climbed into her bunk and let the tears flow where no one could see them.

CHAPTER SIX

Then one morning the surgeon said that Morgan's fever had subsided, and the period of crisis might be over.

"Then you expect your patient to recover fully?" Sophie asked in a shaking voice. Until then, despite her inner turmoil, her deep fear that the dawning promise of happiness for two people was to end in tragedy, she had been able to sustain her pose as a sympathetic fellow passenger.

The surgeon was eyeing her with what might be taken as concern. Was her emotion so apparent then? During these days she had admitted to herself her love for Morgan Carter, relieved that her inner struggles were over. If he died, she had vowed to return to Bordeaux and live out the life of the widow Armonville; if he lived . . .

"I make it a practice never to predict the outcome when such fevers are involved. I've too often been disappointed." The surgeon's deep-set eyes seemed to be looking back over a lifetime of practicing medicine at sea. "They may seem well enough after the disease has passed its crisis—which this one seems to have done—but the next day there is a relapse, and a day or two later they are gone. . . . Madame Armonville are you not feeling well?"

"Oh, no. I'm quite all right. It is just the shock of that sailor's death and then someone so close at hand, that one has got to know, suddenly at death's door."

"Quite understandable. Actually, if I had to bet, I would expect our patient to recover nicely. A strange thing . . ."

"Yes?"

"In the delirium that often follows such a shock to the body, he has spoken out several times in English."

"Is that really so surprising?" Sophie quickly interjected. "All merchants in the ocean trade have a smattering of several foreign tongues. No doubt he was remembering some port of call, some happy memory, some girl . . ."

"Yes, no doubt," said the surgeon, giving her a searching look she could not fathom.

The storm struck in the middle of the night. Sophie was barely awakened by it when she was thrown bodily out of her bunk onto the hard floor of her tiny cabin. Her first thought was for Morgan. If he were dealt such a blow the consequences could be grave.

Slammed back and forth between her bunk and the door, she managed to pull a robe over her nightgown and light a lamp. She careened down the narrow corridor to the dispensary in her bare feet, opened the door and slipped inside. The door closed behind her, and she held the lamp over Morgan's unconscious form. She should have known that the surgeon would anticipate. He was held firmly in the bunk by strips of canvas webbing.

She hung the lamp from a bracket and, holding the edge of the bunk, leaned over Morgan. What unexpected turns life took once the safe harbor was left behind. Here she was alone with him at last, but he was now still and white as a statue. Several days' dark beard contrasted with his pallor. His breathing was regular and deep.

Slowly she lowered her hand to his forehead. It was cool. She leaned over further and brought her lips close to his. They hovered there but went no further. She raised her head, and with eyes closed, breathed a prayer of relief.

"Madame Armonville?"

The surgeon stood in the doorway in his nightgown, a

lamp in one hand and the other holding the doorjamb against the ship's roll. How much had he seen?

"I . . . I was . . . I was thrown from my bunk by the storm and immediately thought of the invalid."

"You know him, don't you?"

"Know him?"

"He has spoken the name 'Sophie' several times."

"I can explain. . . . Yes, I know him. We have a joint commercial undertaking . . ."

"Which is none of my affair." He spoke with the air of one whose business had for long been in the arena of war and death, where intrigue and profit and passion were of small account.

"Then you will not speak of this to anyone?"

"So long as whatever you are involved in is not directed against France."

"You have my word on it. Quite the opposite."

The storm had passed by morning. It had not been a violent one but, as Etienne had warned her, *La Bonne Nouvelle* was made for speed and not for comfort in rough seas.

She came up on deck to a calm sea and perfect blue sky in the wake of the storm. The captain, the ship's officers and the Girards were crowded together at the rail. And then she saw the three ships on the horizon.

"British ship of the line and two frigates," one of the officers curtly responded to her query, "bearing down on us like a surly old bulldog and two greyhounds."

Shortly, the captain gathered his officers and passengers around him on the deck.

"We might be able to outrun all of them, but I do not choose to attempt it. No state of war exists between France and England, and I do not think they will try to board a ship of His Majesty's navy. However, one cannot be sure. Feelings run high in England over the war in America. They know France's sympathies are with the rebels and suspect, no doubt with some reason, that certain French merchantmen carry contraband to the Americans.

"Should they attempt to board us, no resistance is to be offered. I will, of course, protest vigorously. Should they come aboard, no mention is to be made of our encounter with the *Aphrodite*. I have no doubt that these are the very ships that attacked her, and I would give them no clue as to her present location. Now, let us continue on our present course."

The British warships were quickly upon them and signals were sent back and forth.

"They wish to send an officer aboard for an exchange of information. I suppose I cannot object to that," said the captain. "Tell them to come ahead."

The British ship of the line came in so close to them that its huge bulk, with its three decks of cannon, cast a shadow over *La Bonne Nouvelle* from bow to stern. British sailors swung a boat out over the ship's side and lowered it and its complement of six crew, their oars held upright, and two red-coated officers.

"Why, it is not a ship's officer at all," the captain said. "Our visitor wears the uniform of a general in the British army. Decidedly odd."

The man who came up the ship's ladder and swung himself onto the deck was about fifty years old, beefy in his upper parts but still light of leg. Sunlight flashed from the gold braid of his scarlet coat. His hair was thick, matted and dark red, and the backs of his hands were covered with wiry red hairs. His pale blue eyes surveyed the deck and fixed on Sophie standing close at hand. It was, or so it seemed to her, as if he knew who she was and was not surprised to find her aboard the French vessel.

The red-coated aide who followed him up the ladder announced, "Major General Sir George Coburn."

After an exchange of formalities, the British general suggested to the captain that they retire to discuss certain matters, but their captain would have none of that.

"Whatever you have to say, sir, I would have witnesses to."

The British general ducked his head and smiled, as if he were the most reasonable of men.

"Whatever you wish, sir," he said in excellent French. "I only thought it might be useful, after last night's storm, for us to exchange information on what sightings we have had in the last few days. There may be disabled vessels needing aid out there," and he swept the horizon with those pale blue eyes that had fixed on Sophie.

"First, may I inquire why His Britannic Majesty's navy has sent an army general to speak with me."

"Oh, what other use has our navy for me? We landlubbers are merely in the way when it comes to nautical matters."

"And your purpose aboard a ship of the line?"

"A simple passenger, on his way to Canada."

The captain stiffened, and Sophie felt herself do the same. She had been eight when Quebec had fallen to the British. Quite possibly General Coburn had been there that day . . . as had she.

"I see. Be that as it may, we have seen no other ship for five days now."

"And the last you sighted?"

"A Dutch merchantman."

"Ah. Well, in any case, should you come across a French merchantman, the *Aphrodite*, perhaps disabled, you should know that we consider her fair game, loaded as she is to the gunwales with arms for our rebellious subjects in America."

"Consider what you will, sir, but count on France to protect her own interests."

"I have no doubt of it," said the British general, ducking his head again in mock humility. "However, I think you would agree that we would be within our rights to take from a vessel of any flag a British subject accused of high treason."

"Who would be . . ."

"Who would be the so-called American agent in Paris."

"I am by no means certain that my government would any longer consider Americans as British subjects."

"Regrettably. Now, might I ask to be introduced to your cloud of witnesses, perhaps even have a tour of your ship, as you are welcome to have of ours."

"Of course," said the captain, with a dry smile, "except for the cargo hold. I would not want to have it reported to London that you boarded and searched a French man-of-war."

"I quite understand."

Sophie was the last to be introduced to General Coburn, and she had the feeling that he was more interested in learning her name than in knowing what cargo *La Bonne Nouvelle* carried.

She was swept along in the party that made its way through the ship until it arrived, inevitably, at the door to the dispensary. The general peered inside.

"What's the matter with that man?"

"Some strange fever," said Doctor Beauchamp. "I cannot put a name to it, but he has been at death's door for some days now."

The British general, who towered over the others, whipped a handkerchief out of his sleeve, covered his mouth and nose, and quickly moved on.

The party was soon at the rail again and courtesies were being exchanged, when Coburn suddenly turned to the captain. "Might I have a word with Madame Armonville? I believe we have a common acquaintance of whom she might like to have news."

The captain, astonished, could but acquiesce.

Sophie walked with the general a few paces away, until they were out of earshot of the others. Then he turned to her and said in a low voice, "I thought you might want to know, Madame Armonville, that your brother Antoine is well."

"Well?" she said, too astonished to attempt concealment. "I have not seen him since I was a child, nor heard from him in some years." She would have liked to have said much more, asked how this British general knew who she was, how he knew her brother; but her every sense told her to be cautious.

"He is not only alive but prospering in the fur trade, as a result of his firm allegiance to the British crown."

"That was his choice, and so he cut himself off from his family."

"You might profitably follow his example, for your present course can only lead to ruin for your family, your firm and even yourself."

General Coburn's eyes were cold and menacing.

The visit concluded without incident, and *La Bonne Nouvelle* sailed quickly away from the British warships.

"Now, can you explain what that was all about?" said the captain to the company at large.

"I think I can," said Colonel Girard. "General Coburn is, I was told in Paris, the head of British intelligence in North America, and a man who must never be underestimated, as cunning as he is ruthless."

A shadow of suspicion had fallen over Sophie, and perhaps

General Coburn had intended that. She had told the others the simple truth: that Coburn was acquainted with her brother, who had chosen to stay behind in Canada when France had ceded it to Great Britain. But that in itself had quite naturally raised questions in their minds. She had said nothing of the general's warning to her—or call it threat. They would have seen matters in a very different light had they been aware of her ties, and those of Morgan Carter, to the *Aphrodite*.

"I have excellent news this morning," said the surgeon some days later, as they strolled the deck. "Our patient is very much on the mend now. I have withdrawn the grains of opium that I was giving him for the raging headaches the fever brought on, and his mind is clear. Tell me, Madame Armonville, is this not the man sought by the British crown for high treason?"

"Yes." She stood with lowered eyes, awaiting.

"Then I am obliged to inform the captain."

She looked up into his eyes. "Please, Doctor Beauchamp, I beg you. The captain already has some inkling . . ."

"For his own protection the captain must know more precisely. But I think he will judge it a matter that he neither needs nor wants to inquire into further."

"I would be most obliged for your good offices."

"And you may soon pay a call on your friend, if you wish."

The next day she entered the dispensary groomed, carefully dressed, a touch of perfume at her throat and wrists, and as nervous as a young man calling for the first time on his lady in her parlor.

"Yesterday I could not believe my ears, today I mistrust my eyes," were Morgan's first words to her.

She stepped into the cabin and the door closed behind her.

She had expected the surgeon to stay with them. Morgan was propped up on pillows, his face nearly as pale as they. He attempted a smile, the apologetic smile of a man who has never needed to be cared for by others.

"How do you feel?"

"Weak as a newborn kitten, but otherwise well enough."

"You look quite better than I was prepared for."

"Extensive preparations have preceded your visit. I have been bathed, shaved and had my hair washed by the surgeon's mate, provided a fresh nightgown and even a splash of the surgeon's cologne upon my cheeks."

Sophie came forward and stood over him. This was the moment she had been waiting so long for, and she felt emotions too deep for tears. She felt hope. She felt the possibilities of future years. She felt desire. He searched her face for what emotions moved her, but she was not yet ready to yield them up. She retreated to a chair, dizzy with all that she felt.

"Is something wrong, Sophie?"

"No, nothing at all is wrong."

What more could she say than that? In a way she was glad that for now desire was thwarted. Every woman deserved at least once in life a real courtship, the hesitant, shy approaching of the other by slow degrees, the sweet torture of anticipation. For there was no longer any question in her mind as to where they were headed.

"I'm told I may not stay long today."

"There are tomorrows now, Sophie." Already his voice was growing weak. He must have used all his strength to prepare himself for her visit, to greet her with warmth and wit.

She did not reply immediately but savored his last few words as she might have rolled around in her mouth a wine of unexpected character. Not tomorrow, but tomorrows, and these called into existence now, in this small cabin warmed by the presence of their two bodies. Four simple words joined to the name she had been given at birth, saying all, as the signature of a wine was contained in one sip.

"First we must get you well, put you back on your feet. We have work to do when we get to Martinique."

"You and I?"

"Yes, Morgan, you and I."

What curious ways men and women have of declaring that a love is there that they are not yet ready to speak of in full openness.

"The *Aphrodite* has evaded the British then?"

"We do not yet know, but something tells me Archambault will elude them, spliced-together rigging, patched sails and all."

"He must..." and as he spoke his eyelids began to droop. "...must make it...." His voice trailed off. Perhaps he was already asleep.

She sat silently for a while, happy just to have her eyes upon him at last, without having to say anything more this day, without having to choose each word with care, without having to be sure of not saying too little or too much. Then she stole silently out of the dispensary. She was happy with that pure happiness that comes at the beginning of love when all obstacles are but vague possibilities, like reports of icebergs somewhere ahead in the fog, no doubt dangerous but not yet experienced, and perhaps never to be.

"I've come to give you my morning report, madam," said Captain Joubert, joining her at the rail. This had become a kind of joke between them, because of her constant demands for his latest estimate of landfall.

"I now calculate we will sight the island of Martinique on the twenty-eighth of November, give or take a day."

"That is an improvement."

"The trade winds blow steady and well."

The next day she found Morgan, vigorous and again of good color, trying to keep a tray balanced on his knees with one hand while he awkwardly brought a spoonful of soup to his mouth with the other. She firmly took spoon and bowl from him.

"There," she said, bringing the spoon to his lips, "you would soon have spilled your dinner upon the sheet."

"Then you must come to me every day."

"Since you cannot manage for yourself, I suppose I must," she said with mock sternness, to disguise the emotion in her voice. Even touching his lips with a spoon sent a sensual thrill through Sophie's body. As soon as the bowl was empty she retreated to the safety of the chair at the foot of the bed.

"I've brought some books from the ship's library, such as it is: plays by Racine, La Fontaine's fables and the poetry of Ronsard. I thought it might relieve the tedium of your days if I read to you for a while."

That certainly was a motive, but she had another: to avoid conversation. Instead of feeling the sweet torture of anticipation, she was terrified. Her upbringing had left her innocent of the vocabulary of love, her brief marriage had been but the coming together of two eager and very young people, and she and Morgan could hardly discuss bills of lading and exchange.

"What would you prefer?"

"I would prefer," he said with a smile, "to lie here and look at you."

She was startled. He was teasing her. Then she saw by the look in his eye that he realized how tense she was and was trying to tell her something: the approach to love need not always be a matter of high seriousness.

"You may do that while I read," she said, trying not to sound prim.

"Ronsard, then. I believe he writes mainly of love."

"So I understand. My life since I left school has left me little opportunity for reading, and in school Ronsard was not permitted."

"Not permitted?"

"Our teacher, a stern Huguenot woman, said there was too much of rosebuds and pink flesh for the ears of young girls."

"Then, by all means Ronsard."

She looked up from the books she held in her lap, disconcerted. He was still teasing her. She quickly opened the volume of Ronsard and began to read.

Sophie soon felt that the tiny cabin was filled with the imagery of love, that language that no one had taught her to speak. After many poems that brought blushes to her cheeks, now the poet was speaking to his mistress who had sworn she would arise at dawn but still slept.

". . . and I kiss your closed eyelids, there and there, and there and there your pretty . . . nipples, to teach you to get up in the morning."

She closed the book. Her breasts were tingling, the nipples hard.

"I cannot go on."

"No." He was not smiling now.

She crossed the cabin and stood over him.

"Sophie, I truly did not mean to. . . ."

She did not let him finish, but leaned over and with parted lips kissed him fully on the mouth.

Her lips wet and stinging from the kiss, she brought herself upright, threw back with a hand her loose dark hair that had fallen across his face. They stared at each other in surprise. Unable to speak, she fled to her cabin.

That night she reread the poems by candlelight, realizing with a smile that a poet dead two hundred years had put into her mouth words that had so inflamed her she had been able to cross the room and boldly put her lips to Morgan's. Would she be able to go so boldly on? Would she be able to let loose all the passion that she felt? She both desired and feared it. If only there were more time, but in two days, the captain calculated, they would sight Martinique.

She came on deck two days later to find the captain, the surgeon and, to her surprise, Morgan, standing at the rail engaged in conversation. As she approached they stopped talking and looked in her direction. She felt sure their conversation had concerned her.

"I've been released into the fresh air," said Morgan in answer to the question on her lips. Aside from paleness and a not unpleasing thinness of face, he looked as when she had first seen him at Château Ivran.

"Provided he avoids all exertion. But I'll have to look to you, Madame Armonville, to see that Monsieur Duplessis behaves himself. He'll soon be out of my control."

"I'll impose navy discipline on him, you may be sure," said Sophie, rather pleased with herself for responding in a worldly fashion to the surgeon assuming a certain relationship between her and Morgan Carter.

"You may count on my good behavior," said Morgan to the surgeon. "I would not endanger the life you have given back to me. It has suddenly become quite precious."

He did not look at her, but she felt a shiver of excitement—if she correctly interpreted what he had said.

"Madam Armonville," said Captain Joubert, "we were just discussing your situation, that is yours and Monsieur . . . Carter's. Aboard this ship only Beauchamp and I are aware of his identity. But once we are safely in the French waters of Martinique we can dispense with that fiction. And may I say that while officially France remains neutral, you know where our sympathies lie . . ."

"*Terre!*" came a cry from above.

Their gaze turned first to the lookout in the rigging and then to the horizon. There was nothing to be seen, and after so many weeks at sea, Sophie had difficulty in imagining that the world consisted of anything but water.

In a few minutes, however, a speck of green appeared on the horizon. By then Sophie and Morgan found themselves quite alone.

"What do you feel, now that you are about to see your childhood paradise again?"

"I feel many things." She gripped the rail tightly with both hands. "I feel so many strong emotions that I don't see how my body can contain them all."

"Joyful emotions?"

"I feel both joy and dread. Joy that I am returning to Martinique, and dread that it will have changed and I will find it insignificant and lost to me. Joy that we are approaching a resolution of the fate of our enterprises, my family's fortunes and your country's, and dread of what that resolution will be."

"That is all?"

She regarded her white knuckles clinching the rail. "You know that is not all. Indeed, there is hardly room left in my heart for the matters I have just named."

"Then you speak of us."

"I do."

"There too, is joy mixed with dread?"

It was with the greatest difficulty that she looked into his eyes.

"You know that it must be so."

"Why must it?" He looked puzzled and even hurt.

This would not do, would not do at all. However painful it was she must speak and speak now.

"Oh, Morgan, I would so gladly abandon myself to my feelings . . . for you . . ."

He placed a large warm hand over hers on the rail but remained silent. He would have her say the rest.

"My life in recent years has been resistance to those who would possess me. My independence has been bought at a high price. Now that I would be . . ." She dared not say possessed, "I cannot let myself go. Am I not appalling?"

"I think you are admirable. Had you not refused to be the chattel of your family, you would not be the woman . . . I love . . . nor would you be standing here with me today."

She looked out to the horizon where the green peaks of Martinique could now be made out, capped as always with clouds. The word love had been spoken, and it seemed to her to roll like thunder out across the sea and reverberate off the peaks and echo down the valleys of her own island. What better moment could she have chosen?

"Then what am I to do, who knows only how to resist?"

"If Martinique is all that you say it is, the stern ways of the merchant world of Bordeaux will soon seem a dream."

Suddenly all appeared possible. With a few words he had begun the untying of the bonds with which she had, day after day, year after year, bound herself.

CHAPTER SEVEN

As they made their way along the east coast of Martinique, Sophie's eyes were not upon the island's landscape but on Morgan's face. Written all over it was surprise, even dismay, at finding her island paradise to be a mass of inhospitable ragged ridges emerging from clouds above and descending into a jungle of tangled vines and tree ferns, to end abruptly in sheer cliffs against which a giant surf boomed. The isolated small beaches of black volcanic sand only added to this picture of desolation, as did the wretched villages scattered along the cliffs like sea creatures thrown up by the tide.

"Well, what do you think of my Martinique?" Now it was her turn to tease.

"It is not exactly . . . I mean, I can see where one might find a certain wild grandeur . . ."

"But hardly a tropical paradise."

"I have no means of comparison. . . ."

"Morgan, my dear, this is the windward side of the island facing the stormy Atlantic. An hour or two and you will see my Martinique." She fell silent then, eager as a child to please him with the paradise to come, yet fearful that somehow it would not live up to her cherished memories.

When they at last rounded Cap St. Martin, the deep blue-gray of the Atlantic gave way to sea colors exotic beyond anything that her memory held: azure and ice-green, lapis lazuli and ultramarine, and other shades she could find no name for. There were beaches of fine white sand, palm trees, banana plants, and in the distance the majestic shape of the

Mountain, the volcano Pelée, its peak hidden in bright mist.

"Oh, *Mon Dieu,*" she whispered to herself.

Her hand on the rail was again covered by his.

"Welcome home," he said.

He knew, he understood.

"May you find here again the happiness you deserve."

He had echoed almost exactly the last line of Hyacinthe's letter to her. They were both, after all, men who were sensitive to a woman's feelings.

There was no time for other thoughts, and she had so many that she wished to pursue. The town of St. Pierre—her town—was almost upon them. Again the colors were more brilliant than her memory had painted them: red-tiled roofs, green shutters, bright yellow walls, patches of violet and vermilion here and there.

A pirogue filled with boys in all shades of brown came alongside them offering tropical fruits, seashells, mahogany figurines and much else. The captain had a basket lowered to bring up a dozen of those long thin Martinique cheroots that she had quite forgotten. He passed them around and then took one himself, cut off the ends with his knife and lit it.

"Finest place on earth, St. Pierre," he said, puffing contentedly.

"It is," she whispered to Morgan.

"And you will show it all to me."

"All, all."

Sophie felt that cold fear of the unknown that had become associated in her mind with sea voyages: her escape from Canada and her passage to France to be married to a man she barely knew. As on those other occasions fear was mingled with hope, but this time she had no idea what awaited her or how she would deal with it. Were it not for Morgan's presence she would have been near to despair. But then her future relations with him were much of the cause for the turmoil within her.

No sooner were planks lowered to the dock than a young man in officer's uniform came quickly up and stepped onto the deck, smartly saluting the captain.

"I come from the governor, who is on a visit to St. Pierre from the capital and is most anxious to have his dispatches from Paris."

The captain signaled to a ship's officer, who brought from the captain's cabin a leather case, locked and sealed and stamped in gold with the fleur-de-lys of France.

"I am most obliged," said the young man from the governor's staff, "and I am also instructed to bid you and your officers to share His Excellency's hospitality at a reception even now taking place in the hall of arms of the citadel—an invitation that includes any passengers you may bring to our island."

Sophie looked up to the fort of honey-colored stone that dominated the harbor of St. Pierre. She had herself been presented to a governor there, also on a visit from the capital of Fort Royal. At what age? Fourteen or thereabouts.

"My passengers are Colonel Girard," said the captain, "who is joining his regiment here, and Madame Girard; Madame Armonville of Bordeaux, who comes to Martinique on business; and Monsieur Carter, an American gentleman who travels with us."

"Lieutenant Roland," said the young officer bowing. "I look forward to seeing you again within the hour." He turned and descended the ladder with the royal dispatch case.

"This is impossible," Sophie said in a half-whisper to Morgan. "We cannot go directly to the governor without introduction or having the way prepared."

"You have little choice," said the captain, who had overheard her. "It would be taken amiss for those newly arrived in Martinique and already announced to his staff, not to attend the governor's reception."

As they stood on the dock waiting for the carriage that a member of the crew had been sent to hire for them, Sophie looked about her. She had forgotten the extent to which the life of Martinique was dominated by its women: tall and handsome, dressed in skirts and blouses and turbans as brilliant and varied in color as the shades of the sea and the tints in which the houses of St. Pierre were painted; skins ranging from honey to chocolate.

Some of these women had begun unloading *La Bonne Nouvelle*, bringing down boxes and bundles on their heads. Others were taking down the big canvas umbrellas that shaded the morning market, sweeping rinds and peels of fruit away and washing them into the gutters with buckets of seawater. The half-forgotten smell of fermenting fruit sent a shiver down Sophie's spine.

Once inside the carriage, its leather seats smelling of tropical mold, she leaned back with a sigh.

"I am home at last," she said, "and it has not changed. The long dream is over—unless you are a dream." This time she laid her hand on top of his. The cords with which she had bound herself were fast falling away.

"Then I am home."

"What do you mean?" She leaned back in the corner of the carriage and looked at him with a new boldness.

He was now in all ways as he had been when she had first met him; and she thought back to the wine festival, their voyage up the Gironde and Garonne to Bordeaux on a barge, their tempestuous hours together at Château Marivaux, at Fort Colbert. He was still pondering his answer. Born though they were on the same side of the sea, the ocean between two cultures separated them.

"Would it help if I spoke my thoughts?" she said.

"It would, since I appear to be tongue-tied."

"I am free now. It has happened in an instant, as you said it would. You need no longer have concern for the widow Armonville and her nervous sensibilities. She is left behind in Bordeaux, bent over her ledgers."

Morgan's furrowed brow relaxed. "I wish her well there. But what of the Sophie who shares my carriage?"

"She would come to you tonight, if that proves possible."

At this he put his arm around her and his lips to hers, opening her mouth to his, and with his other arm he pulled the curtains. In the dimness of the shaded carriage she arched her body and pressed against the whole length of him with her breasts, the curve of her stomach, her thighs.

They were mounting to the citadel now, the horse's hooves striking cobblestone.

"How am I supposed to prepare bold and persuasive words for the governor when every thought has been driven from my head?" she whispered in his ear.

"The words will come when the time comes," and he kissed her on the lobe of her ear and down her neck.

The great hall of arms of the fort was hung with the flags of French regiments that had served in the West Indies over the last hundred years, some still bright, some tattered and scorched by the fires of battles long past; there were even, high up on the bare stone walls, a few flags saved from the British at the battle of Quebec. Sophie and Morgan proceeded into the hall, speaking to each other in low voices. Both of them, Sophie reckoned, needing to shore up their courage for an encounter that could be the shipwreck of all their plans.

"I am chastened," she whispered.

"How is that?"

"My fear was that I would find everything changed, that the Martinique I remembered would have faded away. Yet I look around me and nothing has changed. What a puny space of time five years is. It is only I . . ."

"Who has changed?"

"Yes, Morgan, or at least I hope so. *Mon Dieu,* I do fear what is to come."

"And it comes quickly," he said, squeezing her hand.

Lieutenant Roland was approaching, an official smile on his face, to lead them through the crowded hall to where the governor stood at the far end, resplendent in full-dress uniform.

A path seemed to open for them through the crowd. The room was warm, the big doors all down the gallery open wide to a blue sky beyond the parapet lined with cannon. November meant nothing in Martinique.

"Morgan, I'm frightened," she whispered. "What we are doing is mad."

"*Sois tranquille,*" he murmured.

Keep calm? And how was she supposed to do that? She moved along in a daze, bowing slightly to the men and women to whom they were introduced, their names but confused sounds until they came to a pause before a tall, blond woman with an aquiline nose and hard eyes. Sophie sensed instantly that she was of that class of women whose beauty is tied to youth, but as their beauty fades force those around them to acknowledge it as unchanged through the power of their positions or wealth. This thought was interrupted by the voice of Lieutenant Roland.

"*Madame La Comtesse, je vous présente Madame Armonville et Monsieur...*"

"Carter," said Morgan with a disarming smile.

"La Comtesse de Brieux," finished the lieutenant hesitantly, sensing that something was not quite right.

To her surprise, Sophie found that this dreaded moment had left her unmoved, in fact had served to calm her; whereas the narrow refined face of the Comtesse de Brieux had turned pale. They exchanged not a word.

The governor was a giant of a man with full black mustaches and hair longer than one was used to see on an admiral, which, Lieutenant Roland whispered to them, the governor had until recently been. As they drew closer Sophie could see that the governor's bronze visage was marked with the bluish-white scars of old battles. Sophie, who in her business had come to know all sorts of naval persons, saw in him a barely-reformed old pirate.

"*Le Vicomte de Laval, Gouverneur de Martinique.*"

"Excellency."

Sophie bowed deeply, Morgan nodded his head.

"I have had reports of you," the governor growled in a deep gravelly voice, "of you both, that is . . ."

Cannon fire shook the glass of the long gallery. Cries of surprise and fright ran through the assembled guests.

"What is the meaning of this?" the governor cried out, the official composure of his face instantly giving way to anger and the alertness of a military man. "Who dares fire a cannon during my reception?"

All eyes turned to sea. The governor called for his spyglass.

A broad-beamed merchant ship approached the harbor of St. Pierre, followed at some distance by three men-of-war exchanging salvos, two against one. The merchantman, Sophie could see without the aid of a glass was the *Aphrodite*. How could Archambault in a half-crippled ship have followed them so closely? She knew the answer. After forty years at sea Archambault could coax every bit of speed out of the winds. But what of this maritime battle astern of the *Aphrodite*?

The governor thrust the glass into Morgan's hands. "What sort of flag is that?" He could have been speaking to a sub-lieutenant aboard his flagship.

"American, I believe, Excellency."

"So I suspected."

Now the *Aphrodite* was entering the harbor, and the battling warships were not far behind. Officers of the governor's staff had crowded around their superior.

"Fire warning shots!" the governor bellowed. "I will not have this foreign war carried into French territorial waters!"

"Warning shots at whom, Excellency?"

"At the British, *imbécile!*"

Orders were quickly given, followed by the sound of running feet coming up stone stairs. Gunners with ramrods appeared on the ramparts and the cannon were expertly loaded as the two British and one American warship drew ever closer, exchanging broadsides with as yet no major damage on either side.

Two cannon roared simultaneously, banging the glass doors back and forth, shattering panes, filling the *salle d'armes* with smoke and the acrid smell of black powder, overturning wineglasses on the long white-clothed and food-laden tables. Some of the ladies shrieked, their gowns lifted up by the force of the blast.

Two geysers of water arose near the closest British warship. "Well done!" cried the governor, transformed from the host of a formal and elegant reception into his more familiar role of warrior. "Hold your fire!"

Already the two British men-of-war were starting to turn course toward the open sea, while the American frigate continued on, headed for the harbor of St. Pierre. The assembled guests poured out onto the parapet to watch the end of this dramatic and totally unexpected scene.

"Come," the governor said to Sophie and Morgan, "while all this commotion is going on. I would have words with you both before I am obliged to resume my official duties, kiss hands, offer toasts to the health of the king, et cetera, et cetera."

"Study," said the governor derisively. "This is nothing more than a cloak room. And in such I must carry on my private business when I come to St. Pierre." He lowered himself slowly into a chair. "My damned back. Sit down. Sit down."

On the ancient table between them and the governor a leather dispatch case, embossed with the fleur-de-lys, spilled out, like a cornucopia, a pile of white envelopes sealed with red wax. Some of the seals had been broken, some not. The governor pointed to one of the envelopes that had been opened.

"That arrived opportunely. You would not have seen me act so decisively a few moments ago had I not just read these new orders brought by the same ship on which you traveled . . ." The governor paused for effect. ". . . orders that instruct me to give all assistance to the American cause short of that which might lead to war with England. Well, monsieur, madame, what do you think of that?"

"The same ship . . ." Sophie murmured. All the time they had been traveling with the letter that Hyacinthe had hoped he would be able to persuade his minister to write.

"Well, aren't you pleased Madame Armonville, Monsieur Carter? Your names are mentioned prominently in my instructions. I believe you are partners in something called The New World Trading Co. Is that not so?"

"It is so," said Carter, recovering from his surprise, which the governor had so clearly enjoyed causing. "Does this mean that we may bring armaments from France to Martinique for shipment on to America."

"It does."

"Does it mean that we may outfit American privateers here to prey on British merchantmen?"

"If done with discretion."

"Does it mean that we may bring British merchantmen into port and auction off their cargoes as prizes of war?"

The governor raised an eyebrow. Sophie was astonished at Morgan's boldness.

"Young man, you have yet to learn not to ask questions to which the answer may be no. For now, let us leave certain things unsaid. What I mainly require of you is discretion. Should you go beyond what I consider permissible, you will hear from me straightway. And you can be sure I will be watching your every move—as will others."

"And what of the firm of Chardin and Co.?" said Sophie, emboldened to speak up for her own interests.

"The parent firm? All I can say is this, Madame, that so long as you are the agent for the supply of French arms to the Americans the trade of Chardin and Co. will not be interfered with. But once that protection ceases . . ."

"But even then, why should my company's trade not be allowed to continue as usual? The charges in your letter to me are a tissue of lies!"

The governor raised an eyebrow.

"Excuse me, Excellency, for my impudence. What I meant to say is that the charges contained in your letter—brought by others—are not true."

"That I fully understand. But do not think that just because the Comte de Brieux is in disgrace, the Comtesse cannot, through the great web of her family connections, do you—and me—grievous harm. Now, shall we rejoin my guests?"

CHAPTER EIGHT

The retreat of the British, the arrival of the American frigate and the *Aphrodite*—with its cargo of arms, of which perhaps even Governor Laval was not aware—had breathed new life into the reception. The governor ordered more champagne brought up from the cellars on this occasion when the British had shown their heels, and strict formality gave way to general merriment.

While toasts were being drunk, Sophie and Morgan slipped into a side room and she penned a note to Archambault advising him of their presence in Martinique and bringing him abreast of events. This a surprised Lieutenant Roland agreed to have delivered to the *Aphrodite*, now tied to the dock below; and they then rejoined the festivities. The sun was low in the sky before Sophie and Morgan were able to take their leave.

As their carriage rumbled down the cobblestone way from the citadel to the town below, the sky turned a brilliant yellow.

"I have never seen such color."

"Ah, just wait, Morgan. There is a saying in Martinique that our sunsets begin as lemon, then turn mango and end as blood orange. We shall have blood oranges for breakfast. They have no equal."

The mention of breakfast gave vivid immediacy to the matter that, despite the dramatic events of the day, was ever on her mind: that she had promised to come to him that night. She nervously sought his hand with hers. It was one thing to speak of such things, but faced with impending actuality she felt desire but also fright. What would such a virile, confident and, yes, worldly, man think of her, of a woman who had never known a man in that way except for a few weeks with a boy, and that more than six years ago?

"I wonder what the widow Armonville is doing?" Sophie said to relieve the tension she felt.

Morgan laughed. "No doubt she is bent over her ledger in her office in Bordeaux. Certainly she is not to be found hereabouts."

Ah, that was not entirely true. A battle for her soul was going on between a bourgeoise gentlewoman of Bordeaux and a girl of Martinique who had vowed to live a life of passion and adventure.

"Oh, Morgan, have we not had a great and most unexpected victory today!"

"Beyond my wildest hopes, and we have Hyacinthe to thank for it."

"We shall toast him tonight," she said. Indeed, a glass or two of wine might help calm her nerves.

"We shall certainly do that. The future looks bright for us, in every respect."

He leaned over and kissed Sophie gently on the lips. No doubt his thoughts too were on the coming evening.

"That is not to say that our way will be entirely smooth."

"What do you mean?" she asked anxiously. Had she assumed too much regarding their relations? Had he perhaps not even understood her meaning when she had said that she would come to him that night? But surely . . . She had so little experience of men.

"What the devil do you suppose happened to the Comtesse de Brieux? When we came out of the governor's study she had disappeared."

"I imagine," Sophie replied, "that she wished to avoid any

conversation with us or with Governor Laval until she is informed on the substance of our private parley with the governor."

So, his mind had not been on the evening ahead but on their business. Aiding the rebellion in America was uppermost in his thoughts, which was no doubt natural. Yet her disappointment was sharp.

"Sophie, look. You are quite right. The sky is now the color of the flesh of those mangoes cut open in the market. I have never tasted one."

"You shall in the morning, and we will have slices of pineapple as well with our breakfast."

Ah, Sophie, she thought, you are not so innocent as you pretend. You are trying to turn his thoughts from war to other things.

"I am your obedient student in all matters concerning your beloved Martinique."

"Oh, Morgan, I will show you everything, everything. Here I am free," and she buried her face in the ruffles of his shirtfront to hide her confusion, pressing her cheek against his chest.

By the time they reached the harbor the sky had, as Sophie predicted, turned the color of the flesh of a blood orange. Lieutenant Roland had arranged rooms for them at an inn on the seafront, just at the edge of town. The inn was a large one, its first floor given over to a tavern, through which they entered. It was dark inside and the air heavy with tobacco smoke and the fumes of rum. At the bar stood Archambault surrounded by a group of naval officers in blue and white uniforms.

"Sophie! Morgan!" bellowed Archambault. "Come meet my American friends."

A New World Won

Sophie had been so wrapped up in her own feelings that she had given no further thought to Archambault, her senior captain, who had safely brought the first shipment of arms for the American rebels into St. Pierre.

"*Félicitations,* Archambault. You have done it again."

To the surprise of the American officers Archambault gave Sophie a big hug.

"I didn't do it—though I came close to outrunning the English. It's these gentlemen here that saved the day. If it weren't for them I'd now be in chains on a British man-of-war with all my crew. This here is the American frigate's captain, Commander Jones, and you other gentlemen will have to give your own names."

Greetings were exchanged in broken French and English and Archambault ordered another round of rum. Then he turned back to Sophie and Morgan.

"Well, we all made it didn't we?" and he slapped Morgan on the shoulder. "But what of my wounded sailor? Did he make it?"

"Unfortunately, no. He died within the hour."

"Poor lad. I could have got him to your surgeon quicker by bringing the *Aphrodite* alongside your frigate, but—even though I had no idea you were aboard her—I didn't dare take any chance of the arms being discovered."

"You did exactly the right thing, Archambault," Morgan said with feeling. "Duty must always come first."

Duty must always come first? Always? This was the very idea that she was fleeing. Duty to her had meant the bourgeois ideal of hard work and responsibility and family. She was on the very eve of giving all that up for . . . yes, love. But duty had been waiting for her, lurking in the shadows, and now revealing itself under its new name of patriotism.

"In any case, I did what I thought I must; but I will have

the loss of that boy on my conscience," Archambault said. "But look here, Sophie, this is no place for a lady. There'll be many a toast drunk here tonight. The Martiniquais don't have any love for the English, and you can be sure the Americans won't be allowed to buy a single drink tonight. Also the word of what you and I and Morgan are up to has got about, and that makes us as good as heroes."

Sophie looked imploringly at Morgan, and he returned her look warmly but shook his head with resignation.

"Archambault . . ." she began but then bit her tongue. This was the last time Archambault would treat her like a child. There were things that she would have to make him understand, but this was neither the time nor place.

"Innkeeper," called Archambault, "have someone show the lady to her room."

But then Morgan intervened.

"I'll see Sophie up," he said, and they were on the stairs before Archambault could say another word.

By the time they reached the door to her room, without having spoken—it seemed to her that he was as tense and uncertain as she—Sophie made a decision. They were bone-tired and emotionally exhausted. In the morning they would be fresh—and, also, she could put off matters for a few hours more. She was surprised at this thought in one who had told herself that she was eager for passion.

Morgan took her awkwardly in his arms. "I'll come to you as soon as I can," he whispered huskily, "but it may be some hours."

"Then come in the morning, when all the rest are asleep from their carousing, and we can be truly alone."

"It is for you to say." She saw that he felt that somehow it was his fault that what should have gone so smoothly had not. With great reluctance he saw her into her room.

She stood breathing heavily, her back against the door, for some time before taking any notice of her surroundings. When she did she saw that her room was as fine as any in a superior inn in France. The floor was of wide boards of mahogany, the glass doors tall and opening onto a wide gallery in the West Indian style.

Her trunks had arrived, and already her clothes had been hung in two tall mahogany armoires. She went out onto the gallery. It was already quite dark, and the moon was just coming up over the sea. Beyond the inn was the black jungle and its thousand sounds, which began, she remembered well, only with the setting of the sun. During the day the jungle was silent.

"Oh, Morgan," she whispered, her fatigue banished by an overwhelming desire to have him with her. Now that it was too late, her indecision had vanished.

Sophie turned from the beautiful tropical night and went back into her room.

The long white muslin curtains billowed in the morning breeze, letting in the soft perfumed air but holding back the brilliant tropical light and reducing it to a diffuse glow that filled the room. For a brief moment she was fifteen again, all the years that had followed dissolved, leaving her free to resume her dreams. Ah, her dreams. . . .

There was a discreet knock on the door.

Sophie slipped out of the big four-poster bed, piled high with linen-covered pillows, and padded across the mahogany floor in her nightgown.

"*Je viens.*"

Was it Morgan or was it only the maid with breakfast? Even as she opened the door a crack she knew the answer, and as she opened it wide she knew that this was what she desired, all that she desired. There was no more hesitation.

What she had not expected was for Morgan to come through the door in a dressing gown, bearing a tray piled with the tropical fruits of Martinique. He was as barefoot as she.

She stood, surprised, as he put the tray down on the small round dining table, turned and closed the door and locked it.

"I took your breakfast tray away from the maid," he said as if he needed to explain. "I regret last night. You see . . ."

"Regret last night?"

"We were to be together, but I could not escape my male companions and all their toasts and talk and boasting and . . . rum. Even now my head throbs."

"Morgan, my darling, what are you talking about? Did I not ask you to come to me in the morning?" She felt tears of joy in her eyes.

"Sophie! Have I offended you, misunderstood . . ." and he took a step toward her but she waved him back.

"Do not mind my tears," she said, gasping. "It is laughter that causes me to shake. Oh, you cannot imagine with what seriousness Madame Armonville viewed last night. And now you come simply into my room . . ."

His eyes narrowed, and his slight smile sent shivers up her spine. He understood all too well what she was saying.

"Well then, shall we have that breakfast we have promised ourselves?"

Sophie hurried to the armoire and covered herself with a robe, while Morgan put two chairs up to the table and began to attempt the peeling of a mango. The aroma from a large pot of coffee permeated the air.

She came across the room, still barefoot, with all the restrained grace that she could muster. Her strict Huguenot background was thrown aside like a gown. Whatever her upbringing, she was a Frenchwoman and did not need to be told that pleasure was to be approached with restrained anticipation and not rushed headlong into.

She slid into the chair opposite Morgan and took the fruit from his unaccustomed hands.

"Let me. I will show you how to peel each fruit, slice it and arrange the pieces on the plate together to form the most pleasing pattern."

"It is an art then?"

"Ah, Morgan, in Martinique everything is an art."

"And you will teach me."

Without lifting her head from the peeling of a blood orange in a single spiral of skin, she looked up at him coquettishly through long dark lashes.

"Of course."

She was surprised at the warm deep tone of her own voice. What had come over her? She had entered into the kind of amorous adventure that had been her consoling fantasy as she had lain awake at nights above her office and warehouse in Bordeaux. Yet this was real, and she felt no more shame than if the high-ceilinged room, the warm tropical breeze, the perfume of the fruit were the stuff of her imagination.

"To begin, one does not peel a mango as though it were an apple. One girdles it around the middle and twists the two halves apart, thus."

"Amazing."

The look upon his face was . . . what? Amused respect, she decided, and desire, yes, that most of all, and some astonishment at her coolness in the circumstances. Now she looked up, and boldly, into Morgan's eyes, let her eyes wander over his form. His chest, bare under the half-open dressing gown, was covered in the same silky dark hair, darker even than hers, that hung loosely about his face, freed from the usual tight pigtail that bound it. Dark hair swirled more lightly down his arm emerging from the sleeve of his dressing gown, and encircled his wrist. His large hand upon the table still held the fruit knife with which he had ineptly tried to peel a mango.

"Next I will show you how to deal with a pineapple."

"I am at least," he said with a touch of good-humored mockery, "competent to pour the coffee."

He filled the two white porcelain cups with West Indian brew as black as tar and took a small loaf of bread, still warm from the oven, from the linen napkin in which it had been wrapped, and broke it in two.

"Et voilà, monsieur," and she handed him a plate on which the slices of blood orange and pineapple, the mango and halves of lime had been prettily arranged. Then she washed her hands in the bowl of warm water provided, in which a frangipani flower floated.

"Oh, how pleasant! How . . . superb!" And he clinked his coffee cup with hers as though they were glasses of the finest champagne.

"To my beautiful Martinique!"

"To Martinique . . . and to us, Sophie."

"To us." She lowered her eyes. "Morgan, I would prolong this forever. I have never known . . ."

"At least we have the whole morning to ourselves." His voice too had deepened with desire.

"Oh, diable!"

"What is it?"

"Archambault expects me this morning for a long talk, which I surely owe him."

"Except that I told him last night, before we parted, that you had said to me that you were most weary and had no intention of rising before noon."

"Noon? You told him I would not rise before noon? What time is it now?"

"Oh, I would say about nine or a little after."

"But that leaves three hours."

"Yes it does, doesn't it?"

"Well then, there is no need to hurry . . ."

"No."

Her heart was beating fast now. To distract his eyes that never left her face she held out her cup for more coffee, though it was still half full. Her hand shook so that the cup rattled in the saucer.

"Merci."

She was about to add some light remark to excuse her nervousness, but then she looked up into his eyes and saw sympathy and gentleness there. There was no need to say anything. Once again, he understood. From where had this American who, as he was first described to her, looked as though he had just stepped out of the forests, got that subtle understanding of a woman's feelings with which he so often surprised her?

"It is not just for this morning, Sophie, that we have no need to hurry. Do you not feel that, whatever weighty matters may hang over each of our heads, we have reached our safe harbor?"

It was exactly what she had wanted to hear him say. She felt the last of the bonds with which she had bound herself over the years slip away. At last she was free.

"Oh, I do, I do. And do you not feel that the light, the color, the perfumed air of Martinique promise a happiness that one could never aspire to in strict and serious Bordeaux?"

"Or gray and rainy Paris. And I do believe that your beauty has blossomed even further here."

"My beauty?"

She felt color rush to her face and stole a glance in the large oval mirror on the wall. With her dark hair hanging loose, her large dark eyes and arched eyebrows, pale complexion and flushed cheeks, high forehead and softly rounded chin she could not deny . . .

She looked back at him but he only smiled, saying nothing. She blushed even more.

"Morgan, we will make time stand still for us. I will show you everything. First of all a beautiful spot in the hills. I own a villa there—though I have been told it has fallen into ruin—where I spent my girlhood years."

"I want to see every place that has known you."

"You shall, and we will discover new places as well."

"But first of all the places that knew you as a girl."

"Why is that?"

"So that I can better understand what has made you what you are."

She was touched by this sentiment and reached out and put her hand over his, stroked the silky hair on his wrist.

"And I would know more of you, Morgan Carter."

"Oh, I am a simple enough man."

"I do not believe that for one instant."

"Then what sort of man am I?"

"One who greatly deserves to be loved by a woman."

She withdrew her hand from his and fluttered her fingers daintily in the bowl of water and dried them carefully on her napkin. It was almost like a rite.

"And how did you find the mango?"

"Excellent, as was all. Indeed, we seem to have consumed everything on the tray."

"Yes," she said. "Well then . . ."

She arose and undid the sash of her robe, slipped it off and hung it on the back of her chair. After turning her back to him, she grasped her nightgown with both hands, pulled it over her head and tossed it on the floor. Then she walked slowly to the bed, glancing again at her image in the mirror, noting the full breasts and slim waist. Yes, she was beautiful and pleased that it was so. Before her beauty had meant nothing to her: there had been no one to offer her beauty to. She was tall, too, almost as tall as he. That also pleased her.

She slid beneath the linen sheet and closed her eyes. It was so quiet that she could hear the wind in the palm trees. Then she heard his bare feet on the floor and felt his weight sink into the other side of the bed. For a long time neither of them moved and only by his breathing could she tell that she was not alone in bed. Now she was not tense at all. It was just that there was no hurry.

"Morgan?"

"Yes."

"I'm glad I'm doing this."

He said nothing, and she had not expected a reply. It was part of her rite, these words that needed to be said. She opened her eyes at last and reached out and touched his face.

He moved over until she could feel the warmth of his body close to hers, put his warm hand on her cool shoulder outside the sheet and ran it ever so lightly down the length of her arm. Just that, but what a thrill of desire it provoked in her body. There was a moment when restraint, however delicious, was no longer possible.

"Oh, mon amour!" And at last, at long last, their bodies came together.

"Sophie, Sophie."

What followed brought her sheer delight but astonishment as well. Her imaginings had not prepared her for the reality of being made love to by one so virile and skillful and ardent, nor had she understood what passion there was within her waiting to be released. She buried her face in the hairs of his chest, she placed little bites on his neck, she explored the inside of his mouth with her tongue, she kissed his eyelids, she did anything and everything that occurred to her. And he did the same to her, and more.

At last she fell back on the pillow, gasping for breath. He leaned over her.

"This is a moment that I have been anticipating ever since you read me that poem by Ronsard aboard ship."

As he lowered his head she looked down at her nipples, pink and hard. She had never seen them protrude so. Then he kissed them both and caressed them with his tongue at length.

"Oh, Morgan, what bliss."

"When you read of such you turned quite scarlet, but now that you have experienced it you blush not at all."

"The time for blushes is past. So, you rogue, you anticipated that moment. Then you knew all along you would have me in bed."

"I never doubted it for an instant. It was only a question of when you would be ready for it."

"God knows, I am ready now," she said in a husky voice and, taking him by the wrist, spread her legs apart and placed his hand firmly between them, to let him feel the warmth and moistness that her passion had engendered. Then she felt for him in the same place and guided him to her.

She was again astonished, that such a man could have entered her so easily.

"Don't move yet," she whispered. "I just want to feel you there for a while, filling me. Oh, Morgan, I've wanted you there so much."

After a while he did move, slowly at first and then with increasing urgency, and she moved with him, clinging to him, arms and legs wrapped about him as tightly as a drowning person would cling to her rescuer. She could not have said whether her eyes were open or closed. All senses but one were suppressed, and she seemed to be hurtling through space.

"*Oh, mon Dieu! Mon Dieu!*" she cried. And then "*Je meurs!*"

"Don't die yet," he whispered in her ear. "Hold on yet a bit longer."

But there was no question of that. All the feeling in her body had gathered in one small place, where it was held for an instant like a note of music, and then released in a flood of pleasure, a pleasure that grew even greater as she felt the same happening to him. And then she floated up slowly through tropical waters until she found herself lying, drenched with perspiration, on her bed.

She opened her eyes. The church bell was tolling noon. The room had resumed its familiar shape, the white muslin curtains still billowed in the breeze, the remains of their breakfast stood on the table like the still life of some Dutch painter, the linen sheet had slid off onto the floor. She rolled over to look for the first time on her lover entire—her lover, now was that not fine?—nothing less than a Greek god, and as naked as any statue of one.

"Morgan?"

"Hm?" He opened his eyes. "Sophie, you are like a goddess."

"I was about to pay you the same compliment. Then have we not just been where such dwell?"

"Paradise, yes."

"Yet for me something more."

"How so?"

"I am like some benighted heathen who did not even know of the existence of such a paradise."

"Sophie, you are crying. Why?"

"For all the wasted years, for knowing that one can only enter paradise once."

He took her in his arms and held her close, speaking to her in a low voice. "*Chérie,* I must correct you on two points. As to those years that you call wasted, had they not existed then you would not be the same Sophie that I now hold in my arms. And this is the only Sophie that I want: no other. Do you understand?"

She nodded her head vigorously, unable to speak, and crying even more copiously.

"As to paradise, one can only enter it once for the first time. That's true enough. But once entered its existence is established. Now, no matter what happens, we know where that place is that will always await us. Is that not true?"

"Yes, yes. Morgan, you are wise."

"Surely I am. Did I not, the first time I saw you at Château Ivran, say to myself that this is no *marchande de vin* but a goddess."

"My thoughts, in my state at that time, I did not fully comprehend. Now I see that they were much the same for you." She sat up in bed and hugged her knees. "It seems then that ours is *une affaire sérieuse.*"

"Most serious, I would judge."

"It frightens me. My passion frightens me. In those last moments I no longer had the least control over myself, and I must tell you I fought against it . . ."

He did not reply and she continued. "What does this passion that we are caught up in auger?"

"I cannot say. I am as much a stranger in this territory as you."

"Truly? No other woman has ever been with you in such territory."

"With no other woman have I even approached the boundaries of such territory as ours. I can think of only one comparison. Like true passion, the unexplored American wilderness is not for the weak of heart. Yet neither Philadelphia nor Boston, no, not even Paris, holds such charm for me as those wild places."

CHAPTER NINE

Sophie dressed in a leisurely fashion, her languid motions reflecting the complete satiety that her body had known for the first time. She savored the pleasant bruised feeling, the feeling that her body had at last been used as it was meant to be. She sat before the mirror, still nude, and brushed out her hair and pinned it up. She had never felt so womanly. She hoped she had not said too much to Morgan about the revelation that she had had of what lovemaking could be. It would be unfair to the memory of André, and besides . . . well, a woman did not wish to appear inexperienced.

She sighed and went to the armoire to choose her clothes. She would have preferred to spend the rest of the day in complete idleness, but Morgan had gone to arrange a private dining room for them and Archambault. There was much to discuss. Her promise to Morgan of making time stand still for them would have to wait. Even so, there was no hurry. In Martinique one did not dine until two o'clock or even three, and after that there was the siesta. She smiled. She would have to introduce Morgan to that custom. She remembered giggling with her girl friends when the adults retired after the main meal of the day. One knew what they did then. Today, however, all the afternoon had to be given over to business.

When she entered the small dining room that had been reserved for them she found Morgan and Archambault waiting for her. Morgan's eyes devoured her. She had taken great care to dress as becomingly as possible for their first meeting after being together, and from this day on she meant to take as much care with her looks as any courtesan.

"My, you look especially pretty today, Sophie," said Archambault, who had always had an eye for the ladies.

She wondered if Archambault had guessed, for it seemed to her that her whole presence must cry out that she and Morgan were lovers. Well, if he hadn't he would know soon enough, for she intended, with Morgan's agreement, for them to live openly together. She wanted no hypocrisy, no sneaking about.

"Here, Sophie, what do you say to this," and Archambault handed her a glass of the white wine he and Morgan were tasting.

Sophie put her nose into the glass and tasted.

"A nice Pouilly-Fumé from the Loire, a '72 I would imagine, but it has lost something in traveling."

"Right on all counts, but still I think it will go right well with the flying fish I have ordered grilled for our dinner, preceded by a plate of sea urchins."

"With lemons for the sea urchins and limes for the flying fish."

"Naturally."

"And the fish charred a bit on the grill."

"Of course."

Morgan laughed. "Only you French. . . ."

Sophie gave him a certain look. "*Justement,* monsieur. Only we French give proper attention to the arts of living. All is in the details." She let her eyes speak the rest.

"Now, while we wait let us consider our situation," Sophie continued. "Our first order of business must be to get Jean out of prison. At his age it is a death sentence."

"I have already inquired after him," Archambault said. "He is faring reasonably well, being a tough old bird. Morgan has told me that the governor is under orders to look favorably on your affairs, and I imagine that a word to the governor's aide will be sufficient to obtain his release. Then . . ."

Morgan interrupted. "I believe there is another matter that needs attention even more urgently."

"Je m'excuse," Sophie said quickly. "What matter is that?" She would have to remember that having a lover was in more ways than one like being married. One had to be careful of the other's feelings and interests.

"The captain of the American warship tells me he sails with the evening tide, which is a matter of only three hours."

"But what is the urgency?"

"That's clear enough, Sophie," Archambault replied for Morgan. "The British frigates may have turned tail when faced by all the guns of the fort of St. Pierre—what prudent captain would not have—but you can be sure that they will soon be back with their squadron, and that the British will be preparing a most unpleasant reception for our American friends when they sail out of French territorial waters. That is, if the Americans tarry here beyond tonight."

"Then by all means they should sail," Sophie said.

"But with what instructions?"

"What do you mean, Morgan?"

"I mean that we are blessed with the chance to get the good news to my government with the shortest possible delay."

"The good news?" Truly, she would have to do better than this if she was to play in the world of men such as these. And she had no doubt that she could. "You mean to say that you would not have your Continental Congress handle these weighty matters without our sage advice?"

He smiled at this sally of hers. She felt a shiver akin to that of lovemaking. To challenge the great world of kings and ministers, generals and admirals with this man would be . . .

A New World Won

Mon Dieu . . . a life of passion and adventure.

A young woman of the islands placed on the table a plate of black-spined, orange-fleshed *oursins*.

"I would propose," Morgan said, "that we send with the captain, whose destination is Philadelphia, a letter that informs the secret committee of the Congress that the large-bore cannon that General Washington so desperately needs have arrived in Martinique."

"And then?" asked Archambault.

"We will tell the Congress that they must immediately send coastal schooners to St. Pierre to take the armaments away in small lots."

"But what about the British and all their men-of-war?" Sophie asked.

"They cannot follow our small craft into the creeks of Florida and the Carolinas."

"Or they run aground doing so," Archambault added.

"Now," said Morgan, "how does one eat these sea urchins?"

"With a spoon," said Sophie, "after a bit of lemon has been squeezed over them."

"Which improves the flavor?"

"It does but also confirms their freshness."

"How so?"

"If they are alive they will wiggle a bit."

"You eat them alive?"

"Bien sur," said Archambault.

The young woman who had served them throughout the meal entered the room once again with a tray containing a pot of coffee, demitasse cups, a bowl of the coarse brownish local sugar and a box of thin twisted cheroots. The coffee was poured and the cheroots passed. Morgan and Archambault each took one and, after a moment's hesitation, so did Sophie.

The young Martiniquaise clipped the ends off the cheroots and lit them for each of them in turn with a big sulfur match. Ignoring Morgan's surprise—what pleasure to at last, at long last, flaunt convention—Sophie addressed herself to the woman who waited upon them.

"Tell me, mademoiselle, is the name Odette Phillipeau familiar to you?"

"*Sûrement,* madame. She is my second cousin's godmother."

"She is still to be found in these parts?"

"Indeed. She is a laundress here in St. Pierre."

"Do these laundresses still beat their washing against the rocks along the river bank beneath the bridge?"

"Where else, madame? It has always been so."

"You could send her to me?"

"Of course. When do you wish to see her?"

"Whenever she is pleased to come. This evening would be convenient."

"*Très bien, madame,*" and the young woman, with skin the color of the lightest café au lait, starched cotton bandanna, blouse and skirt of deep yellow, chocolate and sky blue, curtseyed ever so slightly and left the room.

"Odette Phillipeau? Was not your maid when you were a girl here a Phillipeau?" Archambault asked.

"Céleste Phillipeau, Odette's mother. She's dead now. Odette and I were inseparable playmates all those years. Odette a laundress? That will not do, and I have need of a maid again. You will soon discover, Morgan, that such help is going to be necessary in the role we aspire to play. One must, for example, in this climate change clothes three times a day."

She was surprised at her outspokenness. What a change three hours of lovemaking had made in her.

"These women are not slaves, are they?" Morgan asked, obviously perplexed and ill at ease.

"Not these women. In many ways they might be said to govern Martinique. They carry goods upon their heads from village to village, run both small shops and larger enterprises, even unload the ships, as you saw, yet maintain themselves in a state of fashion that would shame many a Parisienne."

"And lead every Frenchman on the island by the nose," added Archambault.

"That too. The woman who waited upon us no doubt has a French father, and she may choose to raise her own daughter *en chapeau*."

"What does that mean?"

"Her daughter will be brought up wearing a straw hat like a French girl and then will be accepted as such. Or she may choose to wear the bandanna and belong to the other race. It is a matter of no consequence to anyone."

"Yet slavery is still the lot of the majority."

"Not for long, I think, on French territory. Hyacinthe tells me that in private even the king speaks against that institution. The problem is, I fear, Morgan, rather yours in America."

Morgan was about to speak, but Archambault broke in.

"All very interesting, no doubt, but the American warship sails in less than three hours now, and no letters have as yet been written to the Continental Congress."

"Quite right," said Morgan, "and I will go to my room and do so straightway."

"And I will go see if I can raise Lieutenant Roland and have old Jean released from prison before he passes another night there. And you, Sophie?"

"You two brave men having solved all our problems, I will take my siesta."

The next morning Sophie awoke from a long deep sleep, a sleep that had sealed her passage into another world. When she awoke she was a different woman. She had told Morgan that he was free to come to her room when he wanted and need not ask her permission. As she had expected, he had understood that she wanted some time to herself to consider this *affaire sérieuse* into which they had entered. He had not come to her in the night, nor did she expect him this evening either. She was that sure of his sensitivity to her mood. But then there was a knock on the door.

"*Oui?*"

"*C'est moi, Odette.*"

In an instant Sophie was unlocking the door and there Odette stood, a mature woman now and even more beautiful, if that was possible. They embraced and kissed on both cheeks.

Odette held her by the shoulders at arms' length and examined her.

"*Ma foi, Sophie, comme tu es belle.* There must be a man in your life."

No use in trying to dissemble with Odette. "Yes."

"The American?"

"Yes."

"I've seen him. He's a match for you. *Beau comme le diable.* Good, good. I've not been happy with the reports I've had of you from France these last five years."

"That's all finished, Odette. Oh, how I hope it is. Come sit down and let us talk."

They sat down together on a chaise longue and Odette took Sophie's pale hands in her light brown ones.

"What hopes I had for you when you set sail to marry the marquis, but then your family lost its fortune. No dowry, no marquis." Odette laughed in that deep-throated, cascading laugh that Sophie remembered so well. "*Toujours la monnaie, n'est-ce pas,* Sophie? And then the shipping office and the ledgers."

"As you said, it's always a question of money."

"But no life for my Sophie."

"It is over in any case."

"And you are no younger. The American then, is he the grand passion?"

"You were always a gambler, Odette."

"And still am."

"Then you will understand that I have put everything on one roll of the dice. Should that fail, then . . ."

"Then we will not let it fail. Now in what way may I assist you?"

"I have to play a role, a most difficult one. I must at the same time be an attentive lover, a role I have never played before, embark on a dangerous commerce . . ."

"I have heard."

". . . and make myself useful to the governor to protect myself against the Comtesse de Brieux. She frightens me."

"As well she might. A wicked woman. *Très méchante.* I could tell you much about her, and will."

"In sum, I must deport myself in such a way that . . ."

"That you keep friends and lovers with you and put your enemies to rout."

"Exactly."

"That is a campaign to which I would be prepared to lend myself."

"Meaning?"

"Given the situation you describe, you will have need of a

personal maid, accomplice and adviser. And here I am."

Just what Sophie had been about to propose, but knowing Odette of old, it was the moment to pose a question.

"What would you have me do for you in return?"

"Take me back to France with you and see me married to a gentleman."

"So that is your ambition."

"And the years are passing. At age twenty-five . . ."

"I will think upon it," though she knew what her answer would be, "and give you my reply when next we meet."

"And when should that be?"

"Tomorrow morning at this same hour."

"I will be here. And Sophie . . ."

"Yes?"

"You love this man?"

"I do."

"Do not let that blind you to the need always to please him as if you were a calculating mistress."

"When it comes to matters of love, Odette, you may be sure that I would not ignore any advice you offer."

By mid-morning Sophie was in an open carriage pulled by two fine matched bays and surrounded by men: Morgan, Archambault and old Jean, the manager of her St. Pierre office, released from prison with the ease that Archambault had predicted: a good omen of the governor's intentions. She had not seen Jean in five years, but he had aged at the same rate as his twin brother Etienne in Bordeaux. She could hardly have told the difference between them, not even in their speech. She inquired solicitously on how he had fared in prison.

"Well, I wouldn't recommend it as a form of amusement."

That was all he had to say and Archambault guffawed, at

which Jean shot him a venomous look. There had never been any love lost between Archambault the sea captain and the two brothers, "the pen pushers", as he called them.

"There it is," Sophie said, half rising from her seat and folding the linen parasol with which she had shaded her face from the tropical sun. "Oh, dear, it is in a ruinous state."

The offices of her family's firm and the apartment above it where her parents had stayed when a ship was in, otherwise residing in their villa in the hills, was in a deplorable state. The building was almost devoid of paint, shutters falling apart, even the sign that had once borne the family name had disappeared.

"There was no money," Jean said defensively, "though I asked you often enough for funds to keep the place in good repair."

"Well, if you did," Sophie shot back, not about to be bullied, "your messages never got past your brother, for I certainly never saw any request for money."

"Then I was in prison simply on account of working in your employ."

"So, the state of my property is all my fault."

No response. Morgan followed this exchange with some amusement.

"I would see the apartment first," Sophie said, alighting from the carriage.

"But surely," Jean began, "the offices . . ."

"The apartment is my first concern," she said, as she had told Morgan she intended, "because Morgan and I intend to move here as soon as it can be made ready."

The silence was complete and prolonged. Sophie looked defiantly from Archambault to Jean and back again. Neither man dared speak or even meet her eyes. There, that was established.

"And where's the money to come from?" old Jean said at last.

"Morgan?"

"The bill of exchange?" Morgan asked innocently. "Your bank account has been credited with a million livres."

"A million livres?" Jean repeated incredulously.

"Come on then," Sophie said, impatient to launch her new life, "Let's begin. Jean, you take note of what I want done. First, the outside of the building is to be painted the deepest yellow you can find, and there is to be a sign over the door of sky blue with 'New World Trading Co.' printed in letters of chocolate brown." Her choice of colors was taken from the colors worn by the maid who had served them at dinner the day before, a very Martiniquaise choice.

"New World Trading Company," said Jean, writing down what she had said. "But what about Chardin . . ."

"Jean, this is the only way that Chardin and Co. will survive."

They gingerly mounted the rotting outside stairs that led to the apartment and Jean produced a bunch of keys. While he fumbled for the right one, Sophie looked up and down the quay and saw that many eyes were upon them. Good. She meant to throw down a clear challenge to the Comtesse de Brieux.

The men pushed open the shutters while Sophie surveyed the state of the mildewed plaster and the dark, cracked varnish of the woodwork.

"The floors will have to be stripped and revarnished, the walls completely replastered. But first of all everything needs to be washed with a strong solution. There is a dark side even to paradise, Morgan. You have not yet, perhaps, encountered the spiders and giant centipedes and scorpions of Martinique."

"No, fortunately."

"Well, you will soon enough," said Jean. "You should have seen the specimens in the prison."

"Always," Archambault added, "knock out your shoes in the morning before you put them on."

"And the shutters," Sophie said, returning to the task at hand, "we had just as well take measurements while we are here, for they will all have to be replaced."

As Jean, with Archambault's reluctant help, began this task Sophie turned to Morgan and looked into his eyes.

"Yes, *madame la directrice,* you have orders for me as well?"

"Morgan, do not tease me. Let me have my day of triumph. Who knows how long this fairy tale will last?"

"I understand." And she knew that he did.

"Here," and she thrust a key to her room at the inn into his hand.

"When?"

"Would you prefer to come to me at siesta or at dawn?"

"Why don't I come at siesta and . . ."

"And?"

"Stay till dawn. After all, we should get used to sharing a bed."

CHAPTER TEN

Sophie lay propped up among the pillows, wide-awake but motionless. Her body satisfied—ah, how right she had been not to make love again too soon—and now her other senses seemed unusually sharp. She could smell the sea, the lush jungle cooling off as night approached. From the distance came the clacking of shutters being thrown back, the renewed cries of fruit and flower vendors. The light filtering through the closed shutters of the room was turning to the warm glow of early evening. Siesta was coming to an end. As a child in Martinique, when she was made to rest, it was an eagerly awaited hour. Now the coming of evening brought a certain sadness. There was one less time of siesta left to lie with a man she loved deeply and passionately.

She turned her head indolently to look at Morgan lying beside her asleep, his nakedness half-covered by a sheet. He is like a fine prize animal she thought, all muscle and fire, and I alone know his embraces. I, Sophie Armonville, who had given up all hope of passion, know such passion as this. Then why am I sad? Was it only the natural feeling of sadness after making love that she had heard other women speak of? She wasn't sure. She had so little experience. Here I am, twenty-five years old, and I have known love in all its force only twice. She smiled. Both times within the last three days. Or was it that she sensed that such happiness could not last, that Martinique had for her dark places, as yet unseen, like those that harbored the centipedes and scorpions that one did not see until it was too late?

En tout cas, she was starving. Should she get up and dress or should she lie naked abed and have Morgan order supper sent up to them? She took pleasure even in her inability to reach a decision. Siestas, indecisiveness, indolence. The widow Armonville of Bordeaux would have been shocked.

There was a gentle tapping on the door. Now who could that be? She got out of bed, picked up her nightgown from the floor, where this time Morgan had thrown it, and went to the door.

"Who is it?"

"Me, Archambault. Sophie, I can't find Morgan anywhere. Do you know where he might be?"

"Here."

Silence. Perhaps this time Archambault would understand that she was now free of his or any member of her family's control.

"Oh. Then would you tell him that he should come immediately. There's a British merchantman entering the harbor, but she has an American ensign nailed to the mast. I think our American friends have captured her."

"What's that?" Morgan said, sitting up in bed. "I'm coming. Give me but two minutes."

And that was all the time it took him to be in his clothes.

"What luck, Sophie," he said, kissing her hastily on the mouth. "How could they have known that Martinique is now open to American privateers? My message has just begun its journey to Philadelphia.... Well, I will be back as quickly as possible."

And then he was through the door, leaving her standing in the middle of the room in her nightgown. *Tiens!*

Before she could reflect further she realized she was looking through the half-open door into Odette's eyes.

"Puis-je entrer?"

"Yes, of course, Odette, come in."

Odette was dressed in white linen and wore a neat little straw hat upon her head. Céleste's daughter had been raised *en chapeau*. Sophie marvelled again at her beauty, her large luminous brown eyes, a head of thick shining black hair pulled severely back, and skin most attractively washed the palest shade of brown, little more than a touch of sun might have given.

"Your answer, Sophie?"

"Is, of course, yes. It will be like the old days."

"Except now, Sophie, remember that I am your maid. That is the bargain. Now where shall I begin?"

Odette's eyes surveyed the room, the disorder of the bed, the remains of a meal, and then settled on Sophie.

"I could begin by assisting with your bath and washing your hair, and then I will see to the room."

Before she could protest Sophie found herself with her nightgown removed, sitting on a high stool in the tiled alcove over a drain where a large clay jar held water for bathing, her hair being vigorously soaped by Odette.

"So, you would return with me to France?"

"Yes."

"I cannot say when that will be."

"It does not matter. I will wait. So long as I am still of marriageable age."

"You would marry a Frenchman, then?"

"I would."

"You are determined on that course?"

"I am."

"But why? To marry a Frenchman who does not now even exist for you? What of love?"

"My desire is to be a respectable woman and have my children looked up to. As to my future husband, one can learn to love the man one marries."

"You can be a respectable woman here, Odette. Look at your mother."

"She did well for the daughter of a slave. Even then she had the support of a Frenchman, an admirer of many years —my father to be truthful. But there could never be in this society any question of him marrying a *femme de couleur*. With my skin such a marriage would be possible, except that everyone in St. Pierre knows who my mother is. I could marry a Frenchman here, but not of the respectable class. In France I would be just another Creole lady from the islands, and I could aim as high as my looks and spirit could take me."

Sophie could think of nothing to say. This was not the happy view of relations between the races that she had been brought up with and that she had given Morgan. From Odette's perspective things did not look at all the same.

"Still, Odette, in my view it is not always possible to love a man just because one is married to him."

"Ah, madame, but I will choose carefully."

With that rebuke Odette laughed, and as if to end the conversation poured a gourdful of cool water from the clay jar over Sophie's head and began soaping her hair again.

"They say all over St. Pierre that you have turned the governor's head and that he has dismissed the Comtesse de Brieux's charges against you, which before he accepted."

"I have turned the governor's head? That is laughable."

But she was not about to tell Odette the real reason why the governor had decided that her trade with France was not to be interfered with.

"They also say that the Comtesse plans her revenge against you."

"That is more believable. Tell me about her."

"She is *très fâchée,* they say, and relieves this anger of hers by hurting and humiliating others. She is angry, they say, because she was once one of the most beautiful women in France and her beauty is beginning to fade. But she is even more angry because she was once one of the most powerful women in France and now, on orders from the king himself, she may not even set her pretty foot in France. All that is left her is to make her will felt in this small place of exile. Thus, you have offended her on both counts."

"I can see how the governor's reversal could be blamed on me, but how have I offended against her beauty?"

"Oh, madame, is it not obvious? You have but to look in a mirror."

"Odette, please stop calling me madame," Sophie said, flustered. "Our bargain does not require that."

Morgan did not, as he had proposed, come again to her bed that night nor, she thought with some indignation as she dressed, had he consulted her on the question of the British merchantman that had kept him away the entire night. It was, after all, her firm that was the means of . . . Stop, Sophie, she said to herself. Remember Odette's advice. The shield of an innocent and perfect love must at times be that of the calculating mistress.

This dialogue with her image in the mirror, as she did her hair, was interrupted by her attention being drawn to the image itself. What had Odette said? The most beautiful woman in the islands. *Mon Dieu,* what a thought that was. Then she laughed. Odette had not said the most beautiful woman in the islands, but the most beautiful Frenchwoman, not one of whom could hold a candle to the great beauties of the world of *les femmes de couleur.*

Sophie opened the shuttered doors and went out onto the gallery. Voices came from below. She leaned over the railing and spied on the veranda below. Morgan and Archambault were seated under an awning, laughing and talking and drinking wine from a bottle cooling in a clay jar.

Alors, that was quite enough! She went back into the room, closed the shutters, took a parasol from the Chinese vase that stood beside the door and descended the stairs.

"Well, messieurs, what do you have to say for yourselves?"

They were on their feet in an instant.

"The prize is ours," Archambault almost cried out. "The British ship is loaded to the gunwales with merchandise. Have a glass, Sophie."

"Wine when the sun has not yet risen over the mountain? Order me some coffee and brioches instead and tell me of your adventures."

Archambault lowered his head like a schoolboy chastised, but Morgan only looked smilingly into her eyes. It would take more than a touch of cool sarcasm to chasten this one!

"Our adventures, yes," Morgan said, pulling up a chair for her. "We have fought off His Majesty's customs collectors in the course of the night and, better still, the commander of the local contingent of the French army, none other than Colonel Girard, our shipboard companion, who would have claimed the prize for France."

"And what prevented him?"

"Fortunately, Commander Jones, who captains the American frigate that is carrying my letter to the Continental Congress in Philadelphia, knew that Martinique was ready to receive British vessels captured by the American navy. Coming upon a British merchantman when barely over the horizon from Martinique, he swooped down upon her. He then sent the captured merchantman back to St. Pierre with a letter to the governor stating that the British merchantman is an American prize to be handed over to the New World Trading Company. This letter was handed over to Colonel

Girard with the desired effect. Isn't that an auspicious beginning for our enterprise?"

"Indeed. But the governor, who has gone back to the capital at Fort Royal, will not have yet seen the letter. Suppose he does not agree to what Commander Jones proposes?"

"Remember, Sophie," Morgan said, "that when we met privately with the governor I asked about this very matter and he cautioned me against asking questions to which the answer might be no. I propose that we proceed with an auction of the ship's cargo as though the governor had agreed."

"And the sooner the better," Archambault added. "I have discussed the matter with Jean, and he suggests that we not move the cargo to the company's warehouse but hold an auction aboard ship. Of course, the decision is yours, Sophie."

The two men looked at her expectantly. She had misjudged. There had been no intention on the part of either man to act without her. That they had rushed to the harbor to claim the ship and its cargo without stopping to consult her only showed good sense.

"I agree, and I would propose another step. That as soon as the auction is over and money in hand, you and I, Morgan, as the responsible parties, absent ourselves from St. Pierre for a while. That way we will not be available to receive any contrary orders the governor may feel obliged to issue."

"An excellent idea," said Archambault, getting to his feet. "Then if all is agreed, I will go straightway to tell Jean."

As soon as Archambault had turned the corner Sophie leaned across the table and offered half-parted lips to Morgan. Their mouths were still joined when the tinkle of porcelain announced the arrival of Sophie's breakfast. The maid, who this morning wore a costume of lemon yellow and violet with a red bandanna, took not the slightest notice of the intimacy she encountered. Nor would she have, thought

Sophie, had she come upon a moment of even greater intimacy. There was nothing embarrassing about love in Martinique.

"*Mon Dieu,* Morgan, I am happy. This place would turn even the most strait-laced woman into a wanton."

"Is that how you feel?"

"Only a little part of me still resists."

"The widow Armonville?"

"Yes. For instance, I can delay no longer asking what cargo has fallen into our hands."

"A rich one: tea from China, sugar and coffee from the British West Indies, salted meat from Ireland, rum, wine, many bolts of cloth and a quantity of muskets and powder for the British army in Canada. These last I would propose not be auctioned off but sent along with the weapons aboard the *Aphrodite* as a little gift to my country."

"Agreed that the muskets and powder go to the American government, but as a debit against their share of the prize."

"What," he said with a smile, "you would be so strait-laced as not to make a little present from our share to General Washington?"

She bridled a little at this half-joking remark. It was unfair.

"Remember, Morgan, that the two million livres of which we dispose is but a loan from France that must eventually be repaid by your government in either cash or American produce. It is to the advantage of all that there be a strict accounting."

"Oh my. Then what am I to do about the item I took the liberty of removing from the cargo as a little gift for you?"

"What gift?"

"A trunk is being delivered to your room. It is packed full of the most gorgeous gowns made in Paris for the wife of one of the British generals in Canada. I judge her to be almost exactly your size."

"What? The widow Armonville must refuse this gift," she said sternly and then smiled, "but your Sophie accepts."

Still, that too was a bit unfair. He had led her on, brought out the bourgeois self that she was trying to suppress.

"Well then," he said, a little bit uncomfortably she thought, "where are we to hide ourselves from the governor's orders?"

"That was but an excuse invented for Archambault and Jean. They are accustomed to my overseeing every detail of the business, and I would have them become accustomed instead to my long absences in the company of my lover. My real intent is to begin showing you my beloved island."

"But what of the governor?"

"What could he do once the ship and cargo are sold but rebuke us for having done it, and in truth I think he will be right pleased that we proceeded as we did."

"I see." Morgan laughed but he also eyed her quizzically. "And where would you take us on this pleasure trip?"

"I would like to visit my property in the hills, which is in one of the most beautiful spots on the island. We will need to hire mules."

"And a guide?"

"I will be your guide."

"We will need a place to stay and food if we are to be away several days."

"I am told that my villa is uninhabitable, but there is a small village nearby. If need be we can sleep in the open. It is cool and pleasant up there. As for food we can buy what we need from the peasants."

"I put myself entirely in your hands," but he said it hesitantly.

Morgan was mystified. Good. After all she was not a schoolgirl; and in her relations with the man with whom she was desperately in love, a little guile was the least of the weapons she was prepared to use.

CHAPTER ELEVEN

Sophie reached over and laid her hand on Morgan's bare shoulder. He did not wake. She let her hand lie there for a while. For the first time he had stayed the night in her bed, and she vowed they would not sleep apart again. She shook his shoulder gently.

"What? What is it?"

"Time to get up. It's half past four."

"How do you know? It's dark as pitch."

"The giant wood crickets have just stopped their song. They are as precise as any clock. It is how the poor know that they must begin their day, and travelers, if they wish to reach their destination before the sun is at its fiercest. But first hold me."

She pulled her nightgown over her head to offer him her bare body, but she was soon obliged to slip from his embrace. If she did not, she knew that they would soon be making love. Now that desire had been awakened in her it was always with her, and always, it seemed, growing in intensity. She crossed the room naked and lit the lamp.

"*Mon Dieu*, Morgan, I believe I am developing a taste for this thing that a man and woman do together."

He laughed. "Is that not what you French say, *L'appétit vient en mangeant?*"

"That appetite comes with eating? Then I shall make a glutton of myself, I fear."

She dressed in riding breeches and boots and a loose cotton shirt and tried on the wide-brimmed straw hat that she had bought in the market. The picture of herself she saw in the mirror pleased her, as did the happiness she saw in her eyes.

"For the first time in my life," she whispered to herself.

"What is that?"

"Nothing."

There was a knock on the door.

"Our coffee." Sophie turned to display her costume to Morgan.

But instead of the maid from the inn, the tray of coffee and brioches was brought by Odette, looking as fresh and exotic as a tropical flower.

"Bonjour, messieursdames."

"Bonjour, Odette. The inn has placed a maid at our disposal, you know."

"But I have a contract to fulfill, madame." She began to arrange the breakfast things on the table. "You are going up on Mont Pelée today?"

"Yes. I wish to see the state of Villa Chardin."

"You must be careful on the mountain."

"I know. Oh, I almost forgot," and Sophie took from her shopping basket a long curved sugarcane knife.

"This is for you, Morgan. One always carries a machete on the mountain."

"That is not what I meant, madame," Odette said. "You must avoid the road at midday. The *diablesse* has been seen recently."

"The what?" Morgan inquired.

"There is a superstition," Sophie answered, "that among the women who carry loads on their heads across the mountain, one of them, who is tall and very beautiful and seen only at midday, is a she-devil. She tries to lure workers from the sugarcane fields, and anyone who goes with her is never seen again. All nonsense, of course."

"Nonsense? My mother said that you believed it, madame."

"Yes," Sophie shot back, "and it was Céleste who put that rubbish in my head, as every nurse in Martinique does."

"There are many French in Martinique who believe, and not children either," Odette countered.

That was, Sophie knew, true enough.

"And should night overtake you on the road," Odette went on, ignoring Sophie's incredulity and addressing Morgan, "always keep the light of the next wayside shrine in view. Should you see or hear anything, run to the shrine. They will not come near a shrine."

"They?" said Morgan, clearly astonished at what he was hearing.

"Zombies," said Sophie dryly, "the living dead."

"You believe in such things, Odette?"

"Monsieur, have I not seen a zombie with my own eyes, coming into my room in the middle of the night, its eyes shining, and did I not have to climb out the window to escape it?"

"Odette, enough."

"Yes, madame."

At the inn stables mules had been saddled for them, and just as they were about to mount Jean came into view, in as close to a run as he could manage.

"Sophie, before you leave you must know about the auction. I've been up all night recording the results." He handed her a sheet of paper.

"*Mais, c'est incroyable,*" Sophie said. "Our commission alone is more than the profits of Armonville and Co. for the last two quarters."

"Well then, I've got to be going. Lots more work to be done, too much for someone my age, and with my health half-ruined by prison."

"Just remember, Jean, you are now working for yourself as well."

"What do you mean, Sophie?"

"Didn't I show you the articles of the New World Trading Co.?" She asked mischievously. "You and Archambault are each to receive a nice share of the profits."

"*Mon Dieu,* you are certainly not your father's daughter. Well, thanks then, though I don't know what I'll spend it on at my age." The old man walked away muttering to himself.

As they rode out along the shore to where the road across the mountain emerged from the forest, the dawn began to break.

Nothing had changed. The road over the mountain was not much more than a mule-track following a footpath that had existed for uncounted centuries before the French had colonized Martinique—and that was nearly a hundred and fifty years ago. The tropical forest, of course, never changed: a twilight world of green undergrowth, tree ferns and tall trunks up which lianas climbed towards an upper canopy of green that shut out the sun. The cries of night creatures had subsided and the silence of day had set in. The only flowers now were orchids hanging like small pale lanterns from the trees, and the perfume of rotting vegetation permeated the air. How she loved this place!

"One can imagine a *diablesse* here," Morgan said in a voice as hushed as if he were in a church.

At that moment they turned a curve in the road and came upon a tall bronze-skinned woman moving rapidly up the road, feet bare, back straight as a rod, and balancing on her head a basket containing long loaves of bread.

"*Bonjour.*"

"*Bonjour.*"

"Not a *diablesse?*"

"No," Sophie laughed, "a *porteuse*. She will have left St. Pierre long before dawn, as soon as the bread was out of the oven, and she will distribute it to the plantations and villages on the mountain. Then she will take a little food and a brief siesta and return to St. Pierre, the same basket filled with mangoes, papayas and such, arriving in the town well into the night. Today she may cover as much as fifty miles on foot."

"Impossible!"

"I assure you it is true."

"What can drive these women to such superhuman effort?"

"She is free. Probably her mother was a slave. The first thing a freed woman does is move to a village, or the town if she can afford it. If she works hard enough, a *porteuse* can set aside the money to put herself in business, selling fruit in the market, washing clothes, making skirts and bandannas or jewelry. Her daughter may aspire to a comfortable life, her granddaughter to putting her foot a little way into European society."

"Céleste and Odette?"

"Yes."

Sophie fell silent. She knew so much about how things were in Martinique, yet so little. She had returned to her childhood home a woman who had only just begun to understand herself.

They had reached the top of the ridge, and the first plantation came into view. As they moved out into the sunlight the heat was already intense and their big straw hats a necessity. Soon they were passing through fields of sugarcane so thick and tall that nothing could be seen beyond the road that made a tunnel through it. Then the view opened up as they came into the fields where the cane had already been cut. Ahead black men in white canvas pants, either naked above the waist or wearing shirts of blue cotton, were felling the cane with their machetes.

The road was now wide enough that they could ride side by side on their mules. They and their mounts were drenched in sweat. Morgan passed her the gourd of water that hung from his saddle.

"Tell me," he said, and he seemed to have been brooding over the question, "how did these women win their freedom?"

"By their slave mothers sleeping with the owners of these plantations. It is rare in this society that the children of such unions are not released from bondage. And there are many such unions. I must tell you that even the most strait-laced of the planters often has a slave mistress on the plantation or a *femme de couleur* in town, or both."

"I do not like it."

"Neither do I. It is but release from one form of bondage into another, like . . . like forcing a young girl to marry against her will."

"What do you mean to do about Odette?"

"I have promised to take her to France, and with a dowry."

"To which you are so opposed."

"But it is what she wants. It is the only way she sees out of her situation."

"Perhaps there are no solutions." Morgan sighed. "Once the bond of slavery is entered into, it is like a millstone around the necks of both slave and master for as many generations as one can see into the future."

The black men cutting cane neither greeted them nor

looked up, and they passed on into the forest again. They had now reached a height where the cloud that almost always covered the peak of Mont Pelée began as a light mist hanging in the trees.

"We are close to my property," she said. "It is a moment I have long awaited."

"Yet you seem pensive, even a little sad."

"I am a bit afraid of what I will discover here."

"About yourself."

"Yes, about myself."

From the main track a path, so overgrown that Morgan's machete was often needed to clear a way, descended into ever deeper tropical forest, following the spine of a narrow ridge. Despite its present state Sophie knew every step of the abandoned road. Even in the old days the way to the Villa Chardin had never been broad and welcoming. Her parents, and theirs before them, Huguenot traders among Catholic plantation owners, had isolated themselves here, in a haven of peace and quiet; but from this quiet place a commercial empire had once extended from France to the Great Lakes of North America to the West Indies and back to Bordeaux.

They had never cultivated the land, for they could not compete with slave labor; and they would not compete, for they would not own slaves. Yet the Chardin family could have, at one time, bought and sold all these plantation owners, could have, and did, provide their daughter with a dowry so enormous that it brought an offer of marriage from one of the great noble families of France, and then . . .

"Sophie?"

"What?"

"I said, how much farther?"

"Oh. Not much farther."

She looked from under the brim of her straw hat. She could read nothing on Morgan's face, but she sensed that he knew that in awakening love in her he had also awakened all of her old desires and ambitions. Perhaps it would have been better never to have returned to Villa Chardin.

And then they were there. She cried out in dismay. The Villa Chardin was not just, as she had been told, in a ruinous state; it was like the remains of some ancient civilization eaten by the jungle a thousand years ago. The roof had collapsed, even parts of the walls had fallen, and doors, shutters and window frames had long rotted away. A green wave of vegetation broke against what remained of the house like the Atlantic surf breaking against the cliffs on the windward side of the island.

"There," she said, pointing, her eyes filled with tears, "was the most beautiful view of St Pierre and the sea in the whole island, and I had so looked forward to showing it to you, but now . . . now . . . there is nothing but this terrible jungle that devours everything. Here where I was the happiest I have ever been . . ."

"Happier even than now?"

"Oh, Morgan, how unfeeling of me. Of course I have never been happier than now, but how can I explain?"

"The first great happiness of one's life cannot be compared with anything else, is that not it?"

"Yes, yes. You seem always to read my mind."

"A sure sign, they say, that two people were destined for each other."

She looked into his eyes, calm in his face glistening with perspiration in the shade of the wide brim of his straw hat. It was true. This was the man she had been destined for, and by what odd circumstances they had been brought together, and brought back to the very place where she had first divined that she was meant for a special destiny.

"Here, let me help you down. From here on we will have to cut our way through. I must see this place where you were the girl that became the woman who has . . ."

"Has what, Morgan?"

"Has filled the empty place in my heart that I thought would always remain so."

"Then you were not happy?"

"Never."

"Why?"

"Always there was something missing from my life, and now I know that it was you."

"What a fine thing to say."

He lifted her down from the mule and into his arms and kissed her passionately, and she felt towards him something different, deeper than before.

"Now," she said at last, "through that archway, if we can make our way there, there was once a courtyard with a fountain that was fed by a spring higher up on the mountain and that played night and day. You will have to imagine it, I'm afraid."

But when they did reach the courtyard, completely overgrown and inhabited only by lizards and snakes, miraculously the fountain still played.

"It is an omen," she said, overcome with emotion. "To me, as a girl, this fountain was the soul of the house. I could hear it at night as I lay in bed, watch its spray in the first rays of the morning sun as I dressed, sit on its edge in the evening and read a book by candlelight. And all these years while the house fell into ruins and no human voices were heard, it has gone on playing, waiting for me to return. It is speaking to me now, telling me to bring the Villa Chardin back to life. Morgan, I must rebuild my old home."

"A risky undertaking."

"Did you not say that many British prizes will be brought here by American privateers?"

"That is my great hope."

"Then there will be money enough."

"When I said risky undertaking I did not mean the cost, I meant that such things have a way of possessing people."

"Oh, Morgan, do not think of me as a woman of the merchant class obsessed with property. It is a dream of happiness that I would rebuild."

"Perhaps even more dangerous. Much grief has come of trying to recapture the past."

She was hurt that he had thrown cold water on her impulsive idea. Where was his sense of adventure? Or did he sense a rival for her affection, as she did in his devotion to the cause of American liberty? In the end she held her tongue, remembering Odette's advice.

"No house can possess me," she said finally. "I belong only to you." Yet she would rebuild the Villa Chardin.

"Build it then," he said, to her surprise and delight, "and when my duty's done I would be with you here. It's time for me to learn something of the plant life of the tropics. I've counted more than a dozen species of orchids on our ride up."

"Could you be happy here?"

"With you anywhere, but here perhaps most of all. If only it were not so like paradise . . ."

CHAPTER TWELVE

By Christmas Sophie and Morgan had moved into their apartment on the quay above the offices of the New World Trading Co. It was a Sunday, but how different from those long bleak Sundays she had passed alone in her apartment above her offices in Bordeaux.

She looked up from the letter she was writing, put down her pen and regarded the figure of Morgan, shoeless and stockingless on the chaise longue, smoking a cheroot and perusing the previous evening's post. *Mon Dieu,* how she loved that man.

"Morgan?"

"Yes.?"

"For the first time since childhood I feel both safe and happy, deeply happy."

"You deserve all the happiness in the world."

"It is you, and you alone, who brought it to me."

They looked at each other long and lovingly, and there seemed no need for other words. She returned to her letter and he to the post.

"Ah, at last the viper has struck."

"What viper?"

"La Comtesse de Brieux."

"What has she done?"

Sophie was immediately on the alert. The comtesse's silence since their arrival had been more worrying than if she had declared open war.

"She has invited us to *réveillon*—New Year's Eve dinner.

There are two invitations, one for you and one for me, all writ in the best Parisian style. You will not, of course, go into this tigress's den?"

"Certainly I will."

What did he think she was made of? She had not come this far, broken so many rules of her own class, taken a most fabulous American lover, to be cowed by a woman who would have been no more than her social equal had not a bank failed. But her boldness did not extend to saying all this to Morgan, only to saying that she would accept the comtesse's invitation.

"Then so will I." No more than that. One of the things that most pleased her about Morgan was that he never said more than was necessary, often intriguingly less. Odette had been right: they were well-matched. But for that she must constantly be on her toes; yet how she thrilled at this sweet combat between the sexes! And how far she had come in so short a time, making up for all the lost years.

"Well then, let's open the trunk."

"Trunk?"

"The British general's lady's clothes that you so gallantly purloined for me."

"Sophie, what do you have in mind?"

"I would not attend the comtesse's soirée looking less than my best."

"Take care. Her reputation as a beauty is more important to her kind than all her lands and wealth."

"Remember, Morgan Carter, it is you who taught me to be bold."

"A quality that was always there, just needing to be tickled a bit."

"You have put it well."

With Odette's help Sophie tried on a half dozen of the

dresses from the trunk, which did fit her perfectly, and paraded them before Morgan. Finally she expressed her preference for a very low-cut gown of pale blue silk, clearly meant to be worn on only the most special occasions.

"That choice would be bold indeed."

"Then, by all means, I shall wear it."

Both Morgan and Odette laughed.

"Well, why not? If I can arouse some jealousy, so much the better. I bear enmity only to the British, who drove me from my home in Canada, and the Comtesse de Brieux, who without provocation tried to ruin me, and I would not mind using this occasion to taste a little of revenge, one of several emotions that my pious upbringing forbade me."

"Careful, Sophie. Tigresses when provoked show their claws."

"Yet I will wear this dress. Now begone, Morgan. Odette and I have much work to do to get me ready for this evening."

To her surprise it was time to leave for the comtesse's soirée before Morgan returned, and when he entered the room he stopped short.

"Sophie, what can I say? *C'est épatant, splendide, magnifique!*"

"*Merci, monsieur,*" she said with a little curtsey.

"Once I was invited to an evening at the palace of the Duc de La Rochefoucauld, who is sympathetic to the American cause, and many of the most beautiful noblewomen of France were there in all their finery, but even there you would have caused every head to turn."

Sophie smiled. She had been startled herself when she looked in the mirror, after all was complete, to see what a transformation had been achieved by cosmetics and curling iron and that magnificent gown. She had regretted that she owned no jewels, but upon seeing herself in the mirror realized they would have been superfluous.

"Oh! The sight of you made me completely forget. I have double good news. The second of your ships has arrived, loaded with arms, and an American crew has at the same time brought in another captured British merchantman."

"Good news indeed! And now I can feel free to begin work on the Villa Chardin. This is turning out to be quite an extraordinary day."

It was not until they stepped through the door of the Brieux residence that Sophie fully realized that she had very little idea of the situation into which she had so confidently thrown herself. She began to have hints as their carriage made its way along the curved drive made of finely crushed white seashell. The house, perfectly set on a point of land overlooking the moonlit sea, was not as large and certainly not as ostentatious as she had imagined. But every detail of the grounds, lit by torches placed at precise intervals, was perfect. The house itself was a very clever reproduction, on a grand scale, of a native Martiniquaise hut, down to the palm-thatched roof, whitewashed walls and pink shutters.

"Like Marie Antoinette's farm at Versailles," Morgan said. "The comtesse plays the rustic, the better to show her rank and freedom from convention."

Once inside the whitewashed reception room Sophie realized with near horror that she had overdressed. There were perhaps three dozen other guests, and most of the women wore costumes, however costly the fabrics, based on native dress. She knew perfectly well that these people were mainly from noble families, and that they were in Martinique because their behavior and morals were such that fathers or elder brothers were willing to pay them generous allowances to stay out of France. But as Hyacinthe had told her in one of his witty descriptions of his life among this set, bad morals by no means implied bad taste. Rather the opposite. And Morgan, damn him, who owned clothes of fine Parisian cut had chosen to dress as the simple American patriot.

Other shocks were to follow. They were greeted not by the Comtesse de Brieux but by the comte. She knew that these two representatives of great and rich families had nothing to do with each other, and she had hardly imagined that the comte would be present.

"You have done us an honor to join us this evening," the Comte de Brieux said, looking Sophie over. "My wife bet you wouldn't come, and when she sees you she'll be ever so sorry you did. Oh, how delicious!"

As they moved into the room Sophie, astonished, said in a whisper to Morgan, "This kindly-looking, apple-cheeked gentleman is the depraved libertine I have heard so much about? It is hard to believe."

"The king thought enough of the story to exile him from France for the rest of his life."

"*Ma foi,* but appearances are deceiving."

"In the world of these jaded aristocrats for anything to appear as it really is would be considered bad form."

The comtesse had spotted them and approached, closely followed by several young men who had been paying her court. She wore a pink bandanna on her head, a low-cut Martiniquaise chemise, a striped yellow skirt that showed her ankles, and native sandals. With much carefully applied makeup she was still a great beauty.

"A prosperous New Year to you, Madame Armonville, but I hear you are already having one."

"In what way, madame?"

"I'm told another ship has been captured and brought to St. Pierre by the American pirates."

"Privateers, madame."

"*Ah, bon soir, Monsieur Morgan.*" The comtesse fluttered her long painted lashes. "Perhaps I am mistaken, but I understood that nations may have privateers but rebels only pirates."

"As of July 4 we are a nation."

"The British think otherwise."

Morgan smiled, his feet planted wide apart, his hands clasped behind his back, a lock of his unpowdered dark hair falling across his forehead. "Then a trial of arms must prove which opinion is correct."

"Which you appear to be losing."

"The tide will turn." He spoke as calmly as if he could see into the future and knew that America would in the end be free.

"I hope you beat the British," one of the young men said.

The comtesse turned to him, showing a really quite handsome profile. "No one wishes the English well, Armand, but it is the principle that matters. If one rebellion against a crown succeeds there will be others."

"I would not have thought, Madeleine, that you had great reason to be concerned for the long reign of our gracious king."

"Don't be insolent," the comtesse said, waving her fan dismissively at the young man, and turned back to Sophie. "Enough of this tedious talk. That is a quite pretty gown, Madame Armonville. Rather . . . English . . . in style I would say. Where did you find it?"

"I . . . I . . ."

"Well, *n'importe*, I'm sure you will soon have many more. Now I must see to my other guests. Amuse yourselves till supper is served at midnight, with bézique in that room or dancing in the other. Which would you prefer? Bézique probably."

"I'm afraid I don't play cards."

"But I'm sure you dance."

"The simple country dances, yes."

"Ah. I'm afraid my guests insist on the old court dances, but you'll no doubt enjoy watching."

The Comtesse de Brieux turned and swept away trailing her entourage of young men.

"Morgan, she's calculated all of this to humiliate me."

"Of course."

"Why didn't you warn me. You've moved in these circles in Paris."

"You were not too interested in my advice earlier. I told you she would show her claws."

"I want to leave immediately."

"Which is exactly what the comtesse wants and what you must not do."

"I can't stand more humiliation, and there is sure to be more."

"You have not been humiliated, it is she who has . . ."

"*Je m'excuse, madame.*" It was the young man Armand, his hair powdered and beribboned, in absurd contrast to the imitation of a Martiniquais fisherman's garb that he wore. "I have found another couple, and if it pleases you I will teach you the intricacies of bézique. It will be more amusing than those ridiculous old dances that Madeleine insists upon."

"Well . . ." She turned toward Morgan, but he had drifted away.

"I would be delighted," Sophie said, summoning up courage, "if it would not bore you."

"Why would it bore me to accompany the only woman here tonight who is properly attired, and one of dazzling beauty?" and Armand offered her his arm.

A New World Won

★ ★ ★ ★ ★

Sophie quickly picked up the game of bézique, which after all involved calculations based on numbers, which she far better understood than any aristocrat. By the time the *réveillon* supper was announced—to her surprise two hours had passed—she had won a considerable sum of money. She by now understood that the charming behavior of her partners was meant more to annoy the comtesse than to assuage her wounded feelings. As Morgan had often said, she learned quickly.

"You must not deny me the pleasure of your company at supper, Sophie—I may call you Sophie?" the Comte de Brieux said, smoothly slipping his arm in hers. "You found the game of bézique entertaining, I hope, as well as profitable?"

"Indeed, even if I had some suspicion that the other players did not try overhard to win."

"The comtesse will be delighted that you enjoyed yourself."

"She will?" Sophie looked into the comte's pink and innocent face.

"She will be so delighted that she will go to bed tonight with one of her famous sick headaches. Indeed she should be right sick. She could not have made a greater fool of herself."

They passed through the open doors into the candle-lit dining room, where a long table covered in elegant linen was laid for supper, its centerpiece a great pyramid of pastry and cream profiterolles, the traditional New Year's sweet.

"By the way, *ma chère Sophie,* the comtesse travels to Guadaloupe next week with one of her tiresome young men. I will be desolate with loneliness. Will you not join me here for tea and whatever other amusements we might devise?"

"You are too kind, *mon cher comte,* but I imagine that the

amusements that we each enjoy are too dissimilar for that to be a practical idea."

From across the room Morgan, who was conversing with two quite stunning women, bowed ever so slightly to her and she returned the gesture, in the same way they had at Château Ivran that first day, before they had even spoken. Tonight she had held her ground and won and he knew it. Whatever scorpions and spiders she had imagined hiding in the dark places of Martinique to poison her new-found happiness, they were not here. Indeed all her horizons seemed clear.

CHAPTER THIRTEEN

January and then February came and went, and still not the slightest cloud had appeared on the horizon. Sophie was in love and was loved in return, was overcoming the last impediments to complete intimacy and trust with Morgan, and was becoming rich enough that she found it necessary after all to acquire a big lined ledger to keep track of all the transactions flowing from the captured British merchantmen that crowded the harbor. There was in fact too much success, and a curt note from the governor summoned them to the capital of Fort Royal for a tête-à-tête.

"Well, my dears," said Le Vicomte de Laval, splendid in dark blue velvet and lace, "I had no suspicion of what a box of tricks I was opening when I told you that you might use Martinique as a base for your privateering and gun smuggling."

"I hope we have not misunderstood your instructions, sir," Morgan said anxiously.

"No, dammit," the governor said, toying with a goose quill pen, "it's not that, it's just that I did not comprehend the magnitude of the operation I was allowing to be unleashed. All the merchants are complaining that there are no berths for their ships at St. Pierre—all taken up by your British prizes. Half the population of America must be engaged in privateering; and I'd be surprised if there are any weapons left in France for our own army, given the rate at which we're transferring them to America."

"But surely that is what Paris desires."

"Paris?" The governor laughed. "There are as many

Parises as there are ministers, and each orders me about, and in quite contradictory terms. You see, here is a letter instructing me to curb your activities, which have so alarmed the British that they are again threatening France with war; and here is another congratulating me for having turned a blind eye to these same activities. And here is a third addressed to you, which you will note I have not opened, though I could have done so. No one has the right to use the royal courier to communicate with anyone in Martinique without my knowing the nature of that communication."

"I quite agree," Morgan said, breaking the three red seals of the envelope, "and so I shall read it aloud."

He acts shrewdly, thought Sophie, who had so far remained silent, having learned the advantages of playing the role of mistress over that of outspoken businesswoman. When she did speak she would be carefully attended to. Odette would have been proud of her.

"Paris, January 22, 1777. My dear Morgan: A happy New Year to you and to our charming Sophie, and word reaches me that I may now speak of your mutual happiness.

"I wanted you to be assured that whatever noises you may hear out of the capital, the good work that you are doing for the American cause enjoys the full support of Minister Vergennes and therefore of the king. The other news that I have to impart is not so good: that your every move, every arrival and every sailing from St. Pierre, the nature of every cargo, is now quickly known to the British navy. I think this is bound to lead to the loss of some of your shipments. You should be on the lookout for the spy who is providing the British with this intelligence.

"You should also be aware that the British have put into play a scheme to blacken your reputation with your own government, in hopes this will lead to your recall or even arrest for treasonous behavior. Fortunately we have our own highly-placed agent in the British government who keeps us informed of their machinations, but just what is the exact British plan in this case he has not as yet been able to learn. As regards the gov . . ."

"Yes, go on," the governor growled.

"As regards the governor, I leave it to your discretion whether he can be trusted with the secrets I am sharing with you. Affectionately, Hyacinthe."

"*Sacrebleu!* I'll thrash the insolent young pup next I'm in Paris. You did well, sir, to be open with me. I'll not tolerate anyone in my domain in the pay of London."

"You notice," Morgan said as they drove back in their carriage from the capital to St. Pierre, "that His Excellency never got around to the purpose of our being summoned into his presence, which I am sure was to inform us that we were to cool down our operations. Now that he knows that King Louis himself is pleased with our work, I think we may rest easy on that score. However, Hyacinthe's other intelligence is disturbing."

"Indeed."

"I have little worry that the British will be able to blacken my name, but I wonder who it is that is spying so effectively upon us? I suppose old Jean is above suspicion?"

"Absolutely, even were he not our partner in a small way."

"Then it could be anyone who noses about the docks."

"Hm," Sophie murmured. It had occurred to her that whoever it was might be motivated by something other than British gold and might also be involved in the attempt to slander Morgan. She was not so quick as he to discount the success of such a scheme, and she knew that for his compatriots in America to believe him to be other than a patriot would be the cruellest blow that could befall him.

★ ★ ★ ★ ★

Sophie awoke with a great feeling of well-being from a dream in which she had wandered through the newly restored Villa Chardin in a dressing gown of embroidered Chinese silk. She had gazed lovingly at every detail of every room, details from out of childhood memory that awake she had quite forgotten. And to the beloved house had been added a wealth of new furniture, brocades, silver, vases and paintings in the latest French fashion of Boucher and Fragonard. Her dream was nothing less than a design for what she might do with the vine-covered ruin high above them on the slope of Mont Pelée. Surely it was an omen.

She opened her eyes. Morgan was tying his stock in the mirror with great care. Despite his plain honest American ways, he dressed himself with as much elegance as any man in Martinique. He was still something of a mystery to her and she was glad for it. She intended always to hold back something of herself from him, so that she could make a gift of it to him when the fancy took her. Just such had she done at dawn, awakening him from sleep with her nude body, offering it like, she was vain enough to fancy, one of those succulent tropical fruits that they had consumed before making love for the first time.

"Bonjour, mon amour," she said from the luxurious softness of the piled pillows. "You go out?"

"A letter from Jean summoning me, slipped under the door some hours ago I suppose—we have slept away half the morning."

"One must recover from such ardor." She knew that such cool yet warm remarks pleased Morgan, and she meant to keep pleasing him with all the skill she could command. "What news from Jean?"

"The *Artemis* arrived at dawn with her hold entirely filled with barrels of French gunpowder, General Washington's most urgent requirement. Damned clever of the British never to have permitted the establishment of a gunpowder industry in their American colonies."

"Well, I suppose that is very good news, though the only use of powder is to kill young lads facing you on the field of battle."

"You know, Sophie, that were ours not a sacred cause . . ."

He turned and their eyes met. No, neither of them was content with what they were doing, but . . .

"Morgan I've just had the most extraordinary dream. I saw the Villa Chardin just as it will look, in every detail, once I've had it restored."

"Then you are still determined to do so?"

"Yes, and now there's far more than enough money to do it."

"You know that I'll stand behind you in all that you do. . . ."

"But I don't have your blessing, do I?"

"It's not that, it's just that . . ."

He did not finish his sentence, but she knew what he would have said if he did not fear hurting her: that their mission of aiding the American rebellion should consume all their energies. What he would not have said, even then, was that he somewhat feared the Villa Chardin as a rival. Well, she supposed that if a man and woman in love did not have a point or two of disagreement it would be a bland kind of love indeed, and one not to her taste. She had found, to her surprise, that she preferred the sparks to fly from the flint and steel.

As soon as Morgan had descended to the office below, Odette entered, as was her discreet custom, with Sophie's breakfast.

"Tell me, Odette," she said as she buttered a brioche and poured out her coffee, "does not the Comtesse de Brieux have a large domestic staff?"

"Of course, madame," Odette replied, looking up from making the bed.

"And I suppose you would know one or two of them."

"The personal maid to *madame la comtesse* is a godchild of my mother's and my playmate from age three."

"Ah."

"What is it that madame desires?" Odette's beautiful young face was as impassive as though Sophie had asked her to run an errand in the town, to fetch some eggs or a spool of thread.

"Certain intelligence."

"Ah," it was now the girl's turn to say. "That is more difficult than had you asked me to bring you some costly object from her silver safe. The comtesse is greatly feared."

"I understand that, and I would not have asked anyone of lesser talents than Céleste's daughter to undertake such a task," judging correctly that Odette's pride would overcome her apprehensions.

"What information would madame have?"

"I cannot say exactly. If I knew I might not need your help. All I can tell you is that it would concern the comtesse's correspondence . . . correspondence with foreigners, correspondence, or conversations, that would seem to concern England, correspondence that would be mysterious in its content or in some kind of code. . . ."

"Oh, madame, this is a serious matter."

"It is thus far only my intuition, Odette. I could be quite wrong. But I can tell you that this matter, if it does exist, could be most serious for Morgan—and therefore for me."

"In that case, there is no question. La Comtesse de Brieux

will never, as long as I can prevent it, touch a hair of your head. You will hear from me when I have something to report," and Odette went back to vigorously plumping the bed pillows.

Sophie awoke to a world that was neither night nor day. The newly-made clearing, the trees that she had allowed to remain, the house itself, were hidden by the bank of cloud that had crept down the mountain during the night. She turned over. On the other cot Odette slept soundly, as well she might, having danced far into the night around the workers' cooking fire to the beat of hands on halves of old wine barrels. She had pledged to take Odette back to France with her when she returned, but would Céleste's daughter by then still be wearing the European straw chapeau or would she have returned to the bandanna?

She got up, dressed and put on her shoes, after having made sure there were no scorpions lurking inside. Drawing aside the mosquito netting that covered the tent door she went out into the clearing. The cloud was beginning to rise and her foreman, Sardou, was restarting the fire. His race was unknowable: a mixture of French, Spanish, African, Caribe, perhaps even some Dutch. His skills were as varied as his ancestry. He knew something of carpentry, plastering, bricklaying, iron-working and other trades, enough of each to supervise the whole crew of workers.

"Bonjour, madame."

"Bonjour, Sardou. Il fait frais ce matin." She drew her robe closer around her.

"It'll soon be hot enough."

"Then shall we inspect while it is still cool?"

"As madame wishes."

As they made their way to the now nearly restored Villa

Chardin the cloud lifted like a stage curtain revealing, far below, the sea and St. Pierre in the early morning light. The view too had been restored to that of her childhood, except that now the harbor was crowded with British ships captured by American privateers and American sloops loading French arms destined for Washington's army. What a prodigious thing they had accomplished in only eight months!

"Madame is pleased?"

Sophie looked around the courtyard. There was little to criticize. The cobblestones of the courtyard had been reset in sand, the fountain's water now ran clean, the rails of the galleries on both floors had been replaced and the whole was topped by a new tile roof.

"I am very pleased."

"Then madame must choose the colors, for painting is next."

"The same as of old: pink, yellow and green. I will show you where each goes."

Sophie shivered with excitement. She had brought the Villa Chardin back to life!

"Madame."

She turned. The tall handsome *porteuse* who brought bread from the St. Pierre ovens each morning held out an envelope. She took it and tore it open, knowing full well who it was from.

"Sophie, my love, I have endured three lonely days without complaint. Will you not spend siesta with me? Yours, Morgan."

How could she resist such an invitation? She had shockingly neglected Morgan these last few days as the restoration of the Villa Chardin neared completion. She would indeed be with him this siesta.

Sophie looked up at the *porteuse* and Sardou as if they

might have been able to read her thoughts.

"Sardou, have two mules saddled and awake Odette. I am returning immediately to St. Pierre." She was already burning with desire.

"You're unusually quiet this morning, Odette," Sophie said, watching with amusement the girl's attempts to stay awake, her *chapeau de paille* pulled down over her eyes, her hips swaying with the movement of her mule.

"Eh, madame? I am tired this morning. Too little sleep last night."

"And too much dancing. You danced as if the spirits had possessed you."

"One last time. I was making *mes adieus* to that world. I am no more at home there now than you."

They had emerged from the forest onto a promontory overlooking the inn where she and Morgan had first stayed, surrounded by palm trees, the blue-green sea lapping on its white beach. Beyond was the quay and the brightly painted building, its shutters closed, where Morgan awaited her.

Sophie quietly entered the dimly-lit room, wanting to surprise him, but he was already asleep. Perhaps he had thought she would not come, imagined that the Villa Chardin drew her even more strongly than he. Well, she would show him about that.

Unhurriedly she removed her clothes and took the pins from her hair, and then she went to the bed and pulled back the sheet. Morgan was as naked as she.

She stood there for a moment, caught up in strong emotions: an ever-deepening love for Morgan and her desire for the magnificent male body that she looked down upon, which was not by any means the same as love. In only a few months she had discovered not only what it was to be in love but what it was to be a sensual, passionate woman. She had become what she had imagined as a girl she would be. How could she have suppressed her true nature for so many years? But then was she not blessed in having the gift of passion denied her until it could be joined to that of an overpowering love? She gently lay down on Morgan's body.

"What? Sophie!"

"No. It is but the body of the widow Armonville which I use for my pleasure."

"Oh, I see. And who might you be then?"

"The *diablesse* who comes to men in the heat of the day, and if you value your life you will do exactly as I say."

"Assuredly, if you are indeed a *diablesse*."

"I will soon show you that it is my spirit that inhabits the body of this innocent young woman. Now lie quite still."

They came together then, and she was content to lie like that for a while, feeling the deliciousness of his body beneath her and in her. Then she began to move, overcome by a desire to actively make love to him. Indeed, a wanton spirit had in a way come to possess the body of an innocent young woman. Now she moved her hips with an abandon that she would not have been able to permit herself in the beginning. And she had learned how to prolong lovemaking until, in the heat of day, she was bathed in perspiration.

"Now you may move a little," she whispered huskily and then cried out so loudly with pleasure that anyone in the street below might have heard. She did not care.

Afterwards they bathed in the tiled alcove, soaped each other's bodies and rinsed with gourdfuls of cool water from the big clay jar. And as they dressed Morgan made certain comments that, though in oblique language, showed clearly his astonishment and delight at the depths of passion that lay hidden beneath the reserved exterior of a young widow and wine merchant of Bordeaux. No more astonished and delighted, she thought, than I.

All the next morning was devoted to purchasing the last remaining objects needed to bring the Villa Chardin back to not only its original state but to the state of perfection that Sophie had seen in that dream still vivid in her memory. It was amazing what could be found in the little dark shops of St. Pierre, if one insisted on searches being made on high shelves, in back storerooms and attics—and if one was prepared to pay: brass hinges and locks, crystal doorknobs, bronze fenders and andirons for the fireplaces—for the nights could be chill on Mont Pelée—and silk cords and tassels for the velvet curtains.

"Well, it's all done then. Let's be off, Odette."

"Should we not wait for tomorrow, madame? The day is far gone. It is not wise to travel on the mountain after dark."

"Odette, if you intend to go to France and marry well, you had best forget you ever believed in zombies."

"It is not that."

"What then?"

"While you were making your purchases this morning, I was about exchanging gossip—including with my friend who attends La Comtesse de Brieux."

"Ah. What has she been able to learn?"

"A letter was left out, forgotten one night, after a terrible scene between the comte and comtesse. It was written in some kind of code, but with it was a copy made into plain language . . . Does the name Coburn mean anything to you?"

"Coburn?" Sophie started with surprise, but surprise quickly gave way to fear. Odette had stumbled on something sinister. "It has a familiar ring," she said cautiously, her next thought being that she had not mentioned her shipboard conversation with General Coburn to Morgan. At first, she had simply forgotten, she was so taken up by her newly-ignited passion for her soon-to-be lover; and when she did remember, so many days had passed that it was awkward to explain why she had not spoken of it earlier.

"Madame?"

"What?"

"I said did you wish to hear the rest?"

"My mind was elsewhere. I was trying to recall . . . Yes, of course I wish to hear the rest."

"The letter, which is signed 'Coburn', is addressed to 'Madeleine', which is the comtesse's Christian name. It thanks her for the intelligence she sends regularly, states that a certain sum has been deposited in an account and asks for information on certain ships by name—my friend does not remember which, for she dared take only the briefest look at the letter.

"The letter ends—and these are the exact words, for they naturally struck my friend—'How I wish some accident would carry off that wretch Carter and his inamorata.' Your life and that of Monsieur Carter are in danger, Sophie. You must not expose yourself unnecessarily."

"Bah. I do not take that as a threat. Certainly, I have no intention of not going to the mountain this afternoon. But you have done me a great favor, Odette. You understand that this is a matter about which I cannot speak to you, nor should you mention it to Monsieur Carter."

"Of, course, madame."

She needed time alone to think. Perhaps General Coburn's words were no more than an expression of frustration at not being able to stem the flow of arms to America, but perhaps she and Morgan were in real danger. But what concerned Sophie almost as much was how she was going to explain all this to him.

The sunset that evening was a magnificent one, even for Martinique; and when it ended with the red of a blood orange fading away into night, they were still some distance from Villa Chardin. One of the two muleteers who accompanied them lit a lantern from the lamp of a wayside shrine and led them on on foot. Sophie wondered who it was that tended the shrine lamps along this long stretch of road through the uninhabited jungle. The ways of the mountain people were mysterious even to the Martiniquais of St. Pierre.

The jungle night sounds had begun: myriad insect noises, the howls of monkeys, the screams of night birds. Sophie noted with amusement that Odette, on the mule ahead of her, crossed herself every few minutes. An hour passed, and they had just turned down the path that led to Villa Chardin when the muleteer leading the little party stopped dead in his tracks. Two figures in ragged clothes scuttled away into the jungle and moved ahead of them, one to the right and the other to the left of the path. To go on was to pass between them, and Sophie was about to command that they turn back to the main road, such as it was, when a whistle came from farther up on the mountain and was repeated from somewhere below.

At this, the lead muleteer dropped his lantern and fled back down the road, and his mate leaped from his mule and ran after him. The overturned lantern went out, leaving them in total blackness. Sophie was now overcome with panic herself. A certain number of criminals and escaped convicts hid themselves on the mountain, and from time to time a traveler was murdered for his valuables. As she slid down from her mule Odette ran headlong into her. Sophie grabbed her wrist and they began running down the road together.

"*Vite, vite, madam,* we must reach the shrine."

"*Sotte,* those are not zombies. If they mean us harm, in the light of the shrine is the last place we want to be."

It took some force to drag Odette with her into the jungle, and they immediately tripped over vines and fell, and fell again; but Sophie made the girl go on until they were far from the road. They fell exhausted to the ground, scratched and bruised, but safe. Sophie knew that to find anyone in the jungle of Mont Pelée at night was like looking for a needle in a haystack. And there they lay, wide awake, until dawn came.

The two muleteers had vanished, but the mules were all near where they had been abandoned, grazing along the edge of the road. Sophie and Odette mounted two of them, after tying the reins of the other two to their saddles. Within a few minutes they were having coffee at the Villa Chardin.

Sophie could not know whether the two men they encountered in the night had meant them harm, even less whether —as Odette believed, after she accepted that they were not zombies—that they were assassins sent by La Comtesse de Brieux. But that possibility was enough to make Sophie reach a decision on what to do about the comtesse and how to handle the matter with Morgan.

CHAPTER FOURTEEN

"You're nervous as a cat, Sophie," Morgan said from the wicker chair where he indulgently watched her finish dressing for their housewarming, or hanging of the pothook, as she told him it was said in French.

"That has been said about me one other time," she replied as she adjusted the emerald earring in her ear. The pair was but one of the many gifts that Morgan had showered upon her, taken from the cargoes of captured British ships brought into the harbor of St. Pierre. The bourgeois side of her still rebelled at this wanton lavishing of other people's property upon her, but a newer Sophie revelled in being given the kinds of presents some duke might have bestowed upon a great beauty, an opera singer or ballerina.

"*Ah, oui?* When might that have been?"

"It was said by my aunt when I came to meet you alone for the first time, at the Château Marivaux."

"You did not appear overly nervous to me that day; and I remember the occasion well, as you might imagine."

Their eyes met in the mirror. "I could not afford to appear so. I was terribly afraid of losing you."

"What? You knew even then, you guileful woman?"

"I did not know that I knew."

He got up and came to her, put his arms around her waist and kissed her on the back of her neck.

"You have never been so beautiful as this night."

She turned and kissed him warmly and wetly upon the

mouth. "Now that is done, I can put on my rouge. It is almost time."

"I must admire your courage. To invite both the governor and the Brieuxs and to have them both accept. . . ."

"The governor is, I believe, rather attracted to me; La Comtesse dared not refuse, as it would be taken as cowardice by her circle, after the humiliation she tried to inflict on me. Le Comte de Brieux comes to enjoy his wife's discomfiture." In the way she spoke Sophie was following Odette's advice to treat the man one loves, however simply and sincerely, with the skills of a calculating mistress. She only wished that her feelings were as much under her command as her words.

"Now, shall we take a tour of Villa Chardin, to see, before the first guest arrives, that all is in order?"

"I can already assure you that it is beautiful down to the last detail."

"And almost exactly as I dreamed it that night, which now seems so long ago."

Sophie swallowed hard as they left the bedroom for their tour of the house. If Morgan knew why she had invited La Comtesse de Brieux and Le Vicomte de Laval . . . She had decided in the end to tell him nothing. If she accomplished this evening what she planned, he need never know. It was the course Odette would have advised and, for a woman of the world, a sound one; but she was, as Morgan had said, as nervous as a cat.

"Ah, Sophie," Odette said, circling to view her from all sides, "you have never looked more beautiful."

"Just what I told her, Odette"

"Monsieur Carter, you are a lucky man."

"None knows that better than I."

"You must not make me vain," was all that Sophie responded, but in fact she was greatly pleased at their compliments and knew them to be true. "Now, do you have all that you need for this evening, Odette?"

"Everything is in readiness. Come outside and you will see."

They passed through the open glass doors out into the courtyard, where the young Martiniquaise women that Odette had brought to help her were putting the final touches to the arrangements. Silver gleamed in the light of the Japanese lanterns strung across the courtyard, sprays of orchids decorated the long tables covered in white cloths, and the fountain played quietly.

"It is beautiful, isn't it," Sophie said. Just as she had dreamed it might one day be. Dreams could come true, if one worked hard enough.

"You did well, Sophie," Odette said, "to have your reception outside. Today St. Pierre was like the inside of the baker's oven. The mountain air will restore your guests' good humor."

"That and cool fruit juices spiked with rum," Morgan said, flicking the ash from his cheroot. "Ah, we have a guest at the gate already, old Beaudricourt, always the first to arrive. I will go greet him."

When Morgan had left them, Odette turned to Sophie. "Does Monsieur Carter know of our escapade on the mountain?"

"No, and I do not wish him to know."

"But if the comtesse is really . . ."

"Bah."

"Nevertheless, you should take care."

She did not reply; but Odette was no fool, and Sophie's resolve was strengthened to act in the course of the evening.

Other guests were arriving. The road across Mont Pelée was too narrow and rough for carriages, and they came perforce on horseback. Soon the courtyard was filled with the elite of the island, and Sophie was too busy greeting them to think further about her concerns. Then the crowd fell silent and parted to make way for the governor. He stepped through the archway in the full dress uniform of an admiral, flanked by two aides also in dress uniforms.

"Bon soir, madame, et mes félicitations," and Le Vicomte de Laval bowed low and kissed her hand. The next instant he offered her his arm and led her to a quiet corner of the terrace, to the evident surprise of the other guests.

"You may wonder at my costume this evening. It is to emphasize the military aspect of France's relations with America. You see, I have, since last we met, received fresh instructions from the highest level. I am told to offer every assistance to your operations short of provoking war with England. That decision the king reserves to himself. Also, even were you not the most charming woman in Martinique, I would wish to be seen paying you homage by the leading citizens of the island—most of whom seem to be here tonight."

"This is most welcome news, Excellency."

"Good. Then I think we may join your other guests."

This brief conversation steeled Sophie's nerves, and she felt calm and confident when La Comtesse de Brieux appeared. This feeling did not last long in the presence of a woman who had not so long ago made mock at her private soirées of Marie Antoinette of France.

"I had not expected Laval here," La Comtesse de Brieux said, after she had exchanged formal greetings with Sophie. "I suppose he has his reasons."

"You might ask him," Sophie said, her heart beating rapidly, "as I suppose you will wish to greet the governor immediately."

"Naturally."

"And the comte?"

"Indisposed." This was said with the assurance of someone who had gained the upper hand and could now dictate to her spouse where he would and would not go.

"Shall we go to the governor, then?"

"But first, tell me, my child, why did you invite me here?" In the soft light of the Japanese lanterns, and in the finest clothes that Paris could produce, the comtesse still seemed the great beauty.

"Certainly not to humiliate you," and immediately she regretted this attempt at a cutting remark.

"Why then?" the comtesse said with the faintest of smiles.

"I wished an opportunity to speak privately with you."

"Vous m'étonnez, madame."

"I rather astonish myself," Sophie replied, trying to match the comtesse's coolness, but at the same time speaking a truth.

An hour passed, during which Sophie had not a chance to think further of what she would say to the comtesse when she could be alone with her. Morgan was constantly at her side, promoting the interests of The New World Trading Co., being impossibly charming, lavishing every attention on her. Oh, how she loved him, and how she wished he would go away! At last he did, but La Comtesse was nowhere to be found.

Sophie found her at last in the drawing room, seated on a sofa with Jacques Sorel, the head of La Banque de Martinique et Guadeloupe. The banker's glasses had slipped down on his nose and his hand had come to rest on the comtesse's bare shoulder, as they laughed together over some piece of gossip. Sophie Armonville was, however, the largest depositor of the Banque de Martinique, and Monsieur Sorel was quickly on his feet.

"Bring me some white wine, Jacques," the comtesse said, tapping him on the wrist with her fan.

"Of course, Madeleine." Then the two women were alone.

Sophie remained standing, unable to bring herself to sit down beside the comtesse.

"I'll speak but briefly."

Madeleine de Brieux lowered her lashes in assent.

"You must cease your spying upon us and the spreading of false rumors about me . . . or my partner."

The eyes of the comtesse opened wide. "It is hardly necessary to say that I have not the slightest idea what you are talking about . . . but even if I did, why should I pay any attention to this extravagant demand of yours?"

"Because if you do not I will reveal it all to the governor."

"That I am spying on you and spreading gossip about you and your friend? Madame, the governor is not a child, even if you are. Why would he care?"

"He might care about treason."

"Treason?" There was just the slightest twitch to the corners of the comtesse's mouth, as though she had been about to smile but thought better of it. "You go from *sottises* to absurdity. Madame, if you have something serious to say, do so. I had not expected such prattle from one who has a reputation as a shrewd *femme d'affaires*."

"You may find my indignation at the malicious actions you have taken against me—who have done you no harm—but foolishness; but as for the graver matter," and here Sophie had to sit down beside the comtesse whether she would or not, for her legs would no longer support her, "you might consider how you will explain to the governor the interest of your agents in the numbers and disposition of French troops in the West Indies."

In the long silence that followed, Sophie stole a glance at the mirror. Both her face and that of the comtesse were as white as bones bleached in the sun.

"Those are but words," the comtesse said in the faraway voice of someone who has just seen the most unexpected card laid upon the table.

"Words that I am prepared to go to the governor with this minute and repeat, and accompany them with proofs."

"What is it you want of me?" the comtesse said in a voice that for the first time quavered.

"That you cause no further mischief to us, neither you nor . . . your friends."

"Since you ask me to cease doing something that I am not engaged in, I don't suppose I can—as long as we both must inhabit Martinique—object to that."

"You are wise, considering the cards that are now laid on the table."

"Madeleine, your wine . . ." the banker said, coming into the room. "I say, is something wrong."

"Not at all. Madame Armonville and I were discussing a pledge."

"A loan, eh?"

"Something like that." La Comtesse de Brieux turned to Sophie, the color somewhat restored to her cheeks, at which Sophie could but marvel. "Madame, we have our agreement, I believe; and you can be assured that you will be repaid in full, when conditions have changed. Now, Jacques, shall we take our drinks onto the terrace. I find it oppressive in here."

Sophie looked up from the ledger, rubbed her stiff neck,

her sore wrist and laughed. So had it all begun; but now she entered the credits and debits with the lightest of hearts, for now what she entered was to love's account.

She got up from her desk and went down to where Morgan worked in his glass house at the bottom of the garden. There he tended his orchids, nurtured and classified them. He had already discovered one not known before and named it after her, *orchis sophiae,* Sophie's orchid. Tears came to her eyes. Everything, everything that she had ever desired had been realized. Surely the gods themselves must be jealous.

"I've been doing the accounts," she said, "and entry by entry, America is paying back its debt to France."

He looked up from his work. "And entry by entry, the means for Washington to defeat the British on the field of battle are being landed on the American shore, from Charleston in the south to Portsmouth in the north."

"And the profits grow large, Morgan, very large, and with them the possibility to settle all my obligations to my family, old aunts and cousins, my ships' captains, ships' agents, clerks, even Paulot, all those who had stood by Chardin and Co. in its darkest hours. I'm . . . we're rich. What shall we do with all that money when the conflict in America is over?"

"We could lead an idle life, travel."

"Yes, I wouldn't mind that. To Italy perhaps, to Venice, Florence . . ."

"When the conflict's over. But for now let's see what the packet from America has brought," and Morgan dumped a sackful of mail onto the table. "I suppose I should open this one first. From the Congress, and tripled sealed. I would not take amiss a few words of thanks for all that we have done for the cause of liberty from these gentlemen who are so quick to complain when things go ill and ever silent when they go well."

A New World Won

He broke the three red wax seals on the envelope and began to read the letter inside; and as he did his face grew red.

"Morgan, what is it?"

"What slander is this? And it is clear they believe that prince of liars. Oh, I know well enough who their secret informant is."

He was on his feet now, waving the letter about. Already she suspected that it concerned that matter that she had taken such great risks to assure never arose.

"Surely, no news can be that terrible."

"Oh, no? Listen to this," but he was so choked with anger that it was several moments before he could find his voice again.

"Sir. It is our unpleasant duty to inform you that most serious charges have been brought against you before the Secret Committee of the Continental Congress and that these charges are supported by documentary evidence. It is alleged that the sums provided by the government of France during your tenure as American agent in Paris were superior by 500,000 livres françaises to the amounts you reported to this Committee as receiving and to the value of arms supplied. . . ."

Oh, Sophie thought, how we are led astray by our own cleverness. While I was spiking the guns—a phrase of Hyacinthe's that she remembered from the day she first met him—of Madeleine de Brieux, the English had chosen another path to bring Morgan Carter to his ruin.

". . . It is also alleged that you did secretly rendezvous with a British man-of-war in mid-ocean and there have parley with General Sir George Coburn, the chief of British intelligence in North America, and that the brother of your partner in New World Trading Co. is a well-known agent in Canada of this same General Coburn.

"In view of the serious nature of these charges you are instructed to take the first available vessel bound from Martinique for Philadelphia, there to defend yourself before the Secret Committee of the Congress. You should bring with you any documentary evidence bearing on your case..."

"Oh, Morgan, this is indeed terrible, and after all that you have done for..."

"... a pack of scoundrels, the same who dismissed Philip Byrd for his manifest incompetence and that now is all too willing to listen to his lies."

"Who is this Philip Byrd?"

"He preceded me as American agent in Paris, and after he was dismissed he hung on in Paris to see what trouble he could cause, blaming me for his dismissal. This is not the first time he has spread false rumors, but the first time he has got the ear of Congress. And how do these gentlemen comport themselves? They neither tell me who my accuser is or what documentary evidence they possess. And it is clear that I am considered guilty until I prove my innocence. I would receive greater justice under the tyrannical government of George the Third!"

"Morgan, do calm down." Oh, how she had prayed this moment would never arrive. She had been wiser than he in recognizing his vulnerability, but small comfort that was now.

"Why should I be calm under such provocation?" She had never seen such fire in his eyes. He whirled about and fixed his gaze on her. "But wait a minute. What is this business about General Coburn, whom I have never even laid eyes on? I was delirious with fever when, as I was later told, he came aboard *La Bonne Nouvelle*; and everyone from Captain Joubert down can vouch for that. But someone has provided the Congress with the intelligence that Coburn came aboard the vessel on which I lay ill, and certainly that cannot have been Byrd."

"*Vraiment, chéri,* you must calm yourself." She knew now that the Fates were pursuing her. The gods had, with good reason, been jealous; and she had been foolish beyond repair.

"What I don't understand, though, is the claim that my partner—my God, that's you!—has a brother in Canada who . . ."

"I certainly have a brother in Canada, who chose to live under the British rather than go with us to Martinique, and so cut himself off forever from the rest of the family."

"What is this I hear?"

"I have hardly thought of him from year to year. It was only when Coburn told me that he prospered under British rule . . ."

"Coburn told you? When did you ever speak to Coburn?"

He reached out as if to grasp her by the arm, but she stepped quickly back, not a little frightened by this new aspect of her lover.

"Where else but aboard *La Bonne Nouvelle*? He took me aside to tempt me with sharing my brother's good fortune, an idea so ridiculous that I could barely keep from laughing."

"But why did you not tell me this? What am I to think?"

"Morgan, if you do not lower your voice you will be heard all up and down the quay. I did not tell you because I thought it a matter of little account."

"But it is I who must bear the responsibility for your misguided . . ."

"For my what?" She felt her face flushing until it must have been as red as his.

"For your . . ."

"I see that you cannot finish that unworthy thought. What

was it? That I am secretly in league with the British? That my brother and I have some game of our own to enrich ourselves? To think that with all the love and passion I have shown you, you could believe that . . ."

They stood facing each other, breathing hard, like two fighters who have just dealt each other blows until they are stunned.

"Forgive me."

"I'm not sure I can, Morgan. At least not now. Come, let us sit down and both calm ourselves."

They sat opposite each other in chairs, he with his elbows on his knees and his head in his hands. Her heart went out to him for the terrible and unjust blow that he had been dealt, but her pity was tempered by the unjust wound he had just given her.

However, a quiet voice within her said, "Had you but told him the truth in the beginning, had you not tried to deal with the Comtesse de Brieux yourself, had you not . . ." She had woven a web so tangled that who would now believe the truth? In her despair at where her cleverness had got her, she began to blame Odette. Had she remained Morgan's lover, simple and sincere . . . But the quiet voice spoke again: "You have no one to blame but yourself." Well, now she must speak the truth, not the whole truth perhaps, but nothing that was false.

"My brother Antoine was never loved by our father and had every reason, in his mind at least, to stay on in Canada. His demands for half of the family inheritance were rejected by my parents, and his last message to them was that he would one day have his revenge. He went off to the Great Lakes as a voyageur and came back with enough furs to set himself up in business as a fur trader, throwing in his lot with the British. Both our parents died, and in recent years I have heard nothing of him, until that day that General Coburn came aboard *La Bonne Nouvelle*. That is the entire story, and I would gladly tell it to your ungrateful Congress."

Morgan raised his head. All the anger had gone out of his face and had been replaced by bewilderment and shame. "You are quite right to withhold your forgiveness. My behavior to you just now will forever be recalled by me with shame, but I hope I can earn your forgiveness. Tomorrow the packet-sloop that brought the mail sails for Philadelphia, and I mean to be aboard her." He tried to smile. "While I am gone you can realize your dream of recreating the gardens of Villa Chardin as they were."

"Morgan," Sophie said quietly, "you are quite mad. Do you think for a moment that you will travel without me? Do you think for a moment that a thousand Villas Chardin would balance the scales against my love for you?"

"But you just said. . . ."

"You have hurt me deeply, yes, as no doubt one day I will hurt you. A love that cannot survive such blows is of little account, to my reckoning."

"But you cannot sail with me to America. The danger is too great."

"I shall. For five years I did a man's work, and I can face the same dangers as any man."

"No. I cannot permit it."

"Then you will have to prevent me by force from boarding ship, and that would create quite a spectacle on the docks."

He shook his head and laughed, yet he was crying. He went to his knees on the floor, his head in her lap, and she held his face in her hands and felt his tears running through her fingers. Just before she had married André at age seventeen, Archambault had tried in his rough way to give her some advice on relations between the sexes, since her parents certainly had not. She had forgotten most of what he had said, but now one admonition came back to her: "Sophie, never give your heart to a man who is too proud to cry."

Sophie sat at her writing desk and penned a letter to a young merchant's wife of Bordeaux, her closest friend there, asking her to take a young Creole woman in hand and see into her prospects for marriage. Then she wrote a second letter to her St. Pierre bankers and instructed them to issue a bill of exchange in a substantial amount to Odette Phillipeau. She knew now that she might never return to France, but she could see that Odette got there and with a dowry sufficient to assure her a suitable marriage. She had also made provision for elderly relatives. *Mon Dieu,* she thought, it's not as if I am writing my last will and testament. Now I am free to live!

The scorpion that in Martinique lurked in dark corners, that she had looked for everywhere, so unsure was she of her new-found happiness, had emerged from, of all places, an envelope from Philadelphia sealed with red wax, and she had crushed it—God willing—under her heel. But then she thought of the Comtesse de Brieux's last words to her, spoken with venom: "You can be assured that you will be repaid in full."

BOOK II
THE NEW WORLD
1777–1778

CHAPTER FIFTEEN

When at last they sighted the mouth of Delaware Bay, Sophie sighed deeply with relief. It had been a long hard voyage up the American coast. The sloop *Betsey* on which they traveled had been tossed about by summer storms; and always there was the fear of being captured by the British, the hold of the ship loaded with cannon for Washington's army and enough gunpowder to blow them to bits if they should be fired upon. For that reason they dared not fight, and should they be captured their cargo assured that they would all end in a British prison.

Twice they had sighted a British warship on the horizon and sought the safety of the shallow waters of tidal creeks. There, at anchor, swarms of mosquitoes assaulted them, and with the heat and humidity of a Carolina August, sleep, even on deck, became close to impossible.

"At last," Morgan said, putting his hand over hers on the rail, "to be able to get off this infernal boat."

"And to be able to stand upright upon arising in the morning. We cannot, at least, complain that we were not allowed intimacy." They had shared a cabin not much larger than a kitchen cupboard, in which it was necessary to stoop over even to get into their narrow bunk.

"And to have fresh vegetables again," he mused. "I dream at night of crisp green Parisian salads."

Isaac Slocum joined them at the rail. Although captain of the ship, he was hardly more than a boy and mightily impressed to have as passengers the pair who were responsible for the supply of French arms to his country.

"Good morning, madame, sir. I hope you got some sleep in this blustery weather we've been having. But your ordeal will soon be over."

"I am most anxious to get ashore," Morgan said, "and have some news of how the war goes."

"You may not have to wait that long, if you will but turn about."

They turned to see a warship bearing down upon them.

"Don't be alarmed. It's one of ours. She flies the American colors."

The frigate came alongside, and a uniformed officer and sailors with their oars held upright were lowered in a ship's boat, reminding Sophie of that day aboard *La Bonne Nouvelle* when General Coburn had arrived in the same fashion, and of all the grief that had followed that encounter. Would that this were not a similar ill omen!

"Good morning, captain," said the young man in a blue and white uniform, lacking in all elegance, in fact somewhat dingy, who stepped aboard. "Lieutenant Spackman, Continental Navy ship *New Haven*. May I inquire as to your destination?"

"Good morning, lieutenant. We are headed for Philadelphia."

"Then you must turn back. Two British ships of the line block the way a few miles up Delaware Bay, and General Howe has brought his entire army down from New York and clearly means to invest our capital."

"But I must reach Philadelphia," Morgan said forcefully, "under orders of the Continental Congress."

"Unless Washington decides to challenge Howe and can beat him, I doubt you will find the Congress in Philadelphia. They are, of course, all accused of treason to the Crown and are liable to be taken and hanged by the British if they do not soon flee."

"What awful news. How does the war go elsewhere?"

"Badly. Were it not for the arms supplied by France we would by now, I reckon, have been forced to surrender. As it is, we barely hang on."

"It is French arms that I carry," Captain Slocum said, casting an eye on Sophie and Morgan, but deciding from the look on Sophie's face to say no more. "Where am I to put my cargo ashore?"

"It will not be easy. Further north the British army occupies the ports or the British navy blockades them: New York, Boston, Portsmouth, almost all the others."

"Nor are there so many shallows, as in the Carolinas, where I might evade the British."

"Then I can only advise you to turn back," said the lieutenant.

The three men looked glum, and more than that, as Sophie saw from their fleeting glances at her, the possibility of bold and daring action was cut off by responsibility for a woman aboard.

"To turn back to Martinique," the captain finally said, "would be to abandon our mission, and would require sufficient food and water to do so, which I haven't."

"We could let you have a certain amount of both, but I agree that to return to Martinique . . ."

"May one propose a possibility?" Sophie interjected. *Dieu merci*, she had been studying English since their arrival in Martinique and practicing it assiduously with Morgan. The two naval men looked at her in surprise that a woman would attempt to enter into such serious conversation. Morgan, with his knowledge of Sophie, only smiled.

"One may . . . one could," Sophie said, speaking carefully, "sail for that island off Newfoundland, the one colony that remains to France in North America, and there to await developments."

"If you were to make a dash for Miquelon, you might just make it," the lieutenant said, "but the chances of your being intercepted by the British are great."

"*Certainement,* but whichever way we turn, it is the same," Sophie replied. "And I have with me a French flag that my manager in Martinique *insisté* I take with me. Were we to run her up, even if the British come aboard, they could say nothing against a French vessel carrying French arms to French Miquelon. Indeed, the peace treaty between France and Britain provides for such a thing."

"A transparent stratagem," Captain Slocum said, "when both the master of the vessel and its papers are American."

"Ah, but my company, we may say, leases your ship from you. And your crew and officers are French and Spanish, so we may say that one of these is the vessel's master should the British come aboard us."

The captain looked extremely doubtful of this proposal, while the navy lieutenant was obviously perplexed as to who this woman was who spoke with such authority.

"I will hide neither my colors nor my commission from the British," young Captain Slocum said at last.

At this critical moment Morgan spoke up. "Come, Isaac, is it not better to swallow a bit of pride than to risk losing our valuable cargo and our liberty to the enemy? There is no dishonor in playing the crafty fox to the British hounds."

"You may be right, but the fact is that for the New World Trading Co. to lease my vessel would be but to confirm our mission. The British know full well who is behind the supply of French arms to America."

"*Evidemment,*" said Sophie, "but not of necessity every British warship's captain. *En tout cas,* that was not my intent.

I own, in addition to the company formed to transport arms to America, another in my own name, Chardin and Co., that trades regularly with Miquelon, and I have with me its papers and seal."

The two naval men looked at Sophie skeptically, but neither could put forth any argument for an alternative plan. Indeed, as Morgan said, what choices did they have?

And so they changed course for Miquelon, and no sooner had they done so than the weather also changed. The sea became calm, the sky a cloudless blue, and the air a most pleasant temperature. There was even, thanks to the American warship, now some variety in their monotonous diet. But to spend one's nights in an armoire, *Mon Dieu!*

Sophie came up to Morgan and Captain Slocum, leaning on the rail, apparently discussing dreary military and nautical matters.

"Mon capitaine."

"Oui, madame," the captain said, blushing at having been able successfully to get out two words of French in a row .

"One suffocates below at night, in what you call in English a closet; while above the breezes are warm, the sky full of stars. Could we not sleep on deck?"

"With the sailors? There'll be no privacy."

Morgan raised an eyebrow, started to speak, but realized that anything he said would embarrass someone, if not everyone. Sophie stifled a giggle.

By nightfall the captain had had constructed for them, out of bales and crates and barrels of cargo, an enclosure where they might sleep at night away from the eyes of the seamen; and they lay there at night, she quite content, looking up at an infinity of stars.

"Now suppose, *chéri,* that I had not insisted on accompanying you. One day a ship's captain would have arrived in Martinique with news that you never reached Philadelphia. What despair I would have known then!"

"I believe that you did more than insist. As I recall you said that you would have to be bodily carried off the ship on which I sailed."

"And was I not right? Now we are within two days of Miquelon and safety. While you may not have achieved your objective, you will in time. Meanwhile, what does it matter where we are, so long as we are together?"

"It would not matter, except that I must reach Philadelphia, or wherever the Congress is to be found, before I am judged guilty in my absence."

"Surely they cannot expect you to appear as summoned, when the British army and navy surround the city?"

"Logic would say so, but Philip Byrd has friends in Congress, and logic may not prevail. On the other hand," he said with a smile, "there is certainly nothing I can do about it at present, so why not put it out of my mind and instead turn my attention to you."

"Have you not done so?"

"To the small extent that circumstances permitted, but now that we have some freedom of movement I would make love properly under the stars," and he began removing her clothes without waiting for a response.

"You must promise not to cry out, Sophie."

"I cannot promise, but I will bite my lip hard when the moment comes."

The next day they awoke to a dense fog which did not lift for several hours. That was because they were approaching Newfoundland, the captain said. On the morrow they could expect the fog to be even denser and longer lasting, but before evening they would be in Miquelon.

The following morning the fog did not lift until nearly noon. When it did dark shapes began to emerge at all points of the compass. They had sailed squarely into the midst of a squadron of British warships that stretched from horizon to horizon.

"My God, to have been so close!" Morgan brought his fist down on the rail. "Instead, we have sailed right into the lion's den."

"And it is all my doing," Sophie said softly, feeling a numbing chill run from her extremities to her pounding heart and flushed face. "My ill-conceived plan has ruined us all."

"Your plan has not yet been tested," Morgan said, gripping her wrist. "We may still make it to Miquelon—and I can see a thin line of green on the horizon that must be it—if we all play our cards properly. And we must. Everything rides on it."

"Yes, yes. You and I, Morgan, and the future, that a year ago could not have been dreamed of." She threw her arms around him and held him close. He returned her embrace.

"That and the future of America, which a year ago we could not have imagined would, to some small extent, rest in the hands of two people."

Sophie felt another chill run through her body. Their two destinies hung in the balance, but also that of a country being born. She had not counted on that factor when she had given herself to her American lover. The British must not have the two of them, but neither must they be allowed to snuff out the spirit of American liberty. *Mon Dieu, non!* She must concentrate her thoughts. Perhaps her plan would work, but if it didn't?

"Morgan, if they take me, you must fade away, become part of the crew. Your command of French will permit that."

"Are you mad?" He turned to her with a look that suggested that she might be. "Why would they take you, and if they do I will assuredly go with you."

"They might because the name of Sophie Armonville is well known to the British, and I have no false papers. You do."

"Never!"

She searched for an argument that might persuade him. "You must preserve yourself. It is you who are known to the French foreign minister, who have struck this bargain between France and America that may yet save your country. The British would do no harm to a woman, but to you . . ."

"What do you mean?"

Her clumsy words had only confused, perhaps even angered him. What she meant but could not say was that, indeed, she was in no danger of physical abuse from officers and gentlemen, but he would be treated as a rebel prisoner and sent to one of those British prison ships in New York harbor where starvation and death were, she knew from ships' captains calling in Martinique, the common lot. That is, if he was not hanged.

"I mean that you must trust me." Over his shoulder she saw a British warship turning, its sails filling out. They parted then and went to different parts of the rail to watch the approach of the ship. At least they could both agree that they must not be seen together. How badly she had handled things, beginning with her plan that ignored her own vulnerability. She had just assumed that they would not find themselves in the situation that they now did. She could only blame her own cleverness, the same calculating cleverness of one who had been brought up to see everything in terms of profit and loss, that had nearly lost her Morgan in Martinique.

Less than half an hour later a naval officer hoisted himself up the ship's ladder from an elegant barge flying the Union Jack. She felt calm. Once the cards had been played, there was nothing more one could do. The young lieutenant who stepped upon the deck was handsome and poised, to be expected of an admiral's aide.

"Captain, greetings and good health to your sovereign, the King of France," the young man said in impeccable French. "Our commander, Vice Admiral Fraser, would inquire as to the destination of the sloop *Betsey*."

"Out of Martinique, bound for Miquelon," answered the ship's French first officer, as they had agreed on. Captain Slocum was nowhere to be seen.

"And your cargo?"

"Cannon and gunpowder for our fortress there."

"Ah. Is there any assistance that we may render?"

"None, sir."

"Well then, I have but to deliver the admiral's invitation for Madame Armonville to dine with him," and the British lieutenant turned to Sophie with a smile.

"At what hour?" Sophie said in a voice that was surely her own but seemed to come from far away, the voice of one who has lost the game, who is condemned to some dark fate. There was nothing that she could do now but hold Morgan, close at hand, anguish written all over his face, with her eyes, warn him, order him, not to do the rash thing that he was so clearly on the verge of doing. He obeyed her stern look.

"The admiral proposes that you return with me in his barge. His flagship, *HMS Greyhound*, will then run alongside the *Betsey* as she makes her way to the harbor of St. Pierre de Miquelon."

"Yes," Sophie said, "I should be pleased to join the admiral for dinner," and she stepped forward, knowing full well that she was a prisoner, that the British had known that she was aboard the *Betsey*, and that she had been a fool. What she could not be sure of was whether they knew that the American agent in Paris, and chief thorn in their side, Morgan Carter, was also aboard the *Betsey*. Surely they did, but then what was the point of playing cat and mouse? She was surprised that she could analyze her situation so calmly, but she must; and as she stepped forward to be assisted down the ladder she did not look in Morgan's direction.

"Madame," said Vice Admiral Sir Hugh Fraser, bending to kiss her hand, "you are most kind to dine with me. I hope you will not find it in poor taste for me to ask that we dine alone—and in normal circumstances it would certainly be just that—but these are troubled times we are living through...."

"These are times, I believe it has recently been said, that try men's souls."

The wince that this brought to the ruddy face of the large-nosed admiral, with his alert blue eyes and short powdered wig, confirmed that he was not unfamiliar with the latest publication of Tom Paine, much quoted by Morgan. But he did not acknowledge it. Instead he turned to consider the decanters and bottles on a sideboard in his spacious stern cabin, its mullioned windows open to a fine autumn day.

"At my club in London, or among my peers at sea, I am considered something of a connoisseur of wines and spirits, but in the presence of someone with the knowledge that I understand you to possess, I feel like a damned schoolboy. Please, Madame Armonville, do choose a wine to go with our dinner. We will be having veal and mushrooms of the forest, fresh from our last call at Halifax."

"Surely a claret," Sophie said, her heart pounding.

"Yes, but which?"

"A Médoc, I should think."

"Well, I do have one or two. Here, let's try this one," and the admiral applied a corkscrew to a dusty bottle, poured a little of its contents into a glass and handed it to Sophie. She examined it, twirled the glass, sniffed and tasted it carefully.

"Well, what do you think."

"It is excellent, but not, of course, a Médoc, rather a Pomerol. Château Pétrus, whether '67 or '69 it is difficult to say, the sea voyage having blurred its signature."

"Well, well, Madame Armonville, I see we will be able to discuss matters down to the fine points. It's a '67 by the way."

"One of the first points we might discuss is how you knew I was aboard the *Betsey*. I find that most mysterious."

As she said this, Sophie fully faced the fact that for the others aboard the *Betsey* there could be only one explanation: she had persuaded them to sail for Miquelon because she was in league with the British and had arranged to deliver them into the hands of their enemies.

"Well, my dear, in war as in all endeavors, luck is almost always an ingredient of success, if not the principal one. Shortly after your rendezvous off Philadelphia with the rebel frigate *New Haven*, she was engaged by two of our ships, and after a battle that lasted more than an hour, was obliged to strike her colors. When we boarded her we found among her crew a sailor loyal to the Crown who had overheard your conversation with an officer of the *New Haven*. Word of your presence aboard the *Betsey* was sent around the fleet as quickly as possible; for the capture of an American frigate would pale beside the capture of a cargo of French arms destined for our rebellious subjects—and Madame Sophie Armonville. As luck would have it, I was informed only yesterday."

"Then I am yours," Sophie said resignedly, "by an astonishing piece of bad luck."

"Or good luck, depending on your point of view. Here, let us have a glass of this wine that you pronounce excellent. Dinner will be served shortly."

"What will you do with me?"

"The question is rather more complicated. By Jove, this is indeed a fine wine, the first bottle of it I've opened. I say more complicated, because our loyal sailor described a man who was with you, who I have no doubt is Morgan Carter, the ex-American agent in Paris and now, I believe, your business partner. If I were to hand you both over to the proper authorities, Mr. Carter would no doubt be hanged for treason and you would be an embarrassment to His Majesty's government. One doesn't hang ladies. In any case little would have been accomplished except revenge, and in my view revenge is one of the baser motives for action. What we want to see is a diminution of the traffic in French arms and munitions to America. There you could be of help to us."

"What would you have me do?"

"Cancel your contract with the agents of the French government, tell us which ministers of that government authorized this enterprise, so that we can vigorously protest to the King of France's first minister, and give us all details of shipments already made and those underway: cargoes, ships' names, routes, dates, etcetera."

"And in return?"

The admiral turned up his palms. "That is much simpler. Morgan Carter will not hang."

"But some loathsome prison."

"He would have to be detained, of course, but under humane conditions, and you would reside in some comfortable situation in British territory. When the rebels are defeated, you would both be free to return to your former lives. At least that is what I would propose to my superiors, but I have little doubt that they would agree."

There was a knock on the door and two servants entered with covered silver dishes.

"Just put them on the sideboard," Admiral Fraser said, getting to his feet. "I will myself serve."

When the servants had retired, the admiral turned again to Sophie. "I have made you a handsome offer, and I am a man of my word. But we can dine first while you consider."

"That won't be necessary," Sophie said in a dead voice, all the joy that she had known for one brief year extinguished. "I have no choice but to accept. Where will you take us?" She knew this question for what it was, a vain pretense that she and Morgan would be going anywhere together. Only the deep love that she bore Morgan prevented her from bursting into tears.

"To Quebec, where the authorities are located who deal in such murky matters as these, and who will be able to say more precisely what actions and intelligence His Majesty's government require of you."

"Morgan Carter must never know of what I have agreed to."

"Accepted. Well then, shall we dine?"

"Admiral, I have no appetite. In fact I feel rather sick. Could I be allowed to go out into the fresh air?"

"By all means. I will join you."

As they stepped out on deck two British marines crossed in front of them, leading Morgan, his wrists shackled together. He looked at her with an expression of horror and disbelief. All that she could do was to try to convey the truth with her eyes: that she had not betrayed the American cause. But, for his sake, she was about to.

CHAPTER SIXTEEN

She stood at the rail, wrapped in a military cloak the ship's captain had lent her, Sophie Chardin Armonville, a woman who could no longer say that she had not experienced passion and adventure. She had had them to the full for one brief year, and now she was returning to the city where she had been born, a prisoner. She wept a little then for what was to come. If Morgan had died fighting the British she would have borne it, have cherished their year together for the rest of her life, not have felt herself among the unlucky of the earth. But he was alive and a prisoner. If that were not enough misfortune, how could he not be tortured by the belief that she had betrayed him; and now she was on her way to do just that—either that or let him be hanged.

As she had had the luck of the gods for a year, now she must pay bitterly for her happiness. That is how her Huguenot relatives would have seen it. But would she have foregone that year, seen herself back at her ledger in Bordeaux for the rest of her life, a tiny scrap of paper and a dried wildflower never discovered, not to be standing where she stood today? No, she said to herself defiantly, rather this than not to have lived at all. And there must be a way out!

As if to give her a whisper of hope the fog along the St. Lawrence River lifted just enough to reveal the early autumn foliage along the banks, so well remembered from childhood, the dark firs and lighter pines, the reddening maples and, most beautiful of all, the ever quivering leaves of the aspens, like triangles of gold beaten thin as tissue. No sorrow, no fear could entirely dull one's senses to such beauty.

"Pardon, ma'am, but you should make ready to debark," said the serious young officer assigned to look after Sophie, who had come up beside her. "We'll be landing at Quebec port shortly."

They rounded a point and the austere shape of the citadel of Quebec came into view, a pale silhouette above the morning mists, unchanged but for the British flag flying from its topmost tower. "The boat awaits," the red-coated lieutenant said, and she sighed, turned from the view and followed him.

As the boat made its way from the British warship to the dock the fog lifted entirely, and the waterfront she had once known so well came into view. Even the offices and warehouses of Chardin and Co. were unchanged but for a sign, "J. Smythe." A carriage awaited them on the dock, and they were soon rumbling through the narrow cobbled streets of the lower town, but to what destination she had no idea. Her escort remained silent. Soon, however, it became clear where they were headed. The pace had slowed, and the horses were straining now on the steep incline that led to the rocky crag dominated by the great citadel of Quebec.

Red-coated British sentries now flanked the gate of the once proud French fortress and were posted at intervals in the long corridors within. Sophie and her escort ascended several flights of stairs to the uppermost regions of the fort. There they were met by a British major who curtly dismissed the lieutenant and showed her through a great oak door.

A fire crackled in a large carved stone fireplace and a heavy-set man in a splendid scarlet uniform looked out the tall windows that overlooked the city and the river, his hands joined behind his back. She recognized those broad shoulders, the beefy back and narrow legs immediately.

"Well, Madame Armonville," said Major General Sir George Coburn, turning and speaking to her in quite good French, "I can't tell you what a great pleasure it gives me to see you here. You may leave us, major."

"My being here is not of my choosing, as you well know." Sophie would have been hard pressed to explain why she not only felt no fear but a kind of irrational confidence that somehow she would have the better of this man.

"Well, never mind. The important thing is that you are here. May I offer you coffee."

"Yes, why not?"

Her acquiescence had been assumed, for the instant the general rang a little silver bell a servant entered the room with a tray laden with coffee pot and cups and various kinds of pastries.

"Shall we sit here by the fire? In Canada chilly days come early, as I do not need to tell you."

The general poured coffee and they took a few sips in silence.

"I congratulate you on the quality of this brew."

Sophie looked at Coburn in perplexity. What could he mean?

"Comment?"

"We captured one of your ships a while back—I forget the name—and there was a considerable quantity of coffee aboard. My navy colleagues sent me a few bags."

"Oh."

"I hope your voyage here was made comfortable."

"Quite."

"I have just minutes ago received a communication from my good friend Hugh Fraser," and he motioned to an opened envelope on his desk. "He tells me you two hit it off famously, even reached certain understandings. It goes without saying that any pledges that Hugh made you are equally binding on me."

Sophie looked into the general's eyes, which were the same pale blue as Admiral Fraser's. When Fraser had said he was a man of his word she believed him. She felt no such confidence in the man into whose eyes she now looked.

"I also have made pledges, and I am here to keep them," Sophie said. "What information do you require from me?"

"Information?" Coburn replied, holding out a plate of scones to her. "I have far too much of that." He motioned to a large cabinet, its shelves filled to overflowing with folders of papers. "What I need is not more information but some means of making sense of it all."

"I don't understand how I can help with that."

"Ah, but you can. Those papers you see there are filled with reports of what ordinary soldiers and sailors have seen or heard, or the dispatches of spies, which often are not much better. When I have winnowed out those bits of intelligence that may have some value, even then I have but scattered pieces of a puzzle. What I need is to see the pattern that will tell me the intentions and capability of my enemy."

The general took a bite of scone and another sip of coffee before he continued.

"You, Madame Armonville, have been at the center of a conspiracy that more than any other factor threatens my nation's capacity to put down the American rebellion, and you must see a large part of the pattern, even if you do not understand it all. So, you see, your cooperation is important, and if freely given will assure that your great and good friend comes to no harm—though God knows he deserves it."

"My great and good friend?"

"A euphemism for a relationship with which I am thoroughly familiar. Do not suppose that I am unawares of to what lengths you would go in order to save Morgan Carter's neck."

She said nothing, wishing to give him no clue, even by a trembling in her voice that she might not be able to suppress. A master of spies would have many tricks for assuring himself of information that he only guessed at.

"If you doubt the extent of my knowledge, I can tell you that you won exactly four hundred three livres at bézique that evening at the Comtesse de Brieux's."

Sophie gasped, feigning surprise. "How could . . ."

"The number of persons you conversed with that evening is sufficiently large that I take little risk of compromising one of my agents in Martinique, who was among that number."

She had had her first little victory. The general had so far learned nothing, and she had learned that he was not yet aware, might never be—for the comtesse might fear to inform him—that it was Madeleine de Brieux herself who was his agent.

"Since you are already so well informed . . ."

"But the pattern of French intentions and capabilities, Madame Armonville . . ."

"I know little of patterns."

"I will show you that you know more than you think. I believe we will need to have a number of little chats over the coming weeks, get to know each other better."

From the odd look in General Coburn's eyes she thought for a moment that he had her seduction in mind, but then something told her that it was not that. He wanted her in his power, to play with her like a cat with a mouse. She thought he might even be a little mad. Hyacinthe had told her once that those who lived in the world of espionage after some years lost touch with reality. If Coburn was unbalanced there might indeed be some chance that she could get the better of him, as unlikely as that seemed.

"More coffee."

"*Merci, non.*"

"Well then, you must be tired after all that has befallen you in the last few days. We can resume our conversation in a day or two. I have arranged accommodations for you at a French convent not far from here. You will feel more comfortable with your co-religionists, though fellowship you mustn't count on. The sisters of that order have taken vows of silence. You are free to come and go as you please, and I will provide an officer to accompany you when you desire. I do not need to tell you that escape is not to be considered. The Canadian wilderness and our allies, the Iroquois nation, are quite sufficient walls."

Sophie rose and the general rang the bell again. A young officer appeared as quickly as had the servant with the coffee.

"Captain Fontenoy. He is at your complete disposal, and you will find his French far better than the poor sort I speak."

As she was traveling to the convent in a carriage with the captain, whose attempts to be charming she ignored, it occurred to Sophie to wonder why, if the general's intelligence on her was so fine, he did not know that her family was not Catholic, but Huguenot.

As a child the convent that she was now entering had seemed to Sophie a mysterious place, with its high dark walls of stone, its ancient trees and its silence. Except for days set aside for the visit of the families of those within, the doors of the Convent of St. Jude were seldom opened. Now they closed behind her, leaving Captain Fontenoy outside, and she found herself in a stark whitewashed entry hall, bare of adornment except for a massive crucifix on the wall. A young nun beckoned to her, and she was led down a long white-

A New World Won

washed corridor smelling of strong soap to a door that opened into a narrow cell, also whitewashed and with a smaller crucifix on the wall. The door closed silently behind her and she was alone; but her trunk, that Admiral Fraser had ordered be sent with her, had already been delivered to her place of confinement—for that was what it was.

There was a single narrow window, but the view from it was every bit as fine as that from General Coburn's suite: the lower town, the great curve of the river, and the Canadian forests beyond, already touched by autumn color. She lay down on the narrow bed, physically and emotionally exhausted. The bed was as hard as she had imagined it would be. Sophie laughed bitterly to herself. Her situation was no better or worse than when she had lived above her offices on the Bordeaux quay. In fact it was very similar: she had been a kind of nun there, with an account book as her missal. Suddenly she was overcome with a desperate longing for Morgan's body beside her in bed, and lay there recalling their times together in loving detail.

Sophie was awakened from troubled dreams by a gentle knock on the door. The same young nun, averting her eyes, left a tray with a simple meal on the table, which with a single chair and the bed composed the cell's furnishings. After she had eaten, Sophie's practical bourgeois upbringing asserted itself over the confused thoughts and emotions that had almost overwhelmed her. As her father had been fond of saying, within every problem is the seed of its solution. Well then, she would find that seed.

She tried the door and found it unlocked, opened it and went out into the empty silent corridor. General Coburn had said she was free to come and go as she pleased. She would begin by testing that assertion. However, she knew well, Quebecoise born, that the general spoke the truth when he said that a woman could never escape from a city surrounded by wilderness and Iroquois allied to the British. Even her own brother Antoine, who was a skilled woodsman, would have been daunted by the prospect of evading the Iroquois. It was curious that Coburn, after that one reference to him when he had boarded *La Bonne Nouvelle*, had made no further mention of Antoine.

A door at the end of the corridor opened onto a small terrace overlooking vegetable and flower gardens and an orchard. Three nuns were picking apples and pears from the trees. Sophie descended the stairs and wandered about the gardens. For two of the nuns she might have been invisible, but the third stared at her. Sophie returned her gaze and then froze where she stood. Even with the passage of so many years there could be no doubt. It was Amélie, at age eight her closest friend. How many tears they had shed when her family had decided to flee the British and hers to stay behind. But Amélie a nun? Impossible! Yet there she was in a habit on a ladder in a convent orchard. Sophie took a step towards her, but Amélie shook her head and raised a finger to her lips. Sophie turned in confusion and made her way back to her cell. Was the rule of silence so severe as to forbid dear friends who had not seen each other in many years from exchanging greetings?

That night Sophie longed to lose herself in deep sleep, to leave behind for a few hours the insoluble problems she faced and the distressing discovery that her old friend, so full of life, had taken the veil. She felt shame that not once, from the time she had learned that she was being sent to Canada, had she thought of Amélie before discovering her in the garden.

When at last sleep came it was disturbed by bad dreams in which she was a child again, lost in the Canadian wilderness and pursued by wolves loping through the forest, their tongues hanging out, eyes shining, breaths billowing in the frozen air. An owl cried from far away. She opened her eyes. A dark shape passed through the moonlight streaming in the window. There was someone else in the room. Suddenly she was back in Martinique as a girl, seeing everywhere at night the zombies that Céleste had frightened her with. Had all that had happened to her in these last days affected her mind?

"Sophie."

The hair stood up on the back of her neck. Was she still dreaming? But the owl cried again, and it was a real cry, the cry of the great horned owl. Not a sound to be terrified of but a familiar, comforting sound that had lulled her to sleep as a child in Canada.

"Sophie, c'est moi, Amélie."

"Amélie, viens ici," and the dark shape came towards her. Sophie felt a weight on the edge of the bed and two cold hands grasping hers.

"So many years, Amélie. I never thought to see you again, and then when I did . . ." Sophie was almost overcome with emotion.

"And when you did you were shocked and disappointed. I could see it on your face."

"I could not believe that you had found a religious vocation"

"I haven't."

"Then why are you in this convent, you of all people, my Amélie?"

How quickly with a childhood friend one picked up again, as though only days had passed since they last met.

"First tell me why you are here. Never have I been so astonished. Is it true that you are a prisoner of the British?"

"I am."

"How terrible. But why? What have you done?"

"It is a long story."

"As is mine. Five years, five long years . . ."

Amélie began to sob in the most pitiful fashion. Sophie sat up in bed and put her arms around

"What is it? What happened? Tell me, Amélie." She cradled her old friend in her arms

"There was a young man, I was seventeen . . . we wanted to marry, but my family would not agree, my father, my three brothers . . . you remember them?"

"Of course." She remembered most of all that Amélie's brothers had tried to keep them apart because Sophie's family was Huguenot. "Why would your family not let you marry this young man?"

"He was a Protestant . . . and poor."

"Ah." Her family would have taken the same stand if she had wanted to marry a Catholic . . . most especially if he were poor.

"Then my father died and my brothers arranged a marriage for me. I refused. For three years I resisted, then when I saw there was no hope of changing their minds I ran away with Charles. After a few months, the only happy months I have known since you left Canada, they found us. They beat Charles and forced him to flee for his life. They took me home. By then I was with child. When the child came it was given to foster parents and I was sent here. . . . Oh, Sophie, Sophie, I am so miserable. Until you came . . . in all these years no one to share my grief with."

Amélie began to sob again and sank to the floor. The moon was high in the sky, and as Sophie stroked her friend's head she could see the tear-stained face resting on her knee.

"What will you do?"

Amélie sat up and wiped her eyes with her coif. "I will go to him one day. Charles still waits for me, and now at last we are able to exchange letters."

After five years? Was it possible? Or had Amélie's experience left her a bit demented? But then Sophie remembered that she too had endured five years of bitter unhappiness when love and passion had struck like lightning out of a clear sky. Anything was possible. And was it any less grasping at straws for her to believe that she would somehow secure Morgan's freedom and that all would again be right between them? She could not suppress a sob.

"Sophie, you are crying. Why?"

"I am getting rid of my tears." Sophie pulled herself up straight and drew in her breath. "From now on, Amélie, you and I must cry no more. We must help each other, as we did in the old days."

She took Sophie's hands in hers. "You remember the time we got lost in the woods and both got a beating?"

"Yes, I remember." Sophie remembered well, that and many other occasions of harsh and unfair treatment meant to teach the two girls that they must obey. But they had supported each other and been happy children all the same.

"Listen, Amélie, we will get out of here, both of us."

"Like the time they locked us in the cellar."

"Exactly."

"We must be very careful then. Twice I've left the convent and twice my brothers have found me and brought me back. I have a key to the gate at the end of the garden. I've had it for nearly a year but have dared not use it."

"Splendid! We will use it. Just how I don't yet know, and we must be very careful. Now, dear friend you must hear my sad story. . . . Listen! What is that noise?"

"The sisters are beginning to come out of their cells for

midnight prayers. I dare not stay longer. I must not be missed in the chapel."

She gave Sophie a warm hug and rose to leave.

"When will I see you again?"

"Tomorrow night at the same hour."

Amélie opened the door, looked in both directions, and disappeared into the dark corridor. The door closed silently behind her.

Poor Amélie! What chance did she have? She had escaped twice and her brothers had found her twice. They would find her a third time. Her situation seemed hopeless. Sophie tried not to think about her own situation, which she knew any observer would say was equally hopeless.

CHAPTER SEVENTEEN

The next night, however, Sophie found that she was invited to the weekly social evening given by the general officers of the British army in Canada. General Coburn's method of treating prisoners of war was indeed a strange one! She would surely go, if only to see what advantage she might gain in her coming battle of wits with the general. She was now quite calm, the knowledge that someone else suffered cruelly having made her see her own troubles in perspective. Poor Amélie.

When Captain Fontenoy came for her, Sophie was waiting in the room set aside for the nuns to meet with their families. Although the evening was warm she was wrapped tightly in her cloak, for beneath she wore a low-cut gown. She hoped she looked her best—she was prepared to use that weapon too—but the last thing one could expect to find in a convent was a mirror. She had managed her hair well enough without a mirror, she thought, having sleeked it back to form a French knot on the nape of her neck, while allowing a few tendrils of dark hair to curl loose in front of her ears. Before going out to meet the captain she had, lacking makeup, bitten her lips and pinched her cheeks to give them some color.

Once inside the carriage Sophie, commenting on the warmness of the evening, undid the clasp of her cloak and let it fall from her bare shoulders.

The captain drew in his breath. *"Épatante . . . cette robe."*

Yes, it was a stunning dress, but she was satisfied that the captain referred to more than the dress.

"Tell me, Captain Fontenoy, what will the English ladies

think of a notorious enemy agent being present at their soirée?"

"I should imagine that they will be frightfully indignant, but that their indignation will be overcome by their curiosity. And they will tell themselves that old George, who is noted for his eccentricities, has some purpose in inviting you."

"Does he?"

"Possibly, but then he may be doing so just to create a sensation. George used to be a playwright—even acted in some of his own plays—before he bought a commission in the army."

"Really. And you call General Coburn by his Christian name?"

"Since I was a child. My father got him his present appointment. 'It'll keep him from worse mischief,' pater said." Fontenoy laughed in a patronizing way. Sophie stored away this piece of intelligence for future use.

"And what will the men think of my presence tonight?" She was more nervous than she showed, but, thank God, she was now far more a woman of the world than the widow Armonville of Bordeaux.

"What will the men think?" The handsome Captain Fontenoy smiled and fluttered his long lashes a bit. "Madame, you surely have no doubts on that score?"

When Sophie entered the reception room in the citadel on the captain's arm, a total silence fell over the crowd of red-coated officers and their wives. General Coburn came forward to greet her, apparently relishing the awkwardness of the situation; and as he did the women all together moved away from the men to the far end of the room.

"*Ah, ma belle prisonnière.* They wagered you would not come, but I knew better. As you can see you are to be ostracized by the ladies, but never mind, it gives them something to do, and to gossip about for the next week. But my colleagues are most anxious to meet you. Come, let me introduce you."

Coburn offered his arm and as she took it Sophie said, "Why are you doing this, general?"

"Firstly, to amuse myself. There's damned little amusement to be had in Canada, I can tell you. Secondly, my colleagues are anxious to meet you and eventually put to you directly the particular questions they have. They seem to believe that you will be able to answer in great detail their questions regarding the precise number of muskets, the bore of cannon, etcetera, supplied the American rebels. I told them that a woman would hardly keep such details in her mind."

"There you would be wrong, general."

"So much the better. But what you and I will need to discuss—of much greater importance—is personalities."

The generals and colonels to whom she was introduced crowded around her, more out of curiosity at seeing this young woman who had caused so much trouble for the British crown, it seemed to Sophie, than in learning anything from her. But before there could be any conversation, a tight-faced little man in a powdered wig, a lieutenant general to whom the others deferred, spoke up.

"Well, George, you've had your little joke, and a damned awkward situation you've created. Now, gentlemen, I think we must join the ladies and smooth some ruffled feathers. Colonel Bemis, would you be so kind as to take Madame Armonville for a walk in the garden."

Sophie's cloak was brought and she was spirited away as quickly as if it had just been discovered that she had the plague.

"I'm sorry that you have had to be embarrassed. Damned

poor show", Colonel Bemis blurted out. They had reached the end of the garden and from the parapet looked down on the lights of Quebec city.

"It is General Coburn, *n'est-ce pas,* who should be embarrassed?"

"What does he care? He's rich and has powerful friends in Parliament. He behaves as he pleases. The rest of us . . ."

Sophie looked at the British officer in the light of a lantern hanging from the balustrade. He was older than some of the generals.

"How do you find Canada?"

"Lonely."

"You are married?"

"Wife and five children in Sussex."

"*Alors,* you have someone to return to."

"I wish I was with Burgoyne's army, that's where I wish I was."

"And where is that?"

"In Albany by now, I imagine. The American fort at Ticonderoga fell some time ago. There's nothing standing in his way. The war will be over soon, and I'll have had no part in it."

"That is not something to make one sad."

"My last chance for promotion. Now it'll be retirement and five children to support on half pay."

"Then I regret it."

The colonel turned and looked at her. "I shouldn't be talking to you like this. I couldn't say any of this to my own people, but since you're the enemy . . . Funny, isn't it? You know I've never met a Frenchwoman."

"We're not that different."

"That's not what they say. You're beautiful too. It's hard to believe that you could be responsible for shipping all those arms, just you and that American who escaped."

Sophie's heart leaped. Had she heard correctly?

"I suppose they haven't found him?" It was only with great difficulty that she kept her composure.

"Not yet, and it may not be so easy. Anyone who could dive off the deck of a warship and swim to shore with his feet manacled...."

"And where was this?" It was a question that might raise the British officer's suspicion, but she had to chance it.

"Near Three Rivers, they say."

Trois Rivières. As they lay in bed together Morgan had told her many tales of his adventures in the American wilderness, and there had been something about Trois Rivières, but she couldn't remember what.

"Colonel, I see they have begun to dance inside. Would not this be a good time to return me to Captain Fontenoy, who may convey me to the convent? It would spare us all, as you say, further embarrassment."

"I won't hear of it. I'm taking you myself."

As Sophie and her escort crossed the reception room, they passed close to several couples drinking coffee and conversing. The Englishwomen, so very dowdy in Sophie's eyes, tried to avoid looking in her direction, but they could not help themselves. They were, she knew, both fascinated and repulsed at the presence of this—yes, beautiful, she would not deny it—enemy agent. If only they could have seen her bent over her ledger in a shipping office in Bordeaux, wearing equally dowdy clothes! Suddenly, one of the women staring at Sophie stepped forward, her mouth gaping open.

"You ... you ... French whore, that's my dress you are wearing ..."

"And that is my coffee you are drinking, madame. Such are the fortunes of war."

★ ★ ★ ★ ★

Sophie lay on her hard narrow bed, all of the courage that she had summoned for the ordeal at the citadel drained out of her. The owl called to its mate, the moon shone down on sleeping Quebec, midnight had passed and she had missed Amélie's visit, if indeed her friend had come. She so much wanted Morgan. A year before she would not even have understood how she could so want a man to be at her side all the night, breathing steadily, her body pressed against the warmth of his.

The tears began to flow and she did not even try to stop them. She was fearful yet proud of Morgan, who had dived overboard into the St. Lawrence and yet managed to swim ashore with ankles chained. She could only hope he was now safe somewhere in the Canadian wilderness, and that he would not be so foolish as to try to come to her—if he still believed in her faithfulness.

"Sophie."

She awoke with a gasp from a confused dream of descending rapids in one of those huge canoes in which the voyageurs brought their furs into Quebec at the end of summer.

"Amélie."

Moonlight had given way to the cold gray light that precedes the dawn. Her old friend in her severe habit sat on the end of the bed, her face composed. She had let all the pent-up grief come out the night before, and now she seemed to be at peace with herself. Their hands met and joined.

"I came twice in the night," Amélie whispered. "The first time you were not here, the second you slept so soundly I thought it best not to wake you."

"Amélie, what do you know of Trois Rivières?"

Amélie laughed. "Sophie, you have not changed."

"What do you mean?"

"You always, when you wanted something, did not waste your time in polite approaches to the object of your desire. What do you want now?"

Had she really been like that? Was she still?

"What I want is my man."

"Then we are as one."

"But tell me of Trois Rivières."

"It lies halfway between Quebec and Montreal."

"Well, of course, I know that, but . . ." What Morgan had told her and her own childhood memories were fast coming together. "What is it they are noted for there?"

"The making of canoes, *bien sûr*."

"*Bien sûr.*" Even her dream had tried to tell her. A family who had taught Morgan the art of canoe-making and a daughter who . . . but he had been frank about it and she had laughingly, their first weeks together, forgiven him any and all women he had known before they had met.

"Amélie, I learned last night that Morgan Carter, my . . . *amant*, has escaped from the British near Trois Rivières. He may even now be in hiding with friends there, makers of birchbark canoes, a Frenchman, his wife Huron. I must try to get a message to him. He must know I have not betrayed him, may even be in a position to help his cause. . . ."

The thought that she might find herself in a situation where she could be of assistance to the American cause, which had just occurred to her, lifted her spirits somewhat; and she proceeded to tell Amélie of all that had occurred since that day at Château Ivran when she had first laid eyes on Morgan until their capture by the British that now lay like a dark shadow across the once sunny landscape of their relations.

"You have trusted me with secrets, and I will trust you

with mine, Sophie. It may be possible to get a message to Trois Rivières in the same way I get my letters to Charles. Do you have money?"

"Yes." Indeed Sophie had a whole purse of gold and silver coins hidden beneath the false bottom of her trunk.

"Then write your letter and give it to me as quickly as possible with enough money to hire a messenger to take it to Trois Rivières. Soon the baker's boy will be here with the day's bread. I work in the kitchen, and it is one of my duties to receive the bread each morning. It is through this boy that Charles and I are able to exchange letters, and if properly recompensed he will do the same for you."

"Oh, Amélie, thank you, thank you." Sophie quickly got out of bed, hugged her friend, ran to her trunk and took out pen and paper. She sat down at the table, lit a candle and began writing, suddenly full of hope. Yet she knew the chances of Morgan Carter ever seeing the passionate words she penned must be slim. Nor had her friend's situation really changed. But they gave each other courage and hope. Amélie came up behind her and put a robe over her shoulders.

When a message arrived several days later saying that General Coburn wished to see her, Sophie welcomed the news. Better that her interrogation begin, she told herself as she dressed, better to have her wits challenged and mind occupied, than to sit day after day, alone—for she and Amélie had agreed that they should take no more risks by meeting—brooding in the convent over the fate of her letter to Morgan. The baker's boy claimed that he had given her letter to a resident of Trois Rivières who was returning there from a visit to Quebec. But for all she knew her letter might fall into the hands of the British. Already she regretted having sent it.

A New World Won

When the carriage arrived, Sophie was somewhat surprised, and relieved, that there was no Captain Fontenoy but only a driver to accompany her. She needed time to think. A plan had begun to form in her mind of concocting information Coburn might think she possessed—something quite other, he had hinted, than the details of arms shipments—and trading it for her freedom. Then she would go search for Morgan and be rejoined with him, and all would be well again. She sighed. It was only a dream but one she had to pretend to believe, for otherwise . . .

So absorbed was Sophie in her thoughts that they were well past the citadel before she realized that she was being taken out of Quebec into the country. It was a crisp fall day, the sky was a deep blue, and a little river flowed crystal-clear alongside the road, making its way to the mighty St. Lawrence. How happy she could have been on such a day and in such a place with Morgan, had not fate overtaken them!

Their destination proved to be a cottage in a grove of pines at the river's edge. General Coburn waited for her in the doorway of the cottage, dressed in the rough clothes of a country squire on his land.

"Good day, my dear," the general said in a hearty voice. "I'm delighted you could come." Did she have any choice? "The governor has been good enough to lend me his hunting lodge for the day so that we could talk in private, away from the curiosity of my countrymen—and women—and I do apologize for their behavior towards you at our little social evening."

"Were they not right to be offended by my presence?"

"Officers and their ladies should be able to conceal their emotions. Emotions are for the rabble, but wars are won by cold-blooded calculation. Now, come, let me show you the view."

They passed through a room furnished with leather chairs and dark wooden tables and a desk. A fire burned in the grate, over which hung a portrait of King George in court robes. General Coburn opened glass doors at the end of the room, and they stepped onto a balcony that hung out over the river.

"Quite beautiful isn't it. If I were a young man I would be quite enchanted at the idea of spending the day here alone with a beautiful Frenchwoman."

Sophie stiffened, but then she saw that these were but words. Once again it seemed to her that this was a man who was simply not interested in women.

"Now how can I be of assistance to you, general?" She had decided to take the offensive, see if she could put him off balance. The look he gave her was that of someone reassessing an opponent he may have underestimated.

"How? By replying quite truthfully to my questions."

"I would be a fool not to, given the power you have over me."

"Wisely said. You do your part and you have my word that you and Carter will be freed as soon as the rebels are suppressed."

Sophie tried to keep her face impassive. It had not occurred to her that General Coburn was unaware that she knew that Morgan had escaped. Colonel Bemis's indiscretion had given her a different hand of cards to play, but whether a winning one was another matter.

"Well then, shall I prepare us a collation? I find that conversation goes much better with a meal."

Sophie was surprised at the boyish enthusiasm on his rough ruddy face. Another thing that Hyacinthe had said about professional spies was that they enjoyed the game they played like children.

"Some lunch? By all means." In fact she found that she was quite hungry.

"And may I get your opinion on the claret the governor has laid down? My naval colleague tells me that your knowledge of wines is astonishing."

"It is my trade, after all."

"Or was until you took up smuggling arms," said the general dryly. "Shall we go to the kitchen?"

Sophie was surprised at the culinary skill the general, with his large, clumsy-looking hands, showed. He put a copper pan on the stove, added a knob of butter, chopped some fresh herbs, beat several eggs together, and soon turned a perfectly-made omelette out onto a platter.

"Most expertly done."

"Thanks to your countrymen. I was captured at the battle of Hastenbeck in '57 and held for some months in Normandy, in the château of one of your great nobles. I've never lived better in my life—almost regretted being exchanged for a French officer we held in England. My hosts possessed a splendid cook, and to pass the time I had him teach me the French cuisine. An omelette with a loaf of country bread, a green salad and a bottle of claret would meet with your approval?"

"Nothing could be more French."

"Good. Then tell me what you think of this Château Talbot."

Sophie took the offered glass and sniffed it.

"I can tell you from the bouquet alone that what you have here is not a Château Talbot." She tasted the wine. "This is no château at all but a blend of lesser wines in imitation thereof. Quite agreeable, if one had not paid Château Talbot prices. Your governor has been duped."

"Madame," said Coburn with a laugh, "I shall certainly

obtain my claret from your firm when the war is over. Now shall we have our luncheon?"

All through the meal Coburn told amusing stories of his time as a prisoner in France, of his life in London as a playwright, and of how King George himself had asked him to return to the army to help defeat the Americans. It was only at the end of the meal that the general struck.

"Madame Armonville, I think in your country it is over fruit and cheese that one gets down to business."

"That is correct."

"Then may I be allowed to do so?"

"Of course." Sophie's heart was beating fast. Perhaps Coburn was not a bit mad, as she had first thought, just very cunning.

"Quite frankly, I know all about the New World Trading Co. that I need to know. With you and your friend Carter out of the picture, your business will not survive. I have no illusions that the French government will not find other means of shipping arms to the rebels, and this might not be of great importance—if my colleagues are correct in assuming that General Burgoyne will soon be in Albany. Then, they all believe, with General Howe already having captured your capital of Philadelphia, the rebellion will collapse. I do not make such easy assumptions. Stopping the flow of arms to America is still my objective. You have a cousin in the French secret service I believe."

Voilà. The cat was out of the bag. "I have a cousin . . ."

"His name is Hyacinthe de Marivaux."

She pretended to hesitate, but she knew better than to lie. "Yes, he is my cousin."

"Precisely. A very clever young man, who somehow has access to the most secret dispatches of our ministries of war and foreign affairs concerning British plans for preventing the shipment of French arms to America. Clearly there is a traitor at the highest level of the British government."

Sophie remained silent. She was unsure why he was telling her this, which, indeed, she knew to be true from the letter that Morgan had read to the governor in Martinique.

"I believe," Coburn continued, "that you and your cousin are quite close."

"We have always been friends."

"Exactly. So close friends that, when the French government decided clandestinely to supply arms on a large scale to the Americans, he arranged to turn this trade—and profits—in your direction."

"I don't see . . ."

"So close friends that he would share with you British plans to thwart this trade . . . even the name of his source in the British government."

So that was it! Hyacinthe was indeed clever, too clever to give out the names of his agents in the British government to anyone—ever. She almost laughed but caught herself just in time. Perhaps Coburn was both cunning and a little mad.

"Well?"

What was she to do? If she said she did not know, Coburn would either not believe her, or if he did, her value to him would be greatly reduced. If she said she did know, he would eventually find out that she was lying.

"And if I did have this intelligence and gave it to you?"

"It could never be traced to you. My colleagues know nothing of this matter, of which only the king, Lord North and one or two others are aware."

"But should not this intelligence have a much greater price attached to it than just my release at the end of the war?"

"Madame Armonville, I do not have to bargain with you. I

can have Morgan Carter hanged tomorrow."

He was bluffing of course, but Sophie had no doubt that if Morgan were in the general's hands he would regard his life as of no more importance than that of a fly. Something told her that her only hope with this man was to gamble.

"General Coburn, Morgan Carter is a woodsman of exceptional skill."

"And of what significance is that?"

"It is unlikely that you will be able to recapture him. He is even now, I am sure, well on his way to America."

Coburn leaped to his feet. "Damnation! How did you find out that . . ."

"It doesn't matter. What matters is that the price of the intelligence you want is that I am free immediately to leave for America."

She felt the strange calm of someone who has committed a gravely foolish act, and one that cannot possibly be undone.

"That is quite impossible."

"Why? I am of no use to you, and you yourself said that wars are won by cold-blooded calculation not emotion. I am offering you a very good bargain."

Coburn sat down heavily.

"I would have to have proofs of the authenticity of your intelligence."

"And I would have to have proofs that you would keep your part of the bargain."

Coburn managed to smile. "I see your cleverness extends well beyond a knowledge of wines. I will have to think your proposal over." The general's mind was already far away. "You will hear from me in due course."

For the entire trip back Sophie sat stunned in the carriage, horrified at what she had done. Coburn was bound to find out eventually that she did not know who the British traitor was, and then she would never be freed. They might send her back to prison in England. What had she done?

At the door to the convent a blind beggar squatted on the pavement, his filthy hand extended. There were others in the world with worse troubles than any she had experienced. She reached out with a coin only to have some hard object thrust into her hand. She held it tightly until she reached her cell and then opened her hand: her missing gold earring. The last time she and Morgan had made love in their makeshift cabin on the deck of the *Betsey*, he had removed her earrings along with her clothes. Afterwards she had been able to find only one.

Her message had reached Morgan in Trois Rivières.

CHAPTER EIGHTEEN

The day passed, and the next, and Sophie had no word from General Coburn, nor was there any further sign from Morgan. She had taunted Coburn that Morgan would be well on his way to America, but—thanks to her impetuosity—he appeared to be still in Trois Rivières. Oh, how she regretted having sent that letter! If she had it to do over again she would not have penned those passionate lines declaring her love and complete loyalty. It would have been better that he thought her guilty of betraying him and escaped to America, leaving her to her fate. She would never forgive herself if he were recaptured because of her plea for him to come to her.

The following morning Captain Fontenoy arrived at the convent unannounced. She assumed that he had come to take her to the citadel for further talks with General Coburn—which in the end must reveal that she had no secret information to bargain with.

"No," the captain said, "my only orders from the general are to see that you do not become too bored with your cloistered life. I thought you might like to look in on the preparations being made down on the plains for the ceremony in two days' time, when the governor will give out presents to the various Indian chiefs from their Great Father in London."

"Yes, why not?" said Sophie. Anything to distract her from her fears for Morgan and her own uncertain fate.

"Quite a sight, isn't it," Fontenoy remarked, as they strolled through the parade ground halfway down from the citadel to the river.

A New World Won

It was. She had thought so as a child, and it still seemed to her the grandest sight in Canada: the great parade ground, the Plains of Abraham it was called, where in the course of one day's bloody battle France had lost her New World colonies to England. She could have cried for that, but it did not make any less beautiful the view over the mighty St. Lawrence flowing quietly to the sea, dotted with canoes, its banks etched in the gold of aspens. For one who knew Canada, winter was already in the air.

"Looks as though every tribe from here to Les Grands Portages is represented."

Indeed, every type of tribal dress was to be seen; but the difference Sophie saw, comparing this scene with her childhood memories, was how many of the Indians had squeezed their muscular forms into European coats or parts of old uniforms, how many had looking glasses or other ornaments hanging from cords around their necks. Their world was merging into that of the half-breeds and the voyageurs with shrunken legs and huge shoulders from a lifetime of paddling canoes, all now subjects of His Brittanic Majesty.

Late arrivals from the West were auctioning off the last furs of the season: fox, marten, deerskins, but most of all beaver. In front of lean-tos of birchbark on the edge of the forest, smoke rose from the fires of Indian women preparing food.

"I remember these preparations from when I was a child," Sophie said, "except in those days, of course, the Great Father was the King of France. And then the day after the presents were given out they would all be gone, headed in their canoes back to their lands before the snows came."

And everywhere birchbark canoes of all sizes were being repaired or in the final stages of construction. The air was sweet with the smell of spruce gum being heated for caulking.

That last year, the year before the British had come, she had had her own small canoe. Her brother Antoine, almost a man and already estranged from his father, had taught the eight-year-old Sophie how to use the paddles. It seemed unreal now, like a life of which she had only read in some storybook.

Had she thought that before she saw a tall man in buckskins approaching, still far away, or had the sight of him provoked the thought? Afterwards she could not be sure.

The buckskins were dark and greasy, those of a voyageur; and, as he drew nearer, she first noted a long scar up one side of his sunburnt face that ended in a bare section of scalp, and then that the hand that held the pipe he was smoking was missing two fingers. And then with a gasp and a shudder she recognized the person she had been thinking of that very instant.

"Bonjour, ma soeur."

"Antoine," she at last choked out.

"You know this . . . gentleman?" the young British officer asked dubiously.

"He is my . . . brother."

"I did not expect to see you again," the apparition said.

"Nor I you."

"But here we are, after all these years," and then Antoine turned to Captain Fontenoy with a rather contemptuous look, "and might a bit of privacy between brother and sister be permitted?"

"Well, I suppose so," the captain said uncertainly, retreating back two steps, where he stood shifting from one foot to the other.

"I didn't mean here, captain. My store is just over there. You can be assured I will return Madame Armonville to you as soon as we've renewed our acquaintance."

"Well, all right then. I'll wait outside."

The store that Antoine referred to was the old Chardin warehouse, it too with a carved sign above the door, "J. Smythe", the same she had seen on the riverfront office while being rowed to the Quebec landing from the British warship. Antoine turned a large iron key in the lock and they passed into the cold, dank interior.

"Have a seat there," Antoine said, motioning to a dilapidated leather sofa smelling of mildew, "and I'll light a fire and bring some grog."

Sophie cringed at this new word that the British had coined for rum, a beverage that she disliked in any case.

Antoine worked quietly and quickly. He had always moved with the grace of an animal, Sophie remembered. Why had she so closed him out of her mind all these years? Fear, she supposed, that one day he would turn up. And now she found herself his guest. A fire was soon burning, and two rather dirty glasses had been filled from a bottle of Barbados rum.

"To your health," Antoine said in English, raising his glass.

"*A votre santé.* . . . And who is this J. Smythe?"

She saw in his eyes, in which the newly-lit fire was reflected, that both her points had been made in only three words. She had chastised him for speaking English rather than French, and her use of *votre* rather than *ta* reminded him of the distance between them. One did not in French address a brother in the formal way unless all intimacy had been lost. He understood and was not pleased. Had he in his clumsy way wanted to establish intimacy again? She did not dare. All her senses told her that Antoine had become a hardened, dangerous man.

"My English partner, to the extent of twenty percent, for which he does exactly nothing, except lend me his name. If you're French in Quebec nowadays, and don't have an English partner, you're soon out of business."

There was a silence, as Antoine pondered what to say next. He had always been slow with words. The fire was now burning brightly, and Sophie looked around her, up to the rafters, where every kind of Canadian fur hung: beaver, lynx, wolf and bear, caribou, otter, and deer, mink, marten and fox, the red, the blue and the silver. She knew them all.

"You prosper, then?" Those were Coburn's words aboard *La Bonne Nouvelle*, and she probed for what there might be between this man, now a stranger, and the half-mad English general.

"I survive, Sophie. It is you who prospers. You always did, you always were the favorite."

"I've worked hard for what I have."

"You think I haven't?" He looked gloomily into the fire. "They sure gave you a pretty boy as a guard."

"So you know that I am a prisoner of the British?"

"There's very little that I don't know about what's going on here, even if the governor and his generals don't see fit to receive me. I know for instance that you're now a rich woman. I also know that the governor has offered a thousand pounds for Morgan Carter's capture alive—they must want him alive right bad—or a hundred pounds for his scalp."

Her eyes went automatically to Antoine's partly-bare scalp.

"Yes, that's the work of a scalping knife, but I put my knife between that Ottawa's ribs before he could finish the job."

"What do you want of me, Antoine?" She did not want to hear this kind of brutal talk and could spare him no pity. It was her own life that she must save.

"Some justice at last. Even a bastard deserves that much."

"What are you saying, Antoine? A bastard?"

"Oh, I know what he told you, the old hypocrite: a first wife from Normandy, died of the fever, weeping over her grave in the Quebec Protestant cemetery—you'll find no such grave there. . . . She was Catholic and they weren't married. Neither church would say the words, without the one or the other would change religion. She was one of those girls without dowry or prospects that the king's agents picked up on the streets of Paris and shipped to Canada by the boatload as wives for the French settlers."

Antoine paused and filled his glass, and Sophie's, again. "Hypocrites all, the Huguenots, and as far as that goes the whole tribe of John Calvin. Keep your sins hidden from your own daughter—and your money from your own son.

"And did I not have to make my own way in the wilderness from age seventeen, and now, not even forty and already an old man, my joints frozen up by the cold of Canadian winters, sleeping on the ground, and a thousand miles of paddling a canoe every year. But I can't trust my voyageurs to go without me. The tribes want to trade with me. What happens when I can't make it any more?"

"My father—our father—was a cold man," Sophie said, some of her own deep feelings coming out, and despite her resolve, pity for this man who was of her own blood. "I did not myself bear him any great love. Nor did I ever know any affection from him, whose only care for me was to have a bookkeeper without wages, and then to marry me into some noble family to his own advantage."

She was shocked at what she had just said, what she had just admitted to herself for the first time. "If I had not had my mother . . ."

"I had no mother to stand between me and Jean Chardin." Antoine filled his glass yet again.

"In any case he's dead now, and I have done you no

wrong, Antoine. What is it you want of me?"

"What I should ask for is half your business, which is by rights mine, but I'll settle for eighty thousand livres. With that I could set myself up in the wholesale fur trade."

"And what am I to expect in return for eighty thousand livres, should I ever be free to give them to you?"

Antoine grinned. "You've got a point there. I could get you and Morgan Carter out of Canada. Maybe he can hide, but he can't run. By now every Iroquois from here to Albany knows about the reward."

"Then of what use would your help be?"

"I can arrange a boat for us to Miquelon. I know you can draw on funds there."

"You are proposing this while a British officer stands just outside the door? You're mad."

"Not mad, only bold."

"Yes, you were always that."

"Then it's agreed?"

"Agreed." What else could she say? She could not afford to cut off any corridor of escape, however dubious, however dangerous.

"When I'm ready you'll hear from me. Speak of what I've said to the British and we're all done for. You'll be behind bars, not in any convent; Morgan Carter's scalp—however good a woodsman he may be—likely'll be hanging from some Iriquois warrior's belt; and I'll be back to paddling a canoe for someone else. Now go back to your British gentleman before he becomes suspicious."

Sophie let herself out the door, and Captain Fontenoy came forward to meet her. She did not doubt that Antoine was capable of attempting what he proposed, but was their meeting not too much of a coincidence? Antoine could be acting on the orders of General Coburn, and this was perhaps an attempt to lure Morgan out of hiding.

"I'm afraid I'll have to report this meeting to the general," Captain Fontenoy said when he came up to her. "You say this person is your brother?"

"Half-brother. He wanted money," which was true enough, "but in my present situation . . ."

"Well, if he bothers you again . . ."

"If I were you, captain, I would take great care with Antoine Chardin."

Back at her cell in the convent Sophie at last admitted to herself how bleak her situation really was, a lone woman surrounded by clever and unscrupulous enemies, and the only person she had ever loved in mortal danger—thanks to her own reckless behavior. She lay on her hard bed and wept and then fell into an uneasy sleep. During the night she awoke with the feeling that she was not alone, but when she called Amélie's name there was no answer.

The next morning she found a folded piece of paper on the table by her bed, and when she picked it up a key fell out: "Morgan will be waiting for you at the gate at the end of the garden at midnight, while they all are in chapel. You will not see me again, as I am being sent to a convent far from here. They found one of Charles's letters. God bless you and think of me sometimes. Your Amélie."

Morgan waiting for her at the gate? If a thing seems to be too good to be true, her father had often said, it probably is. She must not become the captive of hope, that cruellest of all torturers. At first Sophie was devestated by the news that Amélie had lost what was probably her only chance to re-find happiness, but then a dark suspicion was born; and for the rest of the day she suffered agonies of indecision. Was this some kind of trick? She even began to have doubts about

Amélie. Was it not strange that her childhood friend was in the very place where General Coburn had decided to have her lodged? What an unworthy thought. To suspect a childhood friend was not, however, so grave a matter as to suspect one's lover—and twice. Oh, Morgan, forgive me that thought!

At last she decided that there was no choice but to follow the directions in the note. At midnight, when the nuns had all entered the chapel, Sophie—knowing that she might be stepping into a trap—put on her cloak and made her way through the darkened garden and felt along the wall until she found the gate, fumbled with the key in a rusty lock; and only with the pressure of both hands was she able to turn it. The gate creaked open a bit, and as it did a hand on the other side pushed it fully open; and she was in Morgan's strong arms once more, enveloped in the male smell of him.

"Oh, Morgan, I fear I have betrayed you by asking that you come to me."

"I can assure you I have not been followed," said that familiar warm voice, "but we musn't stay here."

He locked the gate behind them, and they were soon moving swiftly and silently down the series of stone stairs that led from the upper city of Quebec to the lower town. His hand firmly gripped hers, and how wonderful was the feel of it! Minutes later, without a word having passed between them, they entered a smoky tavern, long and narrow, the benches filled with voyageurs, the tables lined with big pewter mugs of ale.

A place was found for them in an alcove at the back of the tavern, and they squeezed themselves into it, Sophie with her back to the room.

"I'd leave the hood of your cape up," Morgan said. "You'll hear no English spoken in this tavern—only Frenchmen here. The innkeeper's trustworthy, I'm told. At the least, he has no love for the English. Still, there's no point in taking chances."

"How can you talk so calmly?" and they both reached out at the same instant and took each other's hands across the table.

"Because I'll run no risks with your precious self, Sophie Armonville, and that means I have to keep calm and alert to every danger."

"Oh, Morgan, Morgan, are we really together again? Would that this were some tavern in Martinique or France, and all that has befallen us but a dream." She drank in just the sight of him like cool water.

"Alas, it is no dream. How long do you dare be away from the convent?"

"Until coffee is brought in the morning, at least so it has been thus far. Though the sooner I return, clearly the less risk we run. And you, where are you lodged?"

"In a small room beneath the attic of this inn."

"There is much for us to talk about."

"Yes."

But it was difficult to begin. They had, she felt, almost become strangers to each other. Certainly Morgan had changed. In his greasy stained buckskins, with his hair in a pigtail, he looked very much the voyageur. This is the real Morgan that I'm seeing, she thought, and he is so strong and so sure of himself in his own world that I'm a bit frightened of him.

"Sophie . . ."

"Yes?"

"Once before I had to ask your forgiveness, but this time I am so ashamed that I choke on the words."

"You thought that I had betrayed you."

"No, I swear it. For those first few minutes, the worst you

can say of me was that the evidence seemed irrefutable and I could not find an explanation for your innocence, which I so desperately wanted to find. That look I gave you, when they were taking me away on that British warship, must have . . ."

"It broke my heart, Morgan," and she began to cry.

"Say you forgive me."

"Of course I forgive you." She wiped her eyes with the back of her hand. "Morgan, I love you more even than before, but nothing has ever hurt me so much as that look."

"Then how am I to be forgiven?"

"Broken hearts mend, and when they do they can love all the stronger. You are fully forgiven, Morgan, but one thing you must not promise me—that the cause of American independence will never come between us again. That is a promise you could not keep."

"But you will accept my promise that never again will I doubt you in any way."

"That I will accept. Morgan, our love will be even stronger. I promise you that. And now I want you to take me to your small room beneath the attic."

"What? But you said that the sooner you return . . ."

"Morgan, do not dispute with me. You see, I must have you tonight. I simply must. The time has come for me to dare, to put aside all calculation. Perhaps, even, the very danger of it fuels my desire." She had never felt like this before.

"Now what are we to do?" he said, closing the door of his tiny room behind them and taking her in his arms.

"You might begin by removing my earrings."

"I meant what are we to do about . . ."

"We can discuss that afterwards."

What followed was unlike anything Sophie had experienced with Morgan. Naked on a bed as narrow and hard as that in her convent cell, her body turned a rose pink by the glowing charcoal in the brazier that heated the room, she felt a wild desire, as savage as the wilderness that surrounded them. That last reserve, that holding back of something that she had always felt on Martinique, was utterly abandoned.

She drew his mouth to her breasts, showered kisses on his body. Then she drew him down on top of her and opened herself fully to him, her legs locked around his back, her hips turning and twisting in the most wanton fashion until she reached a climax of ecstasy that left her breathless, unable even to cry out.

"Where did such passion arise from?" His voice seemed to come from far away. Some time, she felt, must have passed.

Sophie opened her eyes and looked out through her disheveled hair. "That is the real me, *mon chéri*, who has finally, with your skilled assistance, freed herself from the last modesties of the widow Armonville. I am the new Sophie."

"I look forward to getting to know *la nouvelle Sophie* more fully . . . but first we must get her out of Canada."

"That will be difficult and dangerous. We will have to outwit not only General Coburn but my brother Antoine. Let me tell you all that has happened since we parted, and then you can judge what course would be best."

He listened silently while she told him the whole truth, including every scintilla of fact about General Coburn, La Comtesse de Brieux and Antoine Chardin. Of her own vow to do anything to keep from losing him, however, she said nothing, nor would she.

"I don't think we have any time to spare. Whether they are working together or separately, the general or your half-brother, from what you tell me, may make a move at any moment. My guess is that Coburn is consulting on how to react to your offer. By the way, even though you don't, I do have a good idea of who is the French secret service's informant within the British government, which comes from my time in Paris. It is a minister who has large gambling debts, and only French gold stands between him and disgrace. But we must not bargain with his name, for his continued supply of intelligence is vital to the American cause."

Sophie smiled. "You see."

Morgan grinned sheepishly. "You are right. I have two passions. But we do not need to bargain with General Coburn. We will act before he can call your bluff. There is the grand ceremony tomorrow night, at which the governor will present the customary presents to the various Indian chiefs. Do you think you could get yourself invited?"

"Captain Fontenoy has already proposed to take me."

"Excellent. My plan is going to take steady nerves." He looked at her as though he feared for her but could see no other solution.

"Morgan, when I was alone I was very frightened," she said to reassure him, as she must, for there was no other way of escape, "but now that you are here I am not afraid of anything."

"Then I will tell you my plan quickly, for we must get you back to the convent before dawn."

Never once on the way back up the stone stairs that led to the upper city and the convent did Morgan's hand release Sophie's. Strangely enough, they talked all the way back, like new lovers—and in a way they were—of what was most immediate, the constellations of stars in the clear Canadian night. They found, she from her maritime background, he from his years in the American forests, that between them they could name nearly all. It was something unexpected they shared, and as such was a treasure to Sophie.

"I didn't think, until tonight, that I could love you more. You are adorable." And he kissed her with a tenderness that was far removed from the fierceness of their lovemaking, but perhaps was made possible by it. She left him then, without a word; she could think of none worthy of her feelings, slipped through the garden gate and locked it behind her.

CHAPTER NINETEEN

From the edge of the forest beyond the parade ground and from the other shore of the great river, hundreds of camp fires glowed like constellations of orange-red stars. Nearer at hand bonfires shot up their flames to the sky, dimming the cold white light of the stars that usually dominated the Canadian night. Young braves danced around the fires, their shadows flitting like dark ghosts over the mass of humanity gathered along the river's edge; old chiefs smoked their pipes and rose one by one to deliver their long rhetorical speeches; the governor, in a splendid scarlet coat, sat impassive in a throne-like chair on a raised platform, surrounded by his English generals, French bishops and half-breed interpreters. Among those for whom chairs had been provided were Sophie Armonville and Captain Fontenoy, prisoner and guard.

"To write home about isn't it," said Fontenoy. "Civilization and savagery brought face to face."

"Or one could say two sets of tribal customs," Sophie replied dryly. She had no time for the fatuous observations of Captain Fontenoy. There was too much else on her mind. She had said that she was afraid of nothing with Morgan at her side, but where was he? Soon the governor's speech would begin, then presents would be given out, last of which the kegs of rum. That would be the signal for women and children—and any European man who was not foolhardy—to withdraw.

Then she saw a dark shape, but for an instant out of the corner of her eye, slip through the crowd until it was behind her chair.

"Captain, could you bring me a glass of water? My throat is quite dry."

"Certainly, ma'am," and Captain Fontenoy was quickly away.

"Well done," whispered a voice. Sophie's heart fell. It was Antoine's voice.

"Tomorrow at dawn, at the little dock next to the Smythe canoe shed, once that of Chardin and Co., if you remember where that is."

"I remember." She did not turn her head, not wanting to look into that terribly scarred face in the hellish light of the bonfires.

"You'll have Morgan Carter with you, Sophie?"

"Of course."

"Then you know where he is?"

"Yes."

"And where might that be exactly?"

She feigned a laugh.

"You don't trust me?"

"I trust you to prefer eighty thousand livres to a thousand pounds' reward from the British."

"You've developed a sharp tongue since last I knew you."

Sophie made no reply.

"Well then, till dawn tomorrow," and Antoine was gone as swiftly and silently as he had appeared, proof of a lifetime passed in the wilderness.

Some minutes passed before a figure slipped into the chair beside her, most gracefully for its large bulk, not Captain Fontenoy but General Coburn.

"*Je suis désolé, madame.*"

"What desolates you, *mon général?*"

"That I have let days pass without communicating with you."

"I'm sure you had good reason."

"Governor Carleton, if you can call him good reason."

"And?"

"He has decided you must tell your story in London, that it is far too delicate a matter to be dealt with here."

Sophie turned to face him. Even in the dim light it was clear that he was telling the truth and was embarrassed by it.

"When am I to go?" Sophie said carefully.

"*HMS Greyhound*—you will be familiar with her—sails in two days' time."

"I see."

"I cannot tell you how vexed I am that . . . What the blazes is going on?"

Sophie looked to where the Governor and a half-circle of his dignitaries had been sitting opposite an equal half-circle of Indian chiefs. A British officer was bringing forward a young Iroquois to where the governor sat. The Indian chiefs had risen to their feet, the governor's aide had taken something from the Iroquois's hand, a paper was handed to the governor, who read it quickly and then, to Sophie's astonishment, left the dais on which he had been seated and came straight toward where she and General Coburn were talking. There was fire in his eyes.

"George!" Clearly, Sophie's presence was not even noticed.

"Sir?" General Coburn came quickly to his feet.

"When have you last reported to me on General Burgoyne's campaign?"

"Last week, sir."

"Yet every day you report to me on some of your intrigues that you say will win the war. Well now, sir, by God we may have lost it."

"I don't understand. . . ." His voice trailed off. The ever-composed General Coburn, never at a loss for words, could find none that would serve him.

"Well, I'll tell you straightway. This," and the governor tapped Coburn's shoulder with the rolled paper he held, "is a dispatch in Johnny Burgoyne's own hand. He has been totally and utterly defeated by the rebels at some place called Saratoga, and he, every general, every officer, every soldier of His Majesty's army have surrendered with all their artillery and supplies. Not to speak of wives, dogs, mistresses, camp followers and barrels of brandy and wine."

"I could not have . . ."

"I want you and every general officer in Quebec to report to me at my headquarters as fast as you can round them up, even if it takes till dawn."

"Yes, sir."

"And now I must go back and give my speech. God knows what the Indians will do when they find out that the Great Father in London has sent out a pack of bloody fools to do his business in the New World!"

Sophie Armonville sat alone, dumbfounded and totally forgotten. She stood up and looked about the parade ground. From the edge of the crowd a familiar figure beckoned. Nothing prevented her from simply walking away from the now totally disrupted ceremony and going to her lover.

"Sophie." Once again she felt the comfort of his powerful hand enclosing hers. "What the blazes is going on?"

"There's no time to explain. Just walk away naturally. They won't miss me for some time."

She looked over her shoulder. British soldiers were running here and there, officers mounting their horses. The next instant they were in the shadows of a dark alley and then winding their way down stone stairs to the docks. When they came out onto the wharf, dimly lit by oil lamps, there was no one about, not even a night watchman. Everyone in Quebec was at the ceremony.

"We're in luck," Morgan said, looking around them in all directions. "In an hour we'll be far from Quebec. I have a canoe tied up beneath the wharf. We'll have to climb down that ladder. I'll go first and steady the canoe for you."

As Morgan put his foot on the first rung of a ladder, a figure stepped from behind stacked barrels.

"I thought I told you dawn tomorrow, Sophie."

"Antoine!"

"Trying to run out on our agreement?"

Antoine stepped between Sophie and Morgan, who had frozen with one foot on the ladder.

"Agreement?"

In one swift movement Morgan was back on the dock at her side. Just as quickly Antoine had retreated a few paces, and as he did she caught the flash of the knife that he had drawn from his belt and held by the tip. Morgan froze.

"Antoine, no!"

Sophie knew that the knife in Antoine's hand was as deadly as a pistol in another man's hand.

"All right, Antoine," Sophie said in as calm a voice as she could manage, "we do have an agreement. Your eighty thousand livres will be sent you as soon as we're in Miquelon."

"Yes, but we're going in the morning and I'm going with you."

"I'm not taking any more chances, Antoine. We're leaving now." She dared not enflame him further by speaking the truth: that she did not trust him in the least. He seemed to hesitate.

"The only way you can stop us, Monsieur Chardin," Morgan said, and no one would have guessed from the calm tone of his voice the gravity of the words he spoke, "is by killing me. Then you would at best collect a miserable hundred pounds from General Coburn."

"That's better than eighty thousand livres I'll never see."

"You have my word of honor on it," Sophie blurted out.

"And why should I take that?"

"Men have taken my word on the floor of the Bordeaux exchange for a million livres and never once been disappointed."

Antoine looked deeply into her eyes. "All right. Go then." He put the knife back in his belt. "But deposit the money in my name in Miquelon. I don't want the British to know."

Then he simply turned and walked away into the night.

As frightened as Sophie was, she still paused for a moment to watch Antoine go, feeling some compassion for this man who was of her blood, a man life had treated harshly, yet one who had looked into her eyes and believed her.

Sophie moved the canoe paddle surely and steadily, surprised that she still remembered the wrist movement Antoine had taught her as a little girl. She tried to ignore the pain. The wetness she felt on her palms she knew was from the blood of broken blisters, but that could be dealt with later. Though she was bursting to tell her news, she must keep silent and think only of timing her strokes to those of Morgan kneeling in the stern. Guided by the stars, they were putting Quebec farther behind them with each stroke.

He spoke at last. "How are you holding up, my love?"

"I'm fine," Sophie lied. She was so exhausted she did not know how much longer she could go on. But now that he had broken the silence she would wait no longer. "Morgan, I have precious news for you. General Burgoyne has been defeated by the Americans and he and his entire army taken prisoner. That is what all the commotion you saw was about."

There was no reply from the stern of the canoe, and Sophie guessed that Morgan was overcome with emotion.

At last he spoke. "As soon as we reach shore you must tell me all."

Somehow she managed to continue silently her steady paddle strokes until the dawn began to break. Indeed, a kind of light-headedness came over her, and her arms seemed to move the paddle without effort. Perhaps this was the secret of the voyageurs, who spoke of going into a trance and not even knowing that they had been paddling for twelve or fifteen hours.

"There's a small farm near here," Morgan said, "that belongs to my friends in Trois Rivières. They farm it in the summer but have left it now for the winter. I'm hoping that we can spend the day hidden there. You've seen the canoes astern?"

"No." Sophie turned.

In the first light of day three canoes, large ones, could barely be made out through the mists, far behind them as yet; but if they could see them they could be seen. She would have been overcome with terror but for Morgan's reassuring smile. He did not even seem tired.

"Iroquois, I imagine," he said. "We must quickly put ashore. Luckily, there's more fog ahead."

Her heart in her throat, she marveled at Morgan's navigation. They sailed through the fog right into a creek and up to the dock of the abandoned farmstead that he was aiming for. By the time the sun was up they had climbed into a hayloft, pulled their light birchbark canoe and the ladder up behind them and fallen, utterly exhausted, into the hay.

When Sophie awoke it was late afternoon, and Morgan's shadow from the setting sun fell across her. She rubbed her eyes. He had awakened her she knew not how many hours before to tell her that he was going out to "run a few errands in the forest". She had laughed at that and gone back to sleep, knowing that if he left her it was because she was safe in their hiding place. "Where have you been?" She sat up in the pile of hay in which she had been sleeping

"First tell me all about your news, which is so incredible that I almost dare not believe it."

As she described what had happened in detail, beginning with the young Iroquois messenger breaking into the governor's solemn ceremony, until the moment when Governor Carleton declared that at Saratoga Britain could well have lost the war, the intent frown on Morgan's face gave way to a smile.

"You could not have brought me a finer gift. At the least we will not now lose. A new world has been born, Sophie, and it's ours to win!"

He picked her up and twirled her around the loft.

"Stop, Morgan," she cried out, laughing, "you are making me giddy. Put me down!"

"And were it not for our cannon this victory might not have been. When the war's over they'll erect a statue in Philadelphia to Sophie Armonville."

"Before all those fine things, Morgan Carter, you and I must first escape the British."

"Yes, night is almost upon us, and we'd best not linger here. There's an Algonquian camp nearby, and while you slept I smoked a pipe with them. I found out that those canoes were Iroquois. A thousand pounds alive, you say, Coburn offers?"

"According to Antoine."

"I am flattered. And I am also most grateful for your saving my life. That was a bold thing, indeed, that you did." He took her face in his large hands and looked deeply into her eyes.

"Intuition told me . . ."

"Which I will never again undervalue."

". . . that he did not mean to throw the knife. Thank God I listened to my inner voice, for it was right. But I can tell you that had he . . . I once saw, as a child, Antoine pin a butterfly to a tree at ten paces."

"*Mon Dieu*. That makes me rather weak at the knees."

"And what did you accomplish while I slept?" Sophie replied. What she had done she had done. And she knew that had her stratagem failed, Morgan would have thrown himself at Antoine without hesitation. He did not look weak in the knees to her.

"Well, I did a little shopping for you," and he tossed her a bundle he carried. Inside was a short buckskin dress, greasy and smelling of woodsmoke, and a pair of moccasins.

"Put those on and braid your hair Algonquian-fashion and we'll pass, at least at a distance, for a voyageur and his Indian woman. Now show me your hands."

She held out her blistered hands to him. He knelt beside her, unfolded a little packet of birch bark and smeared her palms with a sweet-smelling ointment.

"Gum from the Canada balsam fir, *Abies balsamea,* another gift from my Algonquian friends and the best remedy for cuts and blisters."

"What a resourceful man I have entrusted my fate to."

They reached Rivière du Loup at dawn the next day. Sophie had insisted on continuing to paddle, her blistered hands wrapped in strips of cloth torn from the lining of her discarded gown. Freedom now was almost within their grasp. Morgan had sent word ahead from Quebec that two persons would pay well for passage to Miquelon, no questions asked. And indeed a boat was waiting for them, a fishing boat in appearance, but its hold filled with contraband furs for trading with the French merchants of St. Pierre and Miquelon. Sophie lay down on the furs, aching in every joint, and went immediately to sleep.

The noise that awakened her was the glad sound of the anchor being raised. Sore all over and her hands swollen and throbbing with pain, yet she felt refreshed. She climbed the ladder to the deck and found Morgan at the rail. The sails of their little craft billowed out, and they had already put some distance between them and the shore.

"Look," Morgan said, putting his arm around her, "three war canoes just arriving. Had you not paddled with me all night, they might have found us still in Rivière du Loup."

"Oh, *Mon Dieu!* Has fate not favored us at every turn?"

"I would give greater credit to Sophie Armonville than to fate."

She said nothing, she was so touched; but she knew that were it not for Morgan she would by now have been on the way to England and prison.

The island of Miquelon and the smaller island of St. Pierre, over which thousands of sea birds wheeled, were but two grass-covered mounds rising from the sea and separated by a few leagues of water only from the long coastline of British Newfoundland.

"And that is all that remains of the once vast empire of French North America, which once ran from Newfoundland to New Orleans. It is sad."

Sophie pulled closer around her the lynx fur that one of the fishermen-smugglers had given her against the cold and damp.

"However small," said Morgan, "for us it means freedom. We are safe, Sophie."

"Safe, I suppose, for now, but I wonder if I will ever feel entirely safe from General Coburn, at least until this war is over, which the victory at Saratoga would apparently assure is no time soon."

"I will be close at hand."

"Will you, Morgan?" She searched his face.

"Except when duty requires me to be absent from you temporarily, and as briefly as possible, you can be sure."

"Which is your way of telling me what?"

"Now that we are free, you know that I must continue on to Philadelphia or wherever the Congress has fled to, in order to clear my name."

"Oh, no." Her heart sank. She had known it would be so, but escaping from Canada had driven out all other thoughts.

"Sophie, I . . ."

"And I suppose I am not to go with you?"

"You did the last time and ended up a captive of the British. The next time you would be taken straight to prison in England, of that you can be sure."

Sophie's eyes filled with tears, but she managed a smile. "Oh, Morgan, I love you so much that I suppose I will endure almost anything. But do not ask me to say that this is fair."

"I will be back to you the instant my duty is done, and never again . . ."

"And never say never, Morgan. Am I to wait for you in Miquelon?"

"That we must discuss."

"In any case, *chéri*," and she put her arms around him, "we are free and, for now at least, together. I will enjoy what I have today and give no thought to tomorrow. I want three things," she whispered in his ear, "and in this order: a hot bath, a good French meal and to make love between clean sheets."

She kissed him, and the lynx wrap fell from her shoulders. "Morgan, I am free in more ways than one. I now have all that I ever wanted. Look at this."

She took from her bosom the little oilcloth packet that, with the purse of coins, was all that she took with her the night of their escape. In it were her company documents and a scrap of paper on which was written, ". . . a life of passion and adventure . . ."

"I wrote that when I was fifteen."

"What does it mean?"

"It means I am the happiest woman on earth. And you will come back to me."

"How could I not come back to the most desirable woman on earth."

As they drew close to St. Pierre, the capital of the tiny colony, indeed its only town, she could not get over the impression that it was a toy town, that she could have reached out and picked up one of the houses. There were only three or four substantial buildings, one of which, made of dark rough stone, with tall mullioned windows, would be the governor's residence. In the harbor there was one warship, a spanking-new frigate flying the fleurs-de-lys of France, and a host of fishing boats. Indeed, the only reason that France had struggled so hard to retain this little foothold in the New World was as a base for its huge cod-fishing fleet.

As soon as they were landed they went, dressed as they were, for they had no choice, to the office of the agent of Chardin and Co. After she had proved her identity the agent, who Sophie knew through correspondence but had never laid eyes on, undertook to find them an inn, clothes and arrange for an audience with the governor, to whom, she told him, they brought important news.

"You may ask what a man of my age and dignity," said the Marquis de Fontevraud, "is doing on this speck of rock in the Atlantic Ocean. Have I been exiled here for the commission of some grave crime? Not a bit of it. A year ago I retired from my last royal appointment and was in attendance at one of King Louis's levees. The king came up to me and said, 'Henri, how long have you been in the service of my family?' I replied, 'Sire, since I was your father's playmate at age five. We fought over a rocking horse.' The king laughed and said, 'What reward would you claim of me?' I said, 'Sire, send me back to Canada,' and the king said, 'If it were in my power you would be governor of all Canada and Louisiana, but alas there remains to me in North America but two tiny islands.' 'Then send me there, that I may die in sight of Canada.' And so the king did."

"Your name is well known, Excellency, to all who ever lived in French Canada," said Sophie. The old man, who wore his white hair to his shoulders and many rings on his fingers, smiled.

"And your name, Madame Armonville, is known to me. I knew your father, and I know of your exploits, and those of Monsieur Morgan, in assisting the government of France in supplying arms to the Americans. I applaud you for it and only wish our king could be persuaded to enter the war directly. His ministers are for it, but young Louis holds back."

"Excellency," Sophie blurted out, unable to contain herself any longer, "we bring news that may cause the king to reconsider. We were captured at sea by the British—not far from here—and held prisoner in Quebec. We escaped only a few nights ago, and just before we did so Governor Carleton received word that General Burgoyne has been defeated by the Americans at Saratoga, and he and his entire army are taken prisoner."

"What's this?" The old marquis rose to his feet.

"With my own ears I heard the governor say that now the war might be lost to the Americans."

"Indeed? The opinion of Carleton is to be respected. He has more sense than the Howe brothers and Lords North and Germaine combined. He will now, no doubt, advise King George to make any concession short of independence to save the American colonies for the crown."

"And that must be prevented," said Morgan, he too rising. "Excellency, is it within your power to get word to Paris quickly of this great American victory? My government will send word, but our vessels are always at risk of being captured by the British."

"That frigate in the harbor sails for the French West Indies in a matter of hours. It is not within my powers as governor of Miquelon to change the captain's orders, but as an old friend of the king I believe my request might be heeded."

"This may be a most momentous day in history!" Morgan exclaimed with almost boyish enthusiasm. His face wore a big grin, and Sophie shared his joy for the success of a country she had never even seen.

"I am well aware of that, young man. Now, it is important that Foreign Minister Vergennes hear directly from you two just what has happened, and particularly the remark of Governor Carleton that Madame Armonville overheard, which cannot be known from any other source."

"I would gladly do so, but I have been summoned back to America," Morgan said, his face showing all too clearly the agony of being torn between two goals.

"And you, Madame Armonville? You travel to America as well?"

She looked at Morgan. He did not speak, though she knew what was in his heart.

"If you give me two hours, Excellency, I shall be ready to sail for France."

As they descended the stone stairs spiraling down from the governor's suite, Sophie studied Morgan's tired and tense face in the cold northern light. There was much going on in his head. At last he spoke.

"You should not have done that."

"And you would never have forgiven me if I had not."

"That is not true, that . . ."

"Let me finish, Morgan. You cannot be in two places at once, but you would do both things that are required for that which you value above all else—the liberty of your country. You would return to Philadelphia to defend yourself, but really to preserve your country's relationship with France. You would also take the word to Paris of the great American victory. Since you cannot do both, it is I who must go to France in your place. And do not deny that you would not forgive me if I did not."

"It is you I value above all else, Sophie."

"I will not put that sentiment to the test by asking you to come with me in the safety of a French warship."

"Now it is you who will not forgive me."

"No, if you are killed or captured and sent to rot in a British prison, I don't think, Morgan," and she took both his hands in hers, "that I will forgive you. I am a woman—thanks in part to you—and must see things from a woman's point of view. You are far more dear to me than America's independence."

He raised her hands to his lips and kissed them.

"Yet you sound as though you are taking leave of me."

"Perhaps you are responsible, in part, for that as well.

Twice the experience of love—I am, quite frankly, speaking of the act of love—has changed me. The first time was in an inn of St. Pierre de Martinique, when Sophie Armonville was freed to be herself as she had always imagined. The second time was in a room above a tavern in Quebec, when I was freed to be not only myself but anything I chose. It is almost frightening, Morgan, to have no limits. Do you understand?"

"I understand. I understood that night."

"Then you will understand that I cannot promise you what you will find when we meet again—if you survive."

His response was to take her shoulders in the iron grip of his two large hands.

"I will, Sophie Armonville, come to you as quickly as this matter of honor—as you say in France—will allow. If by then you, so free that you have taken another in my place, tell me that all is over between us, I will tell you that it is not and overturn all that has taken my place."

"And I will pledge you this . . ." She smiled at him ambiguously, for now she was not taking the advice of Odette Phillipeau to an inexperienced woman—which had brought her much grief. Now she had on her own earned the right to speak as the calculating mistress who meant to keep Morgan against any and all odds, including his sacred American cause. ". . . I will get the word to Paris as fast as any man, and if you come quickly to me, you will have your chance to prove what you say. And now I must go to my agent and arrange the transfer of eighty thousand livres to Antoine Chardin."

"You mean to do it, then."

"I gave my word of honor, did I not?"

CHAPTER TWENTY

The day dawned cold and clear, the sky a burnished silver. From the tall windows of her *rive gauche* hotel apartment, Sophie looked out on the empty quays, the dark mass of Notre-Dame cathedral and the delicate tracery of bare trees etched against the sky. All Paris still slept this New Year's Day. A new day, a new year, perhaps even a new era. Before this day was over it might be known whether this new era was to be born. There was much to do, and she was glad for it. There would be less time to brood again over those questions for which she had no answers. She crossed the room and pulled the bell cord beside her bed.

"Bonjour, Odette."

"Bonjour, Sophie, et bonne année."

It had taken some effort to persuade Odette that the relationship of mistress to servant was over. Sophie had told her straightforwardly that she considered them both to have been through enough to consider themselves women of the world—and friends. The fact that one performed certain duties and the other paid certain sums was not to the point.

"And a happy New Year to you. You have made your resolutions?"

"Yes," Odette said, putting the tray of café au lait and croissants down on the table and looking up at Sophie. "I have resolved not to play the fool this year." And she turned to hide the tears that had sprung to her eyes.

Poor Odette. What would have happened to her if Sophie had not arrived in Paris when she did.

"*Et toi,*" Odette said as she began to lay a fire in the grate, "what resolutions have you made?"

"I . . ." Sophie thought over the most tumultuous year of her life, from that New Year's réveillon at the Comtesse de Brieux's in Martinique to the stormy crossing of the Atlantic and all that had happened since her arrival in Paris. She had done nothing she regretted, would have changed nothing that she had done. Yet how joyfully the year had begun to have ended with her separated from Morgan, not knowing his fate or the future state of their relations.

"Madame, what is it?"

Now there were tears in her own eyes. Odette came to Sophie and put her arms around her.

"Would it help, Sophie, to tell me what it is that has been troubling you?"

"Yes, yes, it would. It began a month ago, when I arrived at La Rochelle. . . ."

Had it been only a month ago? And what momentous things had happened since. Those who watched a French frigate slide into the harbor of La Rochelle in the last days of November, 1777, would have been astonished to learn that it had crossed the Atlantic through foul weather and heavy seas for the sole purpose of bringing a young woman to France with a message that could change the course of history.

Sophie Armonville stood at the warship's rail, pale and haggard. Four weeks and more of pitching and rolling, almost constant seasickness, and lack of sleep, had left her weak and numb, with no thought but for putting her feet on dry land and then finding a soft bed and clean sheets. But even in her wretched condition she felt a thrill at seeing her native land again, just as the captain of the ship that had brought her to France for the first time—to a marriage that was not to be— had said he always felt. His name? D'Apremont, was it? . . .

What a long time ago that had been.

"We could have used this fair weather and calm sea a bit earlier, couldn't we?" Captain de Neville had come up beside her.

"Well, at least it's all behind us. I'll be eternally grateful to you, captain. I only hope that you do not have any difficulties as a result."

"I'll have some explaining to do at the Ministry of Marine," the captain said with a smile, "as to why I'm not in Guadaloupe."

He was an older man than d'Apremont—yes, that was the name—and surer of himself, not likely to be intimidated by his superiors' dismay at his having disobeyed orders. He had not hesitated to follow the command, for such it was, of the Governor of Miquelon, knowing the old marquis to be a friend of the king. Still she—and Morgan—owed Captain de Neville a great deal.

"In a few days time, I will be able to explain the importance of my mission to your minister, captain, should that be necessary."

De Neville had not demanded to know what message she carried nor had she offered to explain. Morgan had asked that the news be taken directly and exclusively to the senior of the three American commissioners in Paris.

"Captain de Neville, could I ask one final favor of you?"

"It is for you to command."

"If one of your officers could hire a carriage for me while I see my bankers. I leave for Paris as soon as my business is done—and I have washed my hair."

Much later than she had expected the carriage rolled up to the entrance of the villa in Passy, which she discovered was a suburb of Paris, and not some neighborhood within the walls. Her driver, a lad from La Rochelle, had no knowledge of

A New World Won

Paris nor did she; and they had become lost time after time.

There was a guardhouse, with a lantern hanging from it, and she remembered with some trepidation the difficulty with which she had talked her way into that fort outside Bordeaux, to warn Morgan of his impending arrest. Well, she was a very different woman now.

"My instructions are clear," the guard said to the carriage driver, his tricorne hat pulled down over his eyes, his staff, which would have been defense against nothing more than a stray dog, held up spear-like in one hand, a lantern in the other.

"There's no admittance here after sundown without I know the visitor by sight and name, or the Doctor has expressly told me who I'm to expect."

Sophie drew aside the curtain. "He's expecting me," she said in a voice warm with intimacy.

The guard thrust his lantern through the carriage window and assured himself that the only passenger was a handsome young woman.

"Well, I don't know you, but you do have something in common with other of the Doctor's late night visitors, except you're prettier. So I suppose it's all right then, him still being up. You'll find him in his study. I imagine you'll know where that is."

"Of course." This brazen falsehood surprised even her.

The carriage rolled on down a tree-lined alley into a courtyard with a large house on either side; but a light burned in only one, in a second-story window.

"You're expected?" the night porter said, with the weary look of one who has learned to expect callers of all sorts at any hour.

"Of course."

"And know the way?"

"Naturally."

The porter sighed with relief. He would not have to show her up and could resume his nap.

Sophie made her way with seeming confidence up the marble stairs and down the hall toward the light that came from an open door.

She stood fascinated for a moment before the tableau. An elderly man, well known to her from engravings, slept in a plush armchair before a desk piled high with papers, his double chin resting on his chest, his extraordinarily large head framed by long wisps of gray hair. Reading glasses had slipped down his nose, and one hand still held a goose-quill pen that had paused in mid-sentence. The disorder of papers flowed from the desk to adjoining tables, a whole archipelago of document-islands.

"Dr. Franklin," she said softly. The light snoring continued. And then louder, "Dr. Franklin."

The eyes that opened were immediately alert. A forefinger pushed the glasses up.

"Then it is true after all."

"Sir?"

"That there is a heaven where one is ministered to by angels. You will assure me that I have passed, despite my sins, to that other side where time gives way to eternity?"

"No, sir. You are in Passy, and it is a quarter past one in the morning of the second day of December, 1777."

The old man took a watch from a waistcoat pocket. "Well, that seems to be true enough. Then who are you, my angel? For you are certainly that."

"In a sense, for I bring tidings . . . from America."

The man behind the desk drew himself up, now totally awake.

"Which are?"

"That the British . . ." Sophie's voice broke with emotion

and fatigue. ". . . that General Burgoyne and his entire army have been defeated at Saratoga by General Gates and taken prisoner."

"Taken . . . all?"

"Yes, sir."

"Whoever you are, madame, can you assure me this is true?"

"I can indeed, Dr. Franklin, and am prepared to present you my proofs in detail."

"Then, at long last . . . I had almost despaired. But now . . . why now, if this is true, almost anything is possible."

"It is true. My name is Sophie Armonville, and I have been a prisoner of the British in Quebec but escaped. I heard with my own ears . . ."

Sophie felt her legs begin to give way beneath her and grasped the edge of the desk to keep from falling.

"I must sit down."

Franklin was on his feet in an instant and moved around the desk with surprising agility to help her into a chair.

"Please forgive my lack of courtesy in letting you stand there. You are ill, madame?"

"No, but very tired. I have come all the way from La Rochelle with pauses only to change horses. And then it was not an easy crossing of the Atlantic . . ."

"Shall I ring for some hot tea, and perhaps some biscuits with a little butter and jam?"

"That would be heavenly."

When the tea arrived Franklin pulled up a chair opposite her and crossed his legs encased in white stockings and blue velvet breeches that matched his coat with silver piping.

"Well, well. So you are the famous Madame Armonville, my partner in this desperate enterprise to break the chains that bind America to the British crown. When I heard of your capture by the British I was most downcast, and to see you here, and so beautiful . . . Why, if we have beat Burgoyne at Saratoga, you can take much of the credit, you and Carter, though the French accuse him of some crime."

"What crime?" She put down the teacup that clattered in her hand.

"Oh, missing monies and such, from the time he was American agent in Paris, before we had three commissioners here—two too many, if you ask me. But I turn a deaf ear to the French complaints. When large sums are spent in secret there are bound to be large temptations—or misunderstandings, if you will. What is important is that you and Carter got the French arms to General Washington. That's all that counts. But enough of that. It's your story I want to hear."

Over several cups of strong tea, which greatly revived her, Sophie told Benjamin Franklin everything that had happened from the day that she met Morgan at a wine festival in Bordeaux until the Marquis de Fontevraud escorted her aboard a French naval frigate off the coast of Canada; everything that is except her feeling for Morgan. But perhaps he knew. Certainly she had made no secret of it. By the time her story was finished the teapot was empty and Dr. Franklin's blue velvet waistcoat was covered with crumbs.

"What a story! Would that I were young again and could have had such adventures in your company. But I am old and must spend my days trying to persuade Foreign Minister Vergennes and Undersecretary Gérard that, although we cannot win battles we will win the war, and that France would be wise to join us in the victory. As you can imagine, I have had scant success. But now, madame, you have brought me a new deck of cards, and although I hold trumps this time, I must play my hand carefully. . . . But I am forgetting your exhausted state and keeping you from well-deserved sleep."

"No, please go on. Now that my mission is done I can sleep all next day if I wish, but to talk with you on a night such as this—that is something that one knows only once in a lifetime."

"Well then, if you really want to hear an old man's ramblings . . . The news that you bring has not reached Paris yet from any other source—although it must within the next few days—but it may have reached London. If so, the British will even now be preparing a new peace offer, a much more generous one, but still withholding full independence. Many in Congress will be tempted to accept, but this would be a great mistake. For now—if I play my cards right—we will soon be fighting the British shoulder to shoulder with France. But to win French support before the British can cause mischief, I must play my hand quickly and secretly.

"I have never put much stock in secrecy. From the other commissioners I receive harsh criticism for not taking sterner measures to root out spies among our staff of secretaries and servants. There is at least one British spy on our staff, and no doubt a French one as well. This has not bothered me overmuch. At least both the French and the British—when they send emissaries to me to make peace offers—learn that in public and private, and to both sides, I say the same thing. Now, however, there is great need for secrecy.

"For a few days—at most—I have a piece of intelligence, thanks to your brave efforts, that I share with no one else in France. Now is the time when I might convince Vergennes, and through him the king, that the moment has come for France to throw in her lot with America. Once the other two commissioners learn of what you have told me—for I must say to you that one lacks sound judgment and the other even a sound mind—it will become much more difficult to steer a right course. If only I had more money! The Congress gives us a pittance, and my colleagues refuse to let me spend a penny without endless haggling."

"Dr. Franklin, what you have called my 'assistance' to the American cause has made me a rich woman. Whatever you may need I am able to provide."

"I would for shame refuse your offer, Madame Armonville, were the stakes not so high. But as it is, you are, indeed, the angel who comes to me at the moment when all that is at stake is upon the table. I gratefully accept. Indeed, I would ask one other—and important—favor of you. . . ."

Sophie Armonville did not sleep through the day in the luxurious hotel on the left bank of the Seine that Dr. Franklin had recommended to her, but awoke at noon, refreshed and ravenously hungry. Her duty was done and she had not a care in the world but the very large one that the only man she had ever loved was not only in danger but considered both by the American Congress and the French government to be a scoundrel and a cheat. She did not believe it, and Dr. Franklin did not care . . . but she had so little knowledge of the world outside that of commerce. Because a man cared deeply for her, and she was sure of that, did not make him an angel—and she smiled at Franklin's awakening and calling her that—but what she could not accept was that Morgan had lied to her, if he had. Their relations would then be built on sand. No! It was not true.

A knock on the door announced a maid bringing her breakfast and a large official-looking envelope. The Undersecretary for Foreign Affairs would receive her at four o'clock at his offices in the ministry. As she ate her breakfast from a tray in bed, Sophie read over several times the copy she had made of the letter introducing her to Gérard, which Franklin had written in the small hours of the morning in his study in the Paris suburb of Passy. She would have to appear before Gérard in a less-than-elegant dress acquired in St. Pierre de Miquelon, but perhaps that would lend her story plausibility. She looked forward with some apprehension to her meeting with one of those haughty aristocrats who knew so well how to make the bourgeois feel their inferiority.

In fact Undersecretary Gérard could not have been more gracious, kissing her hand and offering her a seat on a silk-covered sofa in his elegant office. He pulled up a chair opposite her and crossed his legs, very much like Dr. Franklin, and listened intently to her story.

When she had finished Gérard put down the gold letter opener with which he had been toying and crossed his hands on his knee.

"Well, madame, this is indeed splendid intelligence. And my good friend Franklin was well-advised to have you, who are quite unknown in Paris, bring the news directly to me and not attempt himself to see either me or the Comte de Vergennes. The speed of your crossing gives me some hope that we may have some days to work together before all the world knows of this great British defeat. I also approve of Dr. Franklin's suggestion that you might provide us with a discreet meeting place."

"I have made inquiries," Sophie said, "and have been told I may immediately take possession of a small château in the forest of Versailles which is available for lease."

"Excellent. Since the Comte de Vergennes must reside at Versailles with the king, that will be quite convenient. I will leave immediately to see my minister and give him your good news. He will, of course, wish to see Dr. Franklin as soon as possible. Do you think the château could be available as early as tomorrow?"

"I am told so. It is fully furnished."

"We must be careful of servants."

"I will see that none are present except my personal maid, whom I will choose carefully."

"Splendid, Madame Reynaud."

"Sir?"

A smile broke out on the lean aristocratic face beneath perfectly powdered and pomaded hair.

"We must give you a new identity. The name of Sophie Armonville is well known in France."

"It is?"

" 'The heroine of the American Revolution' I believe she is called in certain circles. No, you are Madame Reynaud, a wealthy landowner of the *haute bourgeoisie,* just returned to France for the first time in years from your plantation in the West Indies. You must, of course, avoid the company of any Creoles in Parisian society who could expose our little deception."

Sophie laughed. Her life of adventure was not yet over.

"Well, madame, I will not detain you any longer. I must go straightway to Versailles."

"Sir, may I ask you one question before I leave?"

"Of course."

"It is rumored that my business partner, Morgan Carter, is suspected of some fraud while he was American agent in Paris. Is there any truth to this rumor?"

Gérard raised an eyebrow. Did he know that Morgan was more than her business partner? Quite possibly, since she had lived openly with him in Martinique.

"Not a suspicion, madame, but sure knowledge. He was given a loan, a large one, for the purchase of weapons and supplies for the American army, in fact the funds with which your enterprise was started. A substantial amount—500,000 livres to be exact—was never deposited. Subsequently, our spies in London discovered that Morgan Carter had deposited the money there under the name of William Bertram, a pseudonym he has used."

"I see."

"In your partnership with this man, I would advise you to keep very strict accounts."

"And should he return to France?"

"He would be arrested and made to return the monies he has misappropriated. For my part I would rather see him back in Martinique, continuing the supply of arms to America, but the treasury is not so lenient. You see, the king himself advanced these funds, and His Majesty is deeply affronted that a man who calls himself a patriot would have betrayed his trust in such a way."

During Sophie's long recitation of what had befallen her since her return to France, she and Odette had been sitting on the rug in front of the fire like two schoolgirls.

"So now you know the cause of my sadness."

"I would not care what my man had done if I loved him," Odette said heatedly.

"To love a man you must also trust him."

Odette winced. She had come to France with the dowry Sophie had given her and high hopes of making an advantageous marriage and advancing her station in life. But she had aimed too high. Odette had married a member of the petty nobility with gambling debts, who had spent her dowry and then deserted her. Sophie had found her on Christmas Eve, when she dined at the Paris mansion of one of the great noble families. She was working there as a maid. The alternative for a Martiniquaise girl with no money was prostitution. When Sophie left the dinner she took Odette with her, and it was then that their friendship really began: two women who had learned to count only on their own wits.

"I deserve your rebuke, Sophie."

"It was not meant as such. I speak only for myself when I say I must trust the man I love."

"Perhaps what you were told was not true."

"I can only hope so," Sophie said, without much conviction. "Now we must get ready. The Comte de Vergennes and Dr. Franklin are expecting to dine at our residence at half past noon."

As Odette was helping Sophie to dress there was a knock at the door.

"Ah," said Odette, "they have begun to arrive for their *étrennes*." These were the New Year's presents that every messenger, porter, postman and delivery boy in Paris expected to receive.

But when Odette returned it was with a large bouquet of yellow flowers.

"Madame, a messenger has just delivered these for you. There was no note. But they are beautiful," Odette said, "and to think, blooming at this season."

Sophie took the flowers from Odette and examined them: winter jasmine, *Jasminum nudiflorum*.

The last time it had been a gold earring. Her deliberate ambiguity when they had parted on Miquelon had been answered with equal subtlety. But that mattered not at all, nor did her boast that he would have to rewin her. All that mattered was that Morgan Carter was in Paris!

CHAPTER TWENTY-ONE

Sophie would sit for a moment on one of the chairs covered in powder-blue velvet that lined the wall of the villa's foyer, rise and pace the room, then come to rest again on a chair. Her body was as restless as her mind. For nearly an hour she had waited, while behind the doors of the study Dr. Franklin conferred with Foreign Minister Vergennes and Undersecretary Gérard. Would they emerge smiling, with the news that a treaty of alliance between France and America had been agreed on? It seemed likely. But all she could think of was that Morgan was not with her to hear the news for which he had waited so long and impatiently. *Mon Dieu,* where was he and why had he communicated only with a bouquet of flowers? Did he realize that he was in danger of arrest?

She let her eyes wander over the rich decoration of the light-filled room, with its carved woodwork in white and gold, in which was set a series of paintings of gods and goddesses and nymphs sporting in the sea. The house that she had taken was as elegant as it was small, so small that she could hear Odette washing the luncheon dishes in the kitchen. This jewel of a house, set behind a high wall in the forest of Versailles, had been a gift of the late king to Madame de Pompadour, and their favorite trysting place. Sophie was saddened by the thought that all love is fleeting. Her eyes returned to the round marble table in the center of the room, on which a spray of winter jasmine stood in a crystal vase.

When the door of the study opened, she searched the faces of the three men for the answer to her question. They did not seem elated, as she had hoped. Then Gérard came toward her, while Franklin and Vergennes paused in the doorway, talking earnestly.

"Then it is not settled?".

"I fear not." Gérard shrugged. "Every detail is agreed on, but still the king hesitates. My minister saw him privately this very morning. The king knows that an alliance with America means war with England and recalls that when the late king went to war with England, only a few short years ago, France lost Canada and our colonies in India. He fears, were there a similar result this time, history would judge him harshly."

Comte de Vergennes broke off his conversation with Franklin and crossed the room, resplendent in white wig and court dress. Sunlight glittered in the gold and silver threads of his embroidered coat and the diamonds of a decoration pinned to a wide red ribbon across his chest. He bowed and kissed Sophie's hand.

"Madame, I must beg to take my leave. I join the other ministers at the palace to present our New Year's greetings to Their Majesties. Again I apologize for presenting myself at an informal meal dressed like this. And an excellent meal it was, made the more enjoyable by the knowledge that you prepared it with your own hands."

"*Merci, Monseigneur.*"

"And I'll tell you a little secret. When Louis the Fifteenth visited Madame de Pompadour here, he would often send away the servants and cook supper himself." The minister's eye fell on the vase of flowers. "Ah, I see you share something else with royalty. When I went to Queen Marie Antoinette's apartments this morning—where Their Majesties were breakfasting—to receive the king's instructions, there were flowers just like these on the breakfast table."

"Winter jasmine." She had meant to add the Latin name,

but a rush of emotion choked off the words.

"Ah, that's what they are. Well then, till the next time, for I fear there must be a next time."

"And a next and a next and a next, if necessary," Franklin said quickly. "You will find that I will not lose heart, Excellency."

When the Frenchmen had departed, Franklin turned to Sophie. "I would not have them see it, but today I must admit to discouragement. When you brought the news of Saratoga, I thought within a few days . . . Might I sit with you for a few minutes and rest, while we talk of more pleasant things. These intense discussions with Vergennes exhaust me. Perhaps we might even test a glass of cognac."

When she had finally seen Franklin off at the door, Sophie went to the vase of winter jasmine and stroked the flowers with her hand.

"Oh, Morgan, Morgan, have we not done enough? Let us go away together and leave this new world to give birth to itself. It has brought us nothing but separation and mistrust."

But first she must find Morgan, and now she thought she knew where.

"Odette, see if you can find the driver, and have him bring my carriage around."

Sophie began to appreciate the vastness of Versailles as she was driven along the seemingly endless iron fence to the entrance to the royal nurseries. Here Morgan had worked as botanist to the king, and here winter jasmine had been cut this morning for the queen's breakfast table. It proved nothing, but she knew instinctively that she would find him here.

The carriage gate was closed, but a smaller gate for those on foot stood ajar. There was no one in sight, not even a guard at the gate. Perhaps the thousands who worked at Versailles had all gathered in the courtyard of the palace to receive their New Year's gifts in the name of the king.

"Wait for me here," she said to the driver, getting down from the carriage. "I can't say how long I will be."

Inside, alleyways lined with huge trees seemed to stretch to the horizon, with magnificent fountains in the distance sending up jets of spray. Straight ahead was a long vaulted building, which would be the Orangerie that Morgan had told her about, a hothouse itself the size of a palace.

The scale of everything was overwhelming. Full grown palm trees lined the walls inside the Orangerie, and the air was heavy with the scent of orange blossom from hundreds and hundreds of potted trees bearing both blossom and fruit. But there was not a person in the vast hall. Arches led to other rooms, made mostly of glass, where various kinds of flowers were being forced into bloom.

One room, warmer and damper than the rest, was filled with tropical plants. It was as though she were back in Martinique. And there, in the midst of this jungle, in a leather gardener's apron, pruning knife in hand, stood Morgan Carter. She marvelled at that handsomeness that she had heard remarked on the day they had first met at Château Ivran.

He stared at her in disbelief, and when he spoke all he said was, "Sophie," and that in a barely audible voice.

"Morgan."

She wanted, above all things, to run into his arms; but she had said proud, hard things that day they parted in Miquelon. She had said that he would have to re-win her, in her anger at his leaving her. But now it didn't matter, yet she could not bring herself to fly to his arms. Worst of all, he seemed to read what was in her mind; and he made no move toward her, as if he were not allowed.

"How did you know where to find me?" he said at last.

"The same flowers you sent me this morning you also cut for the queen's breakfast table."

"How could you possibly . . ."

"Le Comte de Vergennes, who just dined *chez moi,* saw them there."

"The Foreign Minister of France just dined with you?"

"Pourquoi pas? Il admire les jolies femmes."

Morgan laughed. The tension eased a little.

"You must have an interesting story to tell, Sophie."

"And so must you. You know that there's an order out here for your arrest."

"And in America. That is why I came back here. It is only here that I can prove my innocence."

"And me, Morgan," she said, anger instantly rising in her, "did you not come back here for me?"

Tears sprang to Sophie's eyes, and she stamped her foot in frustration at having let herself cry.

"Of course I came for you," he blazed forth as angrily as she. "Unless I prove my innocence how can I ever be with you openly. That is why I sent the jasmine, to let you know that I was here and well. Even after I discovered where you were—which was no easy task—I dared not visit you. Why, if it were not for you I would have told the government of France and those *imbéciles* in the Continental Congress to go to hell and gone off to practice botany in Brazil or Sweden or wherever."

Morgan was flailing the air with his pruning knife, and now it was Sophie who laughed. She wiped away her tears and came to him and kissed him then, but on the cheek and with lips tightly closed. It was not going to be all that easy to put things back the way they were those days and weeks after they had first fallen in love, but she disdained any relation with Morgan than was less than that.

"Come, let us sit on that bench there," she said, "and tell each other our adventures."

By the time they had recounted to each other what had befallen them since they had parted on St. Pierre and Miquelon, the sun, on this short New Year's day, was low in the sky. For her part Sophie said nothing about having driven herself to exhaustion and the verge of illness to bring to Franklin—on Morgan's behalf—news of the great American victory. She did not want Morgan's sympathy, only his undivided love.

No doubt Morgan too had passed over in silence hardships he had endured in America, but one he did not. He was embittered at his treatment by the Secret Committee of the Congress. After all that he had done for his country, he was accused, on the basis of anonymous information, of having embezzled a half million livres; and all his protestations of innocence were brushed aside. Had he not slipped away and taken ship for France, he would have been jailed. One thing, however, he had learned. His accuser was not Philip Byrd, but an American, resident in Paris, and most likely a member of Benjamin Franklin's entourage. Whoever he was, Morgan meant to unmask him.

"Morgan, do you swear to me there is no truth whatsoever to this charge against you?"

"Must I swear to you?" he replied in an angry voice, his eyes flashing. "Is my having said so not enough?"

Sophie blushed with shame, but she had her own resentments.

"Morgan, you should know that the Undersecretary of the French Ministry of Foreign Affairs told me that a spy of theirs has discovered the missing money in a London bank account under the name of William Bertram, a name he said you had used for secret matters."

"*Sacrebleu!* Is that your evidence?"

He withdrew his hand that had just, tentatively, touched hers, and stood up. He seemed to tower above her, shaking with rage. Why had she said such a thing, but then why was he in such a temper if what she had said was not true?

"Yes, it is true that I used that name from time to time, but I swear—yes, I swear to you—that I have taken not one sou from the monies that were given to America by the French government. I also swear to you that if someone did take sums from what was entrusted to me and deposited them in London, I will find out who it is and give him every cause to regret it."

"*Pardons-moi,* Morgan." Sophie exclaimed, getting to her feet and taking his hands in hers. "Of course I believe you. It is jealousy and fear that makes me behave as I do. Always I fear that in the end my rival—the American cause—will take you from me forever. Even now, should you prove your innocence, would you not fly back to America to present your proofs? And then what must I expect? That your patriotic duty requires you to go fight with Washington's army and get killed for your cause? Oh, this *maudite* war!"

She was crying now and heedless of her tears. Now he did take her in his arms and held her close.

"No man ever loved a woman more than I love you. And this I swear to you, Sophie Armonville, that in the end I will be entirely yours, no matter what."

"Then I must believe you, *mon amour.*" She was shaking with sobs that had been long suppressed. All of the challenges that she had thrown up to him on the hour of their parting in Miquelon were now revealed as bluff. She was his and always would be.

"And now you must go," he said. "It is growing dark, and the friends here who are hiding me will soon be returning, tipsy with wine, from the banquet that they organized following the presentation of New Year's gifts. I dared not go with them for fear of being recognized. It is only for that reason that you found me here."

"That and fate, which I truly believe brought us together. When will we meet again?"

"Send Odette—let me see—every evening at nine, to the place in the Tuileries gardens where there is a statue of Pan. At the least we can exchange messages until things become more clear."

"I shall pen a reply within the hour of having your letters. I have many things to say to you that today my confusion and emotion kept me from saying."

"Then may we treat, as some small comfort, our correspondence as a kind of courtship?"

Ah, Morgan Carter. Once again he understood a woman's heart. She wanted to be wooed back.

"Versailles, 2nd Jan., 1778

"Ma chère amie,

"I could not express to you then, and cannot even now—with pen, ink, paper and leisure at my disposal—find the words to tell you my feelings when you appeared, pale and silent, in the greenhouse door. My mind leapt back to that fateful day at Château Ivran when our eyes first met and I knew . . . what? . . . to that morning at Château Marivaux when we stormily discussed the matter of American independence, which brought us together then and seems since destined to draw us apart, to that other morning on Martinique when you said, 'Well then . . .' and tossed aside your nightgown.

"You gave me time for such reflections yesterday as you paused and then came to me with slow hesitation. I knew then not that I had lost you, but that I might lose you, a possibility that I had never before contemplated.

Sophie, do you understand me?—no, I know that you do—but give me time to prove myself and the benefit of every doubt, for I may need it.

"Yours,
"Morgan."

"Paris, 3rd Jan., 1778

"Mon cher ami,
"Your letter—and would that it were longer, but I understand your hesitancy in saying more—touched me deeply. I, too, at that moment when we first saw each other again yesterday in the Orangerie, felt all that had gone before between us, both the bitter and the sweet. Give you time? You will have all my patience and the benefit of every doubt, and it may be that I will be obliged to ask the same indulgence of you. Now, let us get about removing that impediment that keeps us apart, the proving of your innocence.

"Yours,
"Sophie."

"Versailles, 4th Jan., 1778

"Ma chère Sophie,
"Help me to prove my innocence? Now that I am here I hardly know where to begin. I am too well known in Paris to move about freely, and certainly I cannot approach Franklin's entourage. Why then not throw away my poor tarnished reputation—I know what I have done for my country and what I have not—and fly with you to some paradisical spot where we may live and love together? Will you?

"Yours,
"Morgan."

"Paris, 5th Jan., 1778

"Monsieur,
"No, sir, you may not throw away your honor for me. Do not think that I am not tempted to fly with you 'to some paradisical spot where we may live and love together'—greatly tempted—but I will see this thing that we began together finished together. I, too, have a sense of honor; and to tell you the truth I have myself become something of a fanatic for the cause of liberty.

"While I will not fly away with you, I do desire most passionately that you come to me. If you will, you will find waiting tomorrow evening at nine not a piece of paper with my ineloquent words upon it but myself. There will be, as well, supper waiting in my retreat in the forest of Versailles.

"Yours,
"Sophie."

"*Sophie, je t'assure,* you have never looked so beautiful."
"Thank you, Odette."
Sophie looked at her image in the cheval glass and could but agree. What she had been through since leaving Martinique had left her slimmer and paler, which went well with rouge and powdered hair. This was not Sophie Armonville, widow of Bordeaux, but the mysterious Madame Reynaud, wealthy Creole landowner, who had just invited her lover to her hideaway, once that of a king's mistress. Was this not indeed "a life of passion and adventure?"

She saw Odette watching her in the mirror and blushed deeply. The girl knew perfectly well that Sophie, so long separated from Morgan, was wild with anticipation for what this night would bring.

"There's someone at the door," Odette said. Shortly she

returned with an envelope.

"No, not that," Sophie whispered to herself, "not that he is unable to come." She tore open the envelope.

"Passy, 6th Jan., 1778

"My dear Madame Reynaud,

"I blush that once again, and at short notice, I must ask you to come to my aid. What you have done so far can never be repaid, so I console myself with the thought that you might advance one more sum to a bankrupt. A meeting of some importance, quite unexpected, has been proposed, and of such a nature that I feel I must keep it from my fellow commissioners.

"Could you extend your good will yet once more, and provide your residence at Versailles for the purpose of my meeting a gentleman tonight at half past eight, myself arriving a few minutes earlier? My presumptuousness having been taken to this length, I do not shrink even from saying that unless I hear to the contrary I will assume that you will be in residence this evening.

"Your obedient servant,
"B. Franklin."

CHAPTER TWENTY-TWO

Franklin came up the lamp-lit steps slowly, leaning on his ivory-handled cane. It seemed to Sophie that he had aged in the little more than a month since their dramatic first meeting. That night he had been fired with an optimism that had gradually faded as the prize of an alliance with France stayed always just beyond his reach.

"My dear," Franklin said, bending to kiss her hand, "were it not for age and infirmity I would be down on my knees begging your forgiveness for the impertinence of forcing my presence on you like this."

"You will never impose your presence on me, Dr. Frankin, as it will, whatever the circumstances, always be welcome."

"You are graciousness itself, and radiantly beautiful this evening, if I may be allowed to say so."

"Why, thank you."

"But I am used to being received by two lovely women. Where is your charming West Indian accomplice in our little deceit?"

"Odette? I have sent her on an errand, but she should return in time to serve refreshments to you and your guest."

Odette's errand was to gain admittance to the royal nursery and tell Morgan that she would not be able to keep her rendezvous with him. She could not refuse Franklin's appeal for aid, but only with the greatest effort could she hide her frustration at her plans being thwarted at the last minute. She had rehearsed the whole evening down to that moment when she would lead Morgan to her bed, as she had that first time in Martinique, but this time she would have him remove her clothes piece by piece. . . .

"What? Excuse me."

"I said, my dear, shall we have a cup of tea while we wait for my visitor?"

"It is already brewed. I will go fetch the tray."

They settled down in the candle-lit study, and Franklin took a sip of tea and leaned back in his chair.

"I owe you some explanation for this imposition. My visitor tonight is an emissary from Great Britain, a gentleman named Wiggins, though that is probably not his real name. In any case, I have a letter from Lord Germaine assuring me that this Mr. Wiggins speaks not only on his authority but on that of King George as well.

"I had rather been fearing this move. My inability to get the French government—or rather King Louis—to take the plunge and sign an alliance, has given the British time to prepare new proposals for peace. These will, no doubt, include handsome new concessions in return for the American colonies again submitting to the authority of the Crown. I can resist these blandishments, but I am not so sure my colleagues would not be tempted. Hence, my urgent request to you to provide a place where I might meet this British envoy privately. Germaine has surely also sent emissaries to America to whisper in the ears of Congress, but they will need some weeks to reach there, weeks that I can devote to further efforts with the French. As for Wiggins, it will do no harm to hear him out."

"Then shall we follow our usual routine? I will introduce myself and then retire?"

"Yes, the usual routine. You know, my dear, our ruse is working admirably. All Paris believes that you and I are having an affair, which is most flattering to the self-esteem of an old man."

"However, I have heard other, perhaps less ill-founded... Wait. I hear carriage wheels."

Sophie and Franklin reached the entryway just as a heavyset man, but light on his feet, descended from a carriage, turned and looked up at the lamp-lit entry.

Sophie gasped and tried to speak, but words would not come. Mr. Wiggins was none other than General Coburn!

At last she blurted out, "That is the man who held me captive in Canada. He must not see me here!"

Sophie turned and ran in the only direction she could, into the kitchen. She shut the door and leaned back against it, her heart beating wildly. At that moment Odette came through the back door.

"I delivered your message, but I have seldom seen a gentleman so unhappy. He said to tell you he obeys your instructions, but with a heavy heart, and awaits an explanation. Sophie, what is wrong?"

"Odette, Dr. Franklin is greeting a visitor at the door. Go quickly to the study and retrieve the tea tray before this gentleman sees it."

The girl threw off her cloak and without hesitation went through the door, returning in seconds with the tea tray.

"They are going into the study now and paid no attention to me."

"Do you know who that man is?"

"No, but I have seen him before."

"Seen him? Where?"

"When I took one of your letters for Monsieur Carter to the Tuileries gardens. There is a certain back street I go down, with coffeehouses, and in one of these I saw this gentleman through the glass. I particularly noticed, because he was sitting at a table with Mr. Bannister, Dr. Franklin's private secretary."

"Oh!" she cried out, and the cry awakened her from a dream so erotic that her face was hot with blushes. She let go of the two pillows that she hugged, one with her arms, the other with her legs, rolled over onto her back and looked up at the cherubs floating in clouds on the ceiling above. She had dreamed of doing things that a woman of her background should not even know about!

Sophie got up and went across the room, lit the fire that Odette had laid the night before, and sat down at the little writing desk without even putting on robe and slippers.

"*Mon amour,*

"I am *désolée* to have been obliged to ask that you not come to me last night. I will explain all when you do come, and I ask that it be within the hour of receiving this note. Morgan, I am afire for you, and it has burned away all the doubts, resentments, reservations, etc. that I have put in your way. All barricades are down. Come!

"Yours,
"Sophie."

Then she rang for Odette and went to the window. Outside dark clouds hung low over the forest.

"Yes?"

"Once again, I must ask you to go to the Orangerie with a message," Sophie said with some embarrassment. The passion that made her breathe hard was all too evident.

"I'll go immediately," Odette said, taking the envelope with lowered eyes. "Also, there is a gentleman below who wishes to speak with you. He asked that I not disturb you, but said that he would wait until you awoke."

"Visitor?" Sophie frowned. Were her delicious prospects to be frustrated again?

"He says that he is your cousin."

It could only be Hyacinthe, the one visitor she would welcome. "Tell this gentleman to come up."

When Odette had left Sophie looked down at her transparent nightgown, which she had acquired for quite another purpose, and got back into bed and pulled the sheet up over her exposed bosom.

"Well, cuz, what do I see here?" Hyacinthe said, standing in the door. "Nine o'clock in the morning and still abed?"

"Hyacinthe, what an unexpected pleasure. Come give me a kiss."

He crossed the room and kissed her warmly on both cheeks, tossed his tricorne hat onto a chair and sat down with legs crossed on the end of the bed. "Still abed, and in Madame de Pompadour's bed, at that. Cheeks and lips rouged, and—what's this—do I detect powder in your hair? What have you done with that sober Huguenot widow of Bordeaux, Madame Reynaud?"

"So, you know. And what are you doing about at nine o'clock, which is hardly your wont, and so elegantly dressed?"

"It is the business of His Majesty's secret service to know, and I will admit to having come to see you with a purpose. But first, what of you? I had the most terrifying report of your fate, and must admit to having censured myself in the harshest terms for having intervened with you on Morgan Carter's behalf. You did receive that injudicious letter I sent you, as you were about to board ship at La Rochelle for the West Indies?"

"It was a most judicious letter, Hyacinthe, and it moved

me to tears. It also gave me the courage to dare to live."

"Then my idle life has not been all in vain. And what of Morgan?"

"He is here in Paris, safe, in hiding."

"Excellent. And you love him."

"Desperately. But we have had serious misunderstandings, almost to the point of breaking off."

The creases of an ironic smile, the only kind that Hyacinthe was known to display, formed around the corners of his mouth and gray eyes. "The man who made this for me," he said, touching the gilded hilt of the sword that hung at his waist, "told me that it is not the white-hot heat under which the blade is forged that assures its quality, but the repeated plunging of it into cold water during the process."

"Hyacinthe, your presence is most welcome."

He inclined his ash-blond head slightly in response. "Now down to business, cuz. A certain party came here last night to meet with Dr. Franklin."

"I'm sure your service knows it was an English envoy."

"Yes, but exactly who we do not know."

"General Coburn, my captor in Quebec, though he did not see me last night."

Hyacinthe whistled. "Well, well."

"I believe that he is a high official of the British secret service."

"Now head of the British secret service, to be exact. He is the agent, directly, of King George, working through Lord Germaine, thus bypassing the Prime Minister, Lord North. A dangerous man and *un peu fou.*"

"That was my impression, too, that he was a little crazy. When I was his captive in Quebec, he took me to a hunting lodge, where he made lunch for me, and tried to find out whether I might have learned from you the name of a French agent, someone high in the British government."

Hyacinthe laughed.

"Is there such a person?"

"There is, but of course I never told you who it was, nor would I now. George Coburn is not only a little crazy, in this case he doesn't even show good sense. But dangerous he is. I had debated whether to show you this," Hyacinthe said, reaching into a coat pocket and taking out a folded sheet of paper, "and decided it would be too disturbing to you. But under the present circumstances . . ."

Sophie took the folded sheet from her cousin and opened it.

"My dear Countess,
"There has been a new development of which you should be aware, though it need not alter our plans. Indeed, it makes them the more likely of success.

"Our friend has flown the coop, just how I do not know, but it does not matter. She is somewhere out in the wilderness, and I have told our savage friends to find her, and that when they do, as they surely will, I care not what happens to her so long as I do not hear of her again. I think you can take it as a given, then, that our plans will not, in the future, be interfered with from that quarter. I would urge you to press your case with all vigor, so that we may put an end to this traffic and you claim your reward.

"Your obedient friend,
"Adonis."

She looked up at Hyacinthe, aghast.

"You understand who the correspondents are, Sophie?"

"General Coburn and la Comtesse de Brieux."

"And the import of this letter?"

"That after I escaped from Quebec, with Morgan's help, Coburn instructed the Iroquois to find me and either kill me or hold me captive."

"Exactly."

"How did you come by this letter?"

"An American privateer took a British vessel headed from Canada to the West Indies. The Americans searched the ship for any official British correspondence, as is their custom, and anything they find they turn over to your agents in Martinique, in this case Archambault."

"Archambault! How is he?"

"Prospering. Since you gave him a tenth share in the New World Trading Company, he is, by his lights, a rich man, and lives in a style befitting his station."

Sophie laughed. "He'll spend it all, if I know Archambault."

"Sophie," her cousin said, his voice turning serious, "can you tell me what happened last night between Dr. Franklin and General Coburn?"

"Afterwards, and we stayed up until the small hours, Franklin told me that the concessions offered by King George were very large—not including independence, of course—and that he had told 'Mr. Wiggins' that they had come two years too late. Now the die is cast, he said."

"Good, in that Franklin has held steady, and in that the personal involvement of King George, through Coburn, in wooing the Americans, may convince our own king to move at last; but possibly bad in that Dr. Franklin's life may now be in danger."

"What do you mean?"

"Franklin is the only American representative who enjoys the trust of France. If something happened to him, an alliance between France and America would, at best, be much delayed. And given Coburn's character..."

"There is one other thing about Coburn, Hyacinthe. By chance I have learned that he is secretly in contact with Franklin's own private secretary, a Mr. Bannister."

"Does Dr. Franklin confide in this private secretary?"

"I believe so."

"To the extent of Mr. Bannister knowing your true identity?"

"It is possible."

"Then, Sophie, your own life may be in danger. Have you told Franklin that his secretary is a traitor?"

"Not yet. I was debating with myself what to say."

"Then don't. Leave Bannister to me. This kind of business requires a cunning deviousness that is alien to Dr. Franklin. Now as to your own safety..."

There was a knock and Odette came through the door followed by Morgan, who stopped in his tracks at the sight of Sophie with a sheet pulled up to her chin and an elegantly-dressed man sitting on the end of her bed.

"Hyacinthe!"

While the two men embraced and kissed on both cheeks in the French fashion, Sophie beckoned to Odette.

"I'm sorry, Sophie. I was about to leave with your note, when Monsieur Carter came through the door. I told him that you had a visitor and gave him the note. But when he had read it he went straight up the stairs before I could warn you."

"It is quite all right. He and my cousin are old friends. Now please get me my gown from the dressing room."

While Odette held up the dressing gown as a screen, Sophie got out of bed and slipped into it.

"Gentlemen," she said, "would you care for coffee and brioches?"

"An excellent idea," Hyacinthe replied, "and then we can settle down to a council of war."

"Then it is agreed?" Hyacinthe said, touching a napkin to his lips. "I will leave first, Sophie, in your carriage, with the curtains drawn, taking your maid with me to point out to me this coffeehouse where she saw Coburn and Bannister together. You and Morgan will leave somewhat later in my carriage, curtains also drawn. You will be taken to a safe place, which the secret service maintains for just this kind of purpose, and stay there until I get in touch with you. I imagine you would not mind being alone together for a while."

This was said without even the hint of a smirk. In the world in which Hyacinthe moved, relations between the sexes were treated with the greatest frankness, and he saw his once unsophisticated cousin as now a part of that world.

"You really believe these precautions are necessary, Hyacinthe," Morgan said, drumming his fingers on the tablecloth.

"I do, and also it does no harm to sow a little confusion in the ranks of our enemies."

"And where is this hideaway you are sending us to?"

"Ah, I'll let that be a little surprise for you and my dear cuz. You won't be disappointed."

"I'll go dress then," Sophie said getting up and ringing for Odette. *Mon Dieu,* she hoped Morgan did nothing to upset these arrangements. As far as she was concerned it was a dream come true. She went into the dressing room and selected a warm wool dress, for it had begun to snow, a fur-lined cape, a fur hat trimmed with red leather, and red leather boots.

"Twenty-three, twenty-four." Odette counted. "At last. Never, have I seen a dress with so many buttons down the back. And you won't have me to help you out of it."

"Oh, that will be easily enough managed, I imagine."

Sophie blushed, and they both laughed.

By the time they were ready to leave, the ground was covered with a powdery snow. Their breaths billowed in the air and their boots crunched the snow as they crossed to their waiting vehicle. As soon as they were inside the darkened carriage, Sophie showered kisses on her lover.

"Oh, Morgan, what a fool I have been. If it were not for all the clothes I am bundled in, you should have me here and now."

He took her face in those large strong hands, the touch of which always thrilled her. He buried his fingers in her hair and brought his lips close to hers. "Anticipation is part of the pleasure, *ma chérie*."

"If I do not die from it," she said, opening her mouth to his kiss.

By the time the carriage came to a halt, Sophie thought that she might, if not die from it, at least faint from frustrated desire. She pulled aside the curtain. They had stopped on one of the Paris quays, now under a heavy blanket of snow.

The driver opened the door and Sophie got down. All along the quay were warehouses, in front of which horses and carts were lined up for loading. At the edge of the quay barges were disgorging their cargoes: barrels of wine, baskets of coal, and all sorts of merchandise. Workmen stamped their feet from the cold and warmed their hands over braziers of charcoal. A man sold roasted chestnuts from a cart. But nowhere was there any sign of a habitation.

"There you are, madame and monsieur," the driver said, pointing to a long, deep barge.

"There?"

"Yes, madame."

"Extraordinary," Morgan said. "A surprise indeed."

The driver helped Morgan guide Sophie across the slippery plank and then went to bring the bag containing Sophie's personal articles. She looked around the one large room into which the barge had been made. The furniture was of the finest quality, including a wide bed of carved mahogany. There were carpets on the floor, tapestries on the walls, and a sideboard filled with porcelain, crystal and silver. A fire burned in a stove, beside which was a basket of food, a case of wine and a stack of wood for the stove.

"But it is quite luxurious."

"Yes, madame," the driver replied, putting down her bag. "We sometimes have persons of high rank stay here. We move the boat from time to time, so that no one gets used to it at any one place. Well, I'll be going now," and he tipped his hat and went out the hatch, closing it behind him.

"Well?" Sophie said, turning to Morgan with a smile.

He smiled and lifted an eyebrow. "Well?"

"Morgan, it has been since Canada," she said in a husky voice.

"Then let us delay no longer." He moved toward her.

"But first you have a small task to perform," and she turned her back to him.

"Twenty-three, twenty-four," he said, having moved from her neck down to her waist, where he now knelt undoing the last button. "There are twenty-four buttons."

Sophie slipped her arms out of the dress and turned. As she did Morgan pulled on her dress. It fell down around her ankles, taking her underclothes with it, and leaving her standing there in nothing but her stockings. He leaned forward and, to her astonishment and pleasure, placed a long, lingering kiss on that warm, wet place where all her desire was gathered. She felt her legs grow weak.

"Take me to the bed," she whispered

He picked her up and carried her across the room to the waiting bed where, to her delight, his desire was so frantic that he was upon her and moving inside her while only half disrobed. But she did not have long to enjoy the movement that joined them, the sensual feel of her silk-stockinged legs wrapped around his body.

"I can't . . . any longer," and at once Sophie felt the hot rush of Morgan's climax beginning within her. At last! At last they possessed each other again!

CHAPTER TWENTY-THREE

Sophie awoke not knowing at first where she was. There seemed to be three moons, all in a row, floating in the semi-darkness. Then she remembered, and the three moons became portholes looking out on the Seine and the blowing snow. The barge, even though securely lashed to the quay, rolled with the gusts of wind. She thought of another barge floating down the Garonne, a handsome American who had approached her, a moon rising, a sprig of winter jasmine, the first overtures of love. It had all led here.

She had awakened from a dream, not erotic this time—her frustration had been well assuaged—but of running through a landscape, part the forests of Canada, part the jungles of Martinique. It was a happy dream. She reached over to touch Morgan, but he was not there. She sat up and looked around her. She was alone in the room, but the fire in the stove had been restarted. Sophie sighed and lay back in the pillows, unconcerned. Morgan had gone out and would be back. She was safe now.

And soon he did return. The hatch opened, and he descended the ladder in a cloak and tricorne quite covered in snow. He brushed these off and hung them up, came to the bed and sat beside her.

"Your lips are like ice."

"And yours soft and hot."

"Where have you been?"

"You will not believe. At the other end of the bridge, on the Right Bank, there is a bookshop, with which I was once much engaged. They were to publish a book by my old friend and botanical mentor, Charles Dupont, but before I could finish this project in his memory, the winds of war swept me away. But I have returned to find that the book has been published." He took the paper and string from a small parcel.

"'The Flowering Trees of North America'," she said, turning the pages, "handsomely bound in leather, and the illustrations are beautiful."

"From his drawings, made into lithographs here in Paris and colored by hand."

"Morgan, there are tears in your eyes."

"And to end being scalped by Indians. Well, at least he shall have this memorial."

Sophie put her arms around Morgan and held to her this man she loved so much.

"You are so strong and determined in defending your country's independence, yet you have a tender side; and it is that side, I believe, that is more truly you. You long to return to your plants, don't you, Morgan?"

"And would, if I could take you with me . . . and clear my name of having stolen a half million livres of my country's money. Now you know. And you, Sophie, what other side do you have? You are not the same woman I met at Château Ivran."

He took her by the wrists and turned over her hands. "There are still the marks there of canoeing down the St. Lawrence. We have been through much together." He leaned and kissed her palms.

"What am I now? A woman who has seen her dream of a life of passion and adventure come true." She could not go on and put the hands that he had just kissed over her face, and let the tears flow.

"Sophie, what is it?"

"I am so happy now."

"But for the future, what do you desire?"

"I am too much overwhelmed by the present to give much thought to that."

"Then what do you desire for the present?"

In reply she pulled her nightgown over her head and threw it to the end of the bed.

"You want to make love again."

"Provided," she said, "it is accomplished very, very slowly."

"*Et voilà, messieurs:* roast chicken, sautéed potatoes and braised leeks."

"Astonishing," Hyacinthe said with genuine surprise. "The successor to Madame de Pompadour is also an accomplished cook?"

"I, for one, have not forgotten my bourgeois origins." Sophie gave her cousin an ironic smile. She was becoming rather good at his game.

Morgan laughed. "Then I shall carve. I have a ravenous appetite."

"And I." She exchanged a quick glance and a smile with Morgan. Prolonged lovemaking did do that.

"Now, Sophie, your opinion on this wine that I have brought," Hyacinthe said, pulling a cork. "And I tremble before your august judgment."

Sophie swirled the wine in the glass and tasted carefully.

"*Mon cher cousin,* you know perfectly well that this is a wine of the very highest quality."

"Which would be?"

"Château Lafitte."

"And the year?"

"Since it is at least a dozen years old, it can only be the vintage of 1764."

It was a merry meal in a cozy, warm room that rolled with the motion of the river, while outside the snow continued to fall. Perhaps it was the warmth of the room, and a little too much wine, that brought back visions of Martinique, not now the Martinique of her childhood, but the Martinique where, how short a time ago, she had first known love. She suddenly wanted desperately to be back there, to be back there with Morgan. She turned her head to hide unexpected tears.

"And now, I suppose, you will tell us," Hyacinthe said, "that there is even dessert."

"Anjou pears stewed in red wine with *crème fraiche*."

"*Ma foi,* is there no end to your talents?" He rose. "I will go fetch the bottle of Barsac that I left to chill outside in the snow. You will no doubt pronounce it young, brash and over-sweet."

Sophie pronounced the dessert wine excellent, and they toasted each other's health with it.

"I never know," Morgan said, as Sophie served coffee, "when it is permissible in French society to discuss serious matters. Over coffee?"

"The problem, my dear Morgan," Hyacinthe said, "is that there is no agreement in French society on what constitutes a serious matter. For some the shade of stocking that one wears when—let's say being tried for one's life—is more important than the verdict."

"The matter of a missing 500,000 livres and warrants for my arrest in two countries is sufficiently serious to me. What am I to do about it?"

"If you had asked me yesterday, I would have said get the money back—it is in a name that you can lay claim to—return it to your Congress, but . . ."

"But what?"

"But today I can tell you that the money is gone. One of

our agents in London has determined that the entire half-million livres has been withdrawn from the bank in which it was deposited, withdrawn in large amounts at regular intervals, until now nothing remains."

"Then I will never be able to clear my name."

Mon Dieu, Sophie said to herself, are we, who are so close to real happiness, forever to have this hanging over our heads? When Morgan proposed to me that he throw away his good name, and that we run away to live and love together, I should have said yes! yes!

"Who else, Morgan," Hyacinthe asked, "had access to the monies the French government entrusted to you?"

"Only my secretary, and then on only one occasion. He took a bill of exchange to Amsterdam to order two frigates built for the American navy. The British protested to the Dutch government, and the money was returned and later spent on arms in France."

"Ah. We might pursue that transaction further at another time," Hyacinthe said, "but there is a more immediate concern—the reason, actually, for my presence here. Your maid Odette, Sophie—and what a beautiful young woman she is—"

"And one from whom you will keep strictly away."

"—led me to the coffeehouse where she had seen General Coburn and Mr. Bannister together. Afterwards I had words with the proprietor, giving him to understand that this was a police matter. It seems that Coburn and Bannister have met there daily for almost a week, but now have their conferences in an upper room. It is the kind of place where intimate suppers are served in upper rooms. They will be meeting again this afternoon, at an hour that would allow us enough time to digest this fine meal you have laid before us, Sophie. Naturally, you have some fine old cognac about."

"Naturally."

A large and shabby black coach, of the kind that brought working people into Paris, came to a stop in a narrow back street. Three dark-cloaked figures climbed down and disappeared into a narrow alleyway. The snow had ceased to fall, but it was already as deep as the streets of Paris had seen for many a year, so deep that it muffled the sound of the wheels of the few coaches and carriages that were abroad. There was no one about to observe the trio that entered the back door of a public house, where a uniformed young policeman saluted them and pointed them up a back servants' stair. At the top of the stair a sergeant of police ushered them into a cold, dark room where they were met by a middle-aged man dressed all in black.

"Inspector Gervais," Hyacinthe said, "may I introduce Madame Reynaud and Monsieur . . ."

"*Enchanté,*" the inspector said, bending to kiss Sophie's gloved hand.

"All is arranged?" Hyacinthe said, with as little concern as if he were asking a groom if his horse had been saddled.

"As best as can be, although things can go wrong, human nature being always unpredictable."

"True enough," Hyacinthe said, "but within the limits of the possible?"

"We've done our best."

"Good. What are we to expect then?"

Sophie for the first time realized that her cousin Hyacinthe, in the secret world in which he lived, was a person of considerable importance.

"What we expect, sir, is that these two gentlemen in whom you are interested will enter the room next to us, sit down to their coffee and begin to discuss whatever they mean to discuss."

A New World Won

"And we can overhear their discussion?"

"View it even. This upper portion of the door connecting this room with the next swings aside, as you can see, leaving only a thin panel of wood through which one can hear a conversation in the next room quite easily. There is also a tiny peephole in the panel."

"Madame, I will need your assistance," the inspector continued, turning to Sophie. "This is a very delicate business, General Coburn being, I am told, the personal representative of King George of England. No one in Paris at my disposal has ever seen this gentlemen. Could you, when I make a sign, put your eye to this peephole and signal me whether the person with Bannister is indeed General Coburn?"

Sophie nodded, quite fascinated at being brought into the world of espionage; and she had to admit not unhappy at the prospect of revenge on the man who would have seen her dead or a captive of the Iroquois.

They waited in silence for nearly half an hour before the door to the adjoining room opened, chairs were moved about, coffee brought, the door closed, and conversation began. It was like being on the front row of a theater; and with the first words Sophie thought she recognized the voice of General Coburn, and it sent a shiver of revulsion through her body.

"Well, Charlie, it's all arranged?"

"Oh, right enough."

"But how?"

"In the cannister of Lapsang Souchong that he takes in the late afternoon when he works on his papers."

"The same tea every day?"

"Always."

"Can the results be traced to the tea?"

"Only by a doctor with some experience of this kind of

thing, or so I am told by the party who supplied me."

"That won't do. You must find some other substance that leaves no trace."

"That is only possible with small doses administered over a long period of time—that is, the method employed by high-born ladies of France for ridding themselves of their husbands."

Inspector Gervais motioned to Sophie who, having removed her shoes, tiptoed to the wall and put her eye to a pinpoint of light. She turned and nodded.

"That won't do either," Coburn's voice went on. "Within days an alliance could be signed."

"Well then, there's no choice. In any case the tea's already been treated, and he'll soon be sitting down to a pot of it."

"You bloody fool!" Coburn's voice exploded, and then came a sound as of a chair being overturned.

"But I thought you said . . ."

Hyacinthe nodded his head, and Inspector Gervais slipped out of the room. Morgan put his eye to the hole just as the inspector's voice boomed out from the other side of the wall: "George Coburn, you are under arrest on charges of espionage and conspiracy to commit murder—if not murder itself."

The heavy black coach in which they had arrived, while hardly a thing of beauty, was just the vehicle to traverse Paris under snow, having been designed for the muddy roads of the countryside. The horses galloped through the nearly deserted streets, their breaths billowing in the air, the coach swaying dangerously at every curve. Neither she nor Morgan spoke, and Sophie knew that he was brooding over the same thought as she: that it was unlikely that they would find Dr. Franklin alive. Already the red ball of the sun was setting behind the

Paris rooftops. If Franklin had already taken his tea, which by this hour he usually would have, there was little reason for hope.

They thundered through the city gate and into Passy, passing through the entrance to Franklin's villa before the watchman even had time to emerge from his box. Morgan lifted Sophie down from the coach and together they ran up the steps, through the hall, up the marble staircase, past a startled butler descending with an empty silver tray, and burst into the study. Franklin was seated at his desk writing, a teapot at his elbow.

"Dr. Franklin, have you tasted your tea?" Sophie cried out.

"Why no, not yet. Madame Armonville, what . . ."

"*Grâce au ciel!* It is poisoned."

"My goodness. Are you quite sure?"

"Quite," Morgan replied.

"And you, sir, are you not Morgan Carter?"

"Yes sir, we met in Philadelphia."

"I am surprised that you have dared to return to France. You know that there is a warrant out for your arrest?"

"I do, but I believe your secretary—whom I believe you know by the name of Bannister—may be able to clear up my problem with the French police."

"Merciful heavens," Franklin said, looking at his teapot, poking it with his finger. "You must have a very interesting story to tell. But first you must hear my news. Gérard was just here to see me . . ."

Franklin held up a piece of paper, and for once he seemed at a loss for words, even on the verge of tears. Finally he spoke.

"The King of France has agreed to the signing of a treaty with America, to include a military alliance."

"*Quelle bonne nouvelle!*" Sophie exclaimed.

"At long last! Now victory will surely be ours!" Morgan stepped forward and shook Franklin's hand. "You've done it, sir!"

"You may thank the British, who by sending an envoy from King George himself to see me greatly alarmed the French government. They feared a reconciliation between Britain and America might be imminent, and so were able to persuade King Louis to give his consent to a French-American alliance. I suppose I may take some of the credit by leaving the letter from London informing me of this Mr. Wiggins' visit lying about. I assumed that whoever on my staff was in French pay would copy it down and pass it along. And that seems to be what happened.

"Well, now I must hear your story. But first, since you tell me the tea is not drinkable," Franklin said, pulling on a bell cord, "I'll order something stronger. I think the occasion might even merit champagne."

CHAPTER TWENTY-FOUR

When the day arrived it was that rarity in the north of France, a spring day that was sunny and warm, indeed almost hot. It came after a long succession of cold days, dark and rainy, and would no doubt be followed by many more of the same. But for today the sun shone, the first fresh green had appeared on the trees, and thousands of pots of flowers had been brought out from the hothouses to line the way.

A large crowd had gathered in front of the king's palace at Versailles; and on the edge of the crowd Sophie stood with Hyacinthe, resplendent in the dress uniform of an officer of the French navy.

"Well, *ma chère cousine,* how does it feel to know that your friend, who was lately wanted by the police, is in a few minutes to be received by the King of France?"

"Only through the kindness of Dr. Franklin in asking Morgan to accompany him."

"While we are disqualified from even observing the ceremony, you as a woman, and I as a spy."

"I could not expect to be present at the levee, with the king still in his dressing gown and having his hair done. But you surely could have arranged to be in attendance."

"My chief prefers that I not appear in public too close to figures like Dr. Franklin, who all the world is watching."

"I do not even know who your chief is."

"No you don't . . . but you still haven't told me your feelings today."

"My emotions are very mixed. I am happy for Morgan that

his ordeal is over at last. His innocence is recognized, the alliance is signed, the British ambassador is leaving for home without even saying his goodbyes, and now, with the king receiving the American commissioners, the strain of keeping all this secret is relieved. Yet I am anxious for the future, most anxious . . . I have been thinking much about the past today, about all that has happened, that has brought me to the point where I have a future to be anxious about. It all began, you will recall, that night in Bordeaux when you tapped on the window of my office. . . ."

Sophie broke off as she heard in the distance the clatter of horses' hooves on cobblestone. Soon a contingent of cavalry appeared, the horses all white, the riders in blue and gold, their swords held at the ready. Then came a succession of carriages, and finally another contingent of cavalry. The procession came to a halt before the palace, and Franklin descended from the first carriage, in what appeared to be a brand-new suit of brown velvet and carrying a white tricorne under one arm.

"Why he's not got on a wig," someone in the crowd exclaimed. "His head's as bare as a pumpkin."

"And as big."

"The grand chamberlain won't admit him. No one appears before the king what ain't bewigged."

"Oh, they'll admit him all right. There's only one Benjamin Franklin."

The other Americans got down from their carriages, all, including Morgan, in court dress and powdered wigs.

"He cuts quite a figure in court dress," Hyacinthe said. "He would make a fine courtier."

Sophie laughed. The last thing Morgan Carter would ever make was a courtier. She remembered his dismay on being told that he would be obliged to wear a wig to the king's levee.

There was a clatter as the cavalrymen sheathed their swords. Franklin ascended the stairs slowly, at the head of the American delegation, as four footmen in the colors of the King of France swung wide the palace doors. The crowd began to applaud.

"Long live Benjamin Franklin!"

Franklin turned and waved to the crowd.

"Long live the thirteen united states of America!"

Frankin waved again, turned and entered the palace followed by the other Americans. The crowd cheered.

"Well, there's nothing more for us to see," Hyacinthe said. "Shall we stroll in the king's gardens?"

They walked in the gardens for a while without speaking, and then Hyacinthe said, "You spoke of my tapping on your window. Can that have been only eighteen months ago?"

"To me it seems a lifetime ago, and in a way it is."

"Well, you've certainly had a lifetime's worth of adventures in the last year and a half."

"And passion, Hyacinthe, passion. I will tell you the truth. I had no understanding of what real passion was. I do now."

"I know. I can see it in a woman's eyes when . . ."

"Yes . . . Why am I telling you these things? I would not speak of them to anyone else."

"Because I am one of those men—fairly rare, I believe —who understands matters of the heart."

"And why is that?"

"Because I understand women, and I understand women because I love them."

"Love them or enjoy them, as the bee enjoys the flower, taking its nectar, and moving on to the next flower?"

Hyacinthe laughed. "In any case, all that is over for me. I have fallen in love, deeply, passionately, hopelessly in love."

"Tell more."

They were now far from the palace, and coming to a fountain sat down on its edge. Sophie played in the water with a sprig of greenery.

"She is married."

"Naturally."

"But young. Only nineteen. Her husband is sixty-one and a duke, the head of one of the most ancient and powerful families of France. You would know the name instantly."

"And your young duchess, she loves you?"

"Undoubtedly."

"Then the only problem would seem to be one of discretion, with which you are well endowed."

"There is another problem. She takes seriously her marriage vows. She is . . . chaste."

"You mean you haven't . . ."

"No, nor do I see any prospect, and her husband has the constitution of a horse. He'll live to ninety."

"Oh, Hyacinthe." Sophie put her hand over her mouth to stifle her laughter.

"I am quite unable to see the humor in my situation, Sophie."

"Why I believe you are serious, Hyacinthe." She put her hand on his. "I did not mean to mock you. I know well enough that true love always carries with it a portion of pain."

"So I am discovering."

"Now I would ask your advice on a matter that troubles me."

"Gladly."

"But first, tell me exactly what you have learned about the missing half-million livres."

"Under questioning Higgins—or Bannister—admitted that he had taken the money that had been deposited in Amsterdam, which was no longer needed there, but instead of buying French arms with it, as Morgan believed, he deposited it in London. Then he bought the arms with new money granted by the French government, and as new sums were continually being advanced by France, he could keep substituting new money for old.

"He planned eventually to return the money in London, after he had made a fortune for himself with it. Using confidential information that he had access to on French government policy, he played the London stock market—and lost everything. He then thought it politic to resign his position with Morgan and move to England. But the British government had become aware of what was going on, and General Coburn threatened to expose him if he did not return to Paris under a false name and seek to obtain a position on Franklin's staff. From spying he went on to poisoning, and would have been hanged for murder if you and Morgan had not reached Franklin in time. As it is he will only spend a few years in prison."

"What will happen to General Coburn?"

"We let him return to England the next day, as we would expect the British to do when they catch one of our top spies."

"Then the 500,000 livres is irrevocably lost."

"Irrevocably."

"Have you told Morgan this?"

"Not yet. I saw no point in it when he had so much else on his mind. In any case, all this was explained to the Minister of Finance, and—as you know—the charges against Morgan have been dropped. A similar explanation has been put in a letter to the American Congress, and should have similar results."

"I fear not. When Morgan appeared before the Secret Committee of the Congress, a majority of the members of the committee took the position that even were he guiltless the money was in his care, and he could only clear himself by restitution of the entire sum."

"There are worse things, Sophie. He can tell the Congress to go hang. He is welcome to stay here in France as long as he likes."

"Unfortunately, there are worse things. As you know, Dr. Franklin has taken a great liking to Morgan, and without Morgan's knowledge Franklin wrote the Congress asking them to appoint him as American representative in Spain. Both Franklin and Vergennes believe that Spain can be drawn into the alliance against England, and they wanted an able American representative in Madrid to plead the American cause. I would have been prepared to go with him, but, of course, Morgan had to tell Franklin that the American Congress would not, unless the money was restored, agree to him being appointed to any position.

"But now Franklin has asked Morgan to go as his personal envoy to England, to meet secretly with members of the opposition in Parliament. If found out he would, of course, be imprisoned, if not hanged for treason. He has given no answer, but I know that in the end honor will require him to say yes."

"Sophie, *ma chère* Sophie, don't cry," and Hyacinthe took out a lace handkerchief and dabbed at her eyes.

"Every time it's the same. Only one more duty for his country, one last time, and then he is mine forever. But it's never the last time, and won't be until he is either killed or captured by the British. Oh, Hyacinthe, what am I to do?"

"Unfortunately, Sophie, this is not a matter of the heart—wherein I might have some advice to offer—but a matter of honor. And with questions of honor . . ." He shrugged helplessly, then took Sophie in his arms and held her while she wept.

A New World Won

★ ★ ★ ★ ★

While Franklin was escorted by the French cavalry back to his residence in Passy, Morgan and Sophie returned by another route. As soon as they were in the carriage, Morgan took off his wig and tossed it on the seat opposite.

"There, I'm done with the wretched thing."

"But you are beautiful in a powdered wig."

"Beautiful is for women."

"To me you are beautiful, whether in greasy buckskins with your hair in a pigtail or in court dress of colored silks and gold thread, and I want you terribly."

She kissed him passionately and only reluctantly let go of him. "Now you must tell me about the king's levee."

"There's not much to tell. When we reached the king's chambers the grand chamberlain was unwilling to allow Franklin into the king's presence without proper attire, but Vergennes had words with him, and he relented. The king was surrounded by courtiers, all come to see Franklin. The king is much as he looks in his portraits, though beginning to go to fat. When Franklin was introduced to him, the king said in a voice for all to hear, 'I wish the Congress to be assured of my friendship, and I beg leave also to observe that I am exceedingly satisfied with your own conduct during your residence in my kingdom.' Dr. Franklin replied that His Majesty could be assured that America would live up to all its obligations under the treaty of alliance.

"After they had talked some more together, the rest of us were introduced, I being last. When I came before the king he looked at me and said, 'I know you from somewhere.' I replied that I had for a time served him as royal botanist. On hearing this the king said, 'Take care, monsieur, that I do not order you to resume your station. The world has too few botanists and too many diplomats.' And everyone laughed. Then the king spoke with others, and after a while it was indicated that the levee was over."

"What a fine ending to a long story whose outcome was ever in doubt."

"Now, if I could only know what has happened to the missing money, so that this story could be truly brought to an end."

"Morgan, there is something I must tell you." And Sophie related how Higgins had lost the money on the London stock exchange, and there was no hope of its recovery.

"If only . . ." Morgan said, shaking his head.

"If only what, my darling?"

"If only the money could have been recovered, I could have taken up the appointment in Spain, and we could have begun to lead a normal life. But as it is . . ."

"You are going to London." Sophie had not meant to say what she was thinking, but she had to get this thing that was destroying their happiness out in the open.

"I have given Franklin no answer."

"I know, but . . ."

"Sophie, you can have no doubt of my love, and I am only too keenly aware of my promises to you. This is a decision that is tearing me apart."

"Cannot someone else on Franklin's staff go?" she said in desperation.

"Besides myself, only Randolph would be capable of this mission."

"Yes! Yes! Young Randolph. I have heard him highly spoken of."

"In fact, it was Randolph who was meant to go to London. But when Franklin learned of my disqualification for the Madrid post, he decided to send Randolph to Spain instead. He leaves tomorrow, while Franklin writes to Congress to make his appointment official."

"I see." She was beginning to lose hope. "This mission is so terribly important that someone must go?"

"If the opposition in the British Parliament can be fully and quickly informed of the significance of the French-American treaty, they will make every effort to bring down the Tory government. And if the opposition comes to power, they would be prepared to treat on the basis of American independence. The war might be considerably shortened."

"I will say no more, Morgan. The decision is yours." She had no more arguments but tears, and she would not use that weapon—that is if she could keep herself from crying. "Let us talk of other things. Now that secrecy is no longer required, we are being asked to vacate our pretty boat. Where are we to go?"

"It is all arranged," he said. "We are on our way there even now."

They passed Franklin's residence, where the French cavalry contingent, having performed its ceremonial duty, was just departing. Then their carriage entered the Bois de Boulogne, and proceeded down a wooded lane until it came to a stop at the edge of a pond. There a giant old willow tree overhung a tiny cottage, with leaded windows, whitewashed walls and thatched roof.

"*Mais, c'est charmante!*" Sophie exclaimed.

"It belongs to one of Hyacinthe's noble friends, who comes here from time to time with his mistress, but they are about to leave on an extended trip abroad. I gather it may be at our disposal for an extended period of time."

Inside, the little *maison de campagne* was simply furnished but in exquisite taste. I could spend the rest of my life here with this man, Sophie thought. I must not give up. I will think of something.

Sophie was awakened by sunlight on her face, pouring through the lozenges of leaded glass. They had made love the night before with a kind of desperation, as if each were trying to lose the reality they faced in the other's body. But in the middle of the night she had awakened to find the reality still there. And only just before dawn had a possible solution occurred to her.

She got up and laid a fire and lit it and then got back beneath the covers. Morgan was just awakening. He too had probably been awake half the night.

"*Bonjour, chéri.*" She kissed him lightly on the lips.

For a long time they lay with their heads on the pillows, looking at each other with sad, solemn eyes.

"I would like," Morgan finally said, "to be alone for a few hours. I thought I would take a walk in the Bois."

So, the moment of decision had come. The sooner this was all over the better.

"Then I shall go into Paris and be fitted for a gown or two. Shall we agree to meet for a late luncheon?"

Sophie descended from the carriage with a wildly beating heart. It was past two o'clock in the afternoon. It had taken her that long to do what she had to do, and she did not know whether she had done the right thing. But she had vowed to do something, anything, to keep Morgan Carter.

He came out of the house to greet her. His face was tranquil, the face of someone who has made an irrevocable decision and can now rest easy.

He kissed her. "Come inside. Your luncheon is waiting." They entered the small sitting room, where a table was set for two. "But first . . ."

Morgan picked up two sheets of paper from the table. She

held onto the back of a chair to steady herself.

He tossed one sheet of paper back on the table, with, it seemed to her, almost contempt. "I have written the American Congress that, whatever message they may have received from Dr. Franklin, I will not accept the position of representative to Spain, or any other official position with the American government. I said that I feel that I have done my duty to my country honorably and well. If they feel otherwise, so be it."

"You have not already sent this letter?"

"It is gone."

"Then you must retrieve it."

"Impossible. Hyacinthe sent it for me with the royal courier, who is even now riding at top speed for Le Havre with Franklin's dispatch to the Congress on being received by the king, which a French frigate is to carry to America. By chance I found Hyacinthe at Dr. Franklin's when I walked over to give him this."

Sophie took the paper with trembling hand.

"My Dear Dr. Franklin,

"You have done me a great honor in asking me to travel to London as your personal representative, to inform the British opposition of recent developments in France. I have given, believe me, the most serious consideration to your proposal and have now reached a decision.

"Everyone owes a duty both to his country and to those he loves. I feel that I have made some contribution to the founding of an independent America, whose founding was meant to assure for its citizens the rights of 'life, liberty and the pursuit of happiness.' I believe the time has now come for me to exercise these rights for myself and the woman I love. I must, therefore, respectfully decline the mission you have asked me to undertake.

"Your humble servant,
"Morgan Carter."

"Oh, Morgan, Morgan." She was both laughing and crying. "Neither of these letters need have been sent."

"What do you mean?"

"You have thrown away a diplomatic career for me, when . . . when you could have gone to Spain."

"I don't understand."

"I have just dispatched a bill of exchange to the American Congress for 500,000 livres."

"You have done what? But that is an enormous sum! The Congress does not deserve such."

"Calm down, Morgan, I have done what I have done."

"And what does that leave you?"

"After settling annuities on some aged relatives who depended on my business, not a great fortune, as once was mine, but enough to . . ."

"We must intercept that bill of exchange."

"Too late. I too sent it by special courier. For all I know it will go on the same ship as your letter to the Congress."

"It is not right that you . . ."

"Do I look as though I regret the money?" And she ran to his arms. "*Dieu merci!* At last we are free."

"But how will we live now? I have no employment, and I cannot live off what remains of your fortune."

Sophie, weak in the knees from so much emotion, sat down on a sofa and Morgan sat beside her.

"How did you leave Dr. Franklin, Morgan?"

"He said he would have done the same thing, and that he was a selfish old man for trying to keep me for himself. He is sending Randolph to London and one of the other commissioners to Spain, until a permanent appointment to Madrid can be named."

"Then all is well between you."

"It appears so."

"Then may I be permitted a suggestion?"

"Yes?"

"If you spoke to Dr. Franklin, and Franklin spoke to the Comte de Vergennes and Vergennes spoke to the king . . . I believe that His Majesty did say there were too many diplomats in the world and too few botanists."

CHAPTER TWENTY-FIVE

It was that hour along the sun-drenched coast of France that faces the Mediterranean when silence falls over all human activity. The sun was beginning its long descent into the sea, and the light was withdrawing slowly from the white tablecloth, the empty wine bottle and glasses, the end of a loaf of bread, the piled-up bones of fishes, and halves of the lemons that this coast so prodigiously produced.

Sophie at last arose, stretched toward the blue-shadowed ceiling and yawned. If this was not Paradise, such did not exist. Morgan had succumbed to the languor of their surroundings and gone off to their bed. She was not ready for that. Where she had been brought up in Martinique, siesta was a necessity to survive the oppressive heat and damp. Here there was heat, but a thrilling dryness to the air that left one's skin fresh, one's mind clear, even in the straight-down light of midday.

She threw open the shuttered doors and stepped out in her bare feet onto the cool earth of the garden. The warm air rushed up beneath the peasant dress, all that she wore, and caressed her bare body. It was a pagan place, even had there not been fragments of ancient sculpture set here and there in the lush foliage: the torso of some god, the shoulder and breast of a goddess. Sophie recalled then some verses from the Greek poets that she had secretly read, passed from one schoolgirl to another, that were much more shocking than the verses of Ronsard that she had read to Morgan in a ship's infirmary. Remembering that moment when she had, without meaning to—or had she?—broken down the barriers that kept them from intimacy, she felt her nipples harden as they had then.

"Merci à vous, maître Ronsard," she said half-aloud, continuing down the swept path between the masses of tropical plants in the king's garden. Had they not been more than amply rewarded? What governments and congresses and kings had taken from them were just those weights which, when removed, had allowed them to float freely away. What if that chemistry between man and woman, which had been so unexpectedly theirs, had not come to pass? Sophie thought of what might have been: an old woman bent over her ledgers in Bordeaux, an elderly congressman in Philadelphia delivering his speeches about . . . well, whatever congressmen delivered speeches about.

As it was, she was the companion of Morgan Carter, botanist to the king, sent to the south of France to inspect the state of His Majesty's gardens and nurseries. An indefinite period had been assigned for this task, while the king's advisors on such matters considered whether some more permanent appointment for Morgan might be found. Their situation was uncertain. She laughed to herself. Who cared? Until she had met Morgan, her life had been governed by a certainty that, were it not for him, would have followed her to the grave.

The path had come to an end in a cul-de-sac, amidst orange trees and banana plants and some long white blossoms hanging down, which Sophie seemed to remember were deadly poisonous. She turned and started back toward the cottage, thinking now of Morgan, still asleep, naked in this climate among the sheets, about to awake from siesta, long and bronzed and hard of limb. She quickened her pace and as she did, she felt her breathing quicken as well at the thought that in minutes she would be feeling ecstasy in his arms.

Rising from their bed, Sophie pulled the simple peasant gown over her head and she was dressed: no undergarments, no shoes. The sun was just coming up over the Mediterranean as she strolled, a towel over one arm and a piece of soap in her hand, through the gardens to where a spring issued from the rocky mountainside. Its flow was channeled through a lead pipe, from which it emerged a jet of water arching and falling into a pool with sides of dressed limestone. From there aqueducts carried the spring water to troughs that spread out and irrigated the lush gardens.

The gardeners would not arrive for another hour. She looked about her and then removed her dress and with a gasp lowered herself into the icy water. There she floated among the water lilies for a while like some nymph from classical antiquity, free of all her own history: childhood, family, marriage, account books, sea voyages, adventures—free to live and love. And yet . . . she longed to come to rest at some one place. She thought of the little apartment above their offices in the harbor of St Pierre in Martinique, of the Villa Chardin in the hills above, lovingly restored but hardly lived in, of Madame de Pompadour's house in the forest of Versailles, a houseboat on the Seine, a tiny *maison de campagne* in the Bois de Boulogne that had known them for only three nights . . .

Would that they could remain even here in the simple cottage that the head gardener had vacated for His Majesty's inspector of gardens. But they must move on to Montpellier and its royal gardens, and then . . . It seemed that her life since the day she had met Morgan had been one of perpetual motion. Sophie pulled herself up onto the side of the pool and began to soap her hair. Now the sun was well up, and she shivered with pleasure at its warm touch on her cold wet back.

A New World Won

When she returned to the cottage, Morgan was no longer there. She looked about her at the whitewashed walls, bluish in the shadows and golden where the sun struck them, the rough tiled floor, the simple furniture, the dried herbs strung above a window, the copper pots hung from the chimney. Yes, she could live this simple life with joy.

Morgan came through the door carrying a long thin loaf of bread in one hand and a basket in the other. How handsome he was! She came to him and kissed him lightly on the mouth.

"I am starved. What have you brought us?"

"Six eggs, butter and milk from the farmer down the road, and some fresh herbs picked from the kitchen garden."

"An omelette, then, for breakfast, bread toasted over the fire and buttered, and café au lait. What could be better? If you will make a fire, I will grind some coffee."

After they had finished their simple meal, they went out onto the little terrace with cups of coffee and sat on the balustrade, Sophie dangling her bare legs over the edge. From the terrace they looked out over the neat rows of potted plants in the sun, the slatted enclosures providing half-shade for more delicate species and, beyond, the roadstead of Toulon. There a mighty fleet of French warships lay at anchor. The king's garden had been located close by, for every ship's captain was under royal orders, whatever his mission, to bring back interesting plant specimens from around the world.

"They sail on the evening tide," Morgan said reflectively, "and then the die is cast. France enters the war on the side of America, and partly because of you, Madame Armonville, they sail."

"Yet, I hate all war."

"I have no love for it, but with Admiral d'Estaing's fleet put upon the scales, they tip to Washington's side, and the war will be the sooner over."

"Do you regret renouncing all part in it," Sophie said quietly, "for me?"

He looked at her with a look that made her shiver. "No, I am at peace with myself. It is enough to know that America is on the road to freedom. France is out in the open now, and the New World Trading Co. may close its doors. And your feelings, Sophie Armonville?"

"I should be the happiest woman on earth," she said, returning his gaze. She laid her head on his shoulder.

"Yet there is some dark cloud still in your clear skies?"

She sighed. "It is wicked of me to raise the slightest complaint, when all has turned out as I dreamed, but . . ."

"Yes?"

"I would settle down. We have adventured enough."

"It weighs upon me that I cannot yet give you what you desire, but I have given my word to follow the king's orders. We can only hope that there is some decision soon on a permanent position for me."

"And that depends on the king's capricious advisors, who have been known to take years to make a decision."

"I know, I know."

"Or even to forget that there was a decision to be made," Sophie said more sharply than she had intended. Now that she felt herself so completely free, she resented Morgan having bound himself—once again—by his word.

"I am only too well aware . . . What's this?"

A carriage had turned into the gate to the gardens, and its horses came to a stop below them. A door opened, and a slim young man in naval uniform leaped lightly down and bounded up the steps.

"Hyacinthe!"

After kissing them both on the cheeks, Hyacinthe held Sophie out at arm's length. "*Mon Dieu,* you look as though you stepped out of the pages of Rousseau—a child of nature."

"It is true," Sophie said with a laugh. "I have thrown off my bonds."

"Which is what I had hoped for you," Hyacinthe said, with a touch of seriousness to his voice, "and knew you to be capable of."

"How did you find us?" Morgan asked.

"You forget that my business is intelligence."

"You have brought news?"

"I have brought you an invitation to dine with me. There is also a lady . . ."

"Aha," Sophie said. *"Toujours une dame.* But what of *la duchesse?"*

"I will tell you all about everything when we dine. But, *ma chère cousine,* you will have to put aside your peasant costume for an hour or two. We are going to a famous establishment on the shore, outside Toulon, known for its delicacies from the mountains and seas hereabouts."

When Sophie returned she was dressed simply but elegantly, and she acknowledged both men's warm compliments with a smile and a nod of her head. While dressing, she had been puzzling over something.

"Tell me, Hyacinthe, you are not, by chance, sailing with the fleet?"

"I am."

"In what guise?"

"As aide to General Washington."

"You, a naval officer?"

"I have certain qualifications."

"Ah."

"Perhaps I will even have the opportunity to match wits once again with Major General Sir George Coburn, who I hear is returning to North America."

★ ★ ★ ★ ★

The establishment where they were to dine was situated in the remains of an old fort, set into the copper-colored rocks along the shore. The tables were laid alfresco, on a terrace protected from the southern sun by a large striped awning. A light sea breeze off the azure Mediterranean whispered in the pines surrounding the terrace and stirred the pebbles at the water's edge.

"Hyacinthe, what a delicious place you have brought us to," Sophie said, charmed with their surroundings.

"I am told that the food is equal to the setting. I only hope that my lady, who was to join us here, has not been delayed." He took out his watch, frowning. "She is traveling from Paris, and her coach was to have arrived in Toulon early this morning."

"Since you sail with the fleet," Morgan asked, "may we be of assistance to your lady, should she be delayed?"

"She too sails with the fleet."

"Really," Sophie said. "To America? Now I am truly surprised."

"You'll be even more surprised when she arrives." Hyacinthe smiled inscrutably. "But since she hasn't, and there's nothing that can be done about that, let us in the meantime look to what can be done for our stomachs. They say the rack of lamb here is excellent, flavored with various herbs of Provence; and I thought we might precede it with a fresh fish—a *loup de mer,* perhaps—grilled over a fire of olive wood and fennel stalks."

Hyacinthe motioned to the man who waited on their table and instructed him to bring them samples of the establishment's best wines for them to choose among. The man soon returned with glasses containing three white wines and three reds. He was surprised when a woman was asked to make the choice, and astonished when, after tasting each, Sophie said, "I think this young Bandol would go nicely with the *loup de mer,* and the '72 Châteauneuf-du-Pape would be perfect with the lamb."

"When shall we see you again, Hyacinthe?" Morgan asked.

"When my tour of duty is up—normally two years—unless, *s'il plait au Dieu,* the English are defeated earlier . . . Ah, there is a carriage approaching. That must be she."

Hyacinthe arose and disappeared out the door, soon returning with a young woman on his arm.

"Odette!"

"Oui, Sophie, c'est moi."

Sophie looked from the girl's face to Hyacinthe's, who seeing her eyes narrow with suspicion, laughed.

"You asked me to find a position for Odette, and I think I have done rather well. She is to be my companion in America."

"Companion?" Sophie said, with an edge of displeasure to her voice. "Hyacinthe . . ."

"Oh, Sophie," Odette said, laughing, "had I wished to lead a life of easy morals, I could have done so with much greater facility and profit in Paris. Hyacinthe and I were married last week."

The grilled fish melted in the mouth, the lamb was equally delicious, and the wine flowed freely. Afterwards, Morgan suggested that they walk along the pebbled beach a while to recover, but only Odette favored this suggestion.

Sophie and Hyacinthe sat alone on the terrace, the other guests having departed, sipping their wine. The sun was beginning to sink in the sky, and the azure of the sea had turned to a deep blue streaked with green. Hyacinthe looked at his pocket watch.

"We must leave soon," he said. "The tide turns at sunset, and we should be aboard well before."

"Hyacinthe, I will miss you greatly. You have been a true friend. Were it not for you, it is hardly likely that I would have ever known happiness, as I now do to the fullest with Morgan."

"I would like to think that this one good deed of mine," he said with a smile, laying his hand on Sophie's, "will weigh heavily on the day of judgment against all my sins."

"Speaking of which, how is it that you came to marry Odette?"

"Sophie, my little duchess taught me about virtue, and that left me for the first time in my life vulnerable to the arrows of love."

"It is only just, Hyacinthe, that after having caused love's arrows to strike so many feminine hearts, the bow should be pointed one day in your direction."

When Morgan and Odette returned from their walk, the two men stood talking together by the door while Sophie and Odette said their goodbyes.

"I wish you all happiness, Odette. Now, is there anything I can do for you?"

"There is nothing anyone can do for me, who have Hyacinthe as my husband. Is there anything that I can do for you?"

"Yes, Odette. You must promise to write me often, and to include all the political and military news from Philadelphia for Morgan's benefit."

"You have my word on it. Sophie, I will be forever in your debt."

"You have long ago discharged any debt to me by your friendship during my dark hours."

The four of them then came together and kissed on the cheeks. After handclasps all around and a few tears from the two women, Hyacinthe and Odette turned to go. But then Hyacinthe turned back.

"I almost forgot to give you this." He handed Morgan a large square envelope, and then they were gone.

Sophie and Morgan sat down again at the table, and she poured out the last of the wine while he broke the red wax seals on the envelope. There were several sheets of stiff paper inside, and Morgan read for some time. Then he looked up at her, but she could not fathom the look in his eyes.

"Well?"

"The last page tells all," and he read aloud:

". . . you are to purchase whatever articles and scientific instruments are required for the performance of your duties, drawing on monies to be provided by His Majesty's intendant in Toulon, up to the sum specified above. This letter will serve as your authority to board any ship of His Majesty's Navy sailing for the French West Indies . . ."

Sophie caught her breath. Morgan paused and looked up enigmatically again, and them resumed reading.

". . . and there you will acquire a parcel of land, wherever in the French West Indian territories you judge most suitable, for the setting up of a botanical garden for the supply of new and different species of tropical plants for His Majesty's gardens in France . . ."

"Oh, Morgan, what does it mean?" Sophie's heart was beating fast. She understood, yet she did not understand.

"It means that my permanent appointment has been made, as the king's botanist in the French West Indies."

"But where . . ."

"Wherever I choose, and I have already chosen." His enigmatic look melted into a smile. "I thought the Villa Chardin on the island of Martinique might be a suitable location."

"Oh, Morgan . . ." But the rest was lost in tears of joy.

They sat together then for a long time in silence. At last Sophie spoke. "This would be Hyacinthe's doing, I suppose."

"I cannot believe otherwise."

"He has been our good angel."

"I see him," Morgan said, "rather like one of those angels one spies carved high on the front of a cathedral, so far up from the people's gaze that the sculptor could allow himself the liberty of putting a sly smile on the angel's face, a look of worldly amusement."

They stayed on until the sun was sinking into the sea, until sails billowed out golden in the sunset, and the French fleet moved out for America. One by one the great ships of the line, the frigates, the transports and lesser craft took their place in a convoy that stretched to the horizon.

"There they go," Morgan said quietly, "to the making of a new world. The day that Dr. Franklin worked for so long has finally come. This must be the proudest day of his life."

"And yours, Morgan."

He looked at her long, and for the first time she saw no conflict written on his face.

"I did what I could, and you alone made that possible. You do know, Sophie, that from this day on the word duty will never pass my lips."

"I know."

"And what do you feel at this moment?"

"My heart is too full to speak. When I think that we too sail for our New World . . . Oh, Morgan, I am the luckiest woman on earth . . ." She could not go on.

He took her in his arms. She closed her eyes and raised her lips to his. She had reentered her lost Paradise.

AUTHOR'S NOTE

Sophie Armonville and Morgan Carter are fictional. What they did is not. There was an American agent in Paris, sent by a desperate Continental Congress to obtain arms from France. Foreign Minister Vergennes did obtain the king's approval of a plan whereby arms would be shipped by a fictitious trading company to Martinique, where a young American would arrange their transfer to American vessels. Had this plan not succeeded the American colonies would probably have lost the battle of Saratoga, and with it the cause of American independence might have been doomed.

Benjamin Franklin's negotiations with Vergennes to bring France into the war on the American side happened almost day by day as described; and the description of Franklin's reception by Louis XVI is just as it occurred.

The company in the West Indian trade was not headed by a young widow—although at that time in France widows often took over a business and competed successfully in a male world—but by a playwright, Caron de Beaumarchais. Beaumarchais received little recognition for his crucial role in saving the American Revolution; but fame did not elude him. He was the author of two plays which, set to music by Mozart and Rossini, are known to us today as the operas "The Marriage of Figaro" and "The Barber of Seville".